D1281763

Praise for "A Place Called Schugara"

From Chicago to the Ohio Valley to the Caribbean, English's characters paint a picture of human frailty and strength. We recognize ourselves in the unfolding....is there ever a real escape or must we carry with us the baggage of our given identity? Reading "Schugara" is, in a sense, exploring the universal themes of good and evil. Great literature forces us to confront injustice and leave our "comfort zone." In "A Place Called Schugara" the power of love teaches us about redemption. Where and when do we find human decency and will it prevail? "Schugara" raises these questions; goodness confronts evil while, at the same time, dignity and worth are found where we least expect. Keep your hands on the steering wheel. You'll need to for the unexpected twists and turns, expertly crafted to keep you moving through life's mysteries. I'm waiting for the movie.

—Roberta L. Raymond

Roberta L. Raymond, Sociologist, is the Founder of the Oak Park (Illinois) Regional Housing Center.

Praise for "A Place Called Schugara"

When it comes to adventure, regarding **A Place Called Schugara**, Jamaicans would say, "It sell off." There's Paradise Lost and Paradise Found, characters as disparate as social climbers and policemen, priests and predators, and priests who are predators. This is story-telling at its best, a tapestry of people united by fractious spirits set in a time when the last worn-out century was ending and its Orwellian successor lurked just around the corner. There's love and drama, fulfilled and unfulfilled desires, the lure of the taboo; there's passion and heartbreak, and the pathos of ordinary men and women struggling to make it through to the next day. You will laugh, you will cry, you will turn the next page; **Schugara** will remain with you when there are no pages left to turn. **Schugara** is for those addicted to the well-written word; it has "good bones," and meaty ones at that.

—Chester Francis-Jackson

Chester Francis-Jackson is a columnist for *The Gleaner* (Kingston, Jamaica). His articles have appeared in the *Jamaican Observer*, the *Jamaican Herald*, the *Caribbean Times*, and *The New York Times*.

Praise for "A Place Called Schugara"

Whether you read A PLACE CALLED SCHUGARA while enjoying a Red Stripe in Negril or Ocho Rios or while sipping a hot toddy near flickering flames and crackling wood by your fireplace, you're going on a raucous trip. You'll spend time with unforgettable characters in unexpected places in this big, ambitious book. If you're a real reader, you'll be delighted you picked it up and thrilled you went along for the ride.

—Monroe Anderson

Monroe Anderson is a veteran Chicago journalist. He has penned signed op-ed page columns for the *Chicago Tribune* and the *Chicago Sun-Times*. In addition, he reported for the *National Observer* and *Newsweek*. He was an assistant editor at *Ebony* magazine. For thirteen years he was Director of Station Services and Community Affairs at WBBM-TV (CBS2), where he was the host and executive producer of its public affairs television program, *Common Ground*.

"Ofrenda"   Carlos Barberena

A Place Called Schugara

Joe English

With a Foreword by Hank DeZutter

Line By Lion Publishing   Louisville, KY

A PLACE CALLED SCHUGARA Copyright ▢2017
Line By Lion Publications www.linebylion.com

ISBN: 978-1-940938-83-7

For Edward S. Salomon: mensch.

"The love of liberty is the love of others. The love of power is the love of oneself."

– William Hazlitt

Foreword

A Place Called Schugara shows us an America (circa 1980s-90s) that is not working—where the solutions are often worse than the problems, where people have lost faith—with their mates, their jobs, their God or gods, and each other—where drinking vodka all day seems to be an attractive option. It's a society that needs change but keeps getting short-changed.

The novel also shows us an alternative society, a new Eden, in the form of a small Caribbean island named Mabouhey—undeveloped, unknown, and hence undiscovered, a small paradise that is lush in its greenery and alluring in its charms.

The rich but fantastic story of this novel brings its main characters to converge on this island—by choice, chance, and need. Most are escaping *from* unhappy and unfulfilled lives in the spiritually-deprived, morally gridlocked United States—but they are also escaping *to* a fresh start at more meaningful life on the island.

This rambling, rumbling beast of a book is also an old-fashioned love story showing love wearing many of its garments—forbidden passions, heartbreaking violence, graphic hetero- and homo-sexual couplings, and selfless service to others. It focuses most, however, on the kind of active love that helps people overcome their cynicism, ennui, and hardened passivity so they dare to reach out to the world despite its imperfections. It's a kind of love that proves the axiom of one of its characters, a priest: namely, that "our failure to love is always the failure to act."

It is therefore an invitation to all of us not to leap before we look, but to leap while we look, with our eyes wide open.

A Place Called Schugara is nothing if it is not a story, a rich old-fashioned story, fiction stranger than the truths it reveals, a wondrous dream, you might say. It is not a documentary, nor a slice of life. If anything it is a big fat juicy, somewhat messy sandwich, sauces and cheese dripping with each bite. And there's a big pot of gumbo next to it—seafood, chicken and spicy sausage in each bite. No, this novel is no ordinary meal, no mere slice of life — it's a banquet filled with tastes both familiar and exotic. It can thrill you and it can bite back.

The adventure is a rollicking odyssey through the perilously rocky moral terrain of late Twentieth Century America that touches intimately on the excesses, the warped appetites, and the headlined controversies and conflicts of these "Me Decades." It includes predatory child-molesting priests and their young victims confused and ultimately alone in their sexual wonderings, it reveals the ruinous and corrupt excesses that is the War on Drugs, it recounts the greed of politicians who pay only lip service to ideals while pocketing federal dollars, and it accentuates the chronic need to save small industries in the rust belt of mainstream America.

This novel not only reveals these problems—sometimes comically and sometimes tragically—but inveighs against them, exploring the day's headlines about the crises and shortcomings of the major institutions of our American lives—including government monopolized urban education, inner city crime, deadening bureaucracies, and the charlatan false prophets and demagogues who offer phony self-promoting solutions.

A Place Called Schugara reveals a world of violent Chicago streets, and of spiritless small-town Ohio canasta games, of exotic, pristine tropical islands, of scheming politicians and avaricious police and priests who prey on those they are obligated to serve. It's a novel where you visit a priest's parish parlor one moment and a sleazy Ohio "adult bookstore" the next.

The novel's more complicated characters—those who end up on the island—include a vodka-swilling academic and scholar, a "burnt out" case that could have stumbled in from a Graham Greene novel; an Ohio factory owner and operator who seems to have lost his will to do anything but unhappily follow the insatiable ambitions of his materialistic and uncaring wife; a Chicago priest who takes his spiritual duties so seriously that he is exiled by his superiors to Mabouhey to get him out of their way; a grubby but loveable insurance investigator, food stains dribbled all over his shirts and corpulent torso, with uncommonly good instincts for both his job and fellow human beings. And there is Marguerite, the lovely darker-skinned Eve of this adventure who was born on the island and whose life and love—her Adam—were destroyed on a tragic sojourn to Chicago.

The story is told in the voices and dialects—and in one case, a diary—of these characters and a variety of minor characters—including less educated, illiterate or preliterate folks who are often wiser than their better educated colleagues. Clever phrases and insights abound: "mi causa es su causa," one character remarks; a stale marriage is described as "a match made in limbo"; a priest tells a young recruit: "The only sure things in this world, my son, are death and taxes. The Catholic Church tries to avoid both and has been mighty successful for going on two thousand years!" And when our heroine, the lovely island native is assaulted on her trip to Chicago and is told, "It's a jungle out there," she simply replies, "No, it is not a jungle."

This is the first novel of a man who has survived the disappointments and joys of the worlds he writes about. Joe English is as busy, as lively, and as wide-ranging in his interests, his commitments and his passions as his novel. The son of a factory manager, English lived in New Jersey, Virginia, Colorado, and Mexico. He won a

Woodrow Wilson Fellowship for his work at Colorado College and earned a Master's degree in English at Rice University. He studied briefly for the priesthood, but left to work outside the clergy. He was an English professor at Triton College in River Grove, Illinois. Since 1970 he has made his home in the Austin neighborhood of Chicago, where he has fought against institutional disinvestment and residential resegregation. English was instrumental in preserving the historic homes in Austin's Austin Village area, which serves as a model for Americans of different colors living together as neighbors. He spends the winter months in his Caribbean home in Sosua, Dominican Republic.*

—Hank De Zutter

Hank DeZutter is a Chicago based journalist who wrote a weekly public affairs column for the *Chicago Reader*. He was the education editor for the *Chicago Daily News* and English professor at Malcolm X College in Chicago as well as co-founder of the Community Media Workshop. Hank and his wife, Barbara Fields, live in Chicago.

*Sosua deserves mention. What today is a thriving international community of 70,000, Sosua consisted of abandoned banana plantations until the advent of World War Two, when it was founded by Jewish refugees fleeing Hitler's tyranny. In July 1938, at the initiative of United

States President Franklin Delano Roosevelt, 32 nations and 24 voluntary organizations sent delegations to a conference in Evian-les-Bains, France, to discuss the refugee crisis of that time: Jews fleeing Nazi Germany. Golda Meir, future Prime Minister of Israel, was permitted to attend the conference as a representative of British Mandate Palestine, but she was not allowed to speak or participate in the proceedings. At the conclusion of the conference, which, with one exception, provided little but lip service to the plight of the Jewish refugees, Meir told the press: "There is only one thing I hope to see before I die and that is that my people should not need expressions of sympathy any more." Jewish leader Chaim Weizmann said, "The world seemed to be divided into two parts: those where Jews could not live and those where they could not enter." At the Evian Conference, only one country stepped forward to open its doors to the persecuted people—the Dominican Republic. The Dominican Republic guaranteed the emigrants freedom to practice their religion and it guaranteed their right to own property. It donated 26,000 acres of land and, in addition, provided a low-interest loan; Sosua was founded. As the Jewish refugees disembarked at the nearby port of Puerto Plata, Dominicans greeted them with loaves of bread and bottles of wine. To this day Sosua maintains a strong Jewish presence. "I now spend my time in two soulful places," English says. "Austin and Sosua. I am doubly blessed."

A Place Called

Schugara

Prologue

1989
Mabouhey

The Caribbean island Mabouhey is not large enough to appear on maps, but it is large enough for the purpose of our story. To Mabouhey, pristine and treasure-laden as the Twentieth Century drew to its close, fled an American of European descent, mourning the death of his nephew. When Matthew was a child, Travers had taken him to the playground, to the movies, the zoo. And then...? And then, like the coming of night, he let his nephew slip away, he let himself slip away. Travers Landeman was thirty-eight years old with nothing in Ohio for him to go back to and much for him to flee. On Mabouhey he was a fugitive from others, from the prison of a loveless marriage, from the lunacy of bureaucrats who tyrannized his failing business, from unknown and unnamed others who promised him harm, but no longer was he a fugitive from himself.

Who among us has not dreamed of going to the corner store for a carton of milk and simply disappearing? It was imperative that Travers Landeman seize the moment and seize it when he did, for it was still dawn and not yet full sun of permanent revolution. Yes, the good news was that Communism was dead, but the bad news was that Capitalism was very much alive. The new millennium would come and with it would come GPS, DNA, voice and face recognition, and, on viaducts and lampposts, the Cyclops blue light of surveillance cameras lurking, to track and tally men, women, and children in the far from unwithered State. In 1989 airplanes had not been crashed into buildings; Travers Landeman could and he did slip away. The question was: would he get away with it?

He had not happened upon Mabouhey by chance, for there was a direct correlation between his nephew's suicide and Travers' journey. He carried with him Bibles, prayer books, and hymnals, gutted and stuffed with cash, and, although he did not know it, his nephew's diary, a tale of betrayal that would call from the past to have him break his vow that he would never go back to his old self, for it tells the true story of his nephew's death.

His first nights on Mabouhey Travers sat by the fire in the middle of the central clearing. There was singing and dancing and stars. He had come to the island to bring provisions to a missionary, Father Chester, who, like

himself, had fled a purposeless life. By the side of a dying
fire, babies bounced on knees and Travers listened as
Father Chester talked, of his priesthood, of Mabouhey, of
the greatest sin of all, the failure to love, which is always
the failure to act. From across the way, in the shadows, a
woman named Marguerite sat on her verandah, between
emotion and response, studying the priest and the intruder
in the bitter ash of her withered heart. She was the color of
coffee with cream, her hair was flowing and black, and her
face was the burn of a wine-red rose. You shall know of all
of this and more: how Travers was attacked by the great
shark, Kintura; how Travers and Marguerite came to love
one another and build their home on the side of a volcano
at a place called Schugara.

For now it is enough to show that under a sky that
was a net of stars Marguerite takes Travers to the bend of
many rocks, where they hide a canoe—there, beneath the
roots of the caoba tree that leans like a scarecrow into the
water. Marguerite had selected this forested place,
stepping stones of moss and root, because it is where the
island of Mabouhey bends and its great river becomes sea,
Caribbean currents churning the waters into angry
whiteness.

"Once Hernando's boat is there," Marguerite said,
pointing to beyond the white fury, "it will be swept around
the bend. To return to search for you, Hernando's sons will
have to fight the mighty currents."

"How long will that take?" Travers asked.

"There will be enough time," Marguerite answered, "…if you do not drown."

An image of his dead nephew came to him. "I will not drown," he said.

"Kintura…"

"The great shark will not harm me again. Kintura has had his way with me."

"How can you know?"

"I cannot say. But I know." Travers reached for her. Under the thousand stars of the caoba tree's leaves they held each other.

In the morning the people of the village came to say their goodbyes. Then it was time. Father Chester raised his hands in blessing. He lifted his face, emblazoned with bold colors of bright paint on his forehead and cheeks, to the sky.

"Great Spirits," Father Chester prayed, "we thank you for our brother, Travers, for his kindness and generosity. Nourish his journey home with gentle wave and tranquil sky. Keep him close in the bosom of your sheltering warmth. We ask this in the name of the forest, in the name of the sea."

"Namaste, Mabouhey!" the villagers chanted. *The Spirit in me respects the Spirit in you.*

Marguerite put a ring of jungle flowers around Travers' neck, and he stepped on to the pallets that floated on the bottom of Hernando's boat. His left leg throbbed; the teeth of the great shark came again to his mind. With

an instinctive touch he reached to his bandaged thigh. Its
pain reminded him of the world he would leave behind.
Hernando's sons poked paddles into the water.

Father Chester and the villagers waved.

"Namaste, Mabouhey!"

Marguerite was no longer on the beach. Good.
Hernando's sons, Eufusio and Rafael, fussed and
discussed in the patois Travers did not understand and
then, in a staccato of white puffs, the small engine of the
small boat coughed itself alive. Like memories, the people
on the shore receded. Overhead came large white seagulls
like kites and other birds whose names Travers did not
know. The ocean burned like the brightest candle. At last!
At last! Hernando's boat came to the bend, just beyond the
place of many rocks. Travers' heart was a land mine buried
in the desert.

"I would like some water, please," Travers said.

Eufusio opened the red cooler nestled between his
knees. Travers stood to walk to him and then Travers was
not in the boat. As he fell, his left leg scraped against the
boat's side, ripping loose the bandage from his thigh. Is this
what death and birth are like: plunging from a world of
sky? The water took him and he felt reborn. Blood poured
from his thigh as pain came, aftershock echoes of when the
great shark had attacked him ten days before. Travers saw
that there was blood in the water and he knew that it was
his blood and he knew, too, that he should be afraid. He
went under the water and stayed as long as he could. In the

red silence he saw clearly: fish, coral, sand. He came to the surface near to where Marguerite waited in the canoe. Then he lay in its bottom as Marguerite paddled into the mouth of the river. Neither said a word, but their eyes spoke: now there was no going back; now we are together forever. My life was one of dying, Travers thought; now, by dying, I shall live. Marguerite's long arms danced with the oar as the canoe moved up the river and was gone.

Hernando's boat, as anxious as a crow, came back around the bend, just beyond the place of many rocks, straining against the currents, slow in its swiftness. The ocean was an unbroken spell, as primal as the eye of burning sun. Eufusio saw it first: grey sheen of triangle, lucent and lethal, a knife in the moon of the water's turquoise dream. Kintura! The Great White Shark! An instant later Rafael saw it too and its deathshadow also.

"Kintura! Kintura!" Hernando's sons shouted in one voice. Then fin and shadow were gone. Hernando's boat bobbed up and down, a steadfast heart, as Hernando's sons stood together, shielding their eyes with salutes of their hands. There was blood in the water. There! A bandage! Eufusio reached over the side. Sudden clouds darkened ocean and sky, yet the ocean became still as stone. In the new calm of gray, Eufusio lifted the bandage leaking red. No longer young, Eufusio and Rafael locked into each other's eyes.

"Namaste, Mabouhey!" Eufusio said at last.

"Namaste, Mabouhey!" Rafael repeated.

The brothers stood in the sma
together in front of their chests. Slowly
hands upwards to the tops of their heads ͺ
There was blood in Eufusio's hand and there   . ın
the water.

"The American is dead," Rafael said.

"Yes," his brother answered, "the American is dead."

*   *   *

Albert Sidney McNab took a final look at the lobby
of the New Papagayo Hotel: stone floor with rectangles of
pink marble, one of the few natural resources indigenous
to the island of Frederique, the Caribbean island he had
come to and come up empty handed; bench-like chairs and
settees of hand-carved caoba; clusters of schefflera and
palms, explorations of pothos and moonflower veining the
thatched roof with trumpets of green fire. His look was one
of instinct. He did not know what it was he was looking
for, this stoop-shouldered white American who seemed, at
first glance, like just another tourist. Had he stood straight,
he would have been six feet tall. He was forty-five years
old. His hair was in the crew-cut style of the nineteen-
fifties. He wore tan shorts, sandals with orange socks, and
a bright blue short-sleeve shirt, crowded with multi-
colored geometric shapes: triangles, circles, trapezoids,
rectangles. His brown hair was thinning. His glasses had
thick black frames and thicker lenses. He was overweight,

proaching obesity, and he had a weary way about him. He looked like a hastily made king size bed. With a tentative grasp of his suitcase, brown leather shiny from use, he headed to the front entrance, where a minivan waited to take him to the airport. Had he come all this way for nothing? To the smaller neighboring island, Mabouhey, he had taken Hernando's boat, a shack with a tin roof, water above his ankles. This risking of his life had continued, yes—there was no end to danger!—as ashore on Mabouhey he traversed jungle on sandals and mule through clouds of kamikaze mosquitoes. And for what? Albert Sidney McNab had no clues, no leads. Nothing. Day followed sunny island day in languishing Caribbean rhythm as if Travers Landeman had never existed. Five months had passed since his alleged demise. Maybe, as Eufusio and Rafael insisted with the intensity of youth, the Ohio businessman was dead. Maybe a shark had eaten him. Yet, even as this possibility skipped about in his mind, like a stone across water, Albert Sidney McNab felt the old feeling, the feeling that was never wrong.

He had to hit the big one and hit it soon. He couldn't go on much longer dealing with two-bit scams. He knew that much. His feet were too sore all the time and his back was too tired. He worked for a company by the name of Middlebury Adjusting, Fire, and Insurance Advocacy. The MAFIA. Working for such an outfit—he smiled at the pun—is a younger man's game, he thought. No question about it. He had to hit the big one and hit it soon. Why not the BIG big one? Why not indeed? Twenty percent of three million dollars is a whole heap of money and in his pocket if...if he found the missing businessman and brought him back alive.

He supervised the manhandling of his suitcase into the luggage space behind the rearmost seat of the van. Then he stepped back to study the New Papagayo Hotel one last time. His eyes gave scrutiny to balconies stretching seaward. He searched the cliff that was the hotel's backdrop. Nothing. He looked out towards the sea and down to the beach, a horseshoe of green crystal cove. Nothing. He stepped into the van. Albert always gets his man, he thought, ...eventually. Posturing or premonition?

"I'll be back," he said in a low voice. Premonition.

"Beg pardon?" the driver asked.

"Nothing." Albert Sydney McNab squeezed himself into the rearmost seat of the van, slipped off his sandals, and massaged his feet. "Nothing at all." Next time, he vowed to himself, I shall bring proper footwear.

BOOK ONE: ESCAPE

Chapter One:
Ace Boon Coon

Joe Rogers
Chicago, Illinois
1986 - 1991

Little did I know when I fled Chicago's winter for a few weeks in the Caribbean sun that I, Joe Rogers, bookseller, an American of mongrel European descent, would return months later Midwest Consul of the world's newest nation, the Commonwealth of the Island of Mabouhey. That I would find a buried treasure. That I would be taken by love.

Until that fateful journey my Chicago life, a mooring of vodka and cinema, of theaters and restaurants, looked neither out far nor in deep. It was a tributary incapable of flood. No more. Now there is Marguerite, the color of coffee with cream, hair flowing and black, beauty tinged with the haunting of deep sorrow. There is a man known as Quince, once the Ohio businessman Travers Landeman, whose life was transformed on Mabouhey even more deeply than mine. There is a priest by the name of Chester, whom I, agnostic when optimistic—considering the Twentieth Century only, we must dread the notion of God—came to respect. There is the unlikeliest of heroes, one Albert Sidney McNab, knockabout ne'er-do-well, erstwhile detective who, like me, had meandered his life along, transformed on Mabouhey, as we all were, by the power of love. We share a bond, Marguerite, Quince (Travers), Father Chester, McNab, and myself and, for you to understand any of this, the strangest of strange stories, I must first explain my own journey: how it came about that I, Joe Rogers, bookseller, Chicago to the core, found myself carried on a stretcher to a place called Schugara to recline high on a balcony like a Roman emperor at a banquet, to be arbiter and alchemist, on the Caribbean island Mabouhey, on the eve of its independence, with my ankle broken, drunk and getting drunker.

My position is that my low tolerance for alcohol is a blessing. I get there quicker and cheaper. In my early twenties, a wise friend, bless him, introduced me to vodka. The best vodka, he insisted, is the cheapest vodka. It is impossible to distinguish the most expensive Lithuanian, purest spring water triple filtered through succulent Florentine juniper, holistic lavender, and exotic lotus leaves, from the cheapest American rotgut. "Just can't be done." Bert would squint his eyebrows together, an eleven in the middle of his forehead, snort his head back, and savor the silver, pedigree or mongrel, as it slid down his throat. My many years of battlefield testing have disproved this egalitarian hypothesis but overproofed another Bertism of true worth: stick to vodka and the hangover tiger becomes a pussycat. In my cups, I am, as my friend Zero Washington puts it, "Ace Boon Coon." *Bosom buddy.* A satisfactory epitaph. Beats: "He had potential."

Even now, after the many long years, my minivacations with vodka have, at least in part, something to do with my ex-wife, Valerie. Stylish, self-confident, accomplished: the essence of WASP. Valerie. By profession, an attorney. Valerie—I called her "the sea urchin"—was, quintessentially, one of the swarms of the supposedly gentle sex who in the 1970's began shoving their way to the front of the line. The walls of the fortresses Success, Accomplishment, Status, were breached; in skirts and high heels, bankers, surgeons, newscasters, politicians, and, yes, attorneys came marching through. A child of the sixties myself, I, vodka (neat or with tonic water) in hand, never doubted that Valerie and her conquering sisters were to be cheered. Saluted. Even this most military of verbs only approximates our unctuous mindset, flower children all, who thought the same correct thoughts at the same correct time. We had the answers. It was easy to have them, too, because we also had a lot of money, or, if we didn't quite yet, never doubted that bounty beckoned just around the corner. Jobs and deferments were plentiful. (A nasty war, otherwise inconvenient, sucked up surplus labor). We squatted like hogs at the trough while the generation to follow would elbow for room. Riding the crest of a very big wave all the way in, we told ourselves that ours was the force of the moon pushing and pulling the waters ashore. We were the post-war generation, the Big One, Baby Boomers, hell-bent to bulge all the way through the snake's belly.

Val's and my marriage was a match made in limbo. Nothing was ever in your face nasty; seldom was anything noteworthy of joy. Flaccidly we trundled along, the sea urchin and I, Joe Rogers stumbling after a Ph.D. in American Studies, which I never got, Valerie Furlong-Rogers excelling and re-excelling at the paper chase of law. I became a drunk and Val became a grunt. Inertia held us together. Then Val passed the bar. The university handed me a Master's Degree on my way out, *decent et decorum est*, and Val and I moved from Manhattan (Bloomingdale's, Lord & Taylor), where we had lived like serfs, to Chicago (Sears Roebuck, Montgomery Wards), where we lived like petite (very much so at first) bourgeoisie. Chicago! The place of stinking onions, etymologically speaking, or, perhaps, as revisionists claim, of stinking garlic. *Allium Tricoccum* to be precise. More to the point, Chicago is the home of Checkers, Strawn, and Calahutty, LLC, Attorneys at Law. Its glorious founding predated the Great Chicago Fire of 1871; it reaffirmed its pre-eminence a century plus later, as I saw it, *primus inter parasites*, by hiring Val.

Our marriage survived an additional two years, years when Val was ever more advancing, while I muddled about, pretending to write, but, in truth, spending most of my time hunting obscure brands of vodka and equally obscure bookstores. I came to realize with sadness that my generation would be the last to love books, fully, passionately, obsessively love them. The promise of paper! The intensity of ink! The electronic beachhead established by cinema and radio before my birth exploded, as I approached adolescence, in the atomic age of television; I found myself staggering around as one of the walking wounded. By this I mean that I am a turner of pages. I read. Newspapers, magazines, and books. Big, bulky, books! My friends are truly amazed. However do I find the time? Their amazement amazes (and depresses) me. They stare as if I have a disease: not communicable.

The marriage survived, as I said, another two years, until my mother died, God rest her soul. I found myself for the first time with some money, thanks to Ma's shrewd and parsimonious ways when it came to her own welfare and her generosity, as expressed in her will, when it came to mine. God bless Icelandic Air Lines!   Icelandic's low fares brought Europe within Ma's vacation reach. The first thing Ma did when she returned from "Cathedrals of Italy, Spain, and France in Twenty Days" was change her will. The Pope had *beaucoup* plenty. I got it all. I told Val of my melancholy bounty. Val said she wanted a divorce. The timing of Ma's passing she found fortuitous. It relieved the sea urchin of any guilt she might otherwise have felt. Val always said that guilt is unproductive. Turns out she was wrong.

"After all, I do have some obligation to you for the law school days. Even if you were drunk most of the time."

I took issue with her use of the word *most*. "*Much* would be more accurate."

"That's what we called *pettifogging* in moot court."
The consonants came at me like bullets from a machine gun.

We divorced. I got the car, half of the furniture and housewares, the stereo set, half the L. P.'s, and most of the books. Val got the newly bought color television set. I kept the apartment, seven months remaining on its lease. Val bought a condominium in the newly constructed "Prairie Towers" in the Loop (Chicago's downtown). Prairie Towers was designed by Z. Z. Goldfube, whom I had met at one of the dinner parties Val dragged me to. Goldfube proclaimed that Prairie Towers captures Chicago's "prairie essence," whatever that is. I told Val the towers reminded me of giant dirty sponges, or, better yet, of a herd of beached whales, chunks of their flesh pecked away by ravenous cranes. I was about to work in, somehow, one of my favorites words, *palmate,* when Val interrupted.

"Well, *pal,* your ex-*mate* is plunking down her money Tuesday." You understand why I miss her to this day.

Inside I found her "condominium"—the word was new then—dark and foreboding. It had low ceilings and skimpy windows. I made the mistake of telling her so. Very rarely is honesty the best policy.

"The concept is sound," Val said.

"What in the hell does that mean?"

"You wouldn't understand, but..."

"Leave me in bliss," I interrupted.

"Here and hereafter, *n'est-ce pas?*"

"*Dum spiro, spero.*"

"Enlighten me."

"'Whilst I breathe, I hope'. For what it's worth, the motto of South Carolina."

That look again. Then, gently, "You must accept the fact that *I* have succeeded in seceding from the union."

We had a great divorce. At the very top of the charts. Every few weeks we'd get together. Of course, the sea urchin's career—no verb suffices—zoomed. I found myself writing more than I had in years, mainly articles for short-lived journals of academic aspiration on topics such as "The Sexual Barter Economy of Fourteenth Century Cornwall"— fascinating!

We had lunch to celebrate the second anniversary of Val's secession at "Shandy's"—"A Place for Eating"—as well as a place to see and be seen until Jimmy Rittenschmidt, its managing general partner, and one of Checkers, Strawn, and Calahutty's clients, was found dead in the alley behind with bullets in his chest. Chicago.

"I have given much thought to your situation," Val said as the entrees were "presented."

"Are thoughts considered the same as telephone calls? So much for each fifteen minute increment?"

"Not in this case. This is strictly *pro bono*. I am the *pro*. You get the *bono*. I have a specific recollection of course of your mother's will not to mention the divorce settlement. Generous as we both were, you're going to run out of money soon."

"Soon?"

"In three years. Maybe four."

"I realize, Val, that to you handmaidens of justice three or four years is a mere blink of the eye, 'expedited' hearings, summary judgments and the like, let alone, God knows, an actual trial. But three or four years is a good chunk of time. After all, we were married for four years." We both laughed.

"You do make a point. Except for that puerile crap about 'handmaidens of justice'. About the marriage. It does seem a long time. I give you high marks for putting up with me."

"And even higher to yourself for putting up with me?"

"*Nolo contendere.* The simple fact is you can't hold down a job. A real job. No, I am not thinking about your bosom buddies, *Smirnoff, Stolichnaya, Kirov, Finlandia.* Which am I leaving out?"

Resolutely I kept my mouth shut. Val threw her hair over her right shoulder with a flick of her neck as she was wont to do, closed her lips over a spoonful of *pasta primavera*, and winked.

"Ah, yes, *absolutely*, the *absolute* truth..."

"In vodka veritas?"

"Something like that. Your absolute lack of seriousness about things. How you don't give a damn. Makes you totally worthless job-wise."

"I object, your honoress. This is hearsay." I finished my vodka and tonic—*Gretchenskaya* if you must know (redheaded lass in pigtails and pinafore on the label)—and signaled the waiter for another. "It's just that I don't like to work. A four letter word ending in 'k' and not my favorite. Seems perfectly sensible to me. When you come right down to it, who does? Besides I did have a job once. Surely you remember."

"How could I forget? When we first arrived in Chicago. You survived all of three months." Val pronounced the name of the Second City (slipping fast, angels hovering over both big shoulders) as if *Chicago* were the name of a bacillus. The gravel of her groveling disdain was like chalk on a blackboard. Val was and always would be the most native of native New Yorkers. "The City News Center. You got fired."

"I object again. The record shows I did not get fired. I quit."

Again the machine gun. "Pettifogging. You knew you would be fired, so you quit. Can't say I blame you."

"A morsel of empathy! You do recall that my assignment, the strawberry as it were that broke this mammal's back, was to survey the anointed of ice-cream fooderies in 'Chicagoland'. As guaranteed by the First Amendment, a free people have the right to know: which tutti-frutti is tutti-fruttier? It was, my editor insisted, *ha-ha*, going to be my big scoop!"

"To be fair," Val said, "let the record also note that it was the hottest July on record. But enough. By your own admission, you prove my point: you can't or won't, doesn't matter, follow orders. You won't do as you're told. D.A.Y.T. The formula for success. You always have a better idea. *New and improved* is generally neither. Employers don't want better ideas. Charlie Calahutty doesn't want better ideas. The Big Double C is scared to death of better ideas, especially mine, if I were foolish enough to let him know I have any. So I don't. I do as I'm told; I adhere to what is expected of me and I make a lot of money. You could, too. Except that you can't. Or won't. As I said, doesn't really matter. Let's face it. You're a nice enough guy and you have more chunks of completely useless knowledge crammed into your head than most of us have red blood cells. About all I can think of is for you to be a perpetual contestant on television game shows except that you'd refuse to follow the rules. You'd just blurt out the correct answer and be disqualified."

"Without saying, 'Simon says'?"

"Something like that. Anyway, the fact is you're unemployable and, sooner or later, your nest egg will run out."

"A runny nest egg is over easy?" *Gretchinskaya* had found her voice.

"Cute. Pay attention. This is what I have decided."

I am a man who acknowledges the superiority of women. Everything would be set right. Mother's warm hands would tuck me into bed. Dishes were cleared and coffee poured.

"Since you can't work for anyone else, you're going to have to go into business for yourself. Here. I have it all worked out." The sea urchin reached under the table, plopped her briefcase in her lap, and handed me a sheet of paper. "I.S.B.D., old boy." The lawyerspeak of C. S. & C, Checkers, Strawn, and Calahutty: I.S.B.D. *It shall be done*.

There were columns of numbers. "What's this?"

"It's a financial projection called a *pro forma*. It shows the taxable profit, which isn't, which is good, good, good, as well as the cash flow for The Yellow Harp, down on Langley, which is yes, yes, yes."

The Yellow Harp! One of the city's oldest book stores. Thousands and thousands of books, wonderful books, old books, out-of-print books, tattered and torn books, classics and masterpieces, titles little known and never heard of, shelves and shelves full, the Kasbah of Chicago book stores, with enough dust to make Lake Michigan the Sahara!

"You see," Val continued, "C. S. & C. is handling the estate, what there is of it. Old Trampwell finally turned his last page."

"I wasn't aware. I'm sorry."

"No need. Trampwell kept the place going—God knows how—these forty years or so, ever since he inherited it from his grandmother, the legendary Cissy San Souci, one of C. S. & C.'s clients way back when. The only heir is some third cousin once removed. What does that mean, third cousin once removed? Shouldn't a third cousin be at least three times removed, in which case he'd be a third cousin *thrice* removed? Sounds redundant. Never mind. Don't tell me, even though I'm sure you could. Anyway, as I was explaining, this however many times removed cousin wants to remove himself one more time. He wants nothing to do with The Yellow Harp. C. S. & C. is handling everything. Wrapping up the loose ends."

"Loose ends?"

"Burying Trampwell. Liquidating the estate."

Val was on her third cup of coffee and I, I think, on my fourth *Gretchenskaya*. "What's happened to you?" I raised my voice perhaps too much. "A man's life. An honorable life. A life given to books. The Yellow Harp: an oasis in the stockyard city. Books among the bile! Books among the blood! And to C. S. & C. Trampwell's death is just a loose end."

"Cute, again. Don't lecture me. If it weren't for people like me and Charlie Calahutty, the entire system would come crashing down. We keep it going. We oil. We are the great lubricators. You and a dwindling raggle of antediluvian others may care about The Yellow Harp, but all the market cares about is dollars and cents. Jacksons and Benjamins. The place isn't worth spit."

"That shows what you know!" I shouted. From across the room two of Chicago's society matrons, diamond fingers and bosoms of pearls, scowled at me. I scowled back. They retreated into their bouillabaisse as I went on in a slightly lower voice. "Who knows what invaluable first edition of Fitzgerald or Hemingway lies hidden in Trampwell's ruin? There very well might be, you know."

"Yes, we've thought of that, Charlie Calahutty and me. The Chancellor of the University asked C. S. & C. to handle this. She—the Chancellor—would like to see The Yellow Harp carry on. Perhaps you remember the protest over the University's expansion a few years ago?" I nodded my head. "Well, the Chancellor is planning another expansion, even bigger. And she doesn't want a bunch of woolly hairs raising hell all over again. Especially over a dump like The Yellow Harp. Specifically because it's located on the wrong fringe at that."

What the sea urchin meant was this. Back in the sixties everyone knew it was merely a matter of time until the University packed its bags and fled Chicago's ever sprawling southside ghetto. The University had, it was widely believed, purchased an option on a large chunk of what now is the suburb of Downers Grove, which back then was mostly farmland. But, wonder of wonders, the University had confounded the experts and cast down its bucket where it was. Ever since, every few years, it gobbled off another bite of adjacent Blackland. Usually just like that; occasionally with unsavory side dishes of ballyhoo, bribery, and bad press. But The Yellow Harp was located just beyond the southwesternmost edge of the University's domain, a lonely outpost at the wrong edge of no-man's land. Protected by Lake Michigan to the east and Washington Park to the west, the University, when it gobbled, gobbled north or gobbled south, clinging to its lakefront life jacket. It did not gobble southwest.

"So the University has no interest in books?"

"Cute. The University has no interest in *Trampwell's* books. A can of worms best left unopened..."

"Pages best left unturned?" I interrupted.

"...but if its inventory were liquidated and the place sold," Val continued without missing a beat, "the Chancellor fears that some fast buck artist would get the building for a song and rent it out to a bunch of lowlifes. Last thing the Chancellor wants anywhere near her domain is another shoe shine parlor, storefront *Church of the Living Rock*, or boogie shop."

"Boogie shop?"

"Wigs, mostly. I think. Moisturizing creams. Potions to whiten. For crissakes, how would I know?"

"No Negroes need apply?"

"Nor pizza joints neither. 'Best to go with the status quo'. That's according to the Big Double C."

"Is Charlie Calahutty ill?" I asked.

Val took me seriously. I made a mental note to find out if sea urchins ever sleep.

"No," she answered with surprise. "Why do you ask?"

"I am intrigued by the notion of Charlie Calahutty's disapproving of fast buck artists. Are C. S. & C.'s clients now busboys and deliverymen?"

"Bus staff and delivery people," Val corrected. "No. Of course not. Don't be ridiculous. People like that don't need attorneys."

"Blessed are the few in number."

"Look, Joe. Be serious. For once in your life."

"I was serious when I married you."

"Well, try again. No, not me. God forbid!" We both laughed.

"Look, if we do nothing and The Yellow Harp becomes a liquor store or another goddamned storefront church, the self-styled 'community activists' will stir their radical pot big time."

"Double, double, toil, and trouble?"

"And then some. They're short of causes right now. The Yellow Harp is the ideal bone for them to chew on to protect their funding sources. It's a matter of self-preservation." Val reached for her napkin and rubbed her hands.

"The worst are full of passionate intensity?"

"Precisely!" Val signaled for more coffee. "Look, this is where you come in. It's perfect. You buy The Yellow Harp, lock, stock, thesaurus, and Cliff Notes!"

"The Yellow Harp does not carry Cliff Notes," I said with a whiff of condescension. The sea urchin ignored me.

"All but anything truly valuable."

"You mean money, I take it."

"Huh? Well, yeah. Duh. Look, we could hire some antiquarian asshole expert who wouldn't know half what you've forgotten about books and pay him a fortune..."

"Pay him or her a fortune."

"...and maybe our client, Trampwell's cousin, might actually behave. He might even pay C. S. & C. without our having to litigate. You have no idea the kind of people we deal with."

"I thought the University was your client?"

"The University *is* our client. It has always been our client. Pray God, it will *always* be our client. But Trampwell's cousin is our client, too. The University recommended C. S. & C. to him. We will represent his ficuciary interest as well. Vigorously."

"No doubt. Fiduciary vigor vigorously fiduciary." The sea urchin sat in the front pew of the Church of Statutory Integrity and Codified Ethics.

"It goes without saying," Val continued, in a lowered voice, "that this is in the utmost confidence. We've advised Trampwell's cousin as to our ongoing relationship with and representation of the University. But, still, you never know. If the expert we hire were to make a mistake, or puts his— or her—hand in the till, Trampwell's cousin might sue. Gross negligence, conflict of interest—despite our disclosures—legal malpractice. It's all the rage right now. There are *beaucoup* sole practitioners without a pot to piss in on late night television shilling their wares. *No fee unless you win!* C. S. & C., let me tell you, gets tired of being a target!"

"No doubt."

"On the other hand," Val paused and looked me straight in the eye, "if there are no first editions of Willa Cather or Gertrude Stein, why, then, we've shelled out a whole pile of Trampwell's cousin's money for nothing. Some junior associate fresh out of law school with Bohunk and Nobody starts yelling, 'Vitiating the estate! Vitiating the estate!' and there you have it. *Litigation.*"

Litigation. Sounds like the name of a disease. As in: *Chronic litigation was epidemic in late Twentieth Century America; there was no known cure.*

"A conundrum."

"Indeed. However, I am looking at the solution. One thing I can say about you, Joe Rogers, one thing I've always said, is that you have integrity. Even when you're drunk. For the life of me I couldn't imagine what use it might be, your integrity, that is, but here is the perfect fit. You buy The Yellow Harp. Keep the place going. Catalogue all of Trampwell's leavings. Anything of value..."

"Monetary value."

"...say any one book worth at least three hundred dollars, you set to the side and we split three ways."

"Three?"

"One-third to Trampwell's cousin. Two-thirds to you."

"That's two."

Val bestowed her most indulgent look, a look that I remembered, that I remember still.

"I have assured the Chancellor that the University can count on your making a generous donation. One half of your cut. After all, the Chancellor did turn us on to this."

So there it was. The answer to the eternal Chicago question: "*Ubi est mea?*"

"The Big Double C is delighted. He is totally on board. His exact response was 'N.S.M.G., old girl.'" C. S. and C. speak again: *Enough Said Among Gentlemen*. "What do you say?"

"I say that I find it all very quaint."

"'Quaint' beats 'can't'. This is win-win-win."

"Indeed."

"Look, it's all here," the sea urchin said. She handed me a stack of papers. "Purchase price based on an M. A. I. appraisal... "

"M. A. I.?"

"Stands for *Master of the Appraisal Institute*. But it really means *Made As Instructed*." Val laughed. "And, if he knows anything, Charlie Calahutty knows how to instruct! The financing is from University Freedom and Trust. An attractive interest rate, you should know. I have assured the Big Double C and he has assured the Chancellor that the man and the hour have met..."

"Are you cognizant of the purport of that allusion?" *Gretchenskaya* liked words like *cognizant* and *purport*.

"Something, if memory serves, that *Ketel One* shouted out at the dinner inaugurating Charlie Calahutty as President of the Chicago Bar Association."

"'The man and the hour have met' was *first* shouted out at the inauguration of Jefferson Davis. You do remember how *that* venture turned out."

"Jefferson Davis you're not. More like...more like...help me out here."

"Modesty prevents," I said modestly. "I should say the post-war William Tecumseh Sherman. 'If nominated I will not run; if elected, I will not serve.' But I gather that I am conscripted and at a time when there is a dearth of unwashed Irishmen newly off the boat."

"Whatever *that* means. No, don't. Look, you'd be with your first, and, if you'll forgive me, your only true love, bookmaster that you are, happily ever after. The cash flow should be sufficient to sustain you in your abstemious lifestyle..."

"*Abstemious*." *Gretchenskaya* and I savored the word. "A word worthy of note. I am compelled to point out that every vowel appears in sequence." Again, the indulgent look, followed by a flash of brightest smile.

"Don't be *facetious*."

One had to be impressed.

Val threw two twenty dollar bills on the table. "I've got a two," she said, glancing at her watch. She kissed me on the forehead and started for the door. I took her by the wrist. "Sorry, Val. There's one more thing." I looked into her eyes.

"Enlighten me."

"I don't know what a third cousin once removed is either!" Val laughed and let go of my hand. With a turn of her head she tossed her long auburn hair over her right shoulder as she was wont to do one last time. It was silk and sunshine, brown and red and gold. Near the door she turned and waved. Val always wore great clothes. She looked the way she always looked—as if she had stepped off the cover of *Vanity Fair*. She cupped her right hand to her mouth and blew me a kiss. Then she was gone. That was the last time I saw her. Six weeks later, on LaSalle Street, she was hit by a Brinks truck and dead in a flash.

*   *   *

Charlie Calahutty handled the closing himself. According to Val this was a great honor. She would be in

Seattle, but I had nothing to worry about. Wear a suit, clean shirt, and tie. Smile. Say "please" and "thank you." Sign wherever the Big Double C said, "Sign." So I went downtown on the "el" and sat at a big oval table in a large room paneled with the finest cherry. It was the habitat of money. On the walls were splashes of colors by names I recognized. Fingers had diamond rings; wrists, gold and platinum watchbands. The scent of caviar and champagne lingered in upholstery and drapes. This is where we hang out, the ghosts of tycoon millionaires whispered, conjuring up images of cigar smoke and brass spittoons. Charlie said I did fine. He was immensely pleased. A good time, it seemed, was had by all. It was a bright August day, in the eighties. There's wasn't a cloud in the sky that stretched through the windows towards the blue gray waters of Lake Michigan, so close I thought I heard its waters lapping. In summer Chicago is the most alluring of lovers. We started at two and were finished by four.

Val telephoned that evening. Seattle was another triumph. The codicils cooperated and the addenda behaved. There was a god, after all: double taxation had been averted. When Val returned to Chicago she would move into a coveted corner office with a full view of the Picasso! How was The Yellow Harp? "Fine," I said. "Except that I have yet to find any of Edith Wharton's erotica." Val said she would make a reservation at Shandy's for Saturday night for my first "progress report." Three days later she was gone.

The funeral was a funeral. We all met at her sister Irma's house afterwards. Irma lives in a garish Moroccan style "villa," as she calls it, in Highland Park, one of Chicago's tony north shore suburbs. It is a short walk to the lake. From its second floor you can see water. Irma got the villa and three children for the exorbitant price, as Irma sees it, of twenty some years of marriage to Hal, a "muckety-muck" who works at the Board of Trade on LaSalle Street. Irma never tires of confiding how "housepoor" she is. But over her dead body will she part with the place, no matter how much they raise the property taxes. Wouldn't give the muckety-muck the satisfaction. When Irma isn't in court trying to squeeze additional alimony out of Hal, she runs "Mongoose Adventures," a travel agency that specializes in custom designed tours "off the beaten path." Irma brags that she has a vested interest in ecology.

Irma and I never really got along, in large measure because I sensed Irma's resentment of her "baby" sister's success. Irma was three years older than Val with forty pounds' extra mileage. Her resentment wasn't overt, but it was there like old clothes in an attic. Irma would grill me about why I was so "stand-offish," but I pretended I had no idea what she was talking about. Another factor, silly as it seems, is how Irma pronounces her name. "Err-Ma." As if it were spelled E-R-M-A. The first time we met, I made the irrevocable mistake of calling her "Ear-ma." Irma hates "Ear-ma." Irma is "Err-ma." It didn't help matters any when once, after more than four vodka and tonics, I lectured that the Spanish verb *ir*, which means "to go," is pronounced "ear." Ear-ma? Or Err-ma? To go or not to go?

I believe you should call a person whatever it is they want to be called. I like "Joe." I do not like "Joseph." Yet I can't seem to remember which it is that Irma demands. Whichever I choose, "Ear-ma" or "Err-Ma," I know I have a 50/50 chance of causing trouble. Once I tried "Sis." Irma *really* hated that. Whenever I guess wrong, about half the time, Irma insists I do so on purpose.

"How Val could ever have married you is something I will never understand," Irma would sputter, like a hot water heater about to explode. She'd jab her spangled arms wildly in front of her ample bosom. Irma wore lots of shiny circles of bright aluminum, iridescent blues, greens, yellows and reds, on her forearms, which looked like the bowling pins you see in ring toss booths at the carnival, rings and all.

As I said, Irma and I never really got along. But as the days passed after Val's death, something approaching warmth happened between us. I made a point of taking her to dinner every now and then when my nephews and niece were with the muckety-muck. I'd telephone from time to time so that Irma could weep and wail about how house poor she was. It made her feel good to rant and rave, so I'd pretend to listen. Irma seemed to me to have remarkable success in squeezing more and more out of Hal, but I never said so.

Val was right. I fell in love with The Yellow Harp. The building was built in 1882, a classic Chicago balloon frame structure, 20 feet wide and 100 feet deep, two full stories plus an attic a person could easily stand up in, and a full basement with eight plus feet of ceiling height. In the forty years of Kincaid Trampwell's stewardship, as I thought of it, books had conquered the entirety except for Trampwell's bed and, as I was soon to discover, a small room in the basement. My father fought against crabgrass his entire life. Trampwell surrendered to Tennyson and Kierkegaard without a fight.

I went from the closing straight to The Yellow Harp. I approached the front door, fumbling with the gangle of keys in an old coffee can that Charlie Calahutty had handed me at the grand finale. Someone—an undergraduate?—had framed the front windows in purple bunting.

"Want it gone, Boss?" I turned. There, hat in hand, stood an enormous Black man. Everything about him was large. He looked to be in his fifties. He was at least six and one-half feet tall.

"I be Zero Washington Roosevelt Lincoln," he said, "and you are Joe Rogers. I've been waitin' for ya." The colossus extended a hand as large and black as a cast iron skillet and crunched mine within. He reached into his pocket and slid a key into the lock. "Want it gone, Boss?" he asked again, pointing to the purple.

"I suppose so," I said. I stepped inside. A few minutes later, as I stood sideways in the only trickle of aisle I could find, overcome with awe, the black giant was back, bunting neatly folded to be presented to me with both hands.

"'Spects we ain't abouts to need this here no more, Boss. Let us pray with favor."

"I hope not," I replied. "Put it there, please." I motioned to the top of a pile of books. Zero Washington

Roosevelt Lincoln made it through the narrow path as lithe as a panther. When he returned, I tried to hand him a five dollar bill. I wanted him to leave, and he knew it.

"Tanks but no tanks, if yous knows what I mean," he said.

"No," I replied, trying to mask my irritation. "I do not knows what you mean. I mean, I do not know what you mean." In spite of myself, I joined in his laughter.

"Well, sir, Boss," he said, "what I be tryin' to say is this. Way I figures, you gonna need help. Now, seein' as how Mr. Trampwell and me was partners as you might put it for nigh on twenty-five years, I was hopin' things would jellybelly go on happylike, like they did before, before he up and died on me just like that." The black giant snapped his fingers. He looked down at me full in the eye with large, liquid eyes, large black eyes in a round black face.

"I don't know who you are."

He looked as if his mother had died.

"I told you," he said, eyes downcast. "I be Zero Washington Roosevelt Lincoln."

"Well, thank you for your help, Mr. Lincoln. Here, please." Again I extended the five dollars. His entire frame stretched ramrod straight. He seemed seven feet tall. I saw the burden of centuries and the weariness of his world.

"Come with me," he commanded.

I'm not sure why, but I made, I think, a conscious decision to do as he said. To get along, go along? He turned and I followed. We went around the side of the building through the gangway that separated The Yellow Harp from its vacant and boarded-up neighbor. We proceeded down a dozen or so steps. He unlocked a steel door and turned on a light. I followed through a dark passage to another door. He opened its padlock—a Master Lock Number 15, he would later inform me, "made right here in the good ole U. S. of A., Milwaukee, Wisconsin." We stepped inside. It was a small, neat room. There was a bed in one corner, a refrigerator and small stove in another, a table, two chairs, a television, a sofa. He motioned in the direction of the sofa as he seated himself on the bed.

"Take a load off," he said. I settled into the quicksand of the sofa's cushions.

"Like Mr. Trampwell used to say," Zero Washington Roosevelt Lincoln began. "The time is upon us now to throw the dead cat flat out on the middle of the table." Again he looked me straight in the eye. "Here's the proposition. You don't knows it, no sir, but I knows it, yes sir. You needs me almost as much as I needs you. Maybe even more. Mr. Trampwell, he let me stay here and he give me four hundred dollars walkin' around money every month. Not a whole lot some might say, but a whole heap lots better than a poke in the eye, which cannot be argued for sure and for certain. This is what my proposition is. I will go on helping like I was doin' for Mr. Trampwell and you don't have to pay me nuttin' for the first month, nuttin' at all. Jess let me keep on keepin' on with the place like I been doin'. Then, you ain't happy for why so for, I will take myself up and git me away with never a how-de-mind, no sir, and I be a man of my word, that's how my daddy raised me, yes sir. You don't knows it yet, no sir, but I knows it already now, yes, sir; you ain't about to be displeased like a frog stuck in a chicken coop, no sir, displeased and disappointed you will not be. But, like I said, to shuck the corn twice in a manner of speaking, if you was unhappy, why there wouldn't be no such problem, not for you, that is. Not at first. But someday soon trouble would come heaps and high-handed as sho' nuff comes the rain. True that. Of course, if I was gone, that wouldn't be none of my potatoes. True that, too. But, to flip the mattress over twice, if you was to ask me to stay on, I do believe I am of a right mind to consider such a request most favored nation status, as you might put it. You could pay me how so much you would wants to, trustin' in all that you're a fair man, which I hopes you are, cause, as my Daddy always testified, the Bible says to build your house on a solid rock footing and not on slippery slope sands. 'Cept I was due for a raise truth to tell."

There was a compelling fascination to this heartfelt peroration. No question about it. The dead cat certainly was flat out on the middle of the table. It was one of those Chicago offers you couldn't refuse. Well, I couldn't. "Okay," I said, the magnets of his eyes pulling the word from me. We shook hands.

*   *   *

Irma thought I was crazy.

"You have lost your mind again," she said. "What exactly do you know about this Zero person? Nothing! There is more here than meets the eye. Or less."

"If less is more, how much is Zero?"

This Irma ignored. She was as literal as a stroke.

"You should have got rid of that Zero person straight off. It's always better to use a shotgun than a pistol. Go in like Ma Barker! Hit'em with both barrels."

"After all," I responded weakly. "The Yellow Harp is his home. He has nowhere else to go."

"And this is *your* problem exactly why?"

It was paper, mine, in the form of a deed, versus Zero Washington Roosevelt Lincoln's twenty-five year homestead. It should have been no contest. It wasn't.

The truth is that Zero and I had entered each other's lives as facts—like shipwrecks. For my part, I thought that Zero would clean the windows and mop the floors. This was an inchoate expectation, the sort of reflexive judgment we make about the strangers we share the planet with, an assessment based on the superficial, a mirror of preconception and prejudgment. We are prisoners of self. Only those who outwardly resemble us, in appearance, or speech, or manners, do we envision as worthy. Zero was Black. He did not speak the King's English. Therefore, he would push a broom. *N.S.M.G.: Enough Said Among Gentlemen.*

It took less than twenty-four hours to put paid to this common wisdom. The next day I went early to The Yellow Harp. Already Zero had waged impressive battle against the army of books that the day before had seemed unconquerable. A few months later Zero told me how he had gone to the library evenings to study the Dewey Decimal System. "Mr. Trampwell" fought him "toofless and nailed," Trampwell preferring his own "I know that book's here somewhere, gimme just a goldarned minute" system. Now Zero was freed to divide The Yellow Harp into sections according to subject matter. He would shelve each book alphabetically according to author. He envisioned a card catalogue. His printing was neat, each letter carefully made, bold and black. "Like me," Zero laughed. He prided himself on his "lettering."

"I may not talk the talk, but I sho' nuff writes the write."

Within a week I jettisoned my plans to hire a graduate student part-time.

A month later, a bright, glorious Wednesday, as Chicago took baby steps towards winter, Zero, when I arrived at The Yellow Harp, was waiting in front, hat in hand. He was dressed in his Sunday best. Then I remembered.

"Why don't we take ourseffs a walkabout?" It was a wonderful idea. We headed to the great plaisance nearby in the middle of the midway.

Chicago surprises. An inland ocean. A lakefront "forever open, clear, and free." Not for nothing Chicago's motto: *Urbs in Horto*—"City in a Garden." Did you know? Grand boulevards connect—Logan, Humboldt, Douglas, Independence, Franklin, Marshall, Garfield, King, Midway

Plaisance, arteries of green song, where balloons, balls, and blankets rule, where young people with dogs chase frisbees and fly kites. To those who know they know better, know this: here you would build? Concrete? Brick? Asphalt? Steel? No. Here our grandparents played; here our grandchildren shall.

Neither of us said a word until we came to Laredo Taft's magnificent sculpture, "Fountain of Time," at the western end of the plaisance. We leaned against the low wall which curves in front of Taft's tight pack parade of humanity. Before the crag-like figure of Time, hooded and carrying a scythe, march men, women, and children. Priest, warrior, child, mother, baker, and, perhaps too bookseller, shoulder to shoulder, forward to oblivion. Carved in stone, the quotation reads:

Time goes, you say? Ah no! Alas, Time stays, we go.

"I will pay you seven hundred dollars a month," I said. "Needless to say I am not going to throw you out of your home. But I think it a good idea to confine the books to the basement and first floor. We'll rehab the second floor into an apartment for you and make a loft type place in the attic for me. It's time we both moved up in the world! Assuming, of course, that this meets with your approval."

The big black man spoke three words that sounded like one: "Sure do, Boss!"

"You know I don't like your calling me *Boss*," I reminded him gently.

"Sure do, Boss!" he said again and we both laughed.

*   *   *

Legions of dollars went missing in action as Zero fussed over the work. Three months later he moved into his apartment. Another three months and my own moving day arrived. Another lifetime—and fortune—passed before towel racks, doorknobs, and window "treatments" were in place. The ancient garage was wrecked and hauled away. The new one, with walls of cardboard (officially "pressed wood") had space for two cars and an attic for storage thanks to a pull down stairway. Zero bought a 1977 Buick—"Deuce and a Quarter, Boss!"—and I had the Volvo Val had bequeathed me when we'd called it quits.

Short-lived summer turned into endless winter. (Spring and Fall do not exist in Chicago.). Zero and I cleaned the first floor until it sparkled. Zero and his buddies had packed nineteen thousand six hundred and sixty-three books and trucked them over to Big O's Moving and Storage on Stony Island. That's the name of a street. Chicago has great street names: Cottage Grove, Arthington, Berenice, Throop, Kerfoot, Le Mal, Wabansia. Davo. Ernst. Flournoy. Hoxie! And, from seventh grade, the three that rhyme with "vagina": Melvina, Paulina, and Lunt.

I'd had misgivings but Zero insisted that the books would be safe at Big O's and they were. Zero and his gang rolled and brushed thirty-five gallons of Benjamin Moore's "Oriental Silk" onto walls and twenty gallons of its "Antique White" onto ceiling, trim, and baseboards. When the books returned and were properly shelved—oh happy day!—Zero said that The Yellow Harp looked as good as "the preacher's wife on Easter Sunday." We made room for two six foot tall ficus and various ferns. Zero worried about closing The Yellow Harp for so long, nearly six months.

"I hope we aint' doing like my Granddaddy," he lectured. "You see, Granddaddy, he had the best still for miles around up there in the hill country, down in Kainttucky. Granddaddy's still was a still that never was still. It would shake like a washerwoman at prayer meetin' time when the spirits took hole. But that there never still still put out the bess golddarn shine that side of the Blue Ridge. Old Granddaddy he jess couldn't keep his still workin' round the clock enuff. But then one day he got this new lady come to live with him outta Nashville with her city airs and all. Loretta. That was her name, Loretta. Well, Loretta talked my Granddaddy, Stetson Davy Crockett Jackson Lincoln—everyone called him the 'Shine King'—into cleaning and polishing and tinkering with that still and fixin' it up and makin' it all shiny like so shiny in fact that you couldn't look at it in the daytime without your eyes meltin' into your cheekbones. It was that shiny, yes sir! And the business was never the same, no sir!"

"The shine had lost its shine," I said mischievously. Zero gave an indulgent look. I thought of Val.

"I can do better than that," he said. "*Still* and all, time will tell. Remember, time stays. We goes."

*   *   *

Finally the big day arrived—the Grand Reopening of The Yellow Harp! For the first few hours we were a big success. Irma and her jewelry came. Charlie Calahutty made his grand entrance. He surveyed the crowd, his eyebrows the ears of a hunting dog: not his kind (the men had long hair and the women short). A grasp of my wrist, a piercing of his eyes, sparse automatic words, and a deft pirouette to retreat to his limousine back to the north side and sanity.

Wine, apple, cheese, and mushrooms floated by. Music pulsed. Multi-hued we danced. Zero, his friends, and I raised paper cups to Trampwell. Most important of all, a mob of students showed up. Once again Zero was right: "They gonna come, Boss, if you feed them free."

A procession of eight pale women appeared, in black, capes and hoods, gypsy skirts of taffeta, thin blouses with billowy sleeves, hair pulled into buns. They did not wear make-up. A gong sounded the party to a stop as the women arranged themselves into a semi-circle, eyes closed, faces transfigured. One smushed a pamphlet into my hand: *The Yellow Harp: Chicago's First Feminist Center* before stepping forward like the conductor of an orchestra. Her sisters hummed like a deep forest. In the crucible of the room, hot in the abrupt stillness, she read from a scroll that shook in her hands.

"A century ago, on this very spot, Cissy Sans Souci founded Chicago's first Feminist Center." Her voice scratched at our ears. "She named it *The Yellow Harp*. You may ask, "Why?"

"Why?" The voices of her fellows obediently asked.

"Why was the sacred name, *The Yellow Harp*, chosen? Other names were not chosen. *The Yellow Harp* was. Not *The Golden Harp*. *The Yellow Harp*. You may ask, "Why?"

"They already did," a slurred masculine voice shouted from the back of the room. "Get on with it."

"Why?" The women nonetheless asked again.

"Because yellow symbolizes femininity. It lies between green and red, between the spectra of birth and death. We may rightly say, therefore, that yellow sustains. That yellow nurtures. That yellow is yin like the moon."

"Yin like the moon," the coven repeated.

"But hers was a more delicate age. Female lushness is tucked safely inside. Yellow in the continuum of its ethereality is symbolic. The harp in its shape is also symbolic. It is uvonic. It is vulval and vulvar, uxorial and uterine. *Yellow Harp* is a double symbol to honor the plaintive cries Cissy San Souci heard for sisterhood justice, for sisterhood validation, for sisterhood power, for sisterhood unity. We, Sisters of the Sisterhood, say: 'You are not forgotten, Cissy Sans Souci. We are the handmaidens of your vision. We are the servants of your Truth. We pledge ourselves to honor your courage and be worthy of your Name'. Now I, Sister Emmeline, call upon Sister Medea."

Sister Emmeline's testimony was clearly news to Zero, for there was a puzzled look on his face which no doubt mirrored my own. Well, the building was more than a century old, I thought. Clearly Trampwell, Zero, and I were the wrongly gendered descendants of the sainted Cissy. The woman identified as Sister Medea stood next to the woman who had identified herself as Sister Emmeline. She threw her head back and closed her eyes. Then, starting in a whisper that grew to a growl and ended in a shriek, she began:

"Wellness of Truth, Cissy Sans Souci!"

The chorus before us moaned: "Wellness of Truth."

"Scorned! Rejected! Shame, Chicago, shame!

The chorus exploded: "SHAME! CHICAGO! SHAME!"

She: "Male genitalia are exposed! Unprotected! Weakness of flesh!"

They: "EXPOSED! UNPROTECTED! WEAKNESS OF FLESH!"

She: "Female lushness is tucked safely inside!"

They: "SO SAFELY INSIDE!"

She: "We have cinnamon ears and lavender thighs!"

They: "CINNAMON EARS! LAVENDER THIGHS!"

All together now: "HOW CAN WE TELL THE FUCKER FROM THE FUCKED?"

I scanned the first lines of *The Yellow Harp: Chicago's First Feminist Center*: "At the turn of the century Cissy Sans Souci ran a literary salon catering to the cognoscenti of the budding metropolis. Her achievements now lost to history..." That's as far as I got for my attention was drawn back to the Sisters of the Sisterhood. A small hibachi grill had appeared, conjured from beneath the robes of Sister

Emmeline. From under her cape Sister Medea presented a book, gripping it with both hands high over her head. It was Norman Mailer's *The Naked and the Dead*. She threw it on the grill, dousing with lighter fluid. Mailer illuminated.

Zero was the first to come to his senses. He leapt towards *The Naked and the Dead* curling in smoke. But before he could reach Mailer afire one of the Sisters tripped over her cape and fell against the grill. Like lightning bugs, bits of burning paper took to the air. The crowd panicked. There was a rush to the door. Hurly-burly, hurry-scurry, shelves came crashing down. The ficus tipped to the floor.

I fought my way forward, but Zero got there first. He made good use of a fire extinguisher he had grabbed off the wall on what remained of Mailer.   Then the real catastrophe. Lights flashing and sirens blaring, fire trucks came to our rescue. Windows and doors were smashed. Glass was everywhere. In great streaming arcs Lake Michigan roared into The Yellow Harp. Symbolism abandoned, Sister Medea was blasted against one of the fallen ficus, her legs scissoring in the tumescent water's thunder. I stumbled my way to a commanding figure in a red helmet.

"Stop! Please stop!" I begged. "The fire, well, it wasn't much of a fire, really, what there was of it, that is, was out before you got here."

"That may be," the red helmet answered, "but we have to be sure. We cannot take chances. This is a bookstore. Books are made of paper. Paper is combustible. In fact, paper is one of the most combustible of combustibles." The red helmet turned to direct another hose in the general direction of Sister Medea. But then he relented. "Okay," he bellowed through a hand held megaphone, "it's a wrap. The party's over."

Sister Medea sputtered to her feet. Zero took her by the elbow to escort her outside, a sequined black sponge glimmering with sharded glass crystals. The firefighters sloshed through the remains of The Yellow Harp for another twenty minutes and then they too were gone.

Zero and I set to work to salvage what we could. Sometime in the middle of the weary night a squirrelly man in his thirties appeared. "Alex Bezanis the name; fire adjusting the game." I didn't know what a "fire adjuster" is or does. The days of the frontier are long gone. We may still be on our own, but we are not on our own alone. We do not fix our own cars. We do not prepare our own tax returns. Our presidents do not write their own speeches. Hired guns for all! Sign on the dotted lines, as I quickly did, and Alex Bezanis would gird himself with measuring tape, camera, and calculator, to do battle on my behalf with the ones in whose good hands I most assuredly as it turned out was not.

He was a wonder of knowledge and energy. He did not say *the insurance company* or *the insurance firm*. He said *theinsurance* and Alex Bezanis could not open his mouth without saying these two words, which sounded like one: *theinsurance*.

He took command. "No! No! No!" he exclaimed.

"First I must take pictures, lots of pictures, for theinsurance. You have to put them back, back like they were before, before. The shelves. How many? How many?"

"Five or six," I answered.

"Theinsurance! Theinsurance! Didn't you think about theinsurance? Turn them all back over." Zero and I began undoing our undoing of the Sisters' undoing. Alex Bezanis snapped away, photo after photo. Alex's board-up crew appeared—$1,850 for eight windows and two doors!

"Theinsurance will pay. You wanna leave this place open all night? In *this* neighborhood?" A look came over Zero's face that I knew only too well.

As it turned out, The Yellow Harp was lucky. We were able to salvage all but thirty-eight books. The cruelest loss was a first edition of Elizabeth Cady Stanton's autobiography. The following afternoon "Sister Loltun" appeared. Zero, his gang, and I had cleaned up the worst of the mess. New glass gleamed, courtesy of Alex Bezanis' cousin, who owned "Second City Glass." Ficus and fern were none the worse, really, from their short course in gender awareness. Carpenters resumed their clamoring in the attic—the finishing touches were never finished—as November, chilly and wet, lay siege to Chicago.

She wore blue jeans and a tee shirt which featured Erté's "Queen of Sheba." Alluring. Zero was sleeping and I was on the telephone with Alex Bezanis, who needed yet another copy of yet another addendum to yet another supplement of The Yellow Harp's insurance policy. At the closing I was handed something Charlie Calahutty had called a "binder." "Blinder" was more like it.

Out of the corner of my eye I saw her fresh breasts breathing. She waited patiently until I was through.

"I have to talk to you," she said quietly. Her hair stretched along the sides of her head into a bun. She did not wear make-up.

"So, talk," I answered coldly. She had long arms and graceful legs.

"I am Sister Loltun. Or I was until yesterday." Her eyes? The loveliest of light browns. "I'm sorry," she said in a whisper.

"Take your sorrow somewhere else." I started to turn. A few freckles sprinkled beneath the softness of her eyes.

"When I found out what we were going to do," she blurted, "burn a book! A book! Well, I couldn't do that. So I stayed in my dorm. I saw the whole thing on television." Gil Scott-Heron has it wrong, I thought. The revolution *will* be televised.

"But, truly, sir, I never, for a second, imagined that it, the book burning I mean, would be done inside...inside The Yellow Harp, sir." You can imagine how I felt about her use of the military salutation.

"Not so safely inside," I said, but she did not hear me.

"The Yellow Harp! Even if..." She did not finish the sentence.

"Even if what?"

"Even if it is being desecrated by male chauvinist mercantilism!"

"That's really none of your business!" I was too fascinated by the curve of her neck to come up with anything better.

"But it is, sir! It is!" she protested, with the vehemence and innocence and purity of youth. When a beautiful woman is being her natural self is there anything in the force of nature equal to her power? I softened.

"Look, I have no doubt you meant well..." She cut me off.

"What I thought was...was that I should at least help fix, well, help fix the damage." Her eyes were wide with feeling.

"That's not necessary," I said. "I too was young once and full of conviction, believe it or not..."

"I believe it," she interrupted. "I really do."

Well, what more is there to say? She loved books. The feel. The smell. Plus...it would be an honor to walk on the same floors once trod by the sainted Cissy. So I relented.

Her name was Alice Treiger. She was given the name "Sister Loltun" in honor of the famous Yucatan cave.

"A powerful womb symbol," she laughed.

"I believe it," I said. "I really do." Disapproval spread across her face.

"My coming to you now is strictly to make amends." There was worse news. She had a boyfriend, Jimmy, who drove a cab. "'Sister Medusa says I'm a collaborationist," she laughed.

"Collaborate away!" I said.

"Strictly to make amends," "Sister Loltun" repeated, breaking the brief lock of our eyes. She walked to the back of the room. To my approving amazement Zero and she soon were humming about like happy bees.

It was just my luck that Jimmy turned out to be a decent fellow. He loved Alice and Alice loved him. So there you have it. Two's company. Three's a crowd. Four's a party. Soon Alice, Jimmy, Zero, and I settled down into a comfortable *ménage a quatre*. I used the last of Ma's bounty to buy the boarded-up building next door, to be used, initially for storage. For, despite Alex Bezanis' best efforts, theinsurance paid nothing. Nada. Zilch. Yes, the policy read:

ATLANTIS FIDELITY INSURANCE
Special Multi-Peril
AAA
Comprehensive Deluxe Business Owner's
Hazard, Fire, Liability, Business Interruption
FULL COVERAGE

But that didn't mean anything. It was, as always, the small print that mattered, and the small print specifically excluded "any loss resulting in any way under any circumstance from any act of any kind of any terrorism, anytime and anywhere and by any one."

"*Anys from Hell*" we call them, Alex Bezanis said. "Like pennies from heaven. Get it?"

I got it: I wouldn't get it. Theinsurance is wonderful, truly. It gives you key chains, flashlights, pencils, pens, scratch pads, paper clip holders, calendars. And what do you do? You mistake its kindness for weakness. You file a claim! Even when, clearly, the Sisters of the Sisterhood are terrorists!

It took two months to rehab that that the Sisters of the Sisterhood's evening of herstory had wrought. (*Rehab* is a synonym for *torture*). Alice graduated with a B.A. in Philosophy, *cum laude*, no less. She was thinking about grad school, she was thinking about business school, she was thinking, God help her, about law school. The Vals already in line would have eaten Alice for lunch.

"I don't think so," I said.

"Well, I have to do *something*. I can't find a job, especially now that I've graduated. *Cum laude* makes it even worse. I am *over-qualified*."

"We are the victims of our own success."

So we decided to fix up the place next door. Zero came up with the name: *Daughters Domain*. Alice and Jimmy would run it. It would specialize in all things feminist. As the months passed everyone thought I was some kind of marketing genius. The symbiosis between The Yellow Harp and Daughters Domain was "great merchandising strategy," according to the *Daily Crimson*, "likely one day to be a case study in urban marketing." Its Grand Opening was a huge success. That is to say the Sisters of the Sisterhood behaved themselves, contented with reciting their chant and taking credit for Alice's, Jimmy's, Zero's, and my hard work. Every day thereafter a stampede of women appeared while The

Yellow Harp's male chauvinist mercantilism babysat their boyfriends next door. Ka-ching!

*   *   *

Three years passed. Alice and Jimmy got married. "Jumped the broom," Zero said. We fixed up the second floor above Daughters Domain, Alice and Jimmy set up house, the money was fine. God was in Her heaven and all was right with the world, except for Chicago's winters. It is a lie that "you get used to them." It is probably also a lie that "they kill germs." So there I was, hunkering down for another six months of nasty cold and short tempers, rereading Richard Wright's *The Outsider* when Irma called. As I said, Irma and I had both mellowed. She wasted no time in setting me up.

"You know," Irma began, her bracelets tinkling in the background like wind chimes, "I have been thinking a lot about Val lately." Instantly I was on guard.

"One thing Val always said about you, Joe Rogers, is you had integrity." Irma said the word "integrity" the way a Century 21 gal says "money." "That"—there was a catch in Irma's voice—"is, I think, one of the highest compliments one human being can pay to another."

"Irma, what is it you want?"

"Simply this," she answered, without missing a beat. "The children and I have been worried about you. What with winter coming on and all."

"I love winter," I lied. "Gives me plenty of time to read."

"Oh, you always have plenty of time to read," Irma laughed. "No one understands it. After all, you *are* a grown man. Well, there's no law against it." There was a cacophony of tinkling loud and louder in the background.

"What is it you want, Irma?" I asked again.

"You know I don't like to be called 'Ear-ma,'" she chastised. "I do believe you do it on purpose."

"I'm sorry," I apologized. "I get confused."

"Let's not go there. Besides I am in a forgiving mood. It turns out, symbiosis king, that there's something here we can do for each other. Isn't that your forté?"

"Where?"

"Right here. I have this teensy-weensy problem and you are just the person to fix it. Besides it would be good for you. You have to start thinking about yourself more." The word *menagerie*, which Irma customarily would have worked into the conversation by now, she forbore. This self-restraint waved the reddest of red flags.

"*Mi causa es su causa?*"

"Precisely! I suppose. Whatever. Now, where was I? Oh, yes, how worried the children are about you. You know, of course, that *you* are their favorite uncle."

"Irma,"—I got it right this time—"Your children are too busy chasing sex to worry about me." Roberta was now 23, Hal, Jr., 20, and Ralph, 19.

"Don't be absurd. But that is just like you: to jump into the gutter when people are only trying to help."

"That usually is the wisest course."

This Irma ignored. "I'm going to pretend that you never said that. I am going to help you in spite of yourself."

"I thought the 'teensy-weensy' problem was yours, Irma." Two in a row!

"Well, of course it is. Why else would I be calling? You see, we have this group of the most fascinating people all set to go to Mabouhey..."

"Where in the world is Mabouhey?"

"In the Caribbean. I'm surprised you don't know. I swear. Val always said you knew everything."

"Val always said I knew nothing."

This Irma also ignored. Clearly I was in serious danger. "You see, this is where you come in. Archie LeBlat broke his leg, poor thing! Slipped on a patch of ice walking his cocker spaniel. It could happen to you! And I have this group, this *assemblage*, as Archie called it, of the most wonderful people, all sorts of *your* kind of people. You know, people who read books. It was all Archie's idea in the first place. Let's take Chicago to the Caribbean! Wouldn't that be 'whiskers,' as he put it! He came up with the name for the tour himself: 'The Prairie and The Island: Together at Last!' Sounded corny to me, but what do I know? The damn thing was fully booked before the ink dried on the brochures. This winter's been a bitch! Anyway, without Archie LeBlat, the whole thing was turning into a complete disaster!"

"Who's Archie LeBlat?"

"Sometimes you do surprise me! Archie LeBlat is the Carnegie Professor of Anthropology. He is a finalist for this year's Pfinster Prize. He wrote *Search for Myself* and *Myself and Jungle*."

Then I remembered. Archie and his entourage of young women, definitely *not* Sisters of the Sisterhood, came to the Grand Opening of Daughters Domain. He wore a Toulouse Lautrec hat. His blond hair came to his shoulders in waves. He smoked European cigarettes with an inlaid pearl cigarette holder, a la FDR. He was in his mid-thirties, slender, witty, nearing the top of the greasy academic pole. Most important, he was *recognized*. He had worked hard on his "brand." Alas, if you are not known to be somebody, you are nobody. It is a self-fulfilling circle: recognition, celebrity, identity, stature, influence. Worth? Alice called him "kissy-kissy." Zero thought he was a used car salesman. I read the first twenty pages of *Search for Myself* and decided that I, you, and everybody else should stop looking.

"Oh, *him!*"

"Beware the green-eyed monster, dearie! I'm sure you could outshine Archie LeBlat if you'd stop wasting time with that menagerie of yours." Forbearance had reached its limit. "After all, *you* were the only one I could think of as being in the same league as Archie!" This was meant as a compliment.

"You think I should get a cocker spaniel, too?"

"Probably not a bad idea. Next, a public relations firm. You'd be on your way! What I am about to propose would be of *immense* help. Where was I? Oh, yes. Archie.

Poor, dear! Well, enough about *him*. Yesterday's news. Put me in a real quandary. That stupid dog! Broke from his leash, the little shitter, and so now I'm supposed to issue refunds? It was just this time yesterday I got the call. I couldn't think what to do! But then Roberta came up with it. Perfect! I don't know why I didn't think of it myself. Perfect! Time for Joe Rogers to take off his warmup suit and get in the game. *You* are the ideal substitute..." Another epitaph possibility, I thought: "The Ideal Substitute."

"...what with your Ph.D. and all..."

"Irma,"—wrong this time—"I do not have a Ph.D."

"*Err-ma,*" she corrected. "*Err-ma.* So what if you never finished that silly paper. That's just pettifogging..."

The clipped sounds of her consonants clattered like high heels on cobblestones: footsteps in the dark. I felt a sharp stab in my chest.

"Just a minute," I said and laid down the receiver. Val was wearing a tinted raincoat, luminous and black. She was laughing. We were drunk and in love in the alley alongside Ristorante Braggia. It was after midnight and we ran after a cab that refused to stop. We held on to each other in the middle of Rush Street, laughing and touching in the orange rain. I rubbed my eyes and forehead and then I was back.

"...so it's decided then. You don't have to thank me. Good. Excellent. Wonderful. You see, there is a world beyond the printed page. I.S.B.D!"

Again I had to catch my breath. There was Val smiling, right in front of me. "Let me think about it," I hedged, knowing it was a mistake not to slam the door completely shut right then and there. But something stirred within. Whenever it felt like it, winter smacked Chicago in the face. The Yellow Harp was in good hands. I would be gone for only two weeks, or so I thought. There was no reason not to go. So I went.

I would find a buried treasure. I would be captured by love. Months later I would return to Chicago the Midwest Consul of the world's newest nation, the Commonwealth of the Island of Mabouhey. Yes, here you will learn a small something of my childhood, and, yes, again, other bits and pieces about me (working on *my* brand, am I?), but what matters is that I am but one of the threads of the tapestry. Mine now is the story of Marguerite, the fish-girl, who had to go beyond, who would go to Chicago and be destroyed, and of Schugay, the blackest boy with the biggest heart, who loved her. It is the story of a priest named Chester, who becomes a man, and of Travers Landeman, née Ohio businessman, reborn on Mabouhey as the carpenter Quince. It is the story of Travers' dead nephew, Matthew, of how the brightness of youth is betrayed, of how we must first love ourselves if we are to love one another, and of how we *must* love one another. It is the story, finally, of the most unlikely of heroes, the investigator Albert Sidney McNab, who always gets his man. All these stories are my story now: raindrops become river, river become sea, on the island of Mabouhey, high on a verandah, on the side of a volcano, at a place called Schugara.

Chapter Two:
Miscategorization

Travers Landeman
Athens, Ohio
1988-1989

Sandbox

Let us go now into major themes
Like money and the death of dreams.
We are diseased with possessions,
Rutted with debts and obligations.
We may not be late for the accountants.
Each day we wrap the shreds of our lives
Around us like hospital gowns
Slugging about in gray
While the lawyers grin
And rub their hands together.

Oh, how I miss playing in the sandbox!

For his thirty-eighth birthday Travers Landeman's wife, Corinne, gave him an espresso making machine. Over the years their language with each other had devolved into a genteel dialect of co-existence.

"I don't know what to say," Travers said. Long ago there had been intimacy, but now words went between them like shuttlecocks in an aimless game of twilight badminton. Corinne returned his desultory serve.

"Well, babykins, how about 'thank you' then?"

"Thank you then."

Corinne began calling him "babykins" when the sex stopped. Travers hated it, and she knew it. His full name was Charleston Travers Landeman. His father and his father's father were named "Travers," but Travers' mother had insisted on "Charleston" because, she insisted, "My son is not going to be just another Ohio Valley hillbilly." Travers hated "Charleston." Gradually, despite Travers' mother's protests, he came to be known simply as "Travers." They dated their senior year. On graduation night Corinne told him she was pregnant. "You must do the right thing," Travers' father said and Travers did. It was the natural thing to do, the responsible thing. Marry your high school sweetheart, settle down, raise a family. It all went together: supermarkets and television sets, split-level homes and cul-de-sacs. The flag. Voting Republican. Two months after the wedding Corinne told Travers she had miscarried.

"I'm sorry," Travers said. "Are you okay?"

"Actually, I'm fine. Peachier than ever. Stuff happens."

"In a few months we can try again."

"It's just as well."

"What do you mean?"

"I'm talking about my job and all."

"Not that again."

"Yeah. That again."

Corinne worked as a cashier at a nearby supermarket. "You think I like standing on my feet all day? That it's a picnic? A woman in my condition shouldn't have to work."

"What condition is that? I thought you had a miscarriage."

"I told you I did, didn't I? I'm talking about my system in general. May I remind you that I've always suffered from nerves? Ever since I can remember. I'm not supposed to overexert myself. A woman of my stature shouldn't have to work. How do you think I feel when Renee Carter plunks down her yogurt and soy on the conveyor belt? She smirks and asks how I'm doing. Big fat cow. If you'd ask your father for a raise, I could quit."

"We've been over this a million times," Travers said. "I'm not going to ask my father for a raise. You never complained about working before we were married. What would you do all day if you didn't have a job? Watch television?"

"What I do and don't do is none of your business, Mr. Afraid to Stand Up for Himself. I'd manage."

A few months later Travers' father called him into his office. "Just because you are the boss's son doesn't mean you're not entitled to a promotion. Congratulations, Mr. Assistant Supervisor!"

"Now I can quit my job," Corinne said. And she did. Travers' hours at work became longer while Corinne watched television. She took up bonsai, canasta, and mah-jong. "I take your suits to the dry cleaners," she said. "I keep a sharp eye on Octavia, who's about as useful as a twit. She never scrubs under the china cabinet, no matter how many times I tell her. I keep asking you to replace her with someone younger, someone who would make a better impression. My image is important to me, even if you couldn't care less, babykins."

Every few years there was a promotion. Every other promotion Corinne found a new house. "Trading up," she called it. The one before did not have sufficient closets; the one after would have a three car garage.

"It's a La Pavoni, imported from Italy," Corinne gloated. "Top of the line, babykins. I'm hosting canasta this week. Boy oh boy!"

Travers returned to the newspaper. Thoughts tried to struggle into coherence, but he would not let them. "Is this all there is?" He would not let them stick him in a thousand places. He turned to the Sports section.

Corinne's voice came from the kitchen. "It's for you, babykins." Travers folded the newspaper into his lap.

"Hi, Uncle T," his nephew's voice came over the wire. "Happy birthday and a whole bunch more. How are you?"

"Fine, Matthew. Just fine. Thanks for calling. It's good to hear your voice. How are you?"

"All right, I guess. Everything's okay, I suppose. But you shouldn't have given me so much money for my birthday. I didn't know that Benjamin Franklin was on the hundred dollar bill!"

Travers remembered taking the infant from his sister's arms when they brought Matthew home from the hospital.

"One hundred dollars!" his nephew repeated. "Thank you, Uncle T. Uncle T, I think you work too hard. When was the last time you went to a movie?"

"To tell you the truth, Matthew, I can't remember."

"We used to go all the time when I was little, you and me. *The Adventures of Sinbad. Fantasia. Twenty Thousand Leagues Under The Sea. Shane* was your favorite, remember?"

"Yes."

"You don't spend time with me like you used to," his nephew said. "Like you did when I was little. Maybe you could come to a basketball game sometime to see me play? I scored twelve points last week against Hutchinson and grabbed six rebounds. Coach said it was my best game yet."

"I read about it in the newspaper," Travers said. "I was really proud."

"You ought to come in person. Why don't you?"

"Well, Matthew, I'd like to. I really would. But I work late on Fridays."

"The game this week is on Saturday. If we win, we go to the State Tournament in Cleveland. We could win the championship. Coach says we have a real chance. It would mean a lot to me if you'd be there."

"Sure," Travers said. "Wild horses couldn't keep me away!"

"That's great, Uncle T. Really great. Oh, and thanks again for the money! And remember, try not to work so hard."

"That's sweet of you, Matthew. I will try to ease up a bit. It's just that...it's just that..." Travers did not go on.

"It's just what, Uncle T?"

"Oh, nothing. Listen, I'm really glad you called. Say hi to your folks for me."

"Sure. And you tell Aunt Corinne hello from me. And don't forget: see you Saturday."

Travers returned to the Sports pages. He had not wanted to tell his nephew: there wasn't much of anything for him to do but work. When his father died two years before, Travers became the owner—the sole proprietor as the accountants put it—of Ohio Valley Screw and Superior Manufacturing, Inc. It was a grandiose name for a not very grandiose business: nondescript squat structures, dour and ancient, situated on the banks of the Hocking River, which Ohio Valley S. & S. M. had polluted for nearly a century. In his grandfather's and great-grandfather's times the company had prospered; by his father's era the business had become that of managing decline. When his competitors had moved their workforces overseas, Travers' father had refused. "What's the point?" he anguished. "I didn't slug it out on Peleliu so that the bastards who killed my buddies and did their damnedest to kill me could take our jobs."

First the Japanese, then the Koreans, more lately the Mexicans took away this line or that product. Travers had inherited an ever dwindling work force, whose hostility grew as its membership decreased, as facilities and equipment day by day became obsolete. It was a global market now, but Travers, despite his mother's fondest hopes, was just another Ohio Valley hillbilly after all. He had finished high school, and, like his father and grandfather before him, gone straight into the family business. All through high school he had promised himself that he wouldn't, but he had. Now, every day it seemed, there was a new twist to his torture: environmental rules that doubled costs overnight, union demands that were thinly disguised featherbedding, accounting tricks that Travers didn't understand but which metastasized, the spawn of paper, into strangulations of filings, reports, and record keeping. Most insidious of all were the ubiquitous attorneys who had more to say about running Ohio Valley S. & S. M. than he did. Travers had come to despise it all, sitting in his glass enclosed office which overlooked the manufacturing floor. Every day he was reminded that every month fewer and fewer machines were in operation. It was only because the business was debt free that he survived, but it was, Travers knew in his bones, only a matter of time until...until...

"What do you think you're doing?" Corinne demanded the following Saturday as Travers laid a turtleneck on his bed. "You can't wear that."

"Why not? It's a basketball game."

"A basketball game? Don't be silly. We're going to the country club for the Braxtons' anniversary party. *They* have something to celebrate. Everyone will be there."

"The Braxtons?"

"Friends of the Gibsons. We met them at Maureen's fortieth, I think."

"You didn't tell me."

Corinne's face coiled in disgust as she reached for her pantyhose. "I wrote it down on the calendar in the kitchen, like always. If you're too scatterbrained, or lazy, or uncaring to check, like I've told you a million times, no, make that two million, well, you can hardly blame me. Forget that stupid basketball game, babykins. We're going to the country club and that's that."

Travers sat on his bed and brought his hands to his face. It was, he knew, either instant capitulation or ultimate surrender, the latter after protracted warfare. Either way, Corinne would have her way. Corinne always had her way. Would an appeal to family reach her?

"I promised Matt I'd be there."

"Matt?"

"Matt."

"Oh, *that* Matt." Corinne pursed her lips for a final dab of lipstick. "He's only a child," she said. "Children are resilient. They adjust. He probably doesn't even remember inviting you. You're so naive. He was just being polite. He probably thought you had nothing better to do. Besides the sooner kids get used to disappointment, the better. I speak from experience, babykins."

"What in the hell is that supposed to mean?"

"Listen, babykins, don't you ever raise your voice to me. Don't. You. Ever." Corinne's eyes were fierce with venom. "It's not my fault that you screwed up again by not checking the calendar."

How easy it would be, Travers thought…

"Get dressed, babykins. I hate being late. All the good appetizers will be gone."

"Matthew…"

"Matthew's not your concern, babykins. He's not your son. Mabel and Arthur have spoiled that kid. Plenty. The happy 'Leave It To Beaver' bunch, Ohio Valley style. That's all that Mabel and Arthur blab about. Beth is the 4H Barnyard Queen! Matthew made varsity! Give me a break. I'm the wife of the President of the biggest outfit in town, for crisssakes. It would be nice if just once you paid some attention to me. It would be nice, if it's not asking too much, if just once you had some concern for somebody other than yourself. After all, it's the Braxtons' anniversary. Wonderful that *they* find *their* anniversary something to celebrate! Everyone's going to be there! And you, all stuck up in your own world, would go instead to some stupid basketball game and a high school one at that! Maybe if it were the Cavaliers, courtside seats, something like that! Something I could impress Maureen with if we begged off at the last minute. THAT would make some sense. I'd love to see the look on her face! But a high school game in some sweaty gym? Bush league. You gotta be kidding. What are you waiting for, babykins? Get in gear." Corinne went to his closet. "Here," she said, "wear the Missioni jacket I bought you at Statlers."

Wearily, Travers rose from the bed and took the outstretched jacket.

"Are you color-blind?" Corinne shouted. Travers was reaching to take a pair of navy blue trousers out of the closet. "The charcoal grey merino! I suppose I'll have to pick out your tie, too. Just like I do everything else around here. Not that I get any credit, any appreciation. Not from *you* anyway."

*   *   *

Most of all, of all the paper men and briefcase women, Travers hated the politicians. The year before the Braxtons' anniversary party, where necklaces, bracelets, and children were appraised and all found brightest and best, one of Ohio's United States Senators, a former outfielder with the Cleveland Indians, came to town. He was there, he proclaimed, "On a matter of National Security: to save the manufacturing base of the Nation's heartland. We cannot go on, year after year, presidency after presidency, exporting jobs while we import cars and cameras, television sets and washing machines. We must reprioritize. We must recognize that American working men and women are the nation's most important resource. American workers are as good as any the world over. No, let me correct myself. American working men and women are better, more productive, more dedicated, more industrious. It is not their fault, it is not your fault, that jobs are taken away so that you are forced to worry if you will be able to support your families, to make your house payments and car notes. What has happened to the American dream? It has been cast to the wind, by a failure of vision, a failure of vision at the very top. We must and we will do whatever it takes to create those partnerships that are vital to ensuring that the job gets done and that what gets done is jobs. The jobs we have not only must stay, they must and they will multiply. We cannot and we will not let ourselves become ever more dependent on foreigners for parts and products that are vital to our national security."

They were in the Palace Hotel, in the grand ballroom, all the movers and shakers of Athens, Ohio, and the nearby towns and farms. Seated near the front Travers listened without enthusiasm. The words, "a failure of vision, a failure of vision at the very top," slapped him in the face. A lot you know, Travers thought, as the Senator's honeyed words continued. It is not vision that has failed, mine or anyone else's. The fault lies not in our eyes; the fault lies in our stomachs. Americans have grown fat and we like it. We're not about to go on a diet just because the rest of the world has had enough of starving.

The Senator concluded his remarks. The applause went on. The President of Ohio Valley Laborers and Fieldsmen, Local 1, AFL-CIO, stepped to the podium. He raised the Senator's arm high in the air. He gave the Senator a plaque. Both politicians shook hands. The next morning there was a large picture on the front page of the *Athens Messenger*.

What came of this, as far as Travers was concerned, was a program called the Reinvestment Development and Partnerships Effort. One of the Senator's aides visited Ohio Valley S. & S. M., returning for a second visit with the Senator's chief of staff. They spent the better part of a day at the plant, talking to everyone. They took Travers to dinner, handing him an application package for the program—a government guaranteed loan at a subsidized rate of interest. It was a great deal, they glowed. He could borrow as much as he liked. It was all *do-able*. With the Senator's help, of course. Definitely *do-able*.

Travers hated their use of the word. What did these talkers know about doing anything? Theirs was a world of press conferences and expense accounts while Travers struggled to meet payrolls and cover insurance premiums. The next morning Travers handed the application package to Madge Drayback, his office manager. Three hours later she was back in his office. There was, of course, an application fee. Audits of the past five years were required, "prepared by a Certified Public Accountant acceptable to the

Department of Commerce." Ohio Valley Screw and Superior Manufacturing would agree to pay "the prevailing union wages to all employees and certify that same was paid to all contractors, subcontractors, and/or providers of all goods and services." A legal opinion "from a law firm approved by the Agency" would certify that Ohio Valley S. & S. M. was "in full compliance with all local, county, state, and federal laws, ordinances, and regulations," that there were "no taxes owed or in dispute." Consultants "acceptable to the Department" would perform "environmental and social audits" to affirm that Ohio Valley S. & S. M. was "in full compliance with all environmental edicts" and did not discriminate "in employment or purchasing or sub-contracting on the basis of race, color, creed, gender, or national origin." Three million dollars of key man's insurance on Travers' life was mandatory, "from an approved carrier." Finally, before any funds were disbursed, signatures were required from a long list of bureaucrats in Athens, Columbus, and Washington, D.C.

"It would take a month to complete the application, if not more," Madge said. "The application fee itself is twenty thousand dollars. With the accounting and legal provisions, the whole thing is to the moon!"   When Madge was at her most exasperated, at the Union, at "Payables," at "Receivables," at the Internal Revenue Service, this was her stock expression.

Travers and his office manager exchanged weary looks. "It would be six months before we'd see any money," Madge continued. "Not to mention the costs going forward for handling the extra paperwork: monthly reports, quarterly reports, semi-annual audits, certified inspection records. I'd have to add on another full-timer and probably a part-timer as well." She put her hands on her hips and shook her head. "There's big penalties, too, for noncompliance. Civil and possibly criminal. Somebody makes a mistake..."

Travers looked up from his desk. Madge Drayback was sixty-two, close to retirement. He knew that she worried as much as he did. What would become of her if Ohio Valley Screw and Superior Manufacturing folded? Forty-one years of hard work and meager pay. For what? Travers tried to smile as Madge handed him the application package. "Don't worry, Madge. Something will work out." He put the package in the bottom drawer of a file cabinet and forgot about it. A few days later the Senator's Assistant Chief of Staff was on the phone from Washington. Could he be of assistance?

"I'm afraid not," Travers said. "We took a close look. I had my people run the numbers. It's not a good fit." Travers paused. "Not at the present time, that is." Travers sensed that it was unwise to be forthright. Even so, he felt a knot tighten in his stomach as he equivocated.

"I'm sorry to hear you say that," came the response. "This is not good news. The Senator will be...let's just say that the Senator will be disappointed." Twenty minutes later the Senator's Chief of Staff was on the line.

"Am I understanding this correctly?" she asked. "Perhaps, Mr. Landeman, I am not getting the complete story. Am I to take it that you are refusing to participate in the Senator's Reinvestment Development and Partnerships Effort?" Her words were sharp and just short of anger.

"It's not that I am refusing," Travers replied. "It's just that at this *particular juncture* the loan assistance the program offers is not a good fit with our needs." He hated the mealy-mouth language, distended, ritualistic.

"What particular needs exactly are you referring to? Your two hundred-year-old assembly lines? The billions of gallons of toxics you're dumping all over the place? Don't give me this bullshit. Everybody needs money. My strong suggestion is that you listen carefully to what I am about to say. Let me lay it on the line. The Senator doesn't give a damn how well R.D.P.E. fits your needs, as you define them. He doesn't give a damn about your particular juncture, as you so eloquently put it. Don't jerk me around. The Senator is out front on the jobs issue, promising that he is going to do something, and, by God, he is, or at least look like he is."

Travers shivered. Here it was all over again. His father had fought off—barely—vultures from a private equity, "alternative asset" management company, Urbane Capital. "They're after our patents and pension fund," his father said. "They'll strip the company bare and fire everyone. There'd be nothing left. Nothing." But this was even more menacing. This was the government of the United States.

Travers tried a strategic withdrawal. "You misunderstand," he said. "I should have made it clear that once we're into our next cycle we intend to devote time to an in-depth analysis of the program. Our analysis now is at best preliminary. But it seems likely that once we are into our new fiscal year the program"—what was it called?—"would, in all likelihood, be beneficial and we'd proceed."

"Do you think I can be put off so easily? There's no need to wait until you file this year's return with the I.R.S. I have no doubt it will be squeaky clean." There was a pause.

Here we go again, Travers thought.

"I also have no doubt that if you revisit your analysis *now*, you will find that R.D.P.E. is *exactly* what—what is the name of your company again?"

"Ohio Valley Screw and Superior Manufacturing."

"I restrain myself," the voice said. "...*exactly* what Ohio Valley Superior Screw needs. You may not give a damn about the average working man, Mr. Landeman, but, I assure you, the Senator does."

Two days later she was in Travers' office. "No hard feelings?"

Participation in the Reinvestment Development and Partnerships Effort would provide a ten-year exemption from new environmental rules set to take effect the following January. An emergency grant could be expedited "to assist with application costs and requirements." Fees and expenses would be packaged into the loan itself—"soft costs." They may be soft to you, Travers thought. You're not the one paying.

"We do it with smoke and mirrors!" the Senator's Chief of Staff boasted. "This is the nineteen-eighties!"

Travers knew he was defeated. He sensed his father and grandfather watching over his shoulder, shaking their fists in condemnation. He remembered with a shudder the aide's mention of the Internal Revenue Service. He was trapped. He attended meetings where he listened and pretended to understand. But not very deep down he knew that nothing they were proposing, that none of the plans they were discussing, dealt with the root cause of Ohio Valley S. & S. M.'s troubles. Mexicans and Koreans worked cheaper than Americans. There was nothing he, the Senator, or the R.D.P.E. could do about that. The borrowed money would permit Ohio Valley S. & S. M. to buy new, phenomenally efficient equipment (made in West Germany,) but the company had to agree, nonetheless, to maintain the same size workforce for ten years. No jobs could be eliminated, even by attrition. Wages would be maintained at their current levels, to be increased by no less than the rate of inflation as measured by the Consumer Price Index. Ohio Valley S. & S. M.'s days were numbered, with or without R.D.P.E. All the loan would do was prolong its deathwatch, ten years or so. To the politician, Travers realized, ten years is an eternity. And what about Madge Drayback? Wouldn't the extra years be an eternity for her, too? Wasn't the proffered loan just an extension of how he'd been managing things all along? Playing for time and hoping for a miracle? Travers thought and thought about all this. When he went home at night, he felt that his hands were dirty. He thought of the Internal Revenue Service, the Environmental Protection Agency, the Office of Occupational Health and Safety Administration, and he did not sleep.

*   *   *

We dare not admit mortality. We pretend that we do not know the final losing score. We let compromise and cajolery, prevarication and procrastination, dribble our lives away. We are free, but we live as if in chains. Travers Landeman had gone along, had done what was expected, had played by the rules; he stopped at red lights, he paid his taxes, and he was drowning. Every time he came up for air, for the briefest of moments, a smothering hand pushed him down. But finally Travers was lucky, for epiphany came. It came in the guise of spilled coffee.

The external auditor for Fidelity Inland Insurance was in his late twenties. His was the correct uniform: dark suit, white shirt, nondescript tie, suspenders, clean shaven, short hair. "Do you get a cut out of every dollar you squeeze out of me?" Travers wondered. "How much?"

"Here is my card," the young man said. He was four years out of business school and still enthralled by the paper proof he now extended, embossed crimson letters on ivory stock, testament that he was somebody:

Thomas Davidson Stroger, M.B.A.
External Auditor
FIDELITY INLAND INSURANCE
A Division of the Atlantis Group

He would do his job.

"Now remember," Madge Drayback warned, "we are required by State Law to carry Workmen's Compensation Insurance. There's no getting around it. The quotes we got from the other carriers are to the moon. Most wouldn't write us at all after that explosion at the steel mill in Toledo. If we can't keep Fidelity Inland, we'll be thrown into the state pool and our premiums will double if not triple."

So the suspenders man would show up, Visigoth or Hun, shake hands, and pick Ohio Valley Screw and Superior Manufacturing clean as a bone. It did not matter that what was audited was the past, a year already gone, a year disappeared into the great swallowing of what might have been, of what had not happened. It mattered not that no one had been injured, no claim filed, not one penny paid out. Fidelity Inland Insurance had collected estimated payments in advance for premiums based on payroll and workforce projections. Now it would take more. It always took more.

What had the tens of thousands of dollars of premiums paid for purchased? Office furniture? A new forklift? Energy saving retrofits? A ream of paper? A kilowatt of electricity? They had purchased...nothing.

Fidelity Inland Insurance should be happy, Travers thought. But happiness is never complete when there is yet another bite left on the apple. Why not take it all? Travers knew that Ohio Valley S. & S. M. would have to dig deeper, would have to cough up more. That was always the bottom line. That was always the way things sorted out. It was in the natural order of things that mistakes that were made were never made in his favor. The premiums that Ohio Valley S. & S. M. had paid were based on estimates, on the amount of payroll projected for each employee category, with separate sacramental costs as ordained by computers in insurance land. Now that the fiscal year was over, the happy time had come for the projections to be compared with the actual, for the tally to be made, for the tablets to come down from the mountain top. The piper would be paid. For Thomas Davidson Stroger it was Halloween, Christmas, and the Fourth of July all rolled into one.

Madge Drayback deposited a stack of manila folders onto the middle of the conference table. The young man in tie and suspenders set upon the feast laid before him.

"Here we have employees that are categorized as *supervisory*," he began. "Yet these time sheets"—his hands pawed around in the pile to emerge in a triumphant grasp— "yet these time sheets show that many of these...ahem...*supervisory* personnel attended to machinery of various sorts, filling in for vacations, overtime, emergencies, that sort of thing. It hardly seems apt to categorize them as *supervisory*."

Travers cleared his throat. "It's a matter of perspective. For the most part our supervisors supervise. The Union is quite strict about job classifications. There may be isolated instances..."

"Hardly isolated," the auditor interrupted. "There is a definite pattern here. Without question this is *miscategorization*."

Miscategorization, Travers thought. *Communism*.

Typhoid. Rape.

Thomas Davidson Stroger was in his zone. His hands swatted papers back and forth from one pile to the other, shoulders hunched, head lowered. He was a human microscope.

"These are definitely C3's, not C2's," he cried in exultation. His right hand jabbed the eraser end of a pencil into a calculator. "Seven point six percent!" he exclaimed, "not four point two. Seven point six. Definitely miscategorization." Travers looked at Madge Drayback, who was clenching her teeth. The auditor seized another folder.

"Here we have what purports to be *clerical. Clerical,*" he repeated, and, again, *"clerical."* He ran his right index finger down a list of names, pausing intermittently to make notes on a spread sheet. "This doesn't pass the smell test," he said. "Many of these *clericals* also work in the loading area, tallying deliveries, doing inventory, signing receipts and, as such, are exposed. Yes, they are exposed. There are forklifts. There are exhaust fumes. There is electricity."

Travers had been fixated on the auditor's business card. He had imagined, for a moment that he saw blood creasing from the corners of the auditor's mouth.

"Electricity?"

"Electricity."

"I'm afraid I don't understand."

"It's not rocket science. There is a large bank of transformers adjacent to the loading area. These have the potential of causing fire or explosion, not to mention the risk of electromagnetic surge to those in pregnant status."

"The transformers are in a separate room..."

"The *separate room*, as you call it, is, in truth, a screened in cage."

"Its wire is industrial strength galvanized quarter inch steel mesh..."

"So you may say. Exposure is exposure. Most of these *clericals* will have to be reclassified. Five point three, not one point two." Again the eraser stabbed at the calculator. This would go on, Travers knew, stab after stab, folder by folder, to Ohio Valley S. & S. M.'s last drop of blood. Travers would sit there, a convicted felon. He was guilty of the crime of employing.

Thomas Davidson Stroger had made it halfway through the stack of folders. With a show of magnanimity he had had made no changes in "Manufacturing," and "Maintenance." Thanks for nothing, Travers thought. "Manufacturing" and "Maintenance" were the highest assessed categories. "Mine is an inexact science," the auditor said. "When all is said and done, there is some room for interpretation. *Janitorial*, however, well, *janitorial* is entirely another matter." Again the eraser stabbed at the calculator.

Travers sat there. The "inexact science" was taking, in heaps and fistfuls, thousands of dollars, tens of thousands of dollars, dollars Ohio Valley Screw and Superior Manufacturing did not have. Travers saw the worried look on Madge Drayback's face and realized that the numbers the young man was conjuring up were even worse than Madge had feared. Then he noticed a stack of folders on the top of the file cabinet in the corner, duplicates of those on the conference table, and he saw the coffeemaker. Its carafe was half full.

"Let me get you some coffee, Mr. Stroger."

Madge started to rise, but took note of the look on Travers' face and remained seated.

"Cream and sugar, Mr. Stroger?"

The auditor, lost in his furrowing, gave a quick wave of his left hand. "Black."

Travers returned to the conference table. As he reached to fill the mugs, he stumbled. The coffee pot crashed to the table's surface, coffee spilling across the folders, spreadsheets, and calculator, to pour, steaming into the young man's lap. Confusion and apology. The auditor excused himself to the men's room. Madge Drayback mopped at the mess with cloth and paper towels. As soon as the auditor left the room, Travers stepped to the file cabinet in the corner. He grabbed a block of the duplicate folders. These he switched for the bottom third of the as yet unaudited stack on the conference table, splattering them with streaks of coffee. He placed the unaudited folders at the bottom of the pile on top of the file cabinet and returned to his seat. Madge Drayback pretended to concentrate on wiping up the remaining traces of spilled coffee.

"I am so sorry," Travers said when the auditor returned. "Clumsy of me. Very clumsy."

"Accidents do happen," the young man replied as he resumed his seat. "When you least expect them. That's why insurance is so important. Suppose I had been seriously injured? You do remember that woman at McDonalds." He laughed. "No harm, no foul." He examined the next three folders, determining that two "indeed" were—the dreaded word again—"miscategorizations."

"Oh, this is familiar!" He put the folder to the side and reached for another. "This too. It seems we have come full circle!"

"Let me have a look," Madge Drayback said as if on cue. She leaned over the auditor's shoulder. "Oh, these are duplicates." She turned and looked at Travers. "I'm sorry, Mr. Landeman. I guess I..."

"That's okay, Madge," Travers interrupted. "Don't worry about it. No harm, no foul. Isn't that right, Mr. Stroger?"

The auditor laughed. "Yes, you could say that. I suppose we all could say that."

Madge Drayback and Travers joined in his laughter. Now they were all the best of friends. It was as if they had gone to battle together and survived. The young man gathered his papers, reached for his briefcase, and rose from the table. "I'll shovel all this into the computer in Cleveland and get back to you in a week or so with corrected numbers. Fidelity Inland will be in touch." Of this Travers had no doubt. Fidelity Inland would definitely be in touch.

Madge Drayback escorted the auditor from the conference room. Travers closed the door. He sat with his feet on the table. Momentarily he felt a glimmer of satisfaction, of having gotten away with it, away with something, finally, with anything, but this tawdry triumph was quickly subsumed into a feeling of disgust. That his life had come down to such petty subterfuge! It was just one more of the absurdities visited upon him day in and day out, one more band of clowns marching by in endless parade with umbrellas and kazoos, while the years, past, present, and future, stretched before him like a desert. He was a shell of a man and he knew it. His father and his grandfather—they were MEN. But Travers was an empty suit, marching to the drumbeat of Fidelity Inland Insurance, to the dictates of the Environmental Protection Agency and the Internal Revenue Service, to the edicts of the Occupational Health and Safety Administration, to the constraints of Ohio Valley Laborers and Fieldsmen, Local #1, to the stupidity of the Reinvestment Development and Partnerships Effort, to filings, audits, and miscategorizations, each day a thousand cuts from a thousand pens by the likes of the young man in tie and suspenders with the crimson embossed ivory business card. And then he thought of Corinne.

*   *   *

Truly there is nothing so wonderful as free money, for that's what it boiled down to. To be sure, the word used was "loan," but a loan is intended to be repaid. If the borrower may plan otherwise, the lender should not. When borrower and lender conspire against repayment, the word takes on an entirely new meaning. Travers was a stranger in a strange land. He learned new words, the most important of which was "nonrecourse." The "loan," which ended up totaling eighty-six million eight hundred thousand dollars, was a "nonrecourse" loan. In financial dictionaries "nonrecourse" is defined as requiring no personal guarantee of repayment. No human being stands as guarantor. No man, no woman has an obligation to repay. If the loan is not repaid, well, then, the loan is not repaid. Mortgages may be foreclosed. Equipment and inventory may be seized, but no breathing being has to belly up to the bar. As Travers began to understand, nonrecourse loans papered the boom years of the nineteen-eighties. Real estate developers built office towers, condominiums, and shopping centers, paying themselves initiation fees and syndicators' fees. It was well and wonderful if repayment lasted beyond the first years, once escrows for "projected initial operating deficits" ran out. It was to be regretted, and it was, if "market conditions changed" and the loans, alas, went into default. Previously lenders had shied away from nonrecourse lending, except to Fortune 500 companies, which, it was thought, were immune to the vagaries of crass markets and their vulgar cycles. For everyone else nonrecourse financing did not exist—until the nineteen-eighties, when this two-tiered system of extending credit, recourse lending for the many, nonrecourse lending for a select few, came to be seen as discrimination, which, undeniably, it was.

In the last half of the Twentieth Century the word "discrimination" came to have only pejorative connotations. It became an ugly word. A new commandment controlled: thou shalt not discriminate against anyone at any time. It came to be thought of as fortunate that the great ocean liner, The Titanic, sank in the first half of the century rather than the second, when its crew would have been thought to have had as much right as women and children to its too few lifeboats. In the second half of the century, discrimination, in all forms, was to be eradicated. Thou shalt not discriminate against those who are drunk in public. Thou shalt not discriminate against the foul-mouthed. Thou shalt not discriminate against those who wander around glassy-eyed harassing for pocket change.

Providing nonrecourse financing to only a select few was discrimination! Politicians sprang into action. All sorts of programs were legislated. Accountants were happy because accounting fees were large. Lawyers were happy because legal fees were even larger. Bankers were happy, too, because they made money "servicing" nonrecourse loans which carried with them governmental guarantees sheltering banks from risk. Many jobs were created known as "consultancies," and these made the academicians happy as well. A dandy and diversified crop of money grew in the fertile soil of nonrecourse lending. Americans no longer manufactured. Americans pushed paper. When Travers asked the Senator's Chief of Staff what a nonrecourse loan was, she answered, "It means you don't have to pay it back."

They—the politicians—had him. Their crisp suits and starched blouses led him through a thicket of absurdities. Travers signed his name many times on the last pages of fat binders until, finally, the great day arrived. The

Senator stood on a podium at the main entrance to the plant. A giant blow-up of a check made payable to

OHIO VALLEY SCREW AND SUPERIOR MANUFACTURING, INC.

sat on an easel, framed by politicians and union officials on either side. The entire town, it seemed to Travers, ooed and aahed at the number, bold and black, in its center:

EIGHTY-SIX MILLION EIGHT HUNDRED THOUSAND

followed by the talismanic word

DOLLARS.

Travers and Corinne stepped to the microphone. The Senator kissed Corinne on the cheek and shook Travers' hand. Travers mumbled a few words. The Senator slapped him on the back. The giant check stretched between them, a bridge, Travers thought, to nowhere.

All this was but months ago and now he was old. The gush of money seemed to make everything right with the world, to everyone but Travers. New machinery was installed. Orders from the Department of Defense came like a blizzard. A new contract was negotiated with the Union; raises and increased benefits for all. It was morning in America. Let the grandchildren pay. Constantly Travers was badgered for donations.   Each cause was the most worthy. His refusal to contribute vast sums was denounced in pubs and on park benches. When Ohio Valley S. & S. M. donated one thousand dollars to the Red Cross, Travers was maligned as a "tightwad."

Corinne bought a second new car. "One for shopping. One for show!" she bragged. The house they had purchased the year before would no longer do. Its swimming pool was not indoors. Nothing assaults the spirit like dead leaves and bird droppings. Now Corinne hunted for the perfect house in the thicket of "upper bracket" listings. "This will be my final horizontal move," she told her canasta group, "I'm simply worn out from redecorating!"

More and more Travers gave way. Madge Drayback presided over two additional bookkeepers. Ensconced in Travers' old office, refurnished in Art Deco style, signed Erté lithographs on its walls, Arnie Williamson, M.B.A., the Wharton School, Class of '76, now Senior Vice President of Ohio Valley Screw and Superior Manufacturing, crunched the numbers. To Travers, Arnie Williamson was from another planet. Arnie was suave, correct, and, most of all, certain. When the first R.D.P.E. "interim" grant was funded, the Senator's Chief of Staff recommended a firm called MacroManagement, Inc., to "smooth things along."
MacroManagement turned out to be Arnie Williamson.
Arnie Williamson turned out to be the husband of the Senator's stepdaughter.

Travers survived by moving his office to the other end of the building and avoiding Arnie Williamson as much as possible. Travers thought of himself as someone who made things, things that were useful, things of pride. There was a time, not so long ago, when rivets and fasteners from Ohio Valley Screw & Superior Manufacturing sustained every refrigerator, toaster, and washing machine in the land, when plating, couplings, casings, and gears poured forth to assembly lines in Detroit and Seattle. To Travers, Arnie embodied all that had gone wrong. Arnie was a numbers man and Travers looked at him the way the Sioux and Comanche looked at the first railroads. Travers did not blame Arnie personally. It wasn't Arnie Williamson's fault that the rules of the game changed. Arnie didn't even know that they had. All Arnie knew was what they had taught him: numbers were all that mattered, in columns that always added up. Yes, Arnie was, pretty much, a decent fellow, but Travers and he had nothing in common. Ohio Valley S. & S. M.'s Senior Vice President triumphed in the blitz of paper and gloried in the sacraments of accelerated depreciation and deferred taxation. Travers liked to—he used to like to—get his hands dirty. Now a state of the art air conditioning system, manufactured in Belgium, ruled. For every one employee working on a machine, two tended to paper. It was a new world and it was not at all brave. More and more Arnie Williamson, Madge Drayback, and the Union ran things. Travers would arrive later and later and leave earlier and earlier. He played golf and bridge at the country club. He made a conscious effort not to think, and, for the most part, he succeeded.

*   *   *

One afternoon Travers left his office at two o'clock. Another posse of politicians was touring the plant. Travers had survived the morning without screaming. He pretended to understand everything Arnie Williamson said. Travers sat in the parking lot, his hands gripping the steering wheel. His chest tightened. Where to go? Not home. Corinne hosted one of her canasta groups on Thursdays. He began driving, meandering idly. Finally he turned into the parking lot adjacent to a one story building, formerly a supermarket. A red neon sign on the roof announced: "JILLIE'S," and, on the side of the building facing the highway:

Adult Videos   Marital Aids   XXX

Travers opened the door. Rows of magazines and videocassettes, of flesh and bone, waited in palpable need. Display cases lined the walls; like silent fireworks racks burst garish colors. Fluorescence hung like a stale mist. In the aisles three shrunken men fingered magazines, their heads down, their shoulders sagging. Travers started for the rear where a cluster of video booths and dark cubicles beckoned.

"Three bucks to enter!"

Inside a cocoon of glass shelves proffering contraceptives, dildos, and lubricants, a fat, hairy man perched on a stool. He turned his head from a television set where, with insinuation and braggadocio, couples on a dating show completed for prizes.

"Now, for twenty points," the host leered, "tell us the most unusual place you have ever made love."

"In da butt!" Contestant Number Two, a young Black man, shouted.

"Three bucks," the hairy man said again. "You get credit if you buy something."

"Uh. Okay." Travers extended a five-dollar bill.

"I ain't seen ya here before. You ain't a cop, is ya?"

"A cop? No. I am not a cop." Travers pocketed the two dollars change.

"Well, then, seeing as how ya ain't a cop, how about some identification? Lemme see your driver's license." Travers felt sweat on his forehead. His hands began to shake. Murky light and bright colors swirled. He threw his body against the door and ran to his car. Somehow the radio was not on its usual station of what was called "Easy Listening" music. Instead a cacophony of metal sounds, blaring and blasting, crashed into his ears as Jillie's faded in the rearview mirror. In an angry clamor, blinding rain assaulted his car. Something large streaked in front, horn blaring and lights flashing. Travers' car spun around to careen into a ditch, as Travers was thrown violently forward, chest touching wheel. A branch slapped against the windshield like a ghost. In slow motion, glass shattered. A waterfall of crystal poured over him. From far away and then nearer and near a siren sounded. Red lightning flashed. Travers unbuckled his seat belt and pulled himself from the car. He could see nothing. Then, like a dream, the outline of a man in a uniform coalesced before him.

"I am sorry, sir, but I am going to have to issue you a citation."

Travers told no one what had happened. His car was in the shop for three days. He borrowed Corinne's "shopping mobile." She didn't bother to ask why. The following Tuesday Travers returned to Jillie's. Soon he was a regular customer. He would go to the back room to a dark cubicle where he fed tokens into a slot in front of a glass wall. On its other side a naked woman gyrated on a king size bed. Its sheets were red and rancid satin, its pillows the shapes of valentines.

*   *   *

The days passed in numbing sameness. Corinne isolated in a world of canasta and new clothes. In the morning they had coffee and orange juice, cereal or English muffins, Corinne in bathrobe and slippers, Travers in suit and tie. He read at the newspaper. It seemed to him, without feeling, that the world was going to hell even more so than usual. Children were tortured by parents, judges were corrupt, athletes assaulted one another or murdered their families. Politicians blathered; there were hurricanes, tornadoes, fires, floods, and earthquakes. Editorials cried out for forbearance while front pages gloried in blood.

"I have news," Corinne announced a few weeks later as Travers trudged through the front door.

What is it this time? Travers wondered. Another new car?

"Wonderful news," Corinne continued sarcastically. "Your sister, Mabel, and that nothing of a husband of hers won the first prize at St. Canasius' raffle, an all expenses paid trip to this fabulous resort down by Jamaica somewhere. The New Papagayo Hotel. What is a papagayo? Well, never mind about that. Probably isn't all that fabulous, really, when you think how cheap Monsignor Kelly is." Travers slumped into the recliner. Corinne would babble on; he would pretend to listen. "But I bet it will seem fabulous to Mr. and Mrs. The All Perfect Catholic Family. Mabel and Arthur wouldn't know Tiffany's from Woolworth's. Ha! Mrs. Humdrum and Mr. Ho-Hum. Can you imagine? Mabel didn't even know what 'en suite' means."

Travers said nothing. He went to the refrigerator for a beer and returned to the recliner. "When do they leave?"

"Oh, not for a month or so," Corinne said. "You know how your sister is: Miss Perfect All The Time. Everything has to be arranged just so, poor thing. Wouldn't do to have loose ends. Well, she really doesn't have much to work with, does she, babykins? Not like you. If you'd start paying some attention to yourself, that is. I keep telling you Pierre has opened a men's spa, but, no, you're always too busy, or so you say. If you don't care about yourself, you could at least have some concern for my feelings. I am your wife, after all. We are seen in public together!" Corinne laughed an ugly laugh.

The vicious tone of Corinne's laughter slapped Travers awake. Had she always been like this? He tried to think, but could not remember. Their past was a void, numb, empty, blank. Travers took himself to the television lounge. Wars waged and famine ruled. He fell asleep.

"Well, they're off," Corinne informed him, two weeks later. "I mean they will be in about ten days."

"Who?" Travers had no idea what she was talking about.

"I swear you don't hear a word I say. I told you all about it. Mabel and Arthur. Off for adventure—Barbara Stanwyck and Errol Flynn, ha-ha!"

I should go away, too, Travers thought. Anywhere.

"Listen, babykins, I need you to do something for me, for a change. I rummaged through my old clothing. All that stuff from those awful designers season before last. Remember? Dresses that looked like burlap bags! Horrid stuff! Thank God that's out. I swear, there for a while, we all looked like prisoners on a chain gang. That's how Maureen Gibson put it: like prisoners on a chain gang. Well, of course, I wasn't about to give her the satisfaction of telling her then, babykins, but she was right! She was right! Oh, and I bundled up all those old shirts and ties you've been wearing since God know when. That stuff your father gave you just before he died. I'm so sick of those wide ties and baggy sweaters I could vomit. God gave you the goods, babykins; everybody says so. For the love of me, I don't understand why you don't want to make the most of it. Never hurts to gild the lily. I've been promising to get you a whole new wardrobe, babykins, for ages. Well, now there's no excuse. I've made an appointment for you this Saturday at Gaston's. And I'm going to call Pierre, too, to see if he can squeeze you in. Don't forget like you forget everything else I say. Okay, babykins?"

Travers retreated to the bathroom. When he returned, Corinne was sitting in front of her dresser, studying herself in the mirror. "This rejuvenating cream is a miracle," she said. "Oh, and by the way, you never asked what it is I need you to do." There was the usual whine of self-pity in her voice.

Hunt for a treasured pair of shoes lost in the caverns of your closets? Take the show car in for service?

"I packed two suitcases full of that awful stuff I was telling you about. For your sweet, dear sister. To take to the natives. Saint Mabel Calkins."

"The natives?"

Corinne glowed with the pride of painless largesse. "Yes, the natives. *They* can look like convicts. Probably are. On some island, somewhere. Some place nobody ever heard of. There is this Father Chester somebody who's been there for years and years. To listen to Mabel babble, he's some sort of saint, like Francis of Assisi or somebody. At some mission something. I'm sure *I* don't know. I'm sure I don't want to. Anyway, babykins, you and I are going to help clothe the naked, as the Bible says. You remember, I'm sure, how involved Mabel and Arthur are in all that Jesus stuff."

Travers opened his mouth, but then thought better of it.

"So, babykins," Corinne went on, "I want you to be a good boy and bring Mabel and Arthur what we no longer need so that others, less fortunate, might...might..." Corinne could not think of what to say next. "...Might, oh, forget about it."

The following evening Travers loaded the suitcases into the minivan Corinne had purchased the month before — the year old station wagon it replaced did not have heated seats. "Don't forget to remind Mabel to get a receipt from that Father Robinson Crusoe whoever. Charity is charity, after all. We're entitled to the deduction."

*   *   *

His sister and her husband were in their living room, on their knees, with their five children, rosary beads in hands. Travers let himself in through the side door. He waited in the kitchen, helping himself to a beer. He did not have much in common with his sister and her husband, he thought. They were family folk. They had each other, their children, and their God. As far as Travers could tell, it worked for them. He let it go at that. We have trouble enough each of us finding our own way home, he thought. God knows, I wish I could find mine. Best not to second guess those who trod firmly on the path ahead. Yet he could not help but wonder: what secret terrors lay hidden behind Mabel's and Arthur's serenest of smiles? Was their life as picture perfect as it seemed? Did he want to know?

Travers took the beer bottle into his hand and studied its label: crystal waters ribboning down snow-capped mountains. Do such places exist? Pieces of prayer came to him from the living room. He felt empty and alone. Finally, they were through. He heard his sister's voice: "Tommy, go to your room and do your homework. ...No, Beth, you may not watch TV. You have to clean up your room first. ...Robert, help your father bathe little Arthur." Mabel burst through the swinging doors that connected the kitchen and dining room.

"The side door was unlocked," Travers said. "I did not want to disturb you. I took a beer from the fridge. Hope you don't mind."

"Don't be silly, you old silly!" Mabel laughed as Travers stood for a hug. She had this simple warmth about her, something welcome and foreign.

"I brought over some things Corinne thought you should have. For your trip—to take to the mission. They're in the van."

"Oh, God bless you," Mabel said. "And God bless Corinne, too. I know he will. Travers, here, let me read this to you."

Mabel fumbled around for her eyeglasses. She went to the refrigerator to remove an envelope held to its side with a small magnet of the Virgin Mary. Its postage stamps were birds of bright colors. Then she sat at the kitchen table as Travers leaned against the counter.

"*My dear sister Mabel,*" she read. "*You cannot know how gladdened our hearts are to learn of your generous care and concern. We pray for you and for your dear ones. We count the days until you are with us in body as you are with us now and forever in the Spirits. We pray for you and your loved ones as you leave the comfort and safety of your home to come to us, my dear Sister. May the Spirits watch over you and protect you. Peace be upon you. Father Chester O'Reilly."*

There was a catch in Mabel's voice. She removed her glasses and looked at Travers with eyes that sparkled through tears. "What does he mean by *Spirits*?" she asked.

I'm sure I don't know, Travers thought. He said nothing.

"Well," his sister said, after a pause, "The Lord does His work in mysterious ways. We must trust in the Lord. We are his humble servants." She returned her eyeglasses to the top of the refrigerator. "I'll get Matthew to help you," she said. "Matthew! Matthew!"

Travers' nephew entered the room. He was fifteen years old. A shock of blond hair fell over his forehead, teasing his brightest of emerald eyes. There was a lanky grace about him. Everyone in the family, Travers knew, bragged about Matthew's good looks.

"Hi, Uncle T!"

"Hi, yourself, Matthew!"

"Give your Uncle Travers a hug," Mabel commanded.

Travers felt his nephew's body against his. Was he imagining a longing, an asking?

His sister brought short his inchoate wondering. "Matthew, please give your Uncle T a hand with unloading Aunt Corinne's van. Aunt Corinne has decided that the natives at the mission Dad and me are visiting should be dressed to the nines! God bless her generosity!"

Travers and his nephew went into the dark.

"Uncle T, can I ask you a question?"

There was an urgency in his nephew's voice that brought panic to Travers' soul.

"I suppose so," Travers responded weakly.

"You don't go to church much, do you?"

"I don't go to church at all."

"Uncle T," Matthew continued, "sometimes I feel like I am going to explode. Like I just can't take it anymore. Mom and Dad, that's all there is for them. Jesus and Mary. Holy Mother the Church. And I can't talk to them. They wouldn't understand. But I know you will."

Travers' stomach tightened and his head ached.

"Uncle T, maybe I could come over some time. We could go to the movies or something. Like we used to when I was little. Just so I could talk to you. Would that be okay?"

"Well," Travers said softly, hoping that his nephew would not detect his fear, "that would not be a good idea. Your parents might not understand. They have their ways and I have mine, but you are still their son." Travers looked away. He knew that once again he was a coward. For a moment, he feared that his nephew was going to cry.

"It's okay," Matthew said at last. "No harm asking."

"No," Travers repeated, "no harm. No harm at all."

But Travers knew that there was harm done and immeasurable damage to them both. In silence Matthew helped unload the van.

"I'm outta here!" Matthew exclaimed once he and Travers were finished in the garage. The kitchen door slammed behind him, swinging empty in the evening's sudden chill. Mabel rose from her chair.

"Matthew! Matthew! Where are you going?" she shouted. But the darkness did not answer.

"He's a good boy," she apologized, "he really is. But lately..." Mabel's words trailed away as tears came to her cheeks. Then she announced, with conviction, "We must place our trust in Jesus. His Will be done."

There are sins of commission and sins of omission. For many nights thereafter Travers did not sleep. He knew he should have responded when his nephew reached out to him. But he could not. He did not want his own bitter emptiness to spread its poison, least of all to his nephew, the closest he would ever come to having a son of his own. Gradually, like oil seeping into sand, the evening in his sister's garage faded from his mind.

Chapter Three:
Betrayal

Excerpts from the Diary of
Matthew James Calkins
(September 13, 1973—January 6, 1989)

September 10, 1988

I don't know. Everything goes around and around. Nothing makes any sense. I try to listen, to understand. Maybe I can change. In history class today Mr. Atkins quoted some famous person who said that if we are ignorant of the past we will keep on making the same mistakes. I felt like I had been punched in the stomach. I wanted to shout: I know all about my past and it doesn't make any difference. I keep making the same mistakes, over and over.

September 13, 1988

Today was my birthday. A whole decade and a half, the big One Five. Everyone was real nice, but all I wanted to do was hide in my room. Mom and my sister Beth made a big cake, orange cake with pineapple icing, they said it was my favorite and they looked at me with these big moony faces and I could tell they were real happy and I knew I should have been happy too. But I wasn't. I just felt like nothing was real, like it was all a dream or something. What is wrong with me?

September 14, 1988

I spoke with him today! He was standing, leaning like, at the water fountain. He had his book bag hanging over his shoulder and he was eating an apple and his yellowy hair fell in front of his eyes and he kept brushing it back with his other hand like he was playing hide and seek with the world and he was laughing. I kept looking at him, leaning and laughing and eating the apple and brushing his hair back. I saw his mouth open wide and his white teeth take the red from his hand and his mouth close and his lips move wet and silent and I felt jumpy all over like I was a horse tied up in a stable trying to get out to go galloping in a meadow somewhere.

I knew if I didn't go up to him right then and there he would be gone and I would yell at myself the whole rest of the day for not going up to him at the water fountain so I walked up behind him like I was getting in line and he moved to the side when he was finished and I lowered my mouth to the cold water and out of the corner of my eye I could see the top of his levis, the buckle of his belt, where his shirt disappeared into his pants. I drank the water for as long as I could and then I heard his words laughing in my ears.

"I don't care if you do," he said. "And I don't care if you don't. I can take it or leave it. I'm that kind of guy." Some girl's voice said something. "Besides maybe I already had plans for Friday night. Maybe I was just going to stay home and watch TV. Maybe I was just gonna kick it with my homies." Whoever she was, she walked away.

I could feel my heart pounding like a jackhammer. I stood straight up. We were alone!

"Hi, ya, Matt," he said.

"Hi, yourself, Tim."

"What's shakin'?"

"Tell you to it nothin' doin'." I watched his eyes as they watched her walk down the hallway. Then, as casually as I could, I said, "Except that yesterday was my birthday."

"Consider the alternative," he laughed. "Mr. Atkins said that in class yesterday. Only he didn't say it first, I don't think. But he said it first as far as I'm concerned I guess is what I'm trying to say." He was talking to me! "You know, it's funny," he went on, his brown eyes looking right straight at me. "You and me been in all the same classes since way back when, starting in Mrs. Myrtle's kindergarten, and I don't think I ever knew when your birthday was. So you're a Virgo! I should have guessed. See, my ma, she's a Virgo, too!"

"What do you mean?" I asked, thinking that somehow he could hear all of my insides rumbling and pounding and shaking. I tried real hard to be casual and easy-like.

"I mean," he said, pinching me on the cheek, "that you're a real sweetie!" Before I could say anything else, he threw what was left of the apple into the trash bin next to the water fountain and turned his back to me and walked down the hall. I was all jumpy like. "A real sweetie!" What did that mean? I watched him walk down the hall, his back

to me. I looked at his narrow waist. I thought he
walked like a soldier. He got to the end of the hall,
turned around, and waved.

September 22, 1988

I think about him all the time. I think about
what he said. How come I want to be with him all
the time? I wonder if he thinks about me even just a
little?

September 26, 1988

I am going to Hell when I die. There's nothing I
can do about it. That's the only conclusion there is.
My immortal soul will burn in Hell forever.
Monsignor Kelly said that eternity is impossible to
even come close to understanding, no matter how
hard you try. If every million years a bird took one
grain of sand from the beach, he said, billions and
billions of years would go by before even a tiny bit of
the beach, "significant in its insignificance," would
be carried away and billions and billions of years
more would pass before every grain of sand would be
carried away and still eternity would just be
beginning to start, like an eye that would blink but
the blink would go on and on and on like a red
light that got stuck so the green light would never
come on. That's how long eternity is! Even longer.
Monsignor Kelly never said why the bird was taking
only one grain of sand at a time, or why the bird
was taking the sand in the first place, which seemed
a strange thing for a bird to be doing, I thought, or
where the bird was taking the sand, but I think
that's all beside the point. The point is that eternity's
infinite. That's how long my soul is going to burn in
Hell. For eternity or infinity, whichever is longer. In

fire and brimstone. I don't have any idea what brimstone is, but I bet it's something really bad. Every night we all get down on our knees in the living room and say the family rosary because the family that prays together stays together. But all the time when I'm supposed to be thinking about Jesus and Mary and how Jesus got pushed around and suffered and how Mary his mother cried in her heart I'm thinking instead about Tim. Like when Jesus drops the cross and the soldiers are whipping him and then Simon comes and helps Jesus carry the cross, I see Tim and me. I know it's all wrong and probably a really, really bad mortal sin as bad as any mortal sin can be. Cause I get all excited when I see Tim and me and the soldiers whipping us and both of us there with our bodies all beaten and bruised and the blood and all. I think about Tim all the time, even when we're saying the Rosary, and I think about what Tim and I did and how my confession is no good because I have to be really and truly sorry and repentant. Even though I try to feel bad and sorry, I'm not really and truly sorry and repentant, inside, where it counts, in my heart of hearts (that's Father Cusack's favorite expression). Everything's all turned upside down, like in a storm. I know Tim and I have sinned in the eyes of Jesus and Mary and Holy Mother, the Church. That's all there is to it.

When I went to Confession I was scared that Father Cusack would know it was me. The body, Father Cusack said, is a temple for the soul and we must not defile it. It is sacred and holy and the image of our Lord and Savior, Jesus Christ. That's why we have to keep it pure. I'm not sure I understand exactly, but it seems to make sense, I think.

I listened as hard as I could. Father Cusack almost made me feel like I could stop piling my sins one on top of another. He said he knew I was sincerely and truly sorry. Wasn't I? I wanted so hard to believe that I told him I was. Then he asked did I vow to go in peace and sin no more? I knew the correct answer was "yes" so there in the dark silence of the confessional I said that I did so vow even though I could feel my pledge melting away just as soon as I said it. Maybe a split second of being sorry is enough if that's all you can manage no matter how hard you try. I sure hope so, so that if I get hit by a beer truck on my way home from Confession my soul will go straight to Heaven where it will be with the angels and Jesus and Mary forever while Monsignor Kelly's bird can take his sweet time taking grains of sand from the beach every billion years one by one.

"Then, for your Penance," Father Cusack said, wrapping it all up, like he had fought this really fierce fight with Satan and come out on top, "say two Rosaries. Go in peace and sin no more."

September 28, 1988

We did it again. Tim's parents were away for the weekend but Mom and Dad didn't know that. All they knew was that I was spending the weekend at Tim's. We hung around the Avonleigh Mall most of the day Saturday playing pinball and video games and stuff like that. Then we went to Tim's house and fixed tacos and drank beer from the basement refrigerator so that Tim's parents wouldn't notice anything missing and we watched TV and went to bed late, around midnight. I didn't say anything about the time before, after the Homecoming sock hop, and neither did he, the day just went by like in a movie. And then in the middle of the night Tim jumped from his bed into mine and grabbed me under the covers and pulled my shorts off and we both were naked and on top of each other and we did things. The night passed and we played music and lit candles and smoked some cigarettes. Tim said he knew where he could get some pot and that next time he would. Next time! Then we took a shower together and went back to bed and did it all over again. I don't know what to call it, what we did. Make love? Have sex? Sin?

The next morning Tim was in the kitchen fixing bacon and eggs and English muffins and there was orange juice and hot chocolate. He already got the newspaper from the front porch and was reading the sports section like I wasn't even there. He didn't say anything about it and so I didn't either. I wanted to, but I didn't. I wanted to talk about next time. Instead I took the front section of the newspaper and pretended to read. So we just sat there eating without speaking. Then we were finished. I said I would help clean up with the dishes and stuff but Tim said no, it was okay, I didn't know where everything went. I could tell that he wanted me to leave so I got my stuff.

"See you around."

"Yeah," he said.

That's all. "Yeah." He didn't turn around. So I left.

September 30, 1988

Why is it so hard to put it into words? Words make it sound cheap. Ugly. But it's not. It's like some kind of something you can't control, like the wind, like liking carrots but hating broccoli. In the gym guys kid around, showing off, teasing, saying things like "I bet you suck dick real good, cocksucker!" We slap each other on the butts with towels. But just let anyone get the slightest inking that maybe somebody is that way, then look out. "Queer!" They get this really ugly way about them. You can be anything but "queer." You could rape your sister. You could steal from your best friend in the whole world. You could piss on a Crucifix. Anything but being "queer." "Queer." A word. No. An atom bomb. But I don't feel "queer." I just feel like I'm me. Like I am the way I am. They look at you like you've got a disease and they could catch it. They keep telling Ernie Thomas that he likes to dress up in stockings and a bra and wear lipstick and stuff like that. I want to shout, "No, it's not like that, not like that at all." But I'm too scared to say anything so I just play along and play it off. No one suspects me, or Tim, either. We're too macho. They just pick on the wispy guys like Ernie Thomas. Sometimes I wonder how many of them are doing it too, just like Tim and me. How many of them, the queer haters, are "queer"?

October 2, 1988

He doesn't want to talk to me on the phone. He said it would be best if we "just chilled" for a while. I knew what he meant, he said. Sure, I said. But now all I think about all the time is him. I don't go to Confession anymore just because of "impure thoughts." They're only a venial sin and that means Purgatory, not Hell. I can handle Purgatory, I think. From what I understand, it's nothing like Hell. Not even close. It's just being apart from Jesus and Mary and all the Saints for a while, sort of like a waiting period or something. Since I'm always thinking about Tim and me all the time anyway there's no use pretending that I could somehow stay in a full state of grace. So I only go to Confession when I just can't help myself and I miss Tim so much that I masturbate and that, for sure, is a mortal sin, without a doubt, though I don't think it's as bad a mortal sin as having sex with Tim. That's a whole lot worse sin. Probably because it's a whole lot better than just "pleasuring" myself. That's what Father Cusack calls it. So it makes no difference, really. Hell lasts forever and forever. One mortal sin counts just as much as any other, which doesn't seem fair. I mean, it's a whole lot worse to kill a whole bunch of innocent people than just one, isn't it? So, once you've killed one person, you might just as well go ahead and kill a whole bunch more. That's probably why there's serial killers. Eternity is eternity. As for me, I'll take my chances with venial sins, impure thoughts, lying, being mean to my sister. Stuff like that. I just got to make sure I get to Confession right away whenever I commit a mortal sin like pleasuring myself or being naked with Tim and be real careful crossing the street on my way to Confession and look out for beer trucks.

October 4, 1988

I tried to talk to him today after biology class. But he said he was real busy.
"Hope you are doin' okay," he said.

October 6, 1988

We did it again. I spent the night at his house. It was just like before, only better. I don't know why it was. Maybe because I was so worried we'd never be together like that ever again. I don't understand it really. Then the same thing the next morning like it never happened. Can men fall in love with men?

October 8, 1988

I went to the library downtown to find books about it. But I couldn't get up the nerve to ask the librarian for help. So I looked through the card catalogue. It took a while, but I finally found something. I remember the title. "The Normative Nature of Homosexuality." The card had a special notation: CUSTODIAL SECTION - SEE LIBRARIAN. I just stood there, holding the card in my hand. Finally I got up the courage to go to the woman at the front desk. She reached for the eyeglasses that dangled on her breasts.

"Custodial Section," she said. "Ah!"

She stared right at me. She pointed to a desk in the corner. "You've got to go over there," she said, "and ask Mr. Keyes to get the book out of the impound section. You don't look twenty-one."

My heart pounded even harder.

"Let me see some identification," she said. "What did you say the title was?"

"I forgot," I said. She looked at me like I was a criminal. A strange little noise came out of her nose. I turned away and pretended to look at the books on the shelves in front of her desk. Then, after a short while, I headed for the door.

"It's for your own protection," she said.

October 12, 1988

Today after gym class Freddie Denmark picked on Ernie Thomas. It was just after we had all showered and were getting dressed.

"Bet you don't want to leave, huh, Ernie?" Freddie taunted. "Bet you really get off on the scenery just about now. Enough meat for you, Ernie? Or can you only feel it real good when you've got your lipstick and panties on, huh? Is that it, Ernie? Do you wear a bra, too, Ernie? Huh? You know, my sister is using this wonderful new perfume. It's called "Pink Magnolia." Or is it "Peach Passion"? I bet you'd really like it. It comes in a great big bottle. It's so divine." Freddie stretched out the syllables. "Dee-vine." "I'll bring you a bottle real soon, Ernie, I promise."

Ernie Thomas didn't say anything. He just kept putting his clothes on. No one else said anything either. We all were laughing along with Freddie, me and Tim included. Finally Ernie slammed his locker shut, grabbed his tote bag, and headed for the exit.

"Say, Ernie," Freddie shouted after him. Ernie turned at the door. "A hard man is good to find," Freddie smirked, grabbing his crotch and laughing. We all laughed with him too. "A great big bottle, Ernie. A great big bottle. I promise. You know you want it." Freddie gave a sick grin that looked like one of the slides we studied in biology class. Ernie didn't say anything. He just left.

"So the faggot runs away," Freddie said, like he was somehow disappointed as Tim and I and the others stayed right with him in his ugly laughter.

October 17, 1988

He says it was just one of those schoolboy things. I'd better not tell anyone or I'd be sorry. He looked horrible and full of hate like he was somebody I didn't even know. He has a girlfriend now. He's not a faggot. I might be, but he isn't. He tried to act like somehow it was all my fault, like I had forced him or something. He says he just wants to forget all about everything, like nothing happened. I went home and stayed in my room with the door locked 'cause I couldn't stop crying. I told my mother I was sick and I stayed home from school. Mom would knock on my door, but I'd tell her to go away and leave me alone. Dad tried to talk to me, too, but he said all the wrong things, like how I could confide in him, tell him anything, he'd understand. He said that he was young once, too. I could talk to him. But I couldn't. I just couldn't.

October 19, 1988

I am being a real martyr. It doesn't matter how Tim treats me, I tell myself. I will wait. I will love him forever. If I am true, Tim will come back to me. I know it. So I try not to cry all the time, especially when people are looking. I found this poem written by John Clare, who was crazy and blind, I think, and wrote lots of poems about birds and trees and rivers and meadows and stuff like that. The introduction said he was a minor Romantic poet, a precursor (I had to look the word up in the dictionary) of the great Romantic poets like Wordsworth and Shelley and I thought his poems were pretty awful until I read this one. It made me think how noble I am and how true. It made me cry, too, but a different kind of tears. Even though I hurt real bad there is a part of me that won't let go, that won't give up and I promise myself that I would hold on to that part real tight, as tight as I can, until Tim comes back to me. Here's how John Clare said it more than two hundred years ago. It was like it was me (except you have to change the part about "woman's" love):

Whence comes this coldness, prithee, say,
If woman's love be this,
Ah, woe is me, and well a day,
A changing thing it is.

To love at morn and doubt at noon,
And at a little shower,
Fold up your petals and so be done
Like any other flower.

Alas! The smile did me betray
The hour we ever met,
For woe is me and well-a-day,
Thee I can never forget.

Upbraidings? I can offer none,
Nor scorn for scorn allow.
I could not love as I have done
If I could hate thee now.

John Clare may be a minor poet but that's a major poem as far as I'm concerned. I copied it down. I'm going to keep it inside my wallet until I got it memorized by heart. I too am going to be true no matter what. Tim will come back to me. I know he will. I miss him so much.

October 23, 1988

Finally I dragged myself back to school. I was to talk with the school psychologist, Mr. Knorr. He wore a brown corduroy jacket with leather patches on the elbows. He sat in a leather chair with chrome arms on its sides. I sat on a sofa and he started in.

"You have everything going for you, Matthew," he began. "Good looks. Very good looks. A mother and father who love you, who take care of you. You're a good student when you put your mind to it. All you need to do is hunker down. When I was your age, we just had to muddle through all by ourselves, but now it's different. Now there's all kinds of assistance available to you. Me, for one. I'm here to help. That's my job. Talk to me. I'll listen."

A glimmer of hope stirred inside me. I started to open my mouth.

"What I'm saying is," Mr. Knorr went on, "well, what I'm trying to say, Matthew, is that I could understand it if you came from a dysfunctional family, something like that. Well, then, there'd be some explanation. Something to go on. But, you see, the truth of the matter is that there's probably nothing much the matter here except normal growing pains. You know, the testosterone kicking in. What's the problem, Matthew? A girl?"

"No," I answered softly. "It's not a girl." I hoped he might pick up on this and, if he did, I promised myself real hard that I would tell him everything, the whole truth, everything. But he didn't.

"Well," he said, "that's probably part of the problem right there. You are at an age now where it's time to start experimenting with the opposite sex. It's natural. I know your family is Catholic, strict Catholic, Matthew, and I would not suggest for even a minute that you do anything against your religion. But some experimentation, as long as it's kept within bounds, is perfectly natural. Repression can lead to serious developmental problems. Are you dating at all?"

"Not exactly," I said, the glimmer stirring again. But he did not ask me what I meant. Instead he sort of shrugged and then just chugged along like a railroad train.

"Well, then," he said, "it's time you should. There are lots of swell girls here at Athens Central who would just love to get to know you better. Why, I bet when you walk down the hall, lots of pretty faces turn your way. You know, you remind me a lot of myself when I was your age, though I must say that I was never the head-turner you are, not even close."

He was off and running now. It was like I wasn't even in the room. He talked all about his first real love, how her parents objected, how his heart was broken, how he couldn't eat or sleep for weeks. Life wasn't worth living. He wanted to kill himself. He cried all the time. Then, one day, at a McDonald's, he met Sally. He would never forget that day. It was rainy and cold, even though it was May and just as he saw Sally for the first time the sun came out. It was like it happened yesterday. He went on and on. I wanted to scream: but what about me? But what about me? But I didn't. I just sat there. Finally he was through.

"So, I guess you could say that what I'm trying to say, what I'm trying to get you to understand, Matthew, is to take it one day at a time. It will get better. For right now, think about what I'm saying. Jump in there and get your feet wet. You've got nothing to be afraid of. What do you say, Matthew?"

The best I could muster was, "I'll try, Mr. Knorr."

"That's the spirit," he said, and slapped me on my back.

November 3, 1988

I guess I am doing better. Kind of. The hurt stays with me but it's not a sharp pain anymore. I eat and I sleep. It's just like it's a part of me, like one of my elbows or toes. I carry it around like we were Siamese twins. When I see Tim at school, he looks the other way. I want to run to him, to touch him, but I know I can't. I follow him around as much as I can get away with, without being too obvious. He doesn't speak to me. How many times does he have to tell me? Am I deaf? That's what he said the last time we spoke on the phone. It's over. Leave him alone. Don't call. Stop my goofy following him around like a puppy dog. He won't come to the phone anymore. I know he's there, but his mother says he's not at home. I try not to call all the time because maybe his mother would figure it out and then what?

November 7, 1988

Mom and Dad have decided that I should talk to a priest. I am to see Father McArtle on Saturday. I can talk to him, Mom says. She's sure of it. All the kids love "Father Art." He is "with-it." He speaks our language.

November 10, 1988

I went to the rectory today at 3 p.m. Father McArtle, "call me Art," smiles as we shake hands. He has tickets to the Cavs. We will drive up to Cleveland, see the game, be back late. He asks me to wait while he showers. "You can watch TV while I clean up, chum," he says. He disappears into the bathroom attached to his room. "They call it a cell," he laughs. Then he winks at me. There was one of those old black and white movies from the thirties on, with Gloria Swanson and Laurence Olivier. I started to actually pay attention to it when "Art" called from the bathroom.

"Hand me those slacks, would you, chum?"

I walked to the bed, picked up the slacks, and went to the bathroom door. He opened it wide and took the slacks. He was naked.

"Thanks much," he said. Our hands touched briefly and then he closed the door. He reappeared a few minutes later wearing a cream colored turtle neck and the slacks I had handed him.

"I didn't know priests could dress like that," I said.

"Well, priests are people too," he answered. He smiled a bright smile and touched me briefly in the middle of my back as we left his "cell." "Do you have a driver's license?" he asked as we walked to his car.

"A learner's permit."

"Well, swell, then. Why don't you take the wheel?"

I had not known that the red Corvette I had seen parked behind the rectory was his. I settled into the driver's seat, adjusted the rear and side view mirrors, and moved the gearshift into "drive." Without my realizing it, my Siamese twin of hurt just melted away. We laughed. We listened to the radio and sang together when a really corny song like "Teen Angel" came on. The miles sped by. We talked and talked. Actually, I talked and talked. It was like there was this wild mustang inside me that had finally broken free. I told him that English was my favorite subject, that I was going to be a writer. I recited one of my poems and he said that he thought I had a real gift. I told him about my diary and how

I try, no matter what, to write something every day.
The whole world seemed bright and sunny. Every
once in a while Art put his hand on my thigh.

As if to make everything perfect, the Cavaliers
came from behind in the fourth quarter and beat the
World Champion Detroit Pistons on a last second
shot that rimmed and rimmed around the basket
before falling through just as the buzzer sounded. I
couldn't help it, but, all through the game, I kept
looking at Isiah Thomas. He looked just like Tim, I
thought, except that he is Black. Art brought plenty
of popcorn and soda pop. The crowd really got into
the game. It had been a long time since I could
remember having such a good time and when, in the
fourth quarter "Zeke" stole the ball and ran down
the court for a lay-up, it was like Tim just faded
away.

I was in a really good mood as we headed for
the parking lot for the return trip home. "I thought
that Joe Dumars would kill us," Art said. "But the
Big D came through. The best offense is a good
defense." Then, it was strange, he put his hand on
my shoulder and looked me in the eye. "And vice-
versa," he said. He laughed as if to himself and slid
behind the wheel. I tried not to let my
disappointment show.

He exited the freeway about an hour south of
Cleveland.

"Ramada Inns are my favorite," he said.
"Always a first class restaurant. You are hungry,
chum, aren't you? Or did all the popcorn fill you
up?"

We talked all through dinner, about the
Cavaliers, about St. Canasius. Art told me how lonely
it was being a priest, how much he enjoyed being
with me, just getting away, if only for a basketball
game. He made me feel important the way he said my

name and calling me "chum." After dessert was finished, he handed me a fifty dollar bill.

"Ask the waitress for the check, will you, Matt, while I pull the car around front. Meet you outside."

"I don't know how much to leave for the tip."

"Well," he answered with a bright smile, "that depends on the services rendered. Ten percent is standard. Twenty percent is generous. You decide." At the time it seemed like such an important decision. Finally, after sitting there a while studying the change, I decided to split the difference. Art met me outside, but the Corvette was still parked where we had left it.

"Slight problem, chum," he said. "Seems the damn engine flooded."

It was the first time I heard a priest swear, but it was not to be the last.

"It'll have to sit for a while, maybe overnight. I'd better call your parents. Go back inside and wait." Twenty minutes later he was back, room key in hand.

"Well," he said, "I guess it can't be helped. We'll have to spend the night here."

I had this strange feeling go all through me, like cold water.

"I told your folks we'd be back first thing in the morning. Is that all right with you, chum?" He put his hand once more on my back, only a little lower, as we walked to the room. There was one king-size bed.

"The only room left," he said. "We were lucky to get it." He reached for the remote and handed it to me. "I'll be back in a jiffy," he said. "Why don't you get comfortable, take a shower, okay?" I watched TV for about twenty minutes. Then he was back, carrying a grocery bag.

"Goodies," he said, locking the chain lock on the door behind him. "Say, I thought you were going to get comfortable." There was a hurt tone in his voice.

"Uh, okay," I said. I went to the bathroom and stepped into the shower.

When I was finished, I brushed my teeth with the toothbrush and toothpaste I found in a little plastic bag on a shelf above the sink, and combed my hair. I dried myself and returned to the bedroom in pants and tee shirt.

"Wow!" Art said. "You are one mighty fine handsome dude!" He was propped against the headboard wearing only his shorts. His chest was real hairy. There was an opened bottle of Jack Daniels Whiskey on the nightstand. He held a glass in his right hand and an unlit cigarette in his left.

"Come on, light my fire!" he said. I picked up a book of matches that was next to the bottle of Jack Daniels Whiskey. I could not help it. I felt tingly all over. My hand trembled as I brought the lighted match to his cigarette. He held my wrist as I lit the cigarette. "Don't worry, chum," he said, in a whisper. "Everything will be fine. Just fine." He was real gentle. Then he handed me a glass filled with ice. "Name your poison."

"Uh, I'll have what you're having," I said.

"That's the spirit!" It was like his eyes were fire. "Why don't you get more comfortable?" I took off my tee shirt and pants and sat on the bed next to him dressed only in my shorts. We sat there a while, propped against the headboard, pretending to watch TV. But it was like there was this storm going on inside my body. My thoughts, which weren't thoughts really, were all jumbled and scrambled and swirling around like a tornado. Then, after refilling our glasses, Art turned off the TV and put on the radio. He started talking.

"You know, Matthew, you are very special to me, already. It's not easy being a priest. We need love, just like everybody else. To love and be loved. Like Jesus said. You can understand that, can't you, Matt?" His hand glanced across my thigh. He raised his glass. "Happy trails!"

We emptied our glasses and he refilled them.

"I would never force you, Matt. I would never force you to do anything you don't want to do. But I am so lonely. I need you, Matt. I need you so much. To reach out to me. To let me know that I am not alone. That there is someone who cares. That you care."

I felt dizzy and excited and afraid. The Jack Daniels Whiskey had something to do with how I was feeling, but I knew it was more than just that. I got real hard and it was like it was not even a part of me anymore, it was all by itself in its own life, jerking and throbbing. I saw that he was looking at it with big wide eyes. I looked at his, which had slipped out of his shorts to one side. Its head was like a big purple and red eraser swelling right as I could see it.

"You can touch it," he said. "Go ahead. Don't be afraid."

"But it's a sin, Father!" The words came out of me from some place far away and long ago, but they came out. When you say something, do the words just go into the air and disappear or do they go inside you and stay?

He got up from the bed in anger and walked around the room. "You know I don't like you to call me that," he said. "Not when we're alone. If we give each other comfort, how can that be a sin? Jesus commanded us to love one another."

"I'm sorry," I said, and meant it. I didn't want him to turn me away. Everything was upside down and inside out. I didn't want him to be mad at me. I don't know why I didn't, but I didn't.

"That's all you can say, 'I'm sorry'?"

"I'm sorry...Art." I struggled with the words. His penis was hard, as straight as an arrow, and I could not take my eyes away.

"Better. Much better. That's more like it." He walked to the side of the bed where I was sitting and stood in front of me.

"Make it up to me." His words were real dark like they had this strange power. He put his hands on either side of my head. "You told me you had a learner's permit," he said. His voice was soft. "Show me. Kiss it."

There was this little drip glistening on its tip and it had this real sweet taste. I wanted more, but he pulled himself from me to reach into a tote bag he'd propped on the night stand.

"Take off your shorts." He had this silver ring in his hand and he put some kind of lotion on it.

"What's that?" I asked.

"It's a cock ring. Helps keep the dick hard. You young guys don't need 'em, trust me," he said. "I can see that." He gave a small grunt-like chuckle. He reached to the lamp on the nightstand and turned it off. He lay down on the bed and pulled me to him.

"That's quite a rocket you've got there," he said. "The complete package. Sixty-nine is my favorite number."

The next morning it was just like it was with Tim. Like nothing had happened. Art chirped merrily on about the Cavaliers, about Joe Dumars—"there's a body for you"—the chicken fried steak at dinner the night before, the pancakes we had for breakfast. He let me drive the rest of the way home, but it was like I was all by myself behind the wheel. I was all confused inside and it was strange because all I could think about was Tim. With Tim it was different, gentle and different. I don't know how to explain it. Now I felt dirty. I pulled the Corvette next to the sidewalk in front of my house.

"Last night..." I began.

"Last night was a whole lot of fun, chum."

"Fun?"

"What would you call it?" I didn't say anything. "Well," he continued, "I for one enjoyed myself. That's for sure. And you did, too. Some things you just can't fake. Believe me. Might as well admit it."

"Admit what?"

"That you're gay. No big deal. Some like bananas and some like oranges." He tried to hand me fifty dollars—two twenties and a ten. "Be a good sport, chum. Take it."

"For services rendered?" I cried. "Is that the standard ten percent, or do I get twenty?"

He laughed a big laugh. "That's pretty good. That's why I'm getting to like you so much. Stupid you're not. I've had my eye on you for quite a while, you know. And you know too that you wanted it, maybe as much as I did, maybe more. I remember how horny I was at your age. Don't try all that high and mighty holy shit with me, chum. It simply won't wash. Word gets around, you know."

I felt a pain in my stomach. "What does that mean?"

"Simply that Tim O'Connell makes his confessions to me, you little snart, that's what." He said this with a vicious laugh. "I wouldn't play the little goodie two shoes role if I were you. Nobody would believe you anyway. I'd have to defend myself, just wouldn't I now? And, like I said last night, the best defense is a good offense. You wanna tell the world you're queer, that's your business. Not mine."

I felt this really heavy pain in my head and I think I must have put my hands over my eyes or something because just then he got all real nice again.

"That's just the way it works out," he said in a soft voice. "Nothing personal. It's up to you. You know I didn't make you do anything you didn't want to do. Your dick was harder than mine. You'll get used to it. The double life, I mean. You'll find a way. It'll get better. It's not the end of the world. I'll tell you one thing for sure. It's a heck of a lot easier on you young guys nowadays than it was when I was coming up. You're lucky. You have guys like me to show you the ropes." He put his hand on my thigh and squeezed.

"Look, anytime you want to go to a basketball game, just give me a holler." He had this real twisted smile on his face as he tried to move his hand farther up my leg. I pushed him away. I thought I was going to throw up. I jumped from the Corvette and ran into the house. Thank God, no one was home. I ran to the bathroom and splashed cold water on my face, over and over. I pulled all my clothes off and jumped into the shower. And then tears came, running down my face, mixing with the water, and I couldn't help it. If I loved Tim so much, how could I have done what I did with Art? How could I have wanted to? Art was right about that. I couldn't get his sick smile out of my mind. "Until next time, keep your rocket in your pocket," he said. Finally I went back to my bedroom and locked the door. I lay on my bed. I hurt all over and all I could think of was that everything was like it was all closing in around me, like I was all alone in a dark cave that was getting smaller and smaller.

November 14, 1988

Yesterday after Mass Art came up to Mom and me. He told her what a fine job she was doing raising a good Catholic family. He was sure our trip to

Cleveland, car trouble and all, had done me a world of good, getting me to face facts, to see myself as I really am, to stop going around in a dream world. Then, as we were leaving and Mom couldn't see, he winked.

November 16, 1988

I keep thinking about Tim and I keep thinking about Art. If I love Tim so much, how could I have done what I did with Art? How come I want to do it again?

November 20, 1988

I ran into Tim in the hallway today. He looked right through me as if I wasn't there. I walked up to him anyway. "Get the fuck away from me!" he yelled. Everybody stared. I drifted through the rest of the day like a ghost.

November 22, 1988

I think about Tim. Then I think about Art. Maybe Art is right. I keep telling myself that I have to stop fooling myself, that, above all, above everything—everything—I have to tell myself the truth, even if, especially if, I can't tell anyone else. The truth, whatever it is, will set me free. Art is right. I did want it as much as he did. I still do.

November 24, 1988

Mom and Dad and the whole family came to the game, hollering every time I touched the ball and jumping up and down whenever I made a basket. There was this guy who played forward for Palmer

Central who looked a lot like Tim. I was at the free throw line and just as I released the ball I saw him, out of the corner of my eye, looking right at me. I thought in that instant that he could tell and I was sure I had missed the basket, but I didn't. The ball slid through the net, all net, without hardly touching. As I turned he ran by me. His arm reached out and he slapped me lightly on my backside and ran down the court and was gone. If we had won we would have gone to the State Tournament, but we didn't. But that wasn't what I was all down about. My Uncle T had promised me he would come to the game, wild horses couldn't keep him away, he said, but he didn't. He didn't even call.

November 25, 1988

I wish I had somebody to talk to. I still think about Tim, but it's not the same. I think about Art even more. And I masturbate. Sometimes I think maybe I have it all wrong. Maybe I misunderstand everything. After all, Art did take me all the way to Cleveland. He bought me a nice dinner and everything and said I could see him again. Maybe he does care about me. I miss talking to him.

November 27, 1988

I have decided to stop going to Confession. For one thing, it's wearing me out. For another, I can't pretend any longer that I am truly sorry for my sins. When Father Cusack asks me for the umpteenth time if I am really and truly sorry, it's just a lie when I say, yes. I think he knows it, too, even if he's unwilling to admit defeat. I can see his point. He's got a lot invested in trying to save my immortal soul. No one likes to lose. I wish it was back in the Dark Ages when you could buy a Permanent Indulgence, which was like a

"Get Out of Jail Free" card, except you can keep on using it, over and over, because it's permanent. Betcha it would be my luck that I'd be too poor to get one. I wonder how much they cost? Probably only kings and queens could afford them. If you stole money from a poor widow so you could buy a Permanent Indulgence, would it still be good? If so, I bet the crime rate was really high. Permanent Indulgences must have made Confession unnecessary. Stands to reason. That's probably why you can't buy them anymore. All the churches would close down. The priests and bishops would be out of work and I don't think there's much else they can do but church stuff like the Rosary and Mass, which most people (except Mom and Dad) find boring.

November 28, 1988

I don't want to go and sin no more. I want to go and sin as much as possible. I want to sin morning, noon, and, especially, night. Sin, sin, sin. Lying is a sin, but I don't think you go to Hell if you tell lies all the time. You just probably have to spend a long time in Purgatory. Maybe until that bird carries away just about the entire beach, all but a small bucketful that some baby was playing with that the bird didn't see, on a far corner, or behind a bush. That's too long, way too long, as far as I'm concerned. Besides what if Purgatory is nearly as bad as Hell? I mean, it doesn't sound all that bad, being deprived of the company of Jesus and his holy Mother, Mary, and the rest of the gang, but suppose it's worse than that? Like being trapped in a fleabag hotel with a million cockroaches and bedbugs? Or sitting in a dumpy movie theater with snot on the floor where everyone has big time body odor and farts all the time and you can't get out no matter how hard you try. I had a dream about this once and it was awful. It's the truth that's supposed to set you free, isn't it? Not lying. So, unless I luck out at the last minute thanks to handy-dandy Extreme Unction, there's simply no way as I see it that I can make it to Heaven. Period. There's no use pretending. If being like I am is a sin against Jesus, why did He make me that way in the first place? Isn't He supposed to know what He's doing? If anyone does? He made me in His own image and likeness, right? Maybe when I was coming down the assembly line He was tired and forgot something, to tighten a screw, for example. Maybe He was simply having a bad day at work or took His eyes off the ball just for a split second. Can God make mistakes? That's what I am. A great big mistake.

December 3, 1988

I keep thinking about it, like I was in some magic spell or something. I have to stay away from Tim 'cause I'm afraid. Afraid of what I might say. Afraid of who might hear. Suppose I blurted out something about Art and me? That would be a big mistake. The truth is I think about Art a lot more than I think about Tim.

December 5, 1988

I told Mom that maybe I should see "Father Art" again. He was someone I could talk to. That much was true. She got this big moony glow on her face, all motherly and bliss. She gave me a big hug. I wanted to shrink away into nothing because I felt crooked and wrong like I had reached my hand into the pitcher she keeps on the top shelf in the pantry and taken money out of her special kitty, the money she keeps for a rainy day, like I had robbed her.

December 7, 1988

Art took me to the basement of the rectory, behind the boiler, where there is this small room with a bed and a refrigerator and a toilet. There is this mirror standing on legs alongside the bed. He was all real gentle. He combed my hair with his hands. He said he was sorry if he'd done anything to hurt me, for anything he might have said wrong. Did I forgive him? Then he took my hands into his and kissed them and put his arms around me and I thought I would explode. I wanted to tell him how all I had been doing was think all the time about...everything. The Cavaliers' game, the Ramada Inn, everything. But he told me not to talk, not to say anything. We would let our bodies speak. He undressed me. He was real gentle. Then we were together again in bed. He had whiskey and ice and all kinds of creams and stuff. He had this little brown bottle with a yellow plastic wrapping that he called "Poppers." He brought the bottle to his nose and then to mine. I got all dizzy and dreamy. Everything got real alive, all jumpy-like. Art says he loves me, he really does. He says that Jesus, the real true Jesus, not the one processed and packaged down through the ages by the philistines and moneylenders who have taken over the temple, but the Christ whose sole commandment is to love, to love one another as I have loved you, says that love can never be a sin. Art will be with me. He will take care of me. There is nothing to worry about anymore just so long as we have each other. We must keep our secret safe to ourselves and for ourselves. And I promise.

December 9, 1988

After school Art leaves the door to the rectory's basement unlocked so I can be with him in the little room. Sometimes the door is locked and then I know that he can't come, even though he wants to be with me more than anything else.

December 12, 1988

Art gives me presents. "Mementoes," he calls them. A basketball signed by Magic Johnson. A shirt from Jamaica with laughing boys playing on the beach. A mug from Stuttgart, West Germany, with a bright red arrow and black sword. I am not to tell anyone where I got them. People are vicious. People are jealous. People are trapped inside their own tiny lives. Because they are unhappy, they want everybody else to be unhappy, too. They can't bear it when they see two people caring for each other, and looking out for each other, and loving each other, because nobody cares for them. They are all dead inside. Who wants them anyway? All dried up like a withered grape. Our love has to be just ours, a secret.

December 15, 1988

Art is going to take me to Chicago, to the Midwest Catholic Youth Crusade, weekend after next! We're going to have a bang-up time. I can hardly wait!

December 17, 1988

There's been a change. Art is very sorry. I think I see tears in his eyes. Monsignor Kelly is going

after all, too. It's not a good idea, Art says, for me to
go. He'll make it up to me. He promises. Then he does
start crying. I felt like it was my fault, somehow. "It's
time you learned what a dildo is," he says.

December 18, 1988

Here's this poem I came across in my poetry
book. It made me think about Tim. I wish I could see
the look on his face if I could recite it to him in
person. It was written by a poet named A. E.
Housman, nearly a hundred years ago:

Oh, when I was in love with you,
Then I was clean and brave,
And miles around the wonder grew
How well I did behave.

But now my fancy passes by,
And nothing does remain,
And miles around they'll say that I
Am quite myself again.

And I am. That's what my Mom says. I am myself
again. She's real happy. I guess I am too.

December 19, 1988

I see Art all the time. It's like we just can't get
enough of each other. Mom says I've "bounced back."
Dad says it was just "growing pains." We're a good
Catholic family, they say. The Lord works in
mysterious ways.

December 20, 1988

Tim came up to me outside the gym. There was
no one else around.

"I've been thinking about you," he said. "A lot."

"Isn't that special!" I said with as much sarcasm as I could. "I should be really flattered. You've actually been thinking about me. The great Tim McConnell! Little old me! Tim McConnell is talking to me! Aren't I the lucky one?"

"Don't be like that. It hasn't been easy for me, either, you know."

"What's that supposed to mean?"

"It's just that, like I said, I miss you."

"What happened? Did Miss Double Splits give you the shaft?" I gave him this ugly look. It felt good.

"Don't...be like that. Please. I know I deserve it and all, but, still..."

"Still there isn't much point in talking you know. Somebody might see us."

"To hell with that..."

"Oh, yes, now you say that. Of course, there's nobody within a mile. Go ahead. Be brave. Talk to me. Say something. What, exactly, is it that you want to tell me, Tim? Are you trying to tell me that...that you love me?" The words sort of jumped out of my throat. I was surprised and happy that they did. I knew that I was in love with Art. I wanted to hurt Tim like he had hurt me.

"I don't know what love is," Tim said. "I do know that I think about you all the time. I remember you. I remember us. I miss you."

"Well, isn't that sweet?" I said. "I'm honored. I really am. But you must understand. It was just one of those—how did you put it?—it was 'just one of those schoolboy things'. I agree that it was fun, for a while, but, as you said, just a passing phase. After all, I'm not queer. Are you?"

"Don't be like that." He looked at me with big eyes. I stared right back, as cold as I could, even though as I did I felt something move inside me. Then I thought about Art and how much we meant to each other, how we had pledged ourselves to each other, how we are going to move to New York or San Francisco just as soon as I was out of school, just as soon as Art could work things out with the diocese. So I threw Tim's words back at him.

"You have a girlfriend. Talk to her."

December 27, 1988

Just two more years! I count each day. It's an eternity. It's forever. But Art says that's just because I'm young, that two years will race by, I'll see. In no time at all, we'll be together all the time. We won't have to sneak around. He shows me magazines where men are dancing with each other, and go to restaurants and parties and live like everybody else. Like ordinary people. That'll be us in two short years, he says. In the meantime, we're happy, aren't we? We have each other. We will look back someday and remember and think of these as our best times because they are ours, only ours. We have each other.

December 28, 1988

I can go too! I tried not to think about it. There was nothing I could do. I knew that my sister Beth and Cathy McBride, her best friend, were going, and Cathy's father and her brother, Rich. We didn't have the money for both Beth and me to go. Mom was real sorry. I smiled and said that I understood, and I did. Beth had been saving up, babysitting and washing

dogs, while I was spending my spare time in the
rectory's basement. Mom just got off the phone with
Mr. McBride. Rich has the flu. The hotel is paid for
and there's room in Mr. McBride's car. I can go! I'll
have to share a room with Mr. McBride, but that's
okay. I'll find a way to be with Art. Somehow.
Someway. "Do I want to go?" Mom asks with a
twinkle in her eye. Does a basketball bounce? Mr.
McBride will pick Beth and me up bright and
early—5 a.m. Boy, will Art be surprised! I'm so
happy I can hardly sleep!

December 29, 1988 — morning

All the way to Chicago, in Mr. McBride's
Oldsmobile, Beth and Kathy babbling together in the
back seat, Mr. McBride's eyes glued to the
windshield, I keep imagining the look on Art's face
when he sees me. I am going to come up from behind
him and tap him on the shoulder. I study the
program. There's sessions throughout the day. "The
Rosary and Today's Youth." "What Mary Means to
Me." "Purity in the Age of Television." "The Catholic
Athlete as Role Model." Something has happened to
me. I am laughing inside. I think of a man we read
about in history class. His name was Winston McCoy.
He was from Cuba. His family were supporters of
Fidel Castro and, when the Revolution came,
Winston volunteered to go to the country to teach the
farmers how to read and write. He used comic books.
They showed all the American ships lined up on the
horizon taking all the minerals out of Cuba while
the people starved. Well, finally he was assigned to
the same town shown in the comic book. He saw all
the Russian ships lined up on the horizon taking all
the minerals out of Cuba. The people in the town
were still starving. So he started to think. Soon he

was arrested for "anti-Castro" sentiment. He was stripped naked and chained to a metal chair in a freezer while he was hosed down with water. But he wouldn't give up the names of the American spies who had turned him against Castro. He couldn't. There weren't any. He had figured it out all by himself. I am laughing inside. Mr. McBride takes everything as seriously as Mom and Dad. But to me it's all a big joke. The priests live in big houses and drive fancy cars. And you're not supposed to say anything, to ask anything. You're not supposed to think for yourself. It's like those late night ads on TV. "Scrubbo" will perform all sorts of cleaning miracles at half the price of the brand name cleansers. Is the tried and true Catholic brand of Christianity better than the new and improved Protestant brands? I couldn't care less. But if sitting through "The Martyr is the Message" is the price I have to pay to be with Art, well, then, I'm happy to reach for my wallet.

December 29, 1988 — mid-morning

We're in the Palmer House Hotel. The conference is at McCormick Place. That's some big hall they have smack dab on Lake Michigan, Mr. McBride says. We don't have anything like it in Athens, heck, in the whole state of Ohio. Chicago is the big leagues, he says. There's a shuttle bus that leaves every hour. I act like I'm in no big hurry, but inside my insides are jumbling around like an earthquake.

December 29, 1988 — afternoon

I am back at the hotel. I can't think. My breaths come in gasps and chokes. My chest feels like it's going to explode. Oh, help me, Jesus. Help me. Art was leading the session, "What It Means to Be a Man:

Crusading for Christ." It was in the biggest auditorium of them all. Every seat was taken. I sat at the back. I didn't want him to see me. When the session was over, I would come up behind him. He would turn around. A big smile would flow over his face, slowly. He would touch me, as if by accident, in the middle of my back, just below the waist, in a way no one would suspect, our secret signal, and then we'd walk out together plain as daylight, as fast as we could without drawing attention, to his room, and Art would lock the door and it would be better than it had ever been before.

Art was in his own galaxy. His every word was golden. His sentences were a wonder of crisp, clear, Catholic logic. You couldn't put a dent in anything he said, not with a sledgehammer. All that is needed is Faith. All we have to do is believe. Jesus laid it all out for us. His life is the Living Word. Art was like a movie star. His smile radiated to the farthest reaches of the hall. He used his hands for the most dramatic effects. His performance took us all and made us whole, made us one. We laughed. We sighed. We were Brothers in Christ. Ours was a select fraternity. We were like the musketeers of old, like the Crusaders, foot soldiers in the Army of Our Lord and Savior, Jesus Christ, who was our Commander in Chief, and of the Apostles, Matthew, Mark, Luke, John, and Peter, our Commanding Officers. Our weapons are Faith, Hope, and Charity. Especially Charity. Another word, Art said in a whisper, for love. For brotherly love. He stood before us, exhausted. He had given us all there is to give. He had given of himself. The great hall thundered, whistling and clapping, in a great roar of saying, "Yes!" And all of us, fine, young, male and muscular, came to our feet, all at once, a mighty army wakened from slumber, a force to be reckoned with, that would not be denied. We whooped and we hollered. We slapped each other on the back. We knew the Truth and it would set us free.

Slowly the room emptied. I sat in the last row and waited for the crush that surrounded Art to peel away. I was just getting to my feet to go around the side aisle and come up from behind him when, through a crack in the bodies, I saw someone, slight and slender and young, with bright blond hair like a girl's, lean against him, close, so close, and I saw Art's hand reach behind him and then all the bodies turned, it was strange, and I could see Art's hand for long, long seconds on the blond boy's back, just below the waist, and I saw them look into each other's eyes as Art's hand fell away, brushing for a second between the blond boy's legs.

I sank into my chair and hid behind my hands. I heard a cry come from my throat. I burrowed my head deeper into my legs. Then a man put his hand on my shoulder and asked if I was all right. I said that I was and he went away slowly, looking back at me as if he were leaving behind someone wounded on a battlefield. Everything became a blur, but the only thing that mattered there in that moment was that Art not see me, not know that I was there in that room, waiting and hoping and seeing. That's all I could think about: how embarrassed I would be and full of shame, like I had been spying on him or something, and then, out of the corner of my eye, I saw him and the blond boy leave. Together. From all the way in the very back of the room I could feel it. They were going to Art's room as fast as they could without calling attention to themselves. Art would lock the door behind them. I hate him. I hate him. I never want to see him again.

January 2, 1989

I tried to see Art today. I reached him on the phone. He just laughed at me. It was fun while it lasted. What about New York? San Francisco? I'm a real riot, he says. Did I really believe all that stuff? I was getting to be a real drag. If he had wanted to get married, he never would have become a priest. Ha-ha. I should grow up. But I was, he had to admit, "a tasty morsel."

January 3, 1989

I tried to talk to somebody, my Uncle T, but it was no good. We were in the garage. I was helping him take stuff out of his car and we were alone. But he wouldn't talk to me. He was all cold and tired and it seemed like somehow he just got old. I promised myself that I was going to tell him everything, about me, about Tim, about Art. I could hardly breathe. I thought he would understand. I really thought he would. When I was little, he took me to the movies. He talked to me. He seemed like he really cared. But that was a long, long time ago, like everything I remembered I only thought I remembered, like I had imagined it or made it all up, like it had all happened to someone else. People change. Art changed. I thought about how I had treated Tim. I changed.

In the garage it was like we were strangers, my Uncle T. and me. He was all blank and empty, like he was frozen or something. He just turned away. I don't know what's happened to him. It's not worth growing old if that's what happens to you. I asked if maybe I could come see him sometime. He wouldn't even let me come over like he wanted no part of me, like I had a disease or something. Maybe he suspects.

That would explain it. He doesn't want anything to do with me because he knows that I am a queer and dirty. I would have talked to him, too. But he wouldn't let me, because he knows that I am a dirty sinner in the eyes of God.

Somehow he knows. I can't say anything to Mom and Dad, that's for sure. That would be the worst thing to do, to shatter the dream world of their perfect Catholic son. All I would do is hurt them. There is no point to anything. It's all a big joke. Nothing matters.

January 4, 1989

To An Athlete Dying Young

The time you won your town the race
We chaired your through the market-place;
Man and boy stood cheering by,
And home we brought you shoulder-high.

Today, the road all runners come,
Shoulder-high we bring you home,
And set you at your threshold down,
Townsman of a stiller town.

Smart lad, to slip betimes away
From fields where glory does not stay,
And early though the laurel grows
It withers quicker than the rose.

Eyes the shady night has shut
Cannot see the record cut,
And silence sounds no worse than cheers
After death has stopped the ears.

Now you will not swell the rout
Of lads that wore their honors out,
Runners whom renown outran
And the name died before the man.

So set, before the echoes fade,
The fleet foot on the sill of shade,
And hold to the low lintel up
The still-defended challenge cup.

And round that early-laurelled head
Will flock to gaze the strengthless dead,
And find unwithered on its curls
The garland briefer than a girl's.

—A. E. Housman

January 5, 1989

Once there was bright sunlight—
there were beautiful birds
in the branches singing.
There were days pillowed
big with clouds as bright
as the full moon,
and I felt the gentle rain
on my skin
like a golden rainbow.

The world was a bucket of wishes
and the world was a basket of dreams.

Now the trees are skeleton trees, all
their leaves are like barbed wire and
in the shadows vultures go about their
business after the battle is won or lost
and it doesn't matter anymore.

What was the cheering for?
The hurrahing? No one remembers.
They say I am a hero,
when what I am is dead.

The world is a pit without bottom.
The world is a sore that won't heal.

January 6, 1989

This is the last time I will be writing in this journal. I have thought about it. There is no other way. Mom comes to me crying. I was doing so well. I should go see "Father Art" again. My laughter is like a knife in her heart. It must be her fault, she says over and over. Because Jesus has enough love to go around. She knows he does. But she is wrong. I am not going to change. I am going to burn in Hell forever. It's like that's what I'm doing now. Maybe you just die. I hope so. Maybe all the pain just goes away. It hurts so much. Mom looks at me through her tears and I hate myself. Why should she suffer? Dad has this real strange look on his face. No matter what, he says, I am his son and he will always be proud of me. But I know he's wrong. We're a strong Catholic family, he says. Jesus will help us. Jesus will carry us through. His Will be done. If I have done something wrong, he says, well, that would be different. But he knows better. He trusts me. I would never do anything to make him ashamed, to make him cast me away like Peter denied Jesus. It's just growing pains. I'll snap out of it. But he is wrong. I see the little room behind the boiler in the rectory's basement. I am being punished for what I did with Art and for how I treated Tim. Why should my family suffer? I am dirty in Jesus' eyes and a sinner. I am a sinner in the eyes of God. There is so much pain. I am dirty. I want to be clean. I am tired. I want to sleep. Goodbye.

Chapter Four:
Malaise

Travers Landeman
Athens, Ohio
1989

The telephone jolted Travers awake. He was in the middle of a dream, in a small boat, in the wilderness, fishing. But the fish wouldn't stay in the water. They flew around like birds, fins splashing the air-water like disembodied wings. Travers threw his line high into the air. The fish-wings would grab it, fly low over the water, and let go. It was his brother-in-law, Arthur, sobbing.

"Come. Come. Please." There were gasps between each word. Then silence. The dial tone drilled into Travers' ear.

There were police cars and an ambulance. Travers was stopped at the door. Then his brother-in-law appeared, in pajamas, their top a red-brown wound. His hair was wild. Tears poured down his cheeks.

"Oh, thank God you are here," Arthur sobbed. "Thank God you are here." Travers followed to the living room. "It's Matthew. My dear, sweet boy, Matthew!" Arthur Calkins fell to his knees at the sofa to bury his face in his reddened hands. "Oh, God! Oh, God! Why has Thou forsaken me?" He jumped to his feet, arms waving wildly, clenching and unclenching his fists. "Why has Thou forsaken me?"

A woman in a white uniform appeared. "Here," she said to the stricken man, "take these." She reached out two pills and a glass of water. Arthur pushed her away, the glass flying against the wall. Travers was numb. Everything was happening in a blur as the nurse produced a hypodermic needle. "Hold him tight," she commanded. "There! He should be out in a minute." Travers helped move Arthur to the sofa. "Your nephew shot himself in the basement sometime this afternoon," the nurse said. "Your brother-in-law couldn't sleep, worrying about his son's whereabouts. An hour ago, he went downstairs and found him. The mother has been taken to the hospital. The children are with family services."

These words came over Travers like a storm. His nephew's face appeared before him as if in a dream: "Uncle T, maybe I could come over some time." Travers sank his face in his hands.

He was a pallbearer four days later. They went from the cemetery to the dead boy's house. There was food.

People came and went. Finally everyone was gone but the dead boy's parents, Corinne and himself, and the priest who had presided over the funeral. "Ours is not to reason why," the priest had said at the funeral. "Where Matthew is, brothers and sisters in Christ, he is feeling no pain, no anguish. Of this we are assured in love and mercy."

"You have been so good to us, Father McArtle," Mabel said, sobbing. "I don't know what we would have done without you. The thought of Matthew lying in unconsecrated ground, forever, we couldn't bear it. Thank you, Father, thank you."

"Yes," the dead boy's father agreed, straining to form each word. "You can never know how much we appreciate all you have done for us. For Matthew."

"Your son was not in his right mind," the priest said. "Holy Mother Church understands and gives dispensation. Matthew is at rest." The words were automatic, but not to the dead boy's parents.

"I will always remember what you said at the Mass," Mabel sobbed, "in...in..." But she could not continue.

An image of the priest standing at the altar came to Travers: arms extended, vestments like wings, like the fish-wings in his dream. He heard again the priest's sonorous words: "A young life ended in the fullness of its prime. We are left to mourn. In our hearts we carry a grief beyond understanding. Even so, we trust in the ultimate goodness of everlasting love. We must go on. We must go on for Matthew's sake. We embrace each other now in tears, but we must also, as the days pass, embrace each other in love and in faith." The words had not moved Travers. He could sense that others responded, but to Travers the words, for all their roundness, were hollow. They reminded him of his own empty words the last time he had seen his nephew, his cowardly words that evening in the garage: "That would not be a good idea." Travers knew now that he was more alone than ever, more adrift, more lost. He remembered his nephew years and years before. During Mabel's pregnancies, he had taken Matthew to the movies, to the zoo, to the park. Popcorn and cotton candy, Matthew's small and then not so small hand in his. Where had the years gone? Why had they stopped? Why had he let them stop? In a great bursting of regret and self-loathing Travers' body heaved in pain. Tears flooded his cheeks. A cry came from his sister; its dark echo shuddered Travers with cold.

"There, there," the priest said. "Ours is not to reason why. We must place our trust in a Higher Power. Matthew is now with Jesus. Some day, too, we shall be with Jesus — and with Matt." The priest reached for his coat and turned to go. The dead boy's father walked him to the front door.

"Pray for us, Father," Arthur said.

"We must pray for each other." And then, as if as an afterthought, the priest turned. "My dear Arthur, my dear Mabel...I do not know if it would be of comfort to you or not, but..."

"But what, Father?" Arthur responded, with life in his voice.

"You remember how I took Matthew to the Cavaliers game? How I had been counseling him? How we all thought I had reached him? How hopeful we all were?" The priest laid down his coat and hat, went to the sofa, and buried his face in his hands.

"You must not blame yourself, Father," the father of the dead boy said. "You tried. Just as Matthew's mother tried. Just as I tried." Again Arthur broke into tears.

"Yes, yes, I know. We all tried. But what I was thinking was, if it would be of some comfort to you, as a memorial to Matthew, I could go through his writings— Matthew was so proud of his poetry!—and put together a small book we might all remember him by."

A look of hope came to faces of the dead boy's parents.

"Oh, Father, could you? Would you?" Mabel asked. "It would mean so much to us."

"Show me his room," the priest commanded.

A few minutes later the priest emerged with two notebooks. "Yes," he said. "These are the poems Matthew told me about. I am sure of it. Let me talk to Monsignor Kelly. I will ask him to find the funds to publish a memorial volume." He embraced the dead boy's parents.

In a daze of remorse, Travers stood witness. Something was not right. It was like a watching a movie slightly out of focus. In grief and self-anger, he could not think clearly. But one thought was clear: it was his fault that his nephew had killed himself. Matthew reached out to me and I turned him away. If only I had listened...

He and Corinne did the dishes while Mabel and Arthur sat at the kitchen table.

"Arthur and I would like you to do something for us," Mabel said.

"Of course," Travers answered quickly. "Anything."

"At times like this, families must stick together," Corinne said. Mabel, she noticed, used a discount dish-washing liquid, not a name brand. I hope it doesn't ruin my nails, Corinne worried to herself.

Mabel and Arthur held hands, the agony of tears on their faces. "Our place is here now," Mabel said, "with our family. With Matt's memory." Sobbing, she let go of her husband's hand.

"Mabel and I would like you to go to Mabouhey for us," Arthur continued. "We cannot abandon Father Chester even though, even though..." Arthur's words stopped. His body shook in sorrow.

Mabel lifted her head. "You know that we made a promise. You remember Father Chester's letter? I read it to you the night you and Matt...you remember."

"Yes, I remember," Travers said softly. "No harm," he heard himself saying, "no harm at all." I remember. I will remember every day of my life.

"We want you to go in our place," his sister said. "We want you to take Matt's things to the mission so that they are put to use. Will you do this for us?"

Before Travers could assent, Corinne spoke. "Of course, ordinarily, we would be happy to go. But I can't. Our club is hosting the annual Ohio Valley Canasta Tournament next weekend. I am the Chairperson. I'm sure you understand. But Travers can go. You will go, won't you, babykins?"

It's little enough that I will do for you, Travers thought. I would go to the ends of the earth if it would make a difference. I cannot bring your son back. I could have saved him. He reached out to me, but I turned him away. I let him drown. "Yes," he said. "I will go for you."

*　　　*　　　*

That weekend Travers and Corinne went again to Mabel and Arthur's house. Corinne had agonized over which vehicle to take. It is an occasion of sorts, she finally decided. She handed Travers the keys to the El Dorado. "Let's be quick about it, huh, babykins? I've got an appointment at Pierre's in two hours."

While Corinne watched television in the family room, her husband and her sister-in-law went through her dead nephew's things.

"I gave Matt this sweater for his birthday," Mabel said. "He hardly wore it." There were shoes and shirts, books and games. There was a coffee mug with a bright red arrow and black sword. There was a basketball signed by Magic Johnson. "Take his radio," Mabel said. "And his tapes— there, that blue bag."

Travers reached for the blue bag. Sharp corners bulged out, preventing its zipper from closing completely. He looked inside. On top of the tapes there was a blue notebook. Matt must have made a catalogue of his music,

Travers thought. He rearranged the cassettes to zip the blue bag shut, cassettes and notebook inside.

"He always liked you," Mabel said. "He always said you were his favorite."

I know, I know, Travers thought. I let him drown. I let him drown.

Travers opened the passenger door for Corinne, put the suitcase in the trunk, and slid behind the wheel. "Glad *that's* over with," Corinne said, as Travers backed the El Dorado down the driveway. Corinne lowered the visor to illuminate a vanity mirror. Yes, she thought, thinner eyebrows, as Pierre was encouraging, might very well make her look younger.

"Maybe you could do something about the Canasta Tournament," Travers said after long moments of silence. "Maybe Magnolia Williamson could take over for you."

"Why in the world would I want her to do that?"

"So you could come to Mabouhey with me."

"Aren't you the sweet one, babykins. But you see, I would simply die if I missed the Tournament. You of all people should understand. And another thing: over my dead body would I let Magnolia Williamson hog all the glory!"

"It would mean a lot to Mabel and Arthur if you'd come. ...It would mean a lot to me." Might as well make one last try, he thought.

"Don't be ridiculous."

"I mean it. Come with me. Please."

"Look, going to the Missions of Jesus of Agony someplace with a zillion mosquitoes is not my idea of a good time, not even close. Thanks for nothing. You like being the big martyr. It's fine and dandy for you to be so concerned with Mabel and Arthur's feelings, but what about *my* feelings? You know how important the Tournament is to me. I guess it's asking too much for you to think of someone other than yourself for a change. I'm having the living room redone. Not that you've been any help. I'm not going and that's final."

What's the use? Travers thought as he turned into their driveway. Then words came from him in a low voice. "Matt's dead. It's like a nightmare."

"Life goes on, babykins." Corinne gave a final look in the vanity mirror. Pierre *is* right, she thought. Thinner eyebrows. Definitely.

Chapter Five:
Cream Cheese and Indoor Plumbing

Joe Rogers
Chicago; Frederique
1991

So there we all were in the temporary international terminal at O'Hare, doomed for demolition sooner or later, its demise already three years behind schedule. It was a garbage dump. Welcome, world, to Chicago! We Mongoose Adventurers consisted of three moneyed couples in their fifties, six unattached women in their forties, and, finally, forlorn and clueless, me. The women—all nine—scratched me with angry glances. They had signed up for two weeks with the glamorous Archie LeBlat. Joe Rogers? Never heard of him.

"Oh, dearie," Irma had purred, "Joe Rogers is one of the most fascinating personalities and brightest stars in the university constellation! I'm surprised you haven't heard of him! He has been hailed by the *Daily Crimson* as a classic strategic thinker whose ideas are destined to be case studies.

He has avoided the limelight, obsessed with his legendary reading. It is a real coup that Mongoose Adventures persuaded him to lead this expedition. You should feel honored." Now, in the decay of the decrepit terminal, the women were able to see the Irmaen bait and switch for themselves.

All of this and more I learned that evening, vodka in hand—*Potempkin*, with an extra "p"—in the bar of the New Papagayo Hotel, as I fought off the drunken advances of one Megan Collins.

"A real treat, my ass. An honor!" Megan slurred as her left hand swatted at my crotch.

"So why'd you come?" I asked, foolishly.

"Oh, you are dumb! Detumescent and dumb. All Mongoose Adventure trips are fully non-refundable, for any reason, at any time, for any one, any way, any shape, any form, if I haven't forgotten any of the any's..."

"Anys from Hell," I interrupted.

"Exactly!" Megan continued. "It's such a great deal, like a landlord bragging about not charging an early charge! Ain't that a bitch? Real clever, that Irma!"

"*Err-ma*," I corrected, clarity bursting through the *Potempkin*, magical and sure, like a rainbow. "*Err-ma* not *Ear-ma*."

But this is getting ahead of myself. There, in the dilapidated gray of Concourse W, I could only begin to sense the women's feelings of betrayal, of lust unfulfilled. The full cup had been brought to their lips and then—cruel fate!—snatched away. It was only human that I be blamed and so blamed I was. It is simple: our species is an amalgam of need; attention must be paid so long as the need is our own. That has been my undoing—my tendency to empathize, to see matters too much from everyone else's point of view. I know that others react instinctively according to their own self-interest, and I know also that I should too. It's the expected thing. It's the polite thing too in that it does not confuse or bring about unsettling exercises of thought as to motive or intent. But in me, the me-first compass is broken. It's as though I hover about at the fringes of the campfire, freezing, worrying that the marshmallows of those up close might get singed. The women, it seemed to me, had every right to be upset, to feel cheated. But my unnatural empathy only served to stoke their disappointment into anger.

Then, in a gush appeared in the flesh that that had been denied: Archie LeBlat made his hobbling entrance. There are crutches and there are crutches. Archie's was of radiant cherry inlaid with mother of pearl and gold leaf. The air percolated with cries of "You poor, poor dear" as the women rushed him with hosannas of concern. Enwombed with womanly worry, Archie kissed each one. It was not your run-of-the-mill fracture! No and no again. All sorts of Latinate bones and sub-bones were shattered: it was a miracle that Archie LeBlat would ever walk unassisted again. It would require months of physical therapy, of discipline, of pain.

Archie LeBlat smiled a brave smile and reached out his hands—well, actually his hand—and, just like that, his performance burned away the women's anger. He was their bright summer sun and, radiant flowers, the women raised themselves to him. They clustered and cooed. Archie presented each of us an autographed copy of his new book, *My Naked Self*. He clasped the women's hands to his chest, as, as if willed by Archie LeBlat in the role of God, words came through loudspeakers in a perfectly timed choreography. We hurried to board long accordion buses, big gray caterpillars, which carried us out to the tarmac.

My empathy has limits. I do not understand those who defame air travel. As long as the plane does not crash, there is no reason to complain. If it does, well, impossible to complain, no? I have never eaten an airline meal that didn't impress me. Of course the food is rot wash, but that's not the point. Think about it: the sheer accomplishment! There you are, thousands of feet in the air, whizzing along at an incomprehensible speed, *eating*? There is salt and pepper. There is ice! You hurtle forward, faster than a speeding bullet. You go to the bathroom and flush! You watch a movie! And even so on Getaways Charter Air Line Service, Flight #768, nonstop service Chicago O'Hare to Castiglione International, Frederique City, Frederique, I stretched out with blanket and pillow to await that uncertain moment of drift when the aircraft's great engines would unflex themselves for landing.

*   *   *

It was a shack that greeted us. Popinjay soldiers in brightly starched uniforms, machine guns and tassels, hovered. Rusting fans hiccupped from a wire mesh ceiling. A polychrome mural of a bemedaled old man, bald and mustached, determination and greed on his face, covered an entire wall. Emblazoned above were the words:

HIS MOST EXALTED EXCELLENCY
GENERALIZZIMO XAVIER LOURDES
CASTIGLIONE
WELCOMES YOU
TO
THE PEOPLES REPUBLIC OF FEDERIQUE

NO DRUGS ALLOWED

The stance was that of heroic warrior: right hand clasped rigid over heart, left arm extended, presumably in welcome. The generalissimo exuded the menacing charm of a Chicago alderman in Knights of Columbus regalia at the St. Patrick's Day parade. Below this notice of welcome and warning men in puffy loud-colored garb played bongo drums, guitars, and Caribbean string instruments whose names I did not know. They smiled hopeful smiles. I put a five-dollar bill in the opened guitar case as the camcorders and cameras of the Mongoose Adventurers went into action.

The plan was for us to survive one night at the New Papagayo Hotel in Frederique City, the capital and only city on Frederique, before embarking the next morning for the neighboring island Mabouhey. It was on Mabouhey that Archie LeBlat had uncovered unusual fragments—possibly from the Arawak era!—the previous digging season. There, when not desecrating the ruins, we would lodge at Hernando's Iguana Guest House, which, Irma boasted, featured "real beds."

Somehow our mountain of luggage, cameras, handbags, radios, pillows, blankets, umbrellas, folding chairs, walking sticks, and helmets made it out of the airport onto a vehicle that once had been a bus. It resembled one of those yellow school buses you still see in the country except that it wasn't yellow any more. It was beyond yellow, way beyond. Sort of a mud-dust-rust color. It had skinny tires. Its windows were covered with grime. Its driver welcomed us with the charm of a pimp as we belched onto a dirt road nearly as worn as the bus's tires.

The New Papagayo Hotel was stuck into the side of a cliff like a button. It was new and yet it was native. I think that was the idea. Lobby with thatched roof. Lots of potted plants. Tile floor gleaming. A crisp reception area with young black faces determined to please. I abandoned my flock at the soonest possible moment, and, after my luggage was deposited into my room, headed for the bar. Yes, they had vodka: Frederique's finest—*Potempkin*, with, as I said, an extra "p." I sat at the bar and raised my glass to the sea that struggled below. Between cultural exchanges three and four Megan Collins, as I also have said, joined me for a desultory while before slouching back to her room. Starlight dazzled through treetops onto the backbones of supplicant waves.

*   *   *

Potempkin and I moved to a table perched at the edge of the cliff. In the crisp, black night the sky was new with stars, the air soft with the scent of jungle flowers. Happy music came on the gentle breeze. The surf washed in the distance below and stretching far. Then it began. To lead the parade: Mamie and Kirkpatrick Judson. I must come at once. It would not do at all. Unacceptable. A deal is a deal. They had been promised two queen size or larger beds. There was but one. What remedy did I propose in the face of such injustice? I sat there, vodka in hand, surveying the stars, and thinking of poems."*And that inverted bowl which mortals call the sky...*" Mamie and Kirkpatrick maintained a steady sputtering, not, I thought, the most appropriate of choruses. Poetry is a disrespected art. "*Where under crawling cooped we live and die...*"

Susan Chambers entered, stage left. Susan was a large woman in her late forties. She had divorced well twice. She wore her hair up. She bolstered an impressive collection of kerchiefs from her travels hither and yon. She looked French to me. At O'Hare, my vodka made the first of many mistakes by addressing her as "Madame." I marveled again at her largesse of surprisingly firm flesh: a challenge to Willy Loman himself. Now, under the watching stars, it was her turn.

"My problem is truly pressing," she lamented, a locomotive on a straight track picking up steam. "The shower in my room is barely a drizzle! A drizzle!"

"Lift not your hands to it for help—for it..."

"We were here first," the Judsons protested. "Only one bed!"

"As impotently moves as you or I!" The majesty of Khayyam demanded the homage of another cultural exchange. I filled my glass.

"A drizzle! A drizzle!"

"Only one bed!"

I studied Susan Chambers' fat lips with awe. Lavender lipstick to match the kerchief about her neck! What an engineering marvel the human body is! Susan Chambers excreted words as if they were torpedoes. "Do you know the definition of minor surgery?" *Potempkin* asked.

"Minor surgery? Did you say minor surgery?" It was Kirkpatrick Judson, prodded by Mamie Kirkpatrick's elbow in his midriff.

"Minor surgery is surgery that is performed on someone else."

"I don't get it," Susan Chambers said. "You're drunk."

I *am* drunk, I thought. I did not respond that she was fat and, as Churchill observed, morning always beckons. But I thought about it.

"Surgery or no surgery, we have only one bed."

Then, again, the Frenchwoman: "My shower, my non-shower to be precise, is barely a drizzle. Yet all you do is sit here getting drunk."

"I am not just sitting here getting drunk," I protested. "That I have already done. What I am doing now is looking at the stars."

At this point others emerged from the night to add spice to this bouillabaisse of discontent: edges of a bedspread were frayed, there was the sighting of a lizard, a ceiling fan made the most horrible noise, as if a cat were being strangled. The suffering masses waited yearning to be freed. An audience! An opportunity to recite one of my own compositions! To take their minds off their troubles? Unlikely. To distract myself from their distractions? Likely. I put down my glass and struggled to my feet. Their murmurs dribbled away. They looked at me with expectant, self-righteous faces. I became happy at the strength of my voice:

> *Shelves are filled with proper toys—rows and rows.*
> *With golden cords and ribbons and bows,*
> *From a package world,*
> *Each comes labeled and guaranteed,*
> *In boxes and bags,*
> *With instructions sheets.*
>
> *But love, my love, is an old tin can—*
> *Bouncing along and up and down,*

Hit with a stick or pulled on a string,
Making up rules as you go along.

*Love, my love, is an **alley** thing.*

That shut them up. Briefly. There was a gratifying mix of puzzled disgust and spoiled incomprehension on their faces.

"Aha!" It was Susan Chambers who broke the spell. "Getting drunk! Looking at the stars! And reciting poetry! An utter waste of time. There must be an adult around here somewhere." She turned her back and disappeared.

"*She walks in beauty like the night...*" I began.

"We're not going to take this lying down!" Mamie Judson protested. It would be nice to think the pun was intentional. I collapsed into my chair and soon, one by one, the disgruntled adventurers skulked themselves away. I burst out laughing. My new best friend, *Potempkin*, accounted in part for my indifference, but the truth of the matter is that there wasn't anything I could have done to right the wrongs of their unsettled world except bounce the unhappy ones back to the uniforms at the front desk whom they had already assaulted to hear repeated heartfelt apologies and sincere assurances that the earnest young faces really were going to do something, intention trumping capability. If one *really* is going to do something, isn't that just as good as actually doing it? I considered pointing out the obvious: that the New Papagayo Hotel isn't the Waldorf, that Frederique City, Frederique, isn't Basel, Switzerland. But that seemed sacrilege in the silence of such close stars.

"You are Señor LaBlat, no?" I squinted but saw no one. "I am here, Señor." A shape emerged from the shadows. "May I join to you?"

Now I was able to see him: a large man, over six feet tall, bulky, with a bushy mustache. His shirt was unbuttoned at the neck, where black hairs scrambled through. He was in his late thirties or early forties. He wore a cream colored guayabera shirt embroidered with birds of blue and burning green. Before I could say anything he sat down.

"Oh, Señor," he said. "I see dat you drink de vodka del país. Dat ease good. Dat ease very too good." The stranger reached for the *Potempkin*, poured, and raised his glass. "I toast to de bread! To de success of our door prize!"

"To the success of everyone everywhere!" I countered, raising the ersatz Russian to the stars. "May beds be many, water gushing, and lizards elsewhere! But I am not Señor LaBlat."

"Oh, but you are, Señor," the stranger responded with impressive certainty.

"Don't know much about history," I started to sing. "Don't know much biology. But I do know my own name. Most of the time."

"Dat ease mere convergence! You are here a man, nothing de more, nothing de less. Here, for me, for you, for de ladies, in dis place and for dis time, you are Señor LaBlat. If you are so not so, den why so are you here?"

"I am here because Señor LaBlat—Professor LaBlat, that is, Ph. D., McGillacutty Chair, etc., broke his leg. As you can see, my leg is not broken." I attempted to stand, but my vodka legs collapsed beneath me. I braced myself against the table with my left arm and slid back down. Not a drop spilled from the glass in my right hand!

"You say your leg eet ease not broken, but even de so you cannot stand eet up. Yes, at any de rate, eet does not make any de matter about de leg, no more so or no less so dan de name. A man ease what a man does. A fisherman, he fishes. A baker man, he bakes. A butcher man, he...*mueres*... how do you so say dis in English?"

"A butcher man, he thumbs," I said.

"So dere in de sense you see, you are Señor Archie LaBlat."

"Run that by me again."

"How eet ease so ease because of de cause dat your leg eet ease not broken so you must become de Señor LaBlat. Alas! Poor Archie..."

"I knew him well, Horatio! So you have known all along that I am not Archie LaBlat!"

"All of deese eet ease de tired and de true meta-feezeeks," he said, as if talking to a child. "I will call you 'Archie'. Eet ease a lot easier. I have here his letter in which eet says all about you, Señor Joe Rogers."

As I said, after the fourth vodka or vodka and tonic, I lose count. By now I must have been on my sixth. The night was cool and clear. Every star was on fire. The breeze was as gentle as a mother's kiss. The unhappy ones were unhappy elsewhere. In the still of the night, we sat there, alcoholics synonymous.

"Now! Down de stairs to de business," my companion shouted, banging his glass on the table. "Tomorrow we take dem to de digs. Archie, leave eet all to me. Archie always did. We take de Hernando's bus to de end of dis, de big, island, den we package dem in de Hernando's boat in de water to de other, de small, island, den we take de Hernando's mules to de diggings, and den, 'Dig we must,' as Archie always said."

A vision of Susan Chambers humping through the jungle squashing an unfortunate mule flashed in my mind. She wore an elegant frock, pastel peach in color, with, of course, matching kerchief. Dust whirlpooled around her. Mosquitoes attacked. She was cursing and shaking her fists.

"It will never work. It will be a natural disaster."

"But, Archie, why ease eet dat you say dis so?"

I recounted the saga of insufficient beds, stingy shower, lizard slither, bedspread frayed and hiccupping fan.

"Ah! De tourists are restless! Deese things eet ease easy to fix. Eet ease no problem!"

"'*Only against death does man cry out in vain*,'" I responded. I admit this was grandiose, but you must remember that I was talking to a metaphysician.

"True dat, Archie," he said. Then he was off, this Señor Adolfo Federico Castiña y Jones. (Somewhere between bottles two and three I had learned his full name.)

"I shall call you *Smith*," I called after him, as he disappeared into the night.

*   *   *

I cannot say how much longer I sat there enjoying the stars, for Smith's confident assertion is the last conscious memory I can muster. The next morning I awoke to bright sun pouring through curtains. The smell of coffee was in the air. From somewhere in the distance soft laughter floated. I showered and shaved. Adolfo Federico Castiña y Jones— "Smith" really was a lot easier—had gathered the Mongoose Adventurers in the lobby. The transformation was a miracle. Their bright faces bubbled as if he were their kindergarten teacher taking them on a field trip.

"Oh, there you are, my dear Joe," cooed Agnes Stearnes. "What a marvelous day! God is in Her heaven and truly all is right with the world!"

"Breakfast?" asked Susan Chambers, her kerchief choice a mellow lime. "There is a buffet. They even have bagels, though there is no cream cheese. No biggie. Who needs cream cheese on a day like this?" She threw her arms to the sun to pirouette like an elephant in a circus.

"A cup of coffee would be swell," I answered with suspicion. The vision of lime bounced off with a wave of her hand.

"Did you know that lizards descended from dinosaurs?" asked Myrtle Barton with a radiant smile. "Gilberto told me so many fascinating things! There is so much we can learn. Such gentle people," she went on, "gentle, and patient and kind. Oh, there he is now!" She ran towards a silhouette in the distance who was waving a straw hat.

Hernando's bus rattled in front, smoke belching, radio blaring. The consensus was that it could wait. It turned out that as I had sat at the edge of the cliff contemplating stars, savoring *Potempkin*, and remembering poems, Smith— you know who I mean—had charmed and cajoled them all, here and there matching and bedding surely and sweetly. Yesterday's news was yesterday's news.

"You will never see de advertising dat says, 'Come to Frederique and sleep alone,'" Smith boasted. "What you Americans need is to get free. Free of de microwave oven. Free of de electrified coffee pot. Free of de seventeen different types of chocolate toothpaste. All you need"—and here he winked—"is love. Instead you have de garbage disposal. Eet ease better to sleep naked with someone dan to sleep alone in silk pajamas."

The cynic in me started to respond, "What is best of all is to put silk pajamas on afterwards," but the sky was too close, eloquent and sure, so I said nothing. None of it had mattered after all—the litany of the horrors of the night before. Osmond had done his best to fix her shower, Susan Chambers patiently explained. Wasn't effort what really mattered? It is a short walk to the river, a lovely short walk, she gushed. Osmond was going to take her there again as soon as she finished breakfast. "Chicago has indoor plumbing," she said.

Chicago: a world class city! Cream cheese and indoor plumbing! With a shrug, I took the coffee from her.

"There is pouring water, and there is pouring water," I replied.

"That is *so* true, Joseph! That is *so* true!"

I *hate* being called *Joseph* but silence was a small price to pay to nourish her good cheer. Thus it was with happy hearts and lifted spirits that we took Hernando's bus to Hernando's boat, where half our party trickled away to follow bare-chested boys with bright white teeth and flat leathery stomachs into the jungle. Eight of us remained. We stumbled into Hernando's small boat and were off, out to the sea, to the island of Mabouhey, in the distance beyond, over the horizon, just far enough away that, squint as we might, we couldn't quite see it.

Chapter Six:

Palpable Self-Loathing

Mr. Zero W. R. Lincoln, Respondent
1991

Interview #3
STREAM OF UNCONSCIOUSNESS
Submitted in Partial Fulfillment of the
Requirements for the Master Of Arts
in
Journalism and Urban Studies

SocioEconomics 203: Informal Urban Structures

Dr. Elizabeth C. Morseby, Ph.D.

Sally Clark, B.A.
February 21, 1991

Excerpts: Pages Three through Fourteen and Pages
Thirty-Six and Thirty-Seven

Page Three

Respondent: Oh, I sees what you be thinking long abouts now. Here's this ole darkie shufflin' along fetchin' for the white man. Beats two pokes in the eye. You plays the hand you dealt with best as you knows how. Way I sees it, everybody shufflin' for somebody. White folks too. Everybody jess shufflin' along like crabs in a barrel climbing over each other trying to get to the top. And we ain't too choicey none neither about who we pulls back down to the bottom if we can't climb up to where they is. I been hearing you college kids hollering and parading around for years. Knows just about everything there is to know about just about everything. Then you graduates. Off you goes to the suburbs and Daddy buys you a Cadillac. America all about color. That's all there is to it. Excepting, and I ain't a young man neither, the color America is all about is green. You tell me: where do all the rich colored folk live now there ain't no laws against it? The athletes? The movie stars? The ones on TV? You plays the hand you dealt with best as you knows how.

Interviewer: How would you characterize your relationship with Kincaid Trampwell?

Respondent: Mr. Trampwell, see there, that's what you been talking about, me calling the white man "Mister" [respondent laughs], well, Mr. Trampwell, see, he wasn't all that bad a sort, especially for a white man. He liked his whiskey and he liked his books. They say he like his boys, too, although I never did understand much about that sort of thing, not that it was any of my business, no how. I don't mean boys like in children. Nothing like that. Young men. "My young men callers," Mr. Trampwell used to say. I can see him in the back of the store with his legs propped up, smokin' his pipe, arguing like the devil about this here or that there and his young men callers giving as good as they got. And sometimes I'd see them sneaking out in the morning with their white faces scrunched up like a handkerchief peeking out of a zoot suit pocket.

Interviewer: Didn't you find such behavior on Kincaid Trampwell's part insensitive to your own cultural norms?

Respondent: Weren't none of my business really.

Interviewer: You didn't harbor any resentment towards him?

Respondent: Way I sees it, Mr. Trampwell takin'
me in and all did me a whole lot more good than
all them who say they doin' good all the time,
all them shouters and marchers. Course I am
partial to myself. We all is, ain't that so?
All them years have come and gone and there's
been all these new laws and all these changes
so they say, and still, you've got to admit it:
the snake ain't sleepin'. Things for colored
folk ain't none the better and a whole lot worse
than they was back before things got better,
except, that is, for rich black folk. They can
go to the opera and sit anywhere they like,
right next to the rich white folk. Rest of us
just like we always been: crabs in a barrel.
Time was black folk knew how to behave in
public, better than white folk. Daddy slap you
upside yo' head if you looked sideways. Now just
look at us! Shower caps and house shoes on the
subway and el! Clothes on backwards! Butts poked
out with underwear showing!

Interviewer: Kincaid Trampwell...

Respondent: The money he give me, Mr. Trampwell, little as it may seem to you, what with the scrapin' and hustlin' I did, I didn't exactly starve none. And I never was on the dole. Never.

Interviewer: You take issue, you disagree, then, with those who would see your and Kincaid Trampwell's relationship as a classic case of racial exploitation?

Respondent: Nobody was holding a gun to my head. I don't hardly have too much complaint with Mr. Trampwell, not really. We stayed out of each other's way most of the time. Except whenever one of us got took with the cookin' spirit. Mr. Trampwell, he made a mean pot of chili and I ain't none too bad myself at smokin' up ribs, if you don't mind me buttering my own bread. Of course, I always use my granddaddy Stetson Davy Crockett Jackson Lincoln's secret sauce. I had me a home and Mr. Trampwell he had him one too. Home is the place where when you go there they have to take you in. That's what Mr. Trampwell said is

Page Seven

true wisdom. It's according to Robert Frost, who was a crusty old codger, Mr. Trampwell said, and of whom you know of, I'm sure. *'Tis better to go down with boughten friendship at your side: Provide! Provide!* Mr. Trampwell sure could quote dead white men good! So that's what we did: provide.

Interviewer: You haven't said anything about your personal life.

Respondent: I loved me a woman once and she loved me. Then some punk shot her in the face in a convenient store and that's all there is to it. I don't likes to talk about it none.

Interviewer: Tell me something about her.

Respondent: No. [gets up to leave].

Interviewer: Please remain seated. The stipend is dependent upon your completing the entire session.

Page Eight

[Respondent returns to his chair]. Let us turn, then, to your relationship with Joe Rogers. How does it differ from the relationship you had with Kincaid Trampwell?

Respondent: It don't. They the boss. They owns the place. Except Joe Rogers' chili ain't as good as Mr. Trampwell's was, not hardly half so.

Interviewer: The Yellow Harp does not have profit sharing. Neither Kincaid Trampwell nor Joe Rogers set up a 401(k) plan for you. Isn't this unfair? It's been your labor, your hard work, that's been invested in The Yellow Harp for over a quarter of a century, that's kept The Yellow Harp viable, that is to say...

Respondent: I knows what *viable* means. Like I said, I ain't got no complaints, not really.

Interviewer: Even as this interview is taking place, your employer, Joe Rogers, is vacationing at a luxury resort in the Caribbean. Is that fair? Don't you work as hard, if not harder, than he does? Doesn't this double standard make you feel resentful? Exploited?

Page Nine

Respondent: No.

Interviewer: Perhaps a little?

Respondent: Like I said, no.

Interviewer: I find that hard to believe.

Respondent: Don't call me no lie. I tells the truth mostly. That's how my daddy raised me. Joe Rogers left me in charge, didn't he?

Interviewer: Precisely my point. Are you getting additional compensation for the added responsibilities you have while he is on vacation? Is your employer paying you overtime?

Respondent: No.

Interviewer: So you are being exploited?

Respondent: Them's your words, not mine. How many white folks you knows goes out of town and gives their keys to a colored?

Page Ten

Interviewer: I beg your pardon. You mean to say, I am sure, "a person of color."

Respondent: Don' t change the fact none. Joe Rogers left me in charge.

Interviewer: There are laws governing these matters...

Respondent: Laws is for folks who have money. I takes care of myself.

Interviewer: Let us turn now to more recent developments...

Respondent: Well, there's that fellow over there in Russia, Gorbachev. Ain't he somethin else! Lenin be rolling over in his glass grave, I betcha. Do you think Gorbachev can pull it off without the whole mess just come crashing down like Humpty-Dumpty, that *glasnost* and *perestroika* business?

Interviewer: My opinions are not relevant. It is you who are the subject here. You are the important one! [Laughs]. I ask the questions. Not you.

Page Eleven

Respondent: Kinda sorta one-sided, don't you think?

Interviewer: You must understand that this is an academic study.

Respondent: That don't make it fair. I'd like to know your opinion. Do you think this Gorbachev fellow is ace boon coon?

Interviewer: I beg your pardon?

Respondent: You know, like white on rice... umm... *stalwart... indefatigable.*

Interviewer: Please try to understand Mr. Roosevelt-Lincoln,..

Respondent [interrupting]: "Roosevelt" is one of my middle names. My surname is "Lincoln." I comes from good stock.

Interviewer: Please forgive me. Please try to understand, Mr...Roosevelt-Lincoln, it would be inappropriate for me to interject my opinions into this research. I am merely a conduit.

Page Twelve

Respondent: Hardly seems fair. If you asks me, brother Mikhail is getting himself into a whole heap of trouble. Like when they brought the mongoose to India to get rid of the snakes. Well, they got rid of the snakes, all right. Now the mongooses are driving them crazy, eating all the grain. Just like my Daddy warned me: be careful what you wish for!

Interviewer: By "recent developments" I meant something closer to home. What can you tell me about the Sisters of the Sisterhood and their efforts to preserve The Yellow Harp as a feminist center?

Respondent: Oh, you means them gals that looked like vampires! Well, they spirits was just a bit too much of the too much. They was like most you college kids are at your age. Didn't really mean no harm none. Things just got out of hand, like letting the dog out after he's been cooped up too long.

Interviewer: What do you think of their demands that the Yellow Harp be preserved as a feminist center?

Page Thirteen

Respondent: Well, it wasn't no how exactly the kind of female center you're thinking about. I don't suppose you are, that is.

Interviewer: Shouldn't the historical importance of the site take precedence over merely monetary concerns?

Respondent: That depends on whose merely monetary concerns they are, yours or somebody else's. It would be real interesting, though, you got to admit: a whore museum. Are there any others?

Interviewer: I beg your pardon?

Respondent: Well, that's what it was in the first place, come to find out. A whorehouse. The Yellow Harp. When them Sisters of the Sisterhood gals tore up the place, as soon as we got it back together, I poked around in the old stuff Mr. Trampwell kept in the front of the basement. I found all these old papers what Cissy San Souci wrote down. Invoices and receipts. Boxes full. They was for sheets and pillowcases and mattresses. Stuff like that. See, when Joe and me cleaned out the place when we were moving on up, we threw out all these moldy suspenders and spittoons and those old-fashioned starched high collars you don't see anymore. Spats, too! Spats! Folk today don't even know what they are. I kept puzzling over where all that stuff came from. Then I put it all together with the boxes of receipts and it come to me: The Yellow Harp was a whorehouse. So that explains that!

Interviewer: I am sure you are mistaken.

Respondent: No. See, there's more. I found this old peg board with keys. With room numbers and all. Then I came across a notebook just about falling apart where she kept track of the payoffs to the cops. There's no doubt about it: The Yellow Harp was a whorehouse. Another chapter of Lost Chicago. We don't have whorehouses much no more, not that I knows of anyway. So maybe the Sisters of the Sisterhood got a point. Maybe it should, if you think about it, be a whore museum. To move forward, it is important to look back. I agrees with you there. Except, like I said, Joe Rogers owns the place and he's jess fine with keepin' it for books.

Page Thirty-Six

CONCLUSION

The subject is a quintessential example of the effect of centuries of American racism. His constricted view of seeing the world through a racial prism is a vital if unconscious survival mechanism. Other than fanciful attempts at grandiose geopolitical musings, his horizons are limited to the narrow confines of his Langley Street world. These presumptuous speculations, while endearing, are simplistic and semi-literate, and serve only to intensify the pathos of his core ignorance. The subject may best be understood as the northern reincarnation of a sharecropper. It is not surprising, therefore, that he does not question established norms. It is in this context that his stunted personal life must be examined. The psychological patterns of self-hatred, catalogued by Dr. Chelsea Perkins-Jones in her landmark study of ghetto life, *American Allopatry*, are manifest in the subject's characterization of himself as [a] darkie as well as in his ubiquitous use of the pejorative *colored.* His name itself [Zero] as well as the genocidal appellation of not one but three white male authority figures for surname [*Washington, Roosevelt, Lincoln*] reference the marginalizing of his cultural heritage. *Turner Garvey Du Bois* he is not. Indoctrinated by his employer and tyrannized by his employer's cultural chauvinism, he quotes Robert Frost, incorrectly and out of context. It may be argued that his efforts to adjust to majoritarian values to the extent permitted by those who control him exhibit a degree of initiative. This rather is more properly understood as an abnegation of the self. His loyalties are misdirected, most significantly, to a series of white employers, who have paid him subsistence wages and kept him confined on premises. He exhibits, not surprisingly, the classic symptoms of an American transplantation of the Stockholm syndrome—this transplantation system in the Twentieth Century North thus replicating, in its psychological imperatives, the plantation system of the Nineteenth Century South: the sharecropping matrix of the Nineteenth and Early Twentieth Century South transplanted into a mere coping system in the Twentieth Century North. As a consequence, the subject's naiveté, almost precognitive, is devoid of even nascent political awareness. His repeated references to his peers as punks, rowdies, low-lifes, ad nauseum, in conjunction with denunciations of his own cultural identity and norms, specifically his renunciation of urban aesthetics, demonstrate a transference away from his true oppressors and, by extension, provide context for his palpable self-loathing.

Chapter Seven:
Things to Be Doing So Now

Joe Rogers
Mabouhey
1991

In the edge of the welcoming sea we were paddled along by Hernando's sons, helping the small craft's aged motor, which hung over its stern like a pogo stick. Eufusio was 16; "Señor, I am going to Ameerica." Rafael was 15; "I am going to Ameerica too." They were smiling and eager, young and bursting with life. Hernando's boat was a shack, really, with a glass bottom, not at all reassuring, and a tin roof. We sat on benches, water up to our ankles. Frederique disappeared slowly behind us. Suddenly dark clouds smothered ocean and sky; lightning menaced the horizon. Angry waves, larger and large, slapped at the small boat's sides, as if it were a toy in a bathtub. Water poured over the sides. Everything happened in a jumble: Hernando lifted an oar high over his shoulder with both hands as wind and ocean bellowed. Eufusio and Rafael jumped out of the boat. I slid wildly across the watery bench, my hands floundering.

"This is where you meet your destiny!" Hernando shouted. The oar remained high over his head like the blade of a guillotine. The boat curled into a wall of water. The Judsons grabbed each other's hands. Marilyn Barton, Constance Halliburton, and I grasped at the poles that supported the clattering tin roof as winds came underneath pushing upwards. The tin canopy, sail-like, on the verge of being ripped off like the lid of a can of sardines, groaned an eerie curse that pierced through the winds' howling. The small craft bounced hard against the surging sea. Visions of skeletons dancing on the sea's bottom raced through my mind. *Full many a gem the dark unfathomed caves of oceans bear.* That too. These were only a few moments of fear, though they seemed an eternity. As suddenly as the dark clouds had entered, they were gone. In an instant all was calm. There came the reassurance of bursting sun. Glory be to seraphim and cherubim and to all God's creatures, great and small. Hernando pointed to the horizon: a faint outline of land glanced in the water. His sons walked along either side of the boat, water up to their knees. Slowly the outline took shape: the island of Mabouhey!

"This is where you meet your destiny!" Hernando said again.

"*Destination!*" we shouted in one voice. "*Destination!*" We all burst into laughter. We laughed and laughed. Because we were alive.

"You Americans is crazy!" Hernando said.

We stumbled from Hernando's boat to the shore, tears rolling down our cheeks until, somehow, we staggered onto Hernando's mules. The narrow path slit through a green kingdom. The only sun was the glow of a shimmering mist. Eufusio and Rafael macheted in front, our overburdened mules following in languid duty. Half an hour later we came to a swatch of drying mud. Here we were to poke around until daylight receded. In the broiling sun, we set to work. At midday Hernando reappeared with tents and chairs, and food and wine and people, Smith among them. We all sang and danced and ended up jumping into a lagoon nestled in a grove of jungle where birds called out to one another. As twilight approached, we left off muddish matters for the "real beds" of Hernando's Iguana Guest House. We collapsed into *hammocks*, too exhausted to decry such, nor squeaky fan, nor detumescent shower.

The days and nights that followed passed like a dream. In an American Express office once I studied a brochure for a resort in Jamaica called "Hedonism." The glossy pictures enticed and titillated, but their package world seemed saccharine and safe. Can pleasure be an end in and of itself? Or must it be a by-product, a consequence of serendipity? The earth spins, the moon waxes and wanes, while we mortals trudge about like blind men banging spoons on empty pots. All we need is love, Smith said. To find our way through the thick of the night, to be safe once more where candles glow and silk sheets beckon, we must hang on somehow, holding close to each other, in spite of it all, giving up and giving way, letting love in, although our hearts have been broken and will be broken again. And there's the rub: in the dream world of Mabouhey it soon came about that it was as if we had stepped outside our costume skins so that our true selves, freed, could prance and dance in full suns and secret nights like children at recess. Where is it written that recess must end? Smith introduced us to a mud-like beverage ladled into clay mugs from a black pot which boiled over an open fire. "Eat ease de prime of de pulque, de incense of de sacred mesquite, mescal," he said, extending a steaming mug to me.

"But I am betrothed to vodka," I protested.

We were sitting under a caoba tree, majestic and strong, leaning against its trunk, on a slight incline that looked down on my by now berry-colored Americans. Their jipijapa sombreros went up and down like fishermen's bobs as they scraped and scoured, sifted and saved.

"Ah, de narrow in de mind of manahgamey," Smith responded. "Dere ease only de one God and Allah or ease eet Jesus? or Jehovah? or Buddha? ease his name. But here de gods are many. De gods of Africa, snatched across de waters, married with de gods of de wood and de rivers. And everything under de sun and on top of de earth to be used to serve and celebrate dem. De god of de yucca and de god of de plantain, de god of de calabash. *May de fathers die before dere sons and not de sons before dere fathers.* I'll drink myself to dis." Smith took a sip from the steaming mug in his left hand and extended a second cup to me.

So, may *Potempkin* forgive me, I drank. Smith and I sat there philosophizing while the planet seemed to slow in its turning. The colors of the trees came even more alive: blues and greens, yellows, reds and purples. From high in their branches birds and monkeys shared the day's gossip. Visions and voices called. I jumped to my feet to throw my arms to the sun.

"Almighty Mother," the words sprang from me, "be with us. Look over us. Give us light. Keep us warm. Stick around."

"Amen to dat and to all of dat!" Smith agreed. I sat back down, propping my back once again against the caoba. "Strip it away de skin of de civilization, of de vitamin pill and de exercise bike," Smith mused, "and all we are ease de hunters and de gatherers still. Like de people who left dere pots here so you come de thousands of miles to dig in de dirt. What's a few thousand couple of de years?" It came to me then that when Archie LeBlat accepted the Pfinster Prize Chicago's media fell over themselves extolling the sagacity of his acceptance speech: "Stripping Away the Skin of Civilization: Hunters and Gatherers Still." Smith smiled. I drained the mug. Big white puffs of clouds passed overhead like sails. "Ah, but de modern woman and her mate," Smith continued, "bustles about wid dee god of dee voicemail. My machine will be in touch with your machine. What's it all about, Archie?"

I looked down at the dig. Constance Halliburton was dancing about, chattering. Apparently she had actually unearthed something. A piece of pottery, perhaps. The others dropped their brushes and magnifying glasses to converge around her like pigeons. I left the caoba tree and Smith as the magnet of Constance Halliburton's joy drew me to her.

"Look! Look!" she shouted, bubbling. She extended her hands. Cradled within: a shard of a glossy blue stone! She began rubbing it with a chartreuse kerchief she must have borrowed from Susan Chambers. Swirls of blue turned into purple. "I found it," she gushed. "Me. All by myself." The others huddled around her, but I stepped away. I was halfway back up the hill towards the caoba tree, where Smith and the god of another steaming mug waited, when the gravel gave way. I found myself sprawled on the ground. There was a sharp pain in my right ankle. I groped for support, my right hand digging into the loosened soil. I felt something. There, barely protruding: an edge of black with lacings of silver! I clawed into the dirt with both hands. Soon I had unearthed the larger half of a mask, embedded in the rock beneath, approximately twelve inches high by six inches wide. The eyes, a red stone of some kind, were the size of quarters. The hair was beaded with shells and worked with silver. The teeth were of a dull yellow metal. The face itself, cheeks and forehead, was of a smooth black stone, probably obsidian. I did not know what to do. Of course Archie LeBlat had instructed me on the rudiments of babysitting the Mongoose Adventurers so that minimum damage would be done in the unlikely event we actually discovered something. Until now, however, all we had found were bits of shards and pieces of splinters. After the first few hours of the first day, it had become routine to photograph and tag their placements, brush carefully, and then, with rubber tipped tweezers, deposit gently into small plastic bags, sorted and numbered. This was entirely different. One by one the others gathered near me, dropping to their knees for a closer look. In the excitement I paid little heed to the pain in my ankle, but it was there, like a distant echo.

"Step to de sides!" It was Smith, come to see what all the excitement was about. He fell to his knees. He studied the embedded mask for long seconds and then stood, wiping sweat from his forehead. We waited for him to speak. "Dere ease only one of de things to be doing so now," he said at length, with a solemnity that impressed us all. "Dere can be none of de doubt dat dis object of the fact is of de greatest of values. Now dat eet has been given back to us by de god of de earth, we cannot allow eet to keep here. But if we take it, what den?"

"Why not deliver it to the authorities?" Kirkpatrick Judson suggested. By profession Kirkpatrick Judson was an accountant. Smith laughed.

"What? So de generalissimo can buy himself another one of de villas in Switzerland? No, dere ease only one of dee things to be doing so now," he said again. "We must take along de mask to Father Chester. Father Chester will know what to do."

"Wait there a hairy minute!" Constance Halliburton said. She spat the words out as if she had tasted sour milk. "After all, I am the one who helped find it, so to speak. If it weren't for me, Vodkaman here would never have come poking around. The way I see it, I deserve some credit. Finders keepers—that's what I say." She looked around for support. No one said anything.

"Look around to you," Smith replied slowly. "You are here abouts in de middle of de jungles. Are you sure dat *finders keepers* ease what you really want? Before de night ease falling de word eet travels back to de big island. Eet ease a matter of de generalissimo's laws dat all of de art of de facts ease de property of de Frederique government. Dat means Generalissimo Castiglione and none de other. Believe in me. You do not ever want to see de inner sides of de Frederique jail."

We waited in the sun, our spirits, only moments before gay and alive, now weighted with greed and fear. Grudgingly, Constance Halliburton surrendered. But not without a final sortie: "There must be some kind of reward."

"Eet ease de doing of de thing dat ease eets own reward, or should be so," Smith answered. There was a weary look on his face. "Bring to me a hammer and de chisel!" he commanded. A few minutes and he had freed the mask from its rocky tomb. "Hernando will take you back to de guests house," he said to the others. "Archie, come with me."

"If it's all the same," I replied, "I will go with the others. Isn't that what Archie would do?"

"You are not Archie. The Spirits did not give de mask to Archie. You must come with me." The path of least resistance it seemed led into the jungle. I hobbled on one foot to a mule, Smith extended a hand, and I fumbled on the top of the patient animal. Then trailless we set off towards the mountains. The tops of trees touched together. Gossamer light sifted over us. Under green umbrellas the dutiful mules trudged forward, steady and slow. Here and there snakes coiled around branches. Smith rode in front, occasionally turning around to check on me. Two hours passed in this Churrigueresque silence. My right foot dangled to the side, little fingers of pain running up and down my leg as it bounced along against the indifferent animal's side. Suddenly the trees parted. We entered a clearing. It was a village: grass huts, hammocks, a central fire. At one side stood a larger, thatched structure. A simple cross, made of sticks, marked its entrance.

"Oyéz! Oyéz! Padrecito Chester! Padrecito Chester!" Smith shouted as we dismounted in front.

A man of medium height appeared in the doorway. He looked to be in his late forties. His hair was thinning and white. He had a sharp nose. His face was streaked with paints of bright colors and his skin was the parchment of old newspapers. He wore a skirt and sandals. Over his bare chest a figurine of black stone hung about his neck on a leather cord. I could feel his quiet intensity. A bright smile spread across his face as he recognized Señor Adolfo Federico Castiña y Jones. He reached out his hands in welcome.

"Namaste, Mabouhey!" he said, his eyes burning into mine. "I am Father Chester."

Chapter Eight:
Roots

Chester O'Reilly
Chicago; Mundelein, Illinois
1944 – 1969

Chester O'Reilly was born in Austin, Illinois, as he was taught from his earliest days, raised in a halcyon time when the triumphant nation wanted nothing other than to return to hamburgers and hot dogs, crabgrass, and runs-batted-in. *Eisenhower: pater familias.* At one time a city in its own right, Austin was Chicago's largest and most populous neighborhood, an urban transplantation of small-town America, a part of—and apart from—the City of Big Shoulders and Hog Butcher to the World. Austin: summer's children dancing in fire hydrant rainbows, rocking chairs on gingerbread front porches. Austin, at the city's farmost western edge: in the inexorable path of the festering inheritance of the nation's original sin that all men are created equal except for the three-fifths who were counted but did not count. Austin: a way of life set to be dust in the wind.

When Chester was five years old, his parents were killed in a traffic accident. Chester, his brother, and his twin sisters went to live with his father's mother, Alana May O'Reilly. His brother was five years older than Chester; his sisters, three. Chester remembered his mother and his father. His mother had light brown hair and freckles. She sang him to sleep every night. He remembered her voice as pure as summer light:

> *Hush, little baby, don't say a word,*
> *Mama's gonna buy you a mocking bird.*

Chester's father was a strong man with lots of black hair all over his body. Chester remembered his father's strong arms wrapping around his mother's waist as she cooked at the big white Chambers stove. He remembered his father's laughter, deep and full of life. Everyone said they were poor. His mother should get a real job. There were weekends and evenings when she could also take in washing. That was the opinion of Mrs. McPartlin, the lawyer's wife.

"They both should be in the harness," she told Mrs. Scalise, whose husband worked at the Chicago Stock Exchange, one Monday when they came to pick up their laundry. Chester asked his mother what a harness was. His mother looked at him with wide smiling eyes. "A harness, Chester me boy, is anything that keeps you down, that don't let you grow. Being free up here"—his mother touched the side of her head—"is what counts." Chester's mother said they weren't poor, not really. They just didn't have money. But they were rich in spirit. She was married to the best man in the world, who loved her dearly, and showed it by bringing home a paycheck every Friday instead of leaving it at Casey's pub.

They lived above Daniels Bakery on Division Street. Every morning Chester woke to the sweet smells of honey and cinnamon. His father was always gone, off to Brach's candy factory on Cicero Avenue. He ran a piece of machinery as big as a house. Monday was Chester's favorite day. As soon as his brothers and sisters were off to school, Chester's mother would roll a white potbelly contraption, tub and wringer, out of the pantry to the kitchen sink. She hooked up hoses while Chester sorted dirty clothes into separate piles. Whites. Coloreds. In-betweeners. Now and then he would tug at his mother's skirt, holding up a shirt, blouse, or pair of pants. Chester's mother would stop what she was doing, measuring detergent or preparing bleach, put a hand on the side of her waist like the handle on a coffee mug, and look down at him.

"What do *you* think, Chester me boy?"

"In-betweener," he said in most cases. "White" or "colored" in others.

"Well, then," his mother always answered, "listen to your instincts, Chester. Listen to your instincts."

The first time she said this Chester asked what "instincts" are.

"Instincts is God's voice inside you telling you what to do," his mother said.

Chester and his siblings crowded in with his grandmother. "There's plenty of love to go around," she said, raising them as well as anyone can be brought up when there is too much week and too few dollars. Usually there was food. From November to May they were cold. The radiators were not on the floors, but suspended from the ceilings, and, as a consequence, provided little heat to what Mr. Boyle, the landlord, called their "garden" apartment.

Chester was an excellent student. He loved to read. His brother and sisters went to St. Lucy's at Mayfield Avenue and Lake Street, kept there on scholarship through the generosity of the Cardinal's Fund for the Poor, as they were frequently reminded. But Chester had not as yet started school when his parents died. The Cardinal was doing enough for one family. The O'Reilly's weren't the only misfortunates in the archdiocese. That autumn Chester O'Reilly was one of the few Catholic children to enroll in Francis Scott Key Elementary School at Parkside and Race Avenues. Protestants went to public schools. Sister Mary Ignatius had taught Chester's brother all about Protestants and he in turn taught Chester. Turncoats, really. Traitors. They had deserted "Holy Mother the Church." They made Jesus cry. They had fallen away from the One True Holy Catholic and Apostolic Church. It was best to steer clear of them, no different than if they had a disease. The only thing to do was to pray for their conversion. As it was, their eternal souls—"Yes, children, Protestants have souls"— would burn in hell forever. Sister Ignatius was close to tears when she said this, his brother said. So Chester stayed to himself the first weeks. But then, one day in the cafeteria, Jonathan Edwalds sat down next to him.

"You live over on Erie, don't ya?"

"Yes," Chester replied.

"I thought so," the other boy replied. "I used to have a friend on Erie but he moved away. Want a bite of my apple?"

Jonathan Edwalds reached the apple towards Chester's mouth. It already had a large chunk missing. Chester looked at the teeth marks. He thought of Sister Ignatius and he thought of germs.

"No thanks."

"What's the matter?" Jonathan Edwalds yelled, angry now. "My apple ain't good enough for you?" He pushed the apple into Chester's face. Chester pulled his head back, lost his balance, and fell to the floor. The cafeteria exploded in laughter. Jonathan Edwalds leaned over. "An apple a day keeps the doctor away," he smirked. Chester jumped from the floor and pulled the other boy by the front of his shirt. Then they fell to the floor, wrestling around, trying to hit each other. Chester rolled under the table, banging his head against one of its benches. A slight flow of blood creased his forehead.

"Stop this! Stop this at once!" It was Mrs. Nelson, the fifth grade teacher. Chester crawled from under the table. Mrs. Nelson was holding Jonathan Edwalds by the collar. She saw the blood on Chester's forehead.

"I am going to have you suspended, Mr. Johnny Edwalds," she said. "Go at once to the principal's office." The boy started to protest, but the teacher cut him off. "That'll be enough of that, young man. I am not going to tell you again. Go to the principal's office." The sweet smell of honey and cinnamon came to Chester. He heard his mother singing. The pot-bellied washing machine shook from side to side. He would listen to God's voice inside him. "It was my fault," he said. From then on Chester O'Reilly and Jonathan Edwalds were the best of friends. Soon Chester was spending nights at Jonathan's house, a big frame Victorian on Race Avenue, with a wrap-around front porch.

Jonathan's father worked for the city in the Department of Streets and Sanitation, but his real job was being a precinct captain for the 37th Ward Regular Democratic Organization.

"You see," he lectured the enthralled boys, "too much bigness is bad. Nobody gets to know nobody else. That's why Jonathan's great-grandfather spent the family fortune when they hijacked Austin." Jonathan's father went on to explain "the great sell out of 1899," when Austin, Illinois, became just another ward in the city of Chicago. "We voted to stay separate, boys," he said, as if the crime had happened the day before instead of decades in the past. "But we was annexed anyway. My father said it was like the Civil War in reverse. My grandfather took it all the way to the Supreme Court, but he lost. He never was the same after that. He would sit right here on this front porch, in his rocking chair, rocking back and forth, never saying a word. I learned from that, boys. Right don't always come out on top just because it's right. It's not like in the movies. You got to fight for what you believe in, boys, else you're not a man at all. But you also got to know when you're licked."

"And what do you do then?" Chester asked.

"You pick yourself up as best you can, dust off your hands, hold your head up high, and don't second guess yourself. Come here, boys. I want to read you something." With a sweep of his right arm, Jonathan's father motioned them into the house. Chester and Jonathan followed through the parlor to a small room off the dining room. It was Jonathan's father's study. Chester had never been inside it before.

"Take a load off."

The boys seated themselves on a sagging sofa covered with a green blanket. Jonathan's father fumbled about at his desk. "Ah, here it is." He put on his reading glasses and swiveled around to face them. "This, boys, is the inscription on the Monument to the Confederate Dead in front of the State House building in Columbia, South Carolina:

This Monument
Perpetuates the Memory
Of those who,

True to the instincts of their birth,
Faithful to the teachings of their fathers,
Constant in their love for the State,
Died in the performance of their duty;
Who
Have gloried a fallen cause
By the simple manhood of their lives,
The patient endurance of suffering
And the heroism of death;
And Who
In the dark hours of imprisonment
In the hopelessness of the hospital
In the short sharp agony of the field,
Found support and consolation In
the belief
That at home they would not be Forgotten.
Let the stranger
Who may in future times
Read this inscription
Recognize that these were men
Whom power could not corrupt,
Whom death could not terrify,
Whom defeat could not dishonor,
And let their virtues plead
For Just Judgement
Of the cause in which they perished.
Let the South Carolinians
Of another generation
Remember

That the state taught them
How to live and how to die.
And that from her broken fortunes
She has preserved for her children
The priceless treasure of their memories,
Teaching all who may claim
The same birthright
That truth, courage and patriotism
Endure forever.

Jonathan's father sat in silence for a few moments before speaking. "Them's beautiful words, boys. Mighty fine words. Birth, faith, duty, suffering, death, and remembrance. You just do the best you can, boys, you just do the best you can. Only make sure you know what it is you're doing your best for, unnerstand?" He paused for a few seconds and then continued: *Plead for Just Judgement of the cause in which they perished.* Real fine words. But what was dat cause, boys? Slavery. Rippin' da babies from their mama's bosom and sellin' them down river. Can you imagine that? I don't know about da truth part"—his finger jabbed into the paper—"but it just goes to show you dat courage and patriotism ain't enough. Not by a long shot. I'm sure dat dose German soldiers at Stalingrad were real brave, too, fightin' and starvin' and freezin'. And what did they die for, boys? Hitler and his gang. Youse got to learn to think for yourself. That's what you got to do. That's what being a man, a real man, is all about, not just fightin' and dyin' because some big shot says so. Beware of bravery without brains, boys. Think about it." He reached into the bookcase to the right of his desk. "Lots of times things are just da opposite of what they seem. Da Sout's defeat, for example. A blessing, for the Sout most of all. Here's what ole Unconditional Surrender himself wrote in his memoirs:

There was not time during the rebellion when I did not think, and often say, that the South was more to be benefited by its defeat than the North. The latter had the people, the institutions, and the territory to make a great and prosperous nation. The former was burdened with an institution abhorrent to all civilized people not brought up under it, and enervated the governing class. With the outside world at war with this institution, they could not have extended their territory. The labor of the country was not skilled, nor allowed to become so.

The whites could not toil without becoming degraded, and those who did were denominated "poor white trash." The system of labor would have soon exhausted the soil and left the people poor. The non-slaveholders would have left the country; and the small slaveholder must have sold out to his more fortunate neighbor. Soon the slaves would have outnumbered the masters, and, not being in sympathy with them, would have risen in their might and exterminated them. The war was expensive to the South as well as to the North, both in blood and treasure, but it was worth all it cost.

Jonathan's father returned the book to its place and his reading glasses to his shirt pocket. "Think about it, boys. Lots of times things are da opposite of what they seem."

They returned to the front porch, where Jonathan's father told them all about his great-grandfather, who rode with Phil Sheridan in "da war to free da slaves." Chester and Jonathan sat on the steps, their backs against the railing. At his feet, Jonathan's father positioned a red cooler filled with Old Style, "Chicago's beer, boys. In Chicago we drink da best." He opened a bottle with a small tin opener and brought it to his lips. Sometimes, when Jonathan's mother was not at home, he would give Chester and Jonathan surreptitious sips. "Da war to fee da slaves. Dat's what my granddaddy called it, my pops said, because that's what it was. A crusade against chattel slavery. He told me dat his daddy always said you couldn't tell him any different. In their bones all those high riding rebels knew it was just plain wrong for one man to own another like he was a dog or a chair—especially in the land of the free and the home of the brave. Even if they was niggers. Just plain common sense which ain't generally common. Common sense ain't commonplace. No sir, boys. So it was a real problem Abe Lincoln had back then. Makes our troubles today seem like somebody set the Sunday dinner table and one of the dishes got chipped. Stupidest thing Jeff Davis did was firing the first shot. Just like the Japs at Pearl Harbor. A real bonehead mistake. Ole Abe Lincoln was just too smart for that high and mighty slavemaster. Which one do you think looks like a president, boys? Jefferson Davis with his chiseled chin or Abe Lincoln with his monkey lips? It's the insides of a man that counts. Remember that. Not the packaging. Now we got movie stars running for office out in California! Tap dancers and pretty boys! Next thing you know Bozo the Clown will be United States Senator. Imagine that! You tell me, boys: see if you can name one good thing that came from California? Just one!" Jonathan's father inhaled a swallow of Old Style and laughed.

Chester tried to think. He liked it when Jonathan's father asked questions, especially when Chester was able to come up with a satisfactory answer. He remembered when Jonathan's father asked who the greatest president was and his look of approval when Chester answered, "George Washington, because he stepped down." But now Chester was stumped. There must be *something* good that came from California, he told himself, but, whatever it was, he sure couldn't think of it. "Now, where was I?" Jonathan's father continued. "Oh, yes. Old Abe. Wouldn't send guns or munitions to Fort Sumter. Just food and medicine. And Jeff Davis and dat ole windbag, Pierre Gustave Toutant Beauregard took the bait. He sure did design a pretty flag, though. Got to give him that much. A great victory for the Confederacy! That's what everybody thought at the time. But it really was their death knell, getting the North all riled up, like poking a rattlesnake with a stick." Jonathan's father reached for another Old Style. "You know, boys, life is funny like that. Like Ole Unconditional Surrender hisself said, lot of times things are just the opposite of what they seem. Like Lincoln's assassination. Worst thing that could've happened as far as the Sout was concerned—except actually winning! Everybody was hollerin' for blood except ole Abe. *With malice toward none, with charity toward all, let us bind up the*

Nation's wounds. Think about that, boys. And they killed him."

Chester never tired of the stories. To hear Jonathan's father talk was like being there. Chester would listen with wonder, imagining himself in one heroic role after the other. "The thing about the past," Jonathan's father said, "is that it is what it is. The past will never change. That's what keeps it alive. The present dies. The future ain't born yet. The past stays as it is, always."

*   *   *

It should have been an ordinary day. Chester and Jonathan were in seventh grade. They came running home from school to Jonathan's house like they always did and threw their bookbags on the kitchen table. There was a strange silence in the house. Jonathan's mother took Jonathan to her, sobbing deep sobs. Then she took Chester to her bosom as well and the three of them cried together.

Chester's brother told him he would be damned in hell for all eternity if he went to the funeral service at Austin Presbyterian, at Waller and Fulton, but his mother and the potbelly washing machine appeared before him and Chester went. It was the first time he had been in a Protestant church. It was strange. Everything was in English! Chester wasn't sure how he felt about that. Tears in his eyes, he followed along in the prayer book. He said "Amen" when everyone else did. Protestants, he thought, said "Amen" a lot more than Catholics. Every time Chester said the word he saw Sister Ignatius point her finger at him and scowl.

After the funeral service Chester did not go to the cemetery. Instead he walked around the corner to St. Lucy's. He knelt in front of the statue of the Blessed Virgin. She wore blue and white robes. Her arms reached out with open hands. "Forgive me, Holy Mother," he prayed. "I know what I did was wrong." He knelt for a long while, tears streaming down his cheeks. He said the "Our Father" and he said the "Hail, Mary." Then he sat in the front pew, studying the statue. The face reminded him of his mother's. Why would God's voice inside him tell him to do something that was wrong? Maybe it wasn't God's voice. Maybe it was the devil's. Anger seized him. His mother said it was God's voice. His mother wouldn't—couldn't—lie. If his mother said it was God's voice, then it was. Chester looked at the statue. He thought the Blessed Virgin was smiling. "I know what I did was wrong," he said to himself as he walked home, "but I'd do it again."

*   *   *

After graduation from Francis Scott Key Elementary School Chester and Jonathan attended Austin High School. "It's one of the best in the city," his grandmother beamed. Chester was not good at athletics; it was Jonathan who had a natural grace, an instinct, he said, for football, basketball, baseball. "It's as if I know where the ball will be a split second before it gets there," he explained. But Chester was clumsy. They both wore maroon Tiger jackets, but it was Jonathan who starred on the field or in the gymnasium while Chester tended to uniforms and equipment. Jonathan had a series of girlfriends, cheerleaders, members of the pep squad. In their junior year Chester started "keeping company," as she termed it, with Diana Weyer. It was nice being with her. Diana wasn't the prettiest girl at Austin. She wasn't even one of the prettiest. Everyone, even Diana's mother, admitted that. But Diana had an easy charm and natural smile. She was kind. There was a pleasantness to her that reached out to everyone. Her favorite subject was Homemaking. Diana talked of growing up, getting married and settling down with a good man who kept a steady job, and raising children. She and Chester would walk to Merrick Park on their lunch hour so she could watch the mothers playing with their babies in the sandbox.

"So why in the world would a general intentionally back his army into a corner with a deep canyon at its back? That's what Mr. Styles asked today in history class. Jonathan raised his hand and said that maybe the general was drunk. Everyone laughed, but Mr. Styles didn't think that was funny." Chester looked at Diana, but he could tell that she hadn't heard a word he'd said. Diana's eyes were not on him, but on a child dressed in a pink and yellow playsuit, sitting in the sandbox. With a bright red shovel and labored intensity the child scooped sand into an equally red bucket. "Oh, isn't that the cutest baby you ever saw?" Diana looked at Chester with beaming eyes. "Just the cutest little baby?" Chester and Diana were sitting on swings, eating strawberry ice cream cones. Chester studied Diana, for the first time, really, as Diana studied the child. Chester saw the pink of the ice cream and the pink of Diana's lips come together and he thought that Diana's lipstick and eye shadow looked silly. Why do women paint themselves? he asked out loud.

"What did you say?" Diana asked.

"I was just wondering why women use make-up. Why do they? Why do you?"

"Make-up?"

"Lipstick. Fingernail polish. Stuff like that."

"Don't be such a silly."

"No, really, I'm serious, Diana. None of that stuff makes you look any prettier. It really doesn't."

A bright smile came to the girl's face. She had misunderstood him completely. "Oh, you are the sweetest boy," she said, "and you say the sweetest things. Thank you very much, very much, I'm sure." Diana took his hand and resumed looking at the child. Chester let his hand stay with hers for an instant and then let go. He never was able to explain about General Greene and the Carolina campaign: how General Greene's army fought like hell once they realized there was no way to retreat.

Chester's first eleven years of school had poked along. But now, before he knew it, he was being measured for his high school graduation gown. Jonathan would attend the University of Illinois, "downstate," on a football scholarship. Chester's brother had left home the year before to seek fame and fortune in California. Lena and Lana, Chester's sisters, lived a not so short distance away in the

Horner Park neighborhood, married to the Peachley brothers, Ron and Roger, the sons of "Peachley and Sons" plumbing. Now Chester and his grandmother rattled around in the basement apartment, so crowded for so many years. Chester had an entire room to himself! For the past two years he worked after school and on weekends at Freeman's Clothing on Chicago Avenue, sweeping up, emptying the garbage, keeping an eye on things when Mr. Freeman was in the back. Now Mr. Freeman offered him a full-time job.

"I have been paying you one dollar an hour for part time," Mr. Freeman said. "I will pay you one dollar and twenty-five cents an hour for full-time. It's a generous offer—twenty-five cents above the minimum wage. But you're a good worker and honest. You are worth it."

"If you go to work for Mr. Freeman full-time," Chester's grandmother said, "you will work there, or someplace like there, for the rest of your life. You have such a good mind. You should go to college."

"There isn't money for college." Chester said these words without feeling.

"Your mother always hoped you, or your brother, would be a priest. 'We should give one of you back to God,' she said."

Chester did not know how to respond. For some time he had known of his grandmother's hopes, but not of his mother's.

"Go to St. Lucy's and talk to Monsignor Maguire. If God is calling you, it would be a terrible mistake to turn away." Chester saw old Mr. Freeman, his back stooped over. A measuring tape sagged between his hands. "Okay," he replied. "I will talk to Monsignor Maguire."

*   *   *

For as long as anyone could remember Monsignor Michael Patrick Maguire had been pastor of St. Lucy's. He was a large man, in his late fifties. No one ever complimented his sermons for their eloquence, but they were much appreciated for their brevity, especially in the summer. The Cardinal understood that Michael Patrick Maguire had no additional ambitions; he was content to run St. Lucy's firmly, efficiently, and profitably as his own personal fiefdom until he retired. The St. Lucy's chapter of the Knights of Columbus was thriving; the Altar and Rosary Society flourished. Eight years before, Monsignor Maguire had retired the mortgage on St. Lucy's—church, school above, parking lot, adjacent rectory, and the convent across the alley on Midway Park. Ever since, Monsignor Maguire had been one of the Cardinal's favorites.

Monsignor Maguire's six assistant pastors knew their places. The Monsignor liked presiding over banquets and political events and officiating at select weddings, baptisms, and funerals. Weather permitting, he played golf three times a week, April through October. In the winter Monsignor Maguire was a frequent and favored guest at the Florida beach houses of corporate executives. He thought of himself as one of them. There were numerous others, the Sisters of Loretto, his assistants, the itinerant Franciscan or Jesuit, to take care of the spiritual side of the business. He devoted himself to keeping things running smoothly and profitably. He was fond of saying that his was a pray *and* pay business. Monsignor Maguire took care of the *pay* part.

He had been a chaplain in the Pacific in World War II, ashore with troops in the third, sometimes the second, wave as islands whose names he would never forget were wrenched from the Japanese. Cupping his hand to his ear, he heard fragments of confessions in the cacophony of amphibious hell on earth. He smeared oil on the foreheads of dying boys; he made the Sign of the Cross over pieces of bodies. As St. Lucy's Pastor, Monsignor Maguire made a conscious effort to forget the horror and the blood. He never spoke about it, and he delegated officiating at memorial Masses to his assistants. He did not attend military reunions.

The Monsignor escorted Chester to his private quarters and motioned him to a leather chair. They were in the Pastor's study, attached to his bedroom and private bath. The luxury surprised Chester, the elegant comfort, carpet and paintings, lamps, sofa, tables. In an alcove of the room stood a safe with black doors and brass hinges, as tall as he was.

"I had this room redone a year ago. Mrs. McCarthy officiated!" The Monsignor laughed, answering Chester's unspoken question. "Others, of course, pitched in with special donations."

Chester's eyes came to the hi-fi set. Receiver and amplifier sat on an elegant mahogany sideboard. Four speakers hung at the corners of the ceiling. He looked more carefully and was barely able to discern the connecting wires. There was a large television set.

"The one in my bedroom is an R.C.A.," the pastor boasted, "but I think that this MagnaVox has a better picture." Monsignor Maguire turned a dial. Chester's eyes opened wide. He pulled himself forward. Color! A color television! It was the first time he had seen one.

"Let's get down to it. Your grandmother tells me you have a vocation!"

"I'm not sure," Chester replied.

"The only sure things in this world, my son, are death and taxes. The Catholic Church tries to avoid both and has been mighty successful for going on two thousand years!" The Monsignor smiled and Chester smiled with him. "Do you believe in God, my son?"

"Of course," Chester answered without thinking.

"Do you believe He sent His Only Begotten Son, Our Lord and Savior, Jesus Christ to save us from our sins?"

Again, "Of course."

"Well, then," the priest concluded, "there's really not much more to it than that. If you believe, you must spread the Word. What could be more obvious? You see, my son, what the Church needs now, most of all, is modern thinking. Oh, I see you looking around, thinking what a fine carpet, what a wonderful TV! But there is no contradiction between doing the Lord's work and taking care of yourself at the same time. None at all. In fact, in this day and age, it's the only way, really, that the Church is going to survive. We have to be in the world, a part of the world, to do our job. The days of separating ourselves high on a pedestal to dispense wisdom to the downtrodden, well, those days are gone forever. More and more, the Church is a business corporation. We provide a service. With a capital "S." For "Soul," if you like. And that's a good thing. Professional. Sound. A part of—not apart from—the Twentieth Century."

To Chester, these were new ideas. An entire world unto itself, Monsignor Maguire's enthusiasm reached out to him, tempting and contagious, in ways Chester could barely begin to understand. Chester thought of his grandmother, her shawl around her shoulders, rosary beads in her hands, praying in front of the statue of the Virgin Mary. Again and again, he looked around the room, as the priest's confident testimonial continued.

"So, Chester, you can see that it's more than holy water, rosary beads, and incense, not that there's anything wrong with ritual. But 'smells and bells' goes only so far. It's the modern age. The Church has to adjust. We have to adapt. The priest today must be a professional, a professional representative of the Greatest Man Who Ever Lived. We are salesmen. Now, as a salesman, I take a personal interest in my territory. I look after my flock and, of course, my flock looks after me!"

The Pastor of St. Lucy's swept the room with his right arm. "My just deserts, Chester O'Reilly, my just deserts! Nothing more, and, you can bet your bottom dollar on it, nothing less!" The priest waited as Chester's wide eyes studied the room. Then Monsignor Maguire reached to the sideboard to push a button. The room filled with song, the heartfelt sincerity of Pat Boone, a singer of the time who looked and sounded like a cryonic teenager. The priest waited. Finally, he leaned over. "Go for it," he whispered. "Go for it."

Chester hesitated. Did he feel something, anything, inside? Nothing came. He thought of how happy his grandmother would be. He nodded his head.

"Swell!" Monsignor Maguire slapped him on the back. *Another feather in my cap!* the Pastor of St. Lucy's thought as Chester departed. Each year there were fewer and fewer seminarians. The shortage of priests was right up there with declining revenues as Topic A at the Cardinal's dinner table. His Eminence would be greatly pleased.

*　　　*　　　*

St. Mary of the Lake Seminary was located fifty miles north of Chicago. A sign to the side of the iron gate at its main entrance read *ORARE ET LABORARE EST VIVERE.* The bus from Chicago with its cargo of twenty earnest faces, most of whom had never before been outside the city limits, drove through the gate to follow a winding road for a quarter of a mile before stopping in front of an old brick structure. Chester stepped from the bus, gripping his one suitcase, and entered the "Old Red Brick" building. A voice came over the din: "Room assignments are posted at the end of the hall! Room assignments are posted at the end of the hall!" Room 17.

Chester was unpacking his suitcase when he heard movement behind him. A young man of medium height stood in the doorway. His light brown hair fell over his forehead; he was in the habit of brushing it back with his left hand. He had a pleasant way about him. He was of the type that blends into the background.

"Is this room 17?"

"Yes," Chester answered. "I'm Chester O'Reilly."

"My name is Charles Zalesie," the other boy said as they shook hands. "Everybody calls me 'Easy.'"

"Why?"

"Well, 'cause of my last name, for one thing. And 'cause I try not to cause any trouble, for another. I've been 'Easy' ever since kindergarten. If you don't like it..."

"No, no," Chester laughed. "'Easy' is just fine." He felt, once again, cheated, somehow. Just one more thing he'd never had—a nickname. "I took the bed by the window," Chester continued. "But we can switch if you like."

"Oh, no," his new roommate replied, "this is just fine." Charles Zalesie was from "da sout side." His family lived in Chicago Lawn, a working class neighborhood close to Midway Airport. He had nine brothers and sisters. His father worked near the stockyards, in a factory that made machines that made sausages. He wasn't sure about his vocation, either.

"Do you miss girls?" he asked Chester a few months later, after they had established a tentative familiarity. It was after "lights out," when they were supposed to be silent.

"I'm not sure," Chester answered.

"Don't be mad, okay? Maybe it's because you like boys?"

Chester knew he was supposed to feel anger. Instead he felt a surge of excitement, which he quickly suppressed. "Maybe you like boys yourself."

"I don't know," his roommate replied. "But you don't have to get so bent out of shape. It's just that my mother said I should find out. About my roommate, I mean."

"I had a girlfriend once," Chester said. "I really liked her, or I thought I did, I think. Then, one day, it just went away. We were sitting on a swing, in the park. She was eating ice-cream. Don't you think that's strange?"

"I suppose. But it really doesn't make any difference, does it? I mean whether you like girls or boys. We have chosen the celibate life. Our bodies are holy temples. They belong to Jesus. We must not defile them." In a monotone these words were repeated as if remembered from the confessional.

Chester lay in his bed, thinking. "Easy, are you asleep?"

"No."

"Want to talk some more?"

"Sure."

"About what you said. Did your Ma really tell you to ask? About me? I mean."

There was a long pause. "No," his roommate answered softly. "No. I wanted to know for myself. I had to know. 'Cause I don't want you to get mad at me. I never had a real close friend before."

"Suppose I had said you know what?"

"That you like boys?"

"Yeah."

"I don't know," his roommate replied. "Do you think it's wrong?"

"Of course it's wrong," Chester replied. "Everybody knows it's wrong. The Bible talks about two men lying down with each other and being damned in the fires of Hell forever. Father O'Brien said it's an *abomination*."

"Do you think it's more wrong for two men than for a man and a woman?"

"Who aren't married?"

"Yes, who aren't married."

"I don't know," Chester said. He thought for a moment. "Anything that displeases God is a sin. I don't think it makes any difference. Sin is sin."

"You're not mad at me, are you, Chester?"

"No, Easy, I'm not mad at you." I think I should be, Chester thought, but I'm not. He could not let go of Easy's words: "I never had a real close friend before." I did, Chester thought, remembering how in grade school he and Jonathan Edwalds slept in the same bed, how at Austin High they had rough housed around in the locker room, how there had been tears in the edges of their eyes when the bus that would take Chester to St. Mary of the Lake pulled from the curb. In the dark now, there was a pang of longing in his chest. As he listened to his roommate's breathing, strange feelings came to him, but he would not let them take conscious form.

*   *   *

The seminary years passed quickly. Chester had a natural gift for language. The Latin that tormented his classmates rolled off his tongue. He excelled at mathematics and literature, as he always had, but also at theology. His grasp of history would have made Jonathan Edwalds' father proud. In the summers he returned to Chicago, working at Freeman's Clothing.

"I will still pay you twenty-five cents more than the minimum wage," Mr. Freeman boasted. "You are to be a priest!"

Chester liked it on Sundays when he assisted at Mass, opening and closing the ciborium, reading the Gospels. He could feel the congregation's eyes on him. It was as if he had been adopted by the entire parish, its pride reinforcing his own. Then, at last, it was his final year. He returned to St. Mary of the Lake with the joy on his grandmother's face alive in his mind.

One night Chester returned late to his room. As he walked by the gymnasium he heard noises inside. He opened the door and walked to the shower stalls. Easy was leaning against one of the walls with his back to the entrance. He did not see Chester. All Chester could see was the back of Easy's head. Was someone kneeling? Perhaps audible, gasps came from Easy, short, sharp, sibilant, or did they? Chester approached no farther. Instead he let go of the shower room door to retreat through the gymnasium. He walked in the direction of his dormitory when he came upon the grotto to the Blessed Virgin. A statue stood in its center, nestled in a cove of greenery. Chester sat in front of the statue for long moments before falling to his knees. "Holy Mother of God," he prayed silently, "forgive your servant, Charles Easy Zalesie."

"You okay?"

It was Easy's voice. Chester stood, brushing the lower part of his cassock with both hands. He turned. "Yeah." In a confusion of anger, curiosity, and excitement, Chester looked into the eyes of his first year roommate. He could not tell what it was he saw.

"You look real strange," Easy said, touching Chester's arm. "Kinda pale. You sure you feel okay?"

Chester pulled away. "Yeah," he said again. "I told you. I'm fine." He turned away.

"By the way," the other deacon asked, "was that you in the gym just now?"

"Me? No." Chester lied. "What would I be doing in the gym at this hour?"

"Suit yourself." Easy's words came over Chester's shoulder, but Chester did not turn around. He went to his room and tossed from side to side, pushing conscious thought from his mind. He concentrated on the words of the

"Our Father" and "Hail, Mary," until, after long hours, he fell asleep.

*   *   *

With anxious steps Chester entered the refectory the following morning. He heard his heart pounding as Father Gregory finished saying the grace. If the old priest ended without saying *Ora pro nobis*, breakfast would be confined to silence. For the first time Chester could remember, he hoped that Father Gregory would not say the words. But he did. The supplication brought forth a great roar of male voices: "Amen!" The room burst into noise. Chester looked around. Nothing was any different. High at one end of the great hall the priests sat like pieces on a chess board. Below, second year students ran around with pitchers of hot coffee and orange juice; third year seminarians wheeled carts of eggs, bacon, and biscuits from table to table. Through pass-through openings Chester could see freshmen sweating in the kitchen. The customary clatter of conversation and cutlery echoed from one end of the refectory to the other. He sat with his fellow deacons, just below the breakfasting priests, but he did not eat. Finally his eyes found Easy's at the other end of the long table. Easy looked away. Moments later he threw his head back and laughed. As soon as he could, Chester fled to his room. He fell to his knees. Then he thought of Father Raulston.

"Please have a seat." They were in Father Raulston's study, one of the two rooms comprising his quarters, simple in its furnishings: a bed, two armchairs and a coffee table. One of its walls was floor to ceiling shelves filled with books.

"What is on your mind, my son?"

For long moments Chester sat in silence. He did not know how to begin. There was something about the dignity with which the old priest carried himself that was intimidating. Everything about Father Raulston seemed holy: his unaffected speech which Chester had first admired in the literature class Father Raulston taught, "Literature of the Victorian Era," the straightforward way Father Raulston looked you in the eye, how he took his time before answering a question, how he pronounced each word with care, as if precision were a sacrament. Father Raulston's bright intelligence sparkled, but it sparkled not out of vanity but from an inner core of peace. Chester studied the gentle man. Father Raulston sat quietly, his hands folded in his lap.

"Take your time, my son."

"Father," Chester began at last, "if I saw someone cheating on a test, say a Latin exam, what should I do?"

"I should think," the old priest answered, "that you should pray." Father Raulston paused, giving Chester time to consider. "But this isn't about someone cheating on a Latin exam, is it?"

"No, Father."

"Even so, let us proceed as if it were, for the time being. Let us suppose that you thought you saw someone cheating. The first thing to do is to establish exactly what did transpire. Are you certain there was cheating? Could you have been mistaken?"

Chester thought back to the night before. What, exactly, had he witnessed? He had seen the back of Easy's head. He had thought then that someone was in the shower stall with Easy. Now, in the presence of the worthy priest, he was not so sure.

"I *think* they were cheating."

"Ah, then," Father Raulston replied, "that is something else entirely. Many an innocent life has been destroyed by suspicion and gossip. History's pages are stained with the blood of righteousness. Holy Mother the Church has not been without blame. Torquemada presided over the Inquisition. The Puritans fled persecution only to persecute women as witches. In our own time Communism, which is the religion of atheism, gave us the torment of show trials. Nor is our own country exempt. Think of Joseph McCarthy. History teaches us the transcendence of the virtue of humility if it teaches us anything at all. Given your uncertainty, there is only one course. To pray. To go about, in your absence of certitude, as if nothing has happened. You cannot reconstruct the events of the past. They are what they are. They do not change." Chester remembered sitting on the wrap-around porch on Race Avenue. "You must leave God's matters to God," the old priest concluded. Again Chester heard Jonathan Edwald's father: "The thing about the past is that it is what it is. The past will never change. And that's what keeps it alive. The present dies. The future ain't born yet. The past stays alive, always." What Chester had seen the night before, or thought he had seen, was very much alive.

"But suppose they were cheating, Father?"

"It is the human condition to co-exist with evil, my son. Why God permits evil to continue down through the ages is a great mystery. Fortunately God gives us the gift of humility, to remind us that we are not the be-all and end-all, that much is beyond our mere human understanding. That is why He also gives us the gift of Faith, Faith that God, in His Infinite Wisdom, has a Divine Plan. Faith is the beacon that guides us through the darkness of doubt. God has the power to triumph over Satan in all his demonic manifestations, avarice, sloth, envy, lust, and so forth, and including, more to the point for the purpose of our discussion today, Ego. If we have humility and Faith, we too will be among God's legions. Have you read Aquinas, my son?"

"A little, Father."

"Read Aquinas. According to St. Thomas, we know that our knowledge is incomplete. It follows, therefore, that our understanding must be deficient as well. Yet we persist in mistaking our role as servants with that of the Deity Himself. Pieces of the puzzle are missing, and will always be missing. Nonetheless, we pretend that we see the whole picture. It was Voltaire, if I remember rightly, who took God to task when a great earthquake struck Lisbon. Thousands of people perished. The earthquake struck on a Sunday morning, when the churches were full. Lisbon, as you know, is a great seaport. A large convoy had arrived the night before, so the brothels were also full, even more so than the churches. Voltaire accuses: most of the churches were destroyed. The worshippers inside were killed while the brothels and fornicators were spared. Those who sinned survived; those who prayed, perished. St. Thomas would say that Voltaire sees only pieces of the puzzle, not the entire picture. What the missing pieces are, only God can say. That is why He gives us the gift of Faith. That is why the Bible teaches that without faith we are empty garments. We do not believe *because of*. We believe *in spite of*. Study St. Thomas, my son. Leave judgment to God. He works in mysterious ways."

Chester went from Father Raulston's study straight to the library. Over the next few weeks he read everything he could by and about the great saint. But whenever he saw Easy approaching, he turned away and he never spoke to him again.

Chapter Nine:

Sore of Foot and Empty-handed

Albert Sidney McNab
New York, New York
1989

Albert Sidney McNab's feet hurt. He sat on the side of the tub, the bottoms of his pants rolled up to his knees, soaking his feet in Epsom salts. "A fine mess I've made of it this time," he said to himself. After fifteen minutes, pain in his buttocks obliterated the pain in his feet. This is the way of the world, he thought. In the land of the blind the one-eyed man is king. He dried his feet, rolled down his pants, and went to the kitchen area, which was but a small corner of his small "efficiency." Like an army of occupation, dirty dishes claimed sink, countertop, and stove. He fumbled about coming up, finally, with an adequately clean looking plate. He set it to the side while he searched among the refrigerator's forest of wine bottles for something edible. Leftover enchiladas from Raul's? How many days ago was that? He unwrapped the tin foil to bring the mashed enchiladas to his nose. Ah! Yummy! Ten minutes later the porridge-enchiladas sat before him on a tray, on an easel type stand set permanently between armchair and television. For correct culinary accompaniment he had discovered some tortillas only faintly green around the edges. Careful with the knife! "Go away, green," he hummed to himself, as he amputated the offending edges. "No gangrene! Green, be gone!" Perhaps mold is actually good for us, he thought. Penicillin and all. Then he thought better of it. Best not to take chances. It's what we don't know that hurts us. Most of the time.

His two and one-half room "efficiency" was close to public transportation. So the ad in the newspaper promised and, yes, the promise was fulfilled with the day and night stereo of elevated trains above and the subway below. The only reason he had moved, a year before, was that the building he'd been living in was condemned. Too many rats, the city proclaimed. Well, he'd left the leathery ones alone, and they had returned the favor. Squirrels, rabbits, and cats were socially acceptable, to say nothing of pigeons. He had never been shat upon by a rat! But, no! Co-existing with rats was not to be permitted. He had had to be protected. He had had to be saved and from those who had done him no harm! When he'd go to the bathroom in the middle of the night, he heard the rats scurrying around, but he was careful not to step on them. Leave and let live: that was his motto!

Albert Sidney McNab worked for Middlebury Adjusting, Fire and Insurance Advocacy, Inc. M.A.F.I.A.

"Nobody fucks with the M.A.F.I.A.," his boss, Carlo Franco Weberelli boasted. For his first forty-five years he had been Charles Francis Weber. When he inherited the business from his uncle, he had had his name and the company's legally changed "for business purposes." *Middlebury Adjusting* smacked of chiropractics. M.A.F.I.A.'s motto was *WHICHEVER SIDE YOU'RE ON, WE'RE ON THAT SIDE TOO!* Carlo had thought it up himself. "People want to feel they're not alone," he said. "They want to belong."

Ensconced in front of the television Albert Sidney McNab watched as a scantily clad woman pointed to lighted squares of brightly colored letters. Three contestants chosen for their apparent normalcy salivated as the host, manicured, mannerly, and mannequin, gave spin to a giant wheel. The audience in the television studio exhaled paroxysms of envy as the announcer extolled the virtues of a cornucopia of prizes: a nesting of hand painted Bavarian dolls, a refrigerator which made ice-cream, his and her lingerie sets.

A few hours later Albert Sidney McNab was awakened by a stentorian voice commanding him to stay tuned for an exclusive interview with the city's latest serial killer. Trains rumbled through, high and low. "You've really done it this time," the realization returned. "You've really done it this time." What he had done this time was mess up a perfectly fine divorce investigation. He had lost his balance to crash into the lilies on the Long Island estate of Percy Armond Lutton, the cosmetics heir. He had positioned M.A.F.I.A.'s newest camera, precariously as it turned out, on top of its oldest ladder and was reaching to adjust the lens. On the other side of the bedroom window Percy and one of the gardeners, a fine young lad no more than twenty, were about to "do the nasties," as Carlo reveled in saying. The police had come, the film was confiscated, the lilies were on life support, and, worst of all, Percy was alerted that his wife, the vivacious and much in the gossip columns Bouffie Angela Lutton intended, not just to divorce Percy, but to pick him clean as a bone in the process. She would threaten to sue Carlo for negligence, the name of his company be damned (she had her own connections). Thus it came about that Albert Sidney McNab's feet were sore. He had had to walk several miles looking for a bus stop once Percy decided not to press trespassing charges. Bus stops in the sidewalk deficient suburbs, Albert learned, are few and far between. Why would anyone want to live in such places? There was more: pedestrians, he soon came to understand, are a suspicious as well as an endangered species. Twice minivans, beehive hair-do's with the glazed look of adrenalinized shoppers, had run him off the road. A police car trailed him for half a mile. "Maybe if I act crazy," it came to him, "they will give me a ride." He waved his arms wildly. He talked to himself. He cackled. He rolled around in the gutter. All this was to no avail. So he went up to the side of the police car to stare as if he had come upon a train wreck. Carlo, who was to have retrieved him, ladder, and camera, came from around the corner. He saw his assistant waving his arms wildly, jabbering to himself, accompanied by a police car crawling along, laughing blue faces inside. He sped away. The fat man trotted as best he could after Carlo's fleeing vehicle, only to see it escape around a corner. Clutching his chest, Albert turned around to see the police car flee as well. Too much later he came to a bus stop to learn from a posted notice that service had been discontinued the previous summer. If he thought such unacceptable (he did), he should write to his Councilman, Assemblyman, State Senator, Congressman, U.S. Senator, and, of course, the Mayor. Names and addresses were thoughtfully provided. Hours later and footsore sorer he returned to M.A.F.I.A.'s office. Carlo was clutching his chest, too, mourning the loss of his favorite ladder, a most wonderful ladder, an heirloom from his uncle's days, an indispensable tool of the trade, gone, gone forever. He would deduct the cost of the ladder—not that it could ever be replaced—from the fat man's next paycheck, if there were one.

"One day the ladder I climb shall be a sturdy ladder," Albert vowed to himself as he turned off the television. "I shall position it securely and I shall climb it to the very top." He stumbled across the room, lowered the Murphy bed, and collapsed soundly into sleep.

*　　*　　*

Albert couldn't go on much longer. He knew that much. He had failed at more jobs than are listed in a trade school catalogue. He had been a waiter, a bus driver, a door to door salesman—of aluminum siding, of cleaning supplies, of magazines. He had been a telemarketer, an usher. In its desperation the City of New York had hired him as a social worker. He did have a degree, even if it was in Medieval Languages. His job was to investigate what was called "welfare fraud." He was fired after three months when the computers determined that his cases had an eighty-five percent record of benefits *increasing*. He protested that he was only doing his job, making sure that his clients received the benefits they were entitled to by law, not a penny more, not a penny less. He took a special pride in discovering, understanding, and promulgating *supplementary* emergency relief grants.

"You idiot!" his boss yelled. "You're supposed to see to it that they get less. Not more. Less!" Soon thereafter Albert had lucked into the job with M.A.F.I.A.

Carlo had decided he would train an investigative assistant. He placed ads in *Newsday*, the *Daily News*, and the *Post* which were supposed to read:

TRAIN INVEST. ASS. MAFIA.
INTERVIEWS THURS. 4 PM. 766 PARNELL

Instead, the ads appeared as follows:

TRANSVEST. ASS. MAFIA.
INTERVIEWS THURS. 4 PM. 766 PARNELL

When he was "between jobs," Albert Sidney McNab volunteered at a soup kitchen down the street from 766 Parnell. At 3:45 p. m. on that particular Thursday he passed in front, with difficulty. Men of various sizes and shapes, dressed in women's clothing, clustered. He couldn't help but notice how brazenly the men stared at each other's posteriors. Even for New York, he thought, this is strange. "The Mafia is looking for ass," a voice said. "But you have to be a transvestite to apply." Not just strange. *Very* strange. *Only* in New York! Carlo came outside.

"Ladies, uh, ladies...or gentlemen," he shouted, "I'm afraid there's been a mistake. Please go home. The interviews have been canceled." An angry undercurrent percolated through the crowd.

"Just because we're friends of Dorothy doesn't mean you can push us around," an angry voice called out. "Am I right, girlfriends?" There was pushing and shoving and a policeman on a horse. A paddy wagon appeared and the men dressed as women ran, high heels striking the shuffleboard sidewalk like ice-picks. Albert Sidney McNab was about to leave, too, when Carlo approached him.

"Are you here about the job?" he asked.

Albert was clumsy, yes, but he was also tenacious, and, for the first time in his life he was, if not a complete success, at least not an utter failure. Carlo assigned him petty insurance cases. A fire in the Bronx where the owner never made repairs, forged receipts, pocketed the settlement, and abandoned the property. The truck driver in Queens and his fender bender, back injury certified and recertified. Might never walk again. Albert videotaped him on Tuesdays and Fridays entering and, two hours later, exiting the Fairlawn Racquet Club, racquet and gym bag in hand. These and other victories in the never-ending war against malfeasance and fraud earned Middlebury Adjusting, Fire and Insurance Advocacy, Inc. a fee of ten percent of recoveries plus expenses. In certain cases, cases that had been written off as closed, the fee was twenty percent.

It was the underbelly of capitalism, the entrails of commerce, of microeconomics, of the great American dream machine that spits out cars and washing machines, stereos and kitchen gadgets, in all sizes, shapes, and colors, from all corners of the world. It was trench warfare. Somebody has to do it, Carlo said. The world was dog eaten. But all Albert Sidney McNab wanted was for everyone to get along. There were cockroaches in his "efficiency," but he made no effort to kill them. He had read that the cockroach is the most noble of creatures, biologically incapable of violence. When he first read about gene therapy, he immediately thought of the cockroach. He spent his weekends in Washington Square reading or playing chess, and he liked to go to the movies, although, more and more, he was disgusted with violence proffered as art. Frequently he walked out of the cinema with loud denunciations, especially when there were children in the audience.

"I just don't get it," he told Max, one of his chess mates in Washington Square. "I just don't get it at all." The night before Albert had walked out of a much praised film, *Taxi Driver*. In the lobby, on his angry departure, he complained to the manager: seated behind him were three girls, none more than twelve years old. "And, consider this,

Max. *Taxi Driver* has an 'R' rating. No one under 18 is supposed to be admitted without a parent or guardian."

Max, a black man in his fifties, drove a bread truck in midtown. He was used to what he thought of as the fat man's quixotic crusades. "What is it this time that you don't get?"

"The film's restricted to an adult audience."

"So?"

"So I told the manager."

"And?"

"And he offered me my money back." The fat man slid his queen four squares forward to capture Max's white bishop. "Check."

"Did you take it? Check yourself."

"Of course I took it. I am too much in the habit of saying 'goodbye' to money not to welcome its infrequent return. I wish it would show up more often. But that's not the point."

"If money's not the point, what is? Remember, you can't do what you don't got. Besides a bargain is a bargain. Check again."

"What is that supposed to mean? What bargain?"

"You are unhappy. You complain. You get money. *Voilá!* Happiness returns. Enough said. Finito."

"An American Masterpiece, Max! Brains splattering and windshield wipers washing red! I wanted to vomit. The little girls were giggling. Check!"

"You could have changed seats."

"That's what the manager said. 'That's not the point,' I told him. 'Children shouldn't be watching this stuff. '"

"I'm sure you did. What did the manager say behind that? Check."

"He said they were not *my* children. That there's worse stuff on TV. That it was none of *my* business. That I was causing trouble. That he didn't want to call the police."

"But he would have," the black man responded. "I make it my business to mind my business. You should too. I keep telling you you've got to stop going around all the time poking your nose into other folk's troubles. Ain't you got enough of your own?"

No part of this conversation was new to either of them. Albert studied the chessboard. He had to do something about Max's black bishop. That much was certain.

"Of course I have my own troubles," he answered. "Well, I suppose I do. You want me to dwell on failure and disappointment, how inadequately I've answered the challenge of the promise of my youth? How I have betrayed bright hopes and noble aspirations? Is that what you're suggesting, Max? You're not a psychiatrist."

"No, nor do I want to be," the truck driver answered. "But I do know when someone is in a world of trouble. And you, my melanin deficient friend, are in a world of trouble." Max slid his black bishop forward. "Checkmate!"

"Unadulterated luck," the fat man said, extending his hand.

"When black folks win," Max replied, "it's luck. We get full credit when we lose."

"Half a loaf is better than none."

"I know a lot more about bread than you do. Especially *white* bread. Half a loaf is not always better, not when it's the moldy half!"

"My grandparents came over from the old country with nothing but crumbs in their pockets," Albert replied. "Undoubtedly moldy crumbs. I have just offered *you* an entire half a loaf!"

"God bless the child that got his own," Max answered. He paused. "Do you know why I like chess?"

"You don't have to be in shape to play?"

Max laughed. "It's because all the corresponding pieces are equally powerful, black or white. Everything is equal."

"White moves first," the fat man said.

"Don't I know it!" the black man replied.

Albert Sidney McNab was a misfit. No use denying it. There wasn't anything he could do about it, not that he wanted to. It was clear to Carlo and magazine covers that men who wear designer clothes and women draped in pearls were better than people like himself, like Max, like old Mrs. Clancy who fed pigeons in the park while he and the truck driver played chess and solved all the world's problems, but Albert Sidney McNab didn't think so. He didn't think the briefcase or the décolletage any better than he or Max or old Mrs. Clancy. They were just different. Not better. "Some day I shall do something grand," he said to himself as, with a wave of his hand, Max disappeared into the IRT. "Some day it will be my turn." Then, as an afterthought: "I knew all along that Max's black bishop was going to cause trouble." Did knowledge not acted upon count for naught? Forewarned, forearmed, he thought. But only if we act. The moment must be seized—he thought of Lenin in October—or it will pass us by forever. I will be ready when the time comes, he vowed. Of this I am sure. I will be ready when the time comes. A week later the Atlantis Fidelity Insurance Company contacted Carlo. An Ohio businessman, one Charleston Travers Landeman, had disappeared.

"This case is a big waste of time," Carlo said. "Better yours than mine."

I might as well chase geese some place warm, the fat man thought as the van to the airport crawled along. Who knows? Giant oak trees from little acorns grow. "If you've got a hundred years to wait around," he laughed to himself. But such as he was, even so, Carlo was the boss and Albert would do as he was told, even unto the unnatural act of flying through the air. A week later Albert Sidney McNab was back in New York, tanned, sore of foot, and empty-handed. "It seems beyond doubt, Carlo, reasonable doubt, let me qualify, that a shark did in fact consume our client's client."

"A classy way to go," Carlo said. "If you think about it."

Albert Sidney McNab did not want to think about it. "I wish that sharks were more like cockroaches," he said.

Carlo had no idea what this meant. He seldom had any idea what anything Albert said meant.

"Absolutely!" Carlo replied.

"For the sake of those who play on the shore. For the sake of sailors and fishermen too."

"Sure, you're right!" Carlo agreed.

I'm right about something else as well, Albert thought. Our fish-eaten friend deserves another look. Not today. But some day. My future is a thing of the past! Frederique and Mabouhey have not seen the last of Albert Sidney McNab!

Chapter Ten:
Flight

Travers Landeman
Athens, Ohio; Mabouhey
1989

Matt had killed himself. Each day brought new agony. In a daze, Travers dragged himself from place to place. He was unable to eat. He told no one about the night in his sister's garage. There was no one to tell. Its memory was an acid of pain. "No harm." His last words to his nephew pounded in his brain. "No harm at all." No harm? Matthew, the sunshine boy with the promise of dreams, was dead because...because Travers' fearing to love had betrayed them both. Is any harm greater than that which comes, like pestilence when there is famine, from the fear to love? "It is my fault," Travers told himself. "I could have saved him, but I let him drown." He thought of the grief etched on his sister's face when he and

Corinne had fetched Matthew's things. He could not let go of the horror he felt at his wife's self-centered insouciance on the drive home. "Life goes on, babykins."

Travers was sitting in the family room reading at the newspaper. The telephone rang; he was not aware that Corinne was home. Travers lifted the receiver; before he could speak, he heard Corinne's voice.

"Far be it for me to gloat," Corinne gloated. "But it just goes to show. The picture-perfect poster board family. Mrs. Ring Around the Rosary! The family that prays together stays together! Aren't we all so very special! Well, let me tell you something. I saw right through Mabel's June Cleaver act, make no mistake about *that*. Maybe all this will bring Miss Goodie Two Shoes down a peg or two. Of course I'm sorry in a way for her, I mean, her son killing himself, blowing his brains out, right there, while she slept in her bed, who wouldn't be? But when you come right down to it..."

Travers slammed the receiver into its cradle. He thought he was going to vomit. He ran to the bathroom. He was standing at the facebowl, washing his hands, when Corinne opened the door.

"I thought that was you, babykins. Are you okay?"

"No, I am not okay." Travers turned to face his wife. "Don't you have any compassion? Any compassion at all? Matt is gone and all you can do is gossip. What kind of monster are you?"

"So that *was* you eavesdropping on what should have been my private conversation, like a peeping Tom,"

Corinne snarled. "Who are *you* to criticize *me*? Don't you tell me how to live my life, babykins. I'll gloat if I want to. I've been sick and tired of Mabel's holier-than-thou prancing around for years. As far as I'm concerned, she got what she asked for. The chicken came home to roost."

Travers gave her a vicious slap. Corinne fell to the floor. He sank to the edge of the bathtub, his face buried in his hands as Corinne fled to the kitchen.

"Police? Police? My husband is trying to kill me. Come quickly. 8941 Manchester Drive. Hurry. Yes, I'll stay on the line."

Half an hour later the doorbell rang. Travers emerged from the bathroom. Two policemen stood in the living room as Corinne poured forth her tale of terror. She sat on the sofa, a plastic bag of ice at her left cheek. The policemen had bored looks on their faces.

"So, do you want to file a complaint?"

Travers felt Corinne's anguish. The scandal! What would the neighbors say? And there was his sister, Mabel, to consider. He walked into his wife's turmoil.

"Look officers," he said. "Everything's okay. Isn't it, Corinne?"

Corinne raised her head slightly. "Yes," she whispered.

"Are you sure, ma'am? We can take him away if you like." Travers saw himself escorted to the police car in handcuffs with the entire neighborhood watching. He chuckled to himself at Corinne's dilemma.

"What's so funny, buster?"

"Nothing," Travers replied, with as contrite and obedient tone as he could muster. "I am very sorry. I did not mean to..."

"It was just a slap, really, officers," Corinne said. "I simply overreacted. My husband has never hit me before. This is all a misunderstanding."

"If you are sure, ma'am..."

"Yes," Corinne said, lifting herself from the sofa. Travers closed the door behind the policemen.

"Don't worry, Corinne. I'll go along with whatever you say—you thought you smelled gas or something. But stay out of my way." Travis took the minivan keys from the coffee table. Twenty minutes later he headed to the back rooms of Jillie's. Chinelle was there. Cubicle number eight. He seated himself and fed tokens into the machine. An hour later he left. He browsed in the front section for a while before heading for the parking lot. As he was adjusting the steering wheel, a small woman approached. It was Chinelle.

"How 'bout a lift?" Travers heart pounded.

"Sure. Hop in." He leaned over and opened the door. "Where to?"

"Where are you going?" Chinelle fumbled with the radio; a nightmare of metal sounds filled the car.

"That is an excellent question," Travers answered. "I don't have the foggiest idea."

"We could go to the Sportsman's."

"The Sportsman's?"

"On Seventeenth." Chinelle slipped her left hand between Travers' thighs.

*   *   *

The Sportsman's belonged to the California style of architecture: boxy and bland. Built in the nineteen-sixties, it was of squat gray concrete, ugly, dingy, grimy, and there. On the side facing Seventeenth Street a neon sign flashed. **SHORT RATES.**

"Get room nineteen. It's my favorite."

A king size bed, a table, a chair, two end tables, a television suspended from the ceiling. A mirror on the ceiling, a mirror on the wall at bed level.

"I need some money."

"Sure."

"I mean right now. To get high." Travers handed her a fifty dollar bill. "Back in a jiffy. Get comfy."

He sat on the bed. Paisley draperies matched the bedspread: blue, yellow, and green swirls of grime. Travers removed his shoes and socks, his shirt and slacks. The carpeting was sticky. Then Chinelle was back. She took a glass pipe from her handbag and kicked off her shoes. Clouds of smoke filled the room.

"It's channel twenty-three for the movies." Chinelle threw her balled underwear into a corner. "Turn off the lights, will you, huh?" On the television, parts of a man's body and parts of a woman's body blurred together. The sound of a pounding beat repeated. Travers took Chinelle by the shoulders with both hands as he moved his knees to either side of her body.

"Oh, no, baby." Adroitly Chinelle unrolled a condom over his erect penis. "No. That's not how we gonna do it. Mama wants to ride the big white horse." She pushed Travers onto his back to squat on top of him, her hands clutching the headboard. Then she reached to the night stand and there were more clouds of smoke. Travers had not known sex for many months. Now, in this squalid, dark place, he began to remember. He turned his head to the side. The wall mirror showed their haunted shapes blurring into and out of smoke.

"Easy. Easy. Easy, baby. Not yet. Not yet." The words came from Chinelle, hollow, dull, but of no consequence. He spilled himself inside the condom inside her. It was as if he were discarding soiled underwear. He felt a part of him go away. For the briefest of moments he knew a strange stillness as if weariness and pain are but the hallucinations of madmen. Chinelle's experienced fingers pinched the condom at the base of his penis as she pulled herself free. Then she stood at the side of the bed between Travers and the mirror, waving the bulging latex in front of her as if stirring a pot of soup.

"Oh, that's a big load. I see you been saving up for little ole me! Next time we use the magnum triple X with the rubbery dots, you hear? Don't want all these yummy-licious vitamins spilling out now, do we?" The woman licked her tongue back and forth across her upper lip. She reached again for the pipe.

Travers thought he would vomit. He pulled himself to the side of the bed, sat for a moment, and then hurried to the bathroom. All of his demons returned. He wanted to be some place else. He always wanted to be some place else. When he returned, Chinelle was propped against the headboard, still naked. She was chewing gum. On the television, men, women, and children smashed storefront windows to emerge with clothing, furniture, and appliances. Travers dressed.

"Ya ain't leavin', is ya?"

Travers handed her two fifty dollar bills.

"Gimme two more, babe, and you can have another go, just as soon as the big white horse is ready to rumble."

"No."

"Okay, one more then. Besides, you're lookable enough and then some. A guy as good-looking as you shouldn't have to be paying for it anyway."

"No."

"Well, I can keep the room, okay? You wore me out."

"It's paid for til nine."

The following afternoon there was a manila envelope on the front passenger seat of his car. *PERSONAL AND CONFIDENTIAL*. Inside, Travers found four photographs of himself and Chinelle in room nineteen of the Sportsman's Motel. There was a typewritten note: *We will be in contact soon.*

* * *

Travers studied the note. He could not think clearly. His forehead covered with sweat and his hands were clammy. His breathing came in sharp chokes. There is nothing left, he said to himself. Nothing at all. What did he mean by this? But he knew. Everywhere he turned: nothing. At work, Arnie Williamson, bureaucrats, and computers. At home, Corinne and canasta. And in his innermost self itself the memory, like a scar, of the night in his sister's garage when his nephew had reached out to him and he had turned away.   I should have chucked it all years ago, Travers thought. And done what? Sling hash in a hamburger joint, wash cars, dig ditches, anything. Corinne would have left him no doubt. He laughed out loud at the irony. He had not taken the road less traveled by. No. He had taken the American superhighway, interstate, four lanes, median strip, Howard Johnson's, and it had taken him straight to Hell. That night he thought of ending it all. Matthew had. Who knew the names of Matthew's demons? Who, now, would ever know? Travers had moved into one of the guest bedrooms months before. Now he lay in its bed, alone in the dark, eyes closed. We all get to die, he thought. Comes with the territory. A freebie. In the Cracker Jack box of life, the certain toy. Why not sooner rather than later? Why not of our own timing? Why not be in charge if only for once? The telephone rang. "We want fifty large," a man's voice said. "Tens and twenties. You have three days."

Travers tried to think. They had pictures. So what? Yet the more he thought about it, the more he knew he was doomed. They would deliver the pictures to Corinne, of course. Big deal. But they would be smart enough, Travers realized, to deliver them as well to Magnolia Williamson and the rest of Corinne's gang of merry canastateers. It would be quite an adventure for Corinne, and she in the starring role! The betrayed wife, the spurned homemaker! She would make him pay. The divorce would be the talk of the town, Corinne basking in attention and sympathy. Maybe he *should* just get it over with. Better yet, maybe he should kill Corinne! How to go about it? Could he get away with it?

He sat up with a jolt. "'What kind of monster are you?'" he had asked his wife a few long hours ago. "Bush league compared to you, babykins!" he now imagined Corinne's replying. He wanted to scream. What is happening to me? It wasn't Corinne's fault he had fucked up his life. Nor was ignorance an excuse. He could have said "no" when his father vetoed Travers' attending college. No, that's not right. I'm the one responsible. I could have done it. I *should* have done it. I could have said "no" when Corinne said she was pregnant. I was just a kid. What business did I have getting married? My life is a horror movie, yes, but I am its director. In this instant something strange took place. From now on, it came to him, there will be no more excuses. No more goings-along. I shall live my life, he pledged to himself, that which remains. I shall live it. Death is not an answer. Not Corinne's. Not mine. In its own time death will come. But not now. Now, finally, it is time for life.

*   *   *

Travers rose from the bed and dressed. He took a laundry bag from the utility room. Twenty minutes later he was in his office. He took a key from a cabinet, walked past silent machines, and opened the door that led to the basement. In the bowels of the building he went to another door, opened it, and entered a small room. Like smoke, dust filled the air as he removed a blanket which covered an ancient safe. He knelt before it, turning dials clockwise and counter-clockwise. He emptied the contents, stacking packages of one hundred dollar bills on the floor before him. He thought back to twenty years before. In the night his father had taken him to this room, had opened this safe. "My father brought me here," Travers' father told him, "when I took my place in the business as now you are taking yours. As his father brought him and his grandfather brought his father." Then Travers' father had opened the safe. Inside: rows and rows of green, with brown rubber bands. "No matter what," Travers' father told him, "keep this safe full. A time will come when only ready cash will do." He closed the safe and took Travers by the shoulders. "When only ready cash will do." Then he told Travers about the Panic of 1893 and the Great Depression of 1930. "It has been my good fortune," he said, "that under my watch I have never had to take from the safe—yet. After I am gone, if the time comes, you will know."

As the years passed after his father's death, Travers did not think much about the money in the safe. It was cash. What good was cash? Maybe it had had utility in his great-grandfather's, grandfather's and possibly his father's day, but now cash was a dethroned monarch. It couldn't be deposited just like that. It had to be explained, accounted for, justified, verified. It had to have a story. Cash was the fingerprint left on the murder weapon. The money stayed in the safe, year after year, but it might as well not have existed. Until now. His father had said he would know when the time came. Now he knew. Wherever he was going, wherever he ended up, the safe's contents would be his salvation. There had to be a place where cash was still king, beyond the reach of accountants, where the question asked was not "Where did it come from?" but "How much do you have?" Such a place existed, it had to, and Travers would find it. He scooped the green piles into the laundry bag.

A week later his sister and her husband drove Travers to the Cleveland airport. Five nights before, he had packed nine thousand nine hundred dollars in a duffle bag to carry with him on the plane. But he could not figure out how to manage the rest of the money. Then he remembered that Mabel was sending along a trunk filled with Bibles, prayer books, and hymnals. He brought it to his basement, emptied, and set to work. He carved out the pages of the Bibles and prayer books to fill their cavities with packets of faded green from his father's and grandfather's safe. Then he repacked the trunk, placing two layers of hymnals on top. He carried the ripped out pages from the Bibles and prayers books in a laundry bag to a dumpster behind a grocery store on the other side of town.

Mabel and Arthur came to the departure gate with him. Then they were gone. He was off. He would no longer be a fly in Arnie Williamson's ointment. Corinne would float along fine in her canasta boat on her country club sea. Do I care? No. He settled back in his window seat as the ground departed and tried not to worry about the trunk in the cargo hold. He began to feel a freedom even as the memory of the night in his sister's garage plagued him with a fever that would not let go.

*   *   *

Father Chester greeted him at the Frederique airport. He was a strong man, healthy in a weathered way. He dressed simply: white cotton slacks and shirt, sandals. Traces of bright colors shone on his face. His hands were large. Travers felt a simple dignity to his being. As they walked through the tin shack of the terminal, Travers tried to appear nonchalant. He had little to fear. None of Travers' luggage was opened. Outside an aging bus waited.

"This is Hernando," Father Chester said, turning to greet its driver. A surge of feeling came into his voice. "Hernando, this is our great friend from America, Travers Landeman. He has left family and friends to come to us."

"It is good that you are here," Hernando said.

"Yes," Travers answered. Then they were off, the bus's roar making conversation impossible. As the bus wound its way through Frederique City Travers felt a sadness. Ronald Reagan, he remembered, had brought derision by declaring that if you've seen one slum, you've seen them all. But it was true, Travers thought. Here in Frederique City's dreary streets, in the trash and unsmiling faces, he recognized the same despair he had seen in American ghettoes as televised on newscasts. Of course, he had never been to an American ghetto. Why would he? We are each of us in our own ghetto, he thought, only we don't know it. He was thankful when the bus left the main road and the city, such as it was, disappeared. Soon fields of calabash and corn gave way to jungle as Hernando's bus bumped and belched its way forward to stop at an aged pier. On his small boat Hernando took the priest, Travers, the hymnals, the gouged out Bibles and prayer books to the island of Mabouhey.

"This is our home," Father Chester said, as they stepped on shore. "'Mabouhey!' It means 'Welcome!'" They rode then on mules for two hours before entering a clearing. Thatched huts clustered around a central gathering space, where an open fire blazed. Father Chester led Travers to one of the huts. There was a small bed with a coil of mosquito netting above, a chair, and a table with a kerosene lantern. A pitcher and wash basin sat on a small dresser. "I hope these accommodations are not too primitive for you," the priest said kindly.

"Not at all," Travers responded. "No. Everything looks just fine." And he meant it. "But I would appreciate it if I could unpack my luggage." He tried to say these words calmly, as if asking for a glass of water.

"Of course," Father Chester replied. He went to the door to motion his arm in the air. Muscular black men carried trunk, suitcases, and duffel bag into the hut. "We will leave you now," the priest said. "Dinner will be in two hours. I will send Marguerite to help you with the netting."

"If it's all right, I would like to take a short nap." Travers put his hand to his mouth.

"Of course. Your journey has been a long one. You must be tired. I will tell Marguerite not to disturb you for an hour."

Alone Travers splashed water on his face. Then he set to work, emptying the suitcases. He opened the trunk, stacking the hymnals on the floor. He opened each Bible and prayer book. Soon the money filled the suitcases in neat green rows. He placed the hymnals at the bottom of the trunk and the clothing that had been in the suitcases on top. He emptied the duffel bag, to add its green to that already in the suitcases. Then he filled the duffel bag with the shells of the Bibles and prayer books. Finally he unpacked the third suitcase. Clothing, toiletries, books. His dead nephew's blue tote bag, which he held for a while. "I let him drown," he said. He hung the dead boy's bag on a peg to the right of the hut's door. He put the suitcases under the bed with the duffel bag in front. Later he would throw the remains of the Bibles and prayer books into the clearing's fire. He stretched out on the bed to retrace his movements. Where had he slipped up? Where was there a loose end, a thread of neglect or incaution, to unravel, to ensnare him, to bring him down, to bring him back? He could think of none. All that remained was to...to disappear. Afar there was singing, the deep-throated chanting of men and the honeyed voices of women. Soon he was asleep.

Her scent wakened him. She was a shadow at the doorway.

"Father Chester asked that I help you with your netting." It was that magical time when day and night come together. She was a silhouette in the remains of the gentle light, slender, long black hair flowing over her shoulders down to her waist. She wore a simple loose garment, but Travers could not discern its color. Something in his memory stirred, but did not take conscious form. He sat up as she waited in the doorway.

"Come closer."

She walked to him. She had a strong face which she kept turned to one side, but every now and then, as the light from the oil lamp on the dresser flickered, one side of her face showed itself a soft burn of scar. Her green eyes were fierce with brightness. Her skin was a soft brown.

"I am Travers," he said.

"My name is Marguerite."

Now he could see that her face was scarred, deeply and burned, but it did not matter. Travers thought she was the most beautiful woman he had ever seen.

"Father Chester is thankful you are here," she said. His sister's words came to him, from that night, that awful night, in his sister's kitchen, the last night he would ever know peace, the night he had turned his nephew away, the kitchen door clattering in the always empty dark.

"The Lord works in mysterious ways," he heard himself reply. A strange feeling came over him. He wanted desperately to say something more.

"Yes," Marguerite said, "there are ways that are the ways of mystery. The ways of sorrow and the ways of pain.

Yet we live." The intensity of these words stabbed into Travers' heart. He sat on the bed to cover his eyes. "No harm. No harm at all." *Matthew* did not live.

"Father Chester asked that I help you with the netting," Marguerite said again. Their hands touched as the netting unraveled but neither gave word to the touching. "Come with me," Marguerite said when the netting was in place.

Travers followed her to the middle of the clearing. It was night now. Women, men, and children came to the fire. Mats were spread. Overhead the sky splattered with stars. Large pots cooked over an open fire. Father Chester motioned Travers to sit at his side. There were perhaps a hundred people in all, Travers saw, as he seated himself next to the priest. Marguerite was nowhere to be seen. Father Chester crossed his legs and raised his bowl to the stars.

"Heavenly Spirits," he prayed. "We thank you for the goodness of our brother, Travers. He has traveled far from the warmth of family and friends that he might come to us. We thank you for his generosity of spirit. We thank you for his courage. Great Spirits, protect our brother, Travers. Keep him close in your hearts. Let the forests protect him and let the mountains guide his every step. Namaste, Mabouhey!" The villagers answered as one: "Namaste, Mabouhey!" Father Chester leaned close to him. "'Namaste, Mabouhey!' 'The Spirit in me respects the Spirit in you.'" Bowls of a brown pudding-like paste were set in front of him. "It is called *burama*," Father Chester said. "It is made from the yam." Chester ate the paste with large chunks of bread.

There were fruits and vegetables. A hot, mud-like beverage was served in earthen mugs, water in glasses made of bamboo. More wood was added to the fire. Old men made music with flutes, guitars, and many drums. Men, women, and children danced. "Are you enjoying yourself, my son?" Father Chester asked.

Travers did not know how to respond. *Enjoy* seemed paltry, unworthy, to describe what he was feeling. Then it came to him that the word must have evolved from the word *joy*. "Yes," he replied. "I am in joy." He looked at the priest. Shadows of the dancers' forms flickered over Father Chester's face; he seemed to move into and out of the fire's light as if he were a spirit himself. A laughing young girl bounced on his knee.

Travers did not know how long he sat there. The mud-like beverage brought images to him. He saw again his sister's face, its doubting sorrow. He thought he heard his dead nephew's voice, but he could not make out his words. The fire shuddered to a bed of embers. The villagers drifted away.

"You are an American?" Travers asked.

"I suppose I am," Father Chester responded. "But I don't think of myself as such. That part of me seems like it belongs to somebody else. It is as if my past self is an entirely different someone. A long lost relative, perhaps. Myself in a former life, as it were. The happenstance of birth. The lottery of geography. Had I been born in India would I be a Hindu? In Japan, Shinto? In Arabia: *A Salaam Alaikum* instead of *Dominus Vobiscum?* It is the biologist Richard Dawkins, if I am not mistaken, who observes that God is thoughtful to arrange matters so that wherever you happen to be born the local religion turns out to be the one true one. I came here, I was sent here actually, only six years after I completed seminary. I was still a young man. It was long before there was an airport on Frederique. It was some journey, let me tell you. I remember, even now, feeling as if I had traveled to the very end of the earth, to an entirely different planet."

"Didn't you want to come?"

"Not at all," Father Chester laughed. "It was supposed to be a punishment. A life sentence. For my sins. For my one great sin in particular, the sin of disobedience. You see, I did not take well to authority. As my superiors saw it, my disobedience would not—could not—stand. Disobedience they believed to be a contagious not to say a fatal disease. Without question a mortal sin. I have since come to learn that there are much worse sins. Much worse!"

"Which is the worst sin of all?" Travers asked.

The priest stroked the face of the sleeping child. "I should say it is the failure to love," he said. These words stabbed into Travers' soul. A cry came from his lips. "Please forgive me," the priest said, misinterpreting Travers' anguish. "I should have seen that you are tired from your long journey. I should not have run on so long." He began to raise himself to go.

"No, Father. Stay, please." Travers reached his hand to the priest's forearm. "I am no longer tired. I have been tired, very tired, for a long time, for a very long time. But now I am awake. I am awake as I have never been awake before. Please, tell me how it is that it came about that you are here."

Father Chester lay the sleeping girl on a mat next to him. A shooting star traced through the jungle sky. In the seasound's sweep the fire's bed flamed into new worlds of red and gusts of orange. "It would mean a great deal to me," Travers said. "I would very much like to listen and to learn."

"Very well then," Father Chester said, folding his hands on his lap. "This is the story of my priesthood."

Chapter Eleven:
Change

Chester O'Reilly
Chicago
1970 – 1971

With his eyes closed Chester O'Reilly lay at the foot of the altar. He thought of his own inadequacy and doubt even as he felt the joy that filled Holy Name Cathedral: the sweetness of the choir, the hush in the congregation between prayers. Then he was kneeling before the Cardinal. As he was clothed in the vestments of a priest, Chester wanted to shout: Stop! This is a mistake! Instead he mouthed the correct responses, as if in parentheses, to the Cardinal's prayers. The Cardinal kissed him on both cheeks. He was a priest. Monsignor Maguire's words came to him: "a salesman for the Greatest Man Who Ever Lived." But I do not want to be a salesman, Chester screamed inside. I have enough trouble living my own life; I have no business telling others how to live theirs. Doubt. A wound that does not heal. "There is a fundamental distinction between uncertainty and neutrality," Father Raulston said in one of their counseling sessions. "Uncertainty is a gift from God. It keeps us humble. We know, when all is said and done, that we do not know. That only God knows. We trust in Him. He gives us the gift of Faith, our armor and shield, in the fight against Satan in all his manifestations. Faith girds us so that we take a stand for righteousness, so that we do not waste our lives on the sidelines."

Chester heard himself say, "Amen!" He faced the congregation to raise his hand in priestly blessing. In the silence he could hear their applause, their self-affirmation. He was one of them and now he was not one of them. He stepped to the altar and did as he had been taught to do. He raised the chalice and elevated the Host. He said the words. Brass sounds of bells trembled. With great show an honor guard of the Knights of Columbus escorted his grandmother to the communion rail: bright purple tunics, matching creased pants with white piping, musketeer hats with white feathers like roosters'. Bronze swords flashed at their waists. Chester's grandmother knelt slowly, her head bowed. She did not open her eyes as she raised her head and opened her mouth. Chester stood there. The serene joy on the old woman's face pulled him from the quicksand of doubt, but only for a moment. He made the Sign of the Cross with the Host and placed it on his grandmother's tongue. To be a priest, act a priest. We are what we do, he heard Father Raulston say. Best get on with it.

There was a party afterwards, a celebration. Chester, now Father Chester, sat in the middle of a long table at the front of the room, his radiant grandmother seated next to him. They were in the parish hall, the Pine Room, in the basement of St. Lucy's, where the Cardinal had assigned him "to begin your priestly voyage." There was food and drink. The room swelled with pride and congratulations. Monsignor Maguire gave a toast and made a short speech in his folksy style. He reminded them all how years before they had taken little Chester to their bosoms when he was orphaned, how they all had been, therefore, his parents, before he became their "Father." "Ladies and Gentlemen, it is my great pleasure to present for the first time: Father Chester O'Reilly."

Chester looked down at the faces looking up at him. Could he find it in himself to be worthy of their Faith? He was supposed to guide them, to show them the way, not the other way around. They waited. He began reciting the words he had memorized the day before, but now they seemed empty. He said them anyway. This was, he came to understand as the long weeks and months passed, his first lesson in the great benefit of preaching to the converted. He could have been reading a grocery list. So long as he did not break with the expected code of accepted dogma, spoon-fed and inbred, whatever he said would have brought forth the highest and most sincere praise. He told them about Faith, Hope, and Charity. "And the most important of these," he concluded, "is Faith. Without faith we are a ship without a rudder, adrift on the sea of mortality, the hurricane of happenstance blowing us first one way and then the other until we wreck on the rocks of despair. But Faith is like a lighthouse showing us the way, in storm and in shadow, the one true way to our heavenly destiny. It casts a steady beam to bring us through the tempests of temptation and doubt. Yes, we must have Faith, Hope, and Charity, but all good things that follow, follow from Faith. With Faith, all things are possible. Without Faith..." There were no more words. Chester stood before them, the glow of adoration in their faces shining at him. In that moment he saw that such a thing as faith does exist even if he could not find it within himself. "Without Faith," the words returned, "we are nothing." Chester heard his own words coming back at him as if they had ricocheted off those who heard and believed. The women nodded. With their mouths closed and foreheads tightened, the heads of the men jutted like rams. They had needed no persuading and so they found him persuasive. Chester was the one who needed to believe, but, so far as his own soul was concerned, his words were like the prettily wrapped packages Mr. Freeman put in the windows for the Christmas selling season. Chester knew they were empty inside.

From the start things did not go well with Monsignor Maguire. Chester's grandmother insisted that Chester take a large part of her life savings and buy himself a car. So he went to the Austin branch library on Race Avenue to study the special automotive issue of *Consumer Reports*. The following Saturday he took the Metra train to the suburb of Carol Stream, for a century a small town thirty miles northwest of Chicago. Now it was another link in Chicago's suburban chain. Chester thought he was being practical. The salesman provided profuse and detailed reassurance: the Datsun 510 station wagon was compact yet roomy, fuel-efficient yet peppy. It had a radio. It would run forever. "You are making a wise driving investment decision, Father," the salesman said.

Throughout the nineteen-fifties Japanese products, trinkets for the most part, trickled into the land of their conquerors. *Made in Japan* was synonymous for goods that were cheap and shoddy. With a collective determination, however, the Japanese studied their mistakes; quality improved and markets expanded. As the second decade of their economic invasion began, the Japanese broke out of the beachhead they had painstakingly established, key chain by pocket knife. In the nineteen-sixties they conquered clocks, cameras, and cookware. In the nineteen-seventies Nissan, Toyota, and Mitsubishi took dead aim at Detroit. The unthinkable, after all, had happened. After a thousand years the Japanese had been vanquished. Their sacred islands were occupied. So they emulated the ways of their conquerors, barbarians though they were, and by the nineteen-seventies capitalistic Japan, liberal and democratic, replicated the United States of three decades before. The Japanese intensified their single-mindedness of purpose to subjugate the needs of the individual to a higher collective good. They began to see themselves as the new Americans;

they were *new and improved*, well aware that Americans have a short attention span. The future would be theirs. The conquered would prevail. To build the great pagoda at Kyoto took centuries, the present's trust in the future. September, 1945, would be a mere footnote; the war wasn't over then, not by a long shot.

Chester took his grandmother for a ride, cruising on Lake Shore Drive. The city by the lake was a picture postcard. It was Chicago summer, brilliance intensified by brevity. Put on a happy face, the breezes off Lake Michigan sang. You won't be smiling when my big brother, winter, gets here and he's just around the corner. An hour after Chester returned to the rectory, there was a vicious knock on his door.

"What is that jap thing doing in my garage?" It was Monsignor Maguire.

"I beg your pardon?"

"As long as I am in charge here, no jap car...it's a disgrace. Park that damn thing on the street. Do you understand me?"

Chester did not understand. Nevertheless he moved the Datsun to the street. He wasn't sure but he thought he detected the smell of liquor seeping through the door.

The months passed. There were first communions, weddings, confirmations, funerals. The business of being a priest. Is this what it's all about? Chester wondered. There had to be more to it than this. It was a comfortable life, one that, at first, appealed to him. Chester had a spacious room with his own private bathroom. Mrs. McGrath was an excellent cook and an efficient housekeeper. The other assistant pastor, Father Schuler, was like an older brother.

Then it was Chicago winter. "We are punished, saint and sinner alike," Chester mused as the temperature dropped below zero and the week's accumulation of snow froze into stale icing. "The cold stops everything," he thought, "so there is a kind of cruel beauty to it. But when it starts to thaw, everything will be slush and grime." Which is worse? he wondered, cold or its aftermath? as he and Father Schuler tried to start his "dependable" Japanese vehicle. Long orange cables ran from the engine of Father Schuler's Chevrolet to disappear beneath the Datsun's opened hood. That's supposed to be easy, Chester thought, as the engine of the Datsun began belching weak stirring sounds. Of course, an assault on the spirit is worse than mere physical pain. But try telling that now to Father Schuler! His freezing comrade gave a thumbs-up signal for Chester to turn the ignition key one more time. The little Japanese station wagon chugged into life.

"Now that it's started," Father Schuler advised, "drive around for an hour. Then you'd best move it into the garage. Mind, don't tell Monsignor Maguire when he gets back next week. On his behalf, however, respect must be paid to Detroit's superiority!"

"Thank you for your chivalry and thank you, too, for your Chevrolet! Will that do?" Father Schuler laughed.

Chester drove to the Eisenhower Expressway, east to the Loop, north to Evanston, and then returned. Monsignor Maguire had left that afternoon for Sarasota. What you don't know won't hurt you, Chester thought, as he parked the Datsun alongside Monsignor Maguire's Sedan de Ville. Besides it was an emergency. He was sure that Monsignor Maguire, had he known, would have understood. He was wrong. A few hours later there was a knock on his door. It was Mrs. McGrath. "The Monsignor wants you in his study." As soon as the Pastor of St. Lucy's opened his door, Chester could see that he was drunk.

"The goddamn flight was canceled," his superior slurred. "They let us get all the way out to O'Hara and then they cancel the goddamn flight. Runways too icy. Some damn nonsense. Here. Have a drink. Rum and coke, no? *Cuba Libre*—isn't that what they call it?"

Chester stood there in amazement. "Yes. Rum and coke, and, yes, it's called a *Cuba Libre*."

Monsignor Maguire handed his Assistant Pastor the drink. "Sit down," he commanded. "Now I am going to talk and you are going to listen. I don't expect to have to say things twice around here. For better or for worse, and lately that's all it's been, for worse, this is *my* place. Not yours. Not the Cardinal's, bless his Immortal Soul if he has one. Mine. Michael Patrick Maguire. *Monsignor* Michael Patrick Maguire. *Pastor Monsignor* Michael Patrick Maguire. Da boss! As far as you are concerned, that's for sure. Da boss! Now, tell me, WHAT IS THAT GODDAMNED JAP CAR DOING IN *MY* GARAGE?"

Chester vacillated. "Father Schuler thought it would be a good idea if..."

"You know," his inebriated superior interrupted, "that's just what I would have expected from a pantywaist like you. You sneak around, behind my back, wait until I'm gone, or you think I'm gone, and then, whamo! the jap car is in my garage and you, coward that you are, try to foist the blame on Father Schuler! Pathetic!" These words burned in Chester's ears. He felt small and ashamed, not that he had disobeyed Monsignor Maguire and been found out, but that he had tried to implicate Father Schuler.

"I'm sorry," Chester said. "Not about the Datsun. About bringing Father Schuler into it. He was only trying to help. It's entirely my fault. But it's ten degrees below zero out there. If you want my car to start in the morning so that I can get to Loretto Hospital for rounds, the jap car, as you call it, had better stay where it is." Chester surprised himself with these words. It had been a long sixteen months since his ordination, months of kowtowing, of bowing and scraping, of walking on eggshells, of looking over his shoulder. He had begun to despise the Pastor of St. Lucy's. Like the worm inside the apple ate the knowledge that Monsignor Maguire was nearly as responsible as Chester himself for the fact of Chester's priesthood. Nine years before Monsignor Maguire's color televisions and babbittry had seduced him and now Chester loathed himself for the ease with which he had surrendered. He was, it was true, most of all angry with himself. Monsignor Maguire might be a tyrant. He might be a drunk. He might be more of a disciple of Dale Carnegie than of Jesus Christ. Even so, there was a directness about him that Chester admired.

Monsignor Maguire would never have tried to stab Father Schuler in the back.

"Once again you are wrong," Monsignor Maguire snarled. "The jap car will not stay where it is. You will move it. I don't care where you move it. Move it to hell, for all I care. That's where it belongs. Just move it out of *my* garage. You can take the bus to Loretto. Or walk. They walked on Bataan, but that's ancient history to you and your kind. I watch you younger breed. Smart. Sophisticated. With-it. With what? This country used to stand for something. Hard work. Family. Thrift. Obedience. Now what? It's all going to hurry in a hand basket. People used to know their place. That was good. Gave everybody an inner compass. Didn't have to think. Security. People would pull together when they had to, then go back to their own kind. You had the Polacks at Milwaukee and North, the wops in little Italy, the briar hoppers in Uptown, the niggers on the south side, but, when the chips were down, everyone, and I mean everyone, remembered they lived in the greatest country on Earth and pulled together as Americans, all in the same direction, shoulder to shoulder. The crash in '29. Pearl Harbor. D-Day. We got the job done. We paid the price. And for what? So that dandified know-it-alls like you can drive around in jap cars, when they're working, that is." Monsignor Maguire sneered these last words.

Chester sensed that his presence in the room no longer mattered. Monsignor Maguire filled his glass and stared out the window. A branch slapped against it. The Monsignor thought of Iwo Jima. "We held the flag high so that you and your kind can drive jap cars. Ain't that a bitch! Lucky for you we did, too. You wouldn't be cruising up and down Lake Shore Drive in your Tojomobile if things had gone the other way. You'd be humped over on some mosquito-infested island, that's where'd you be, that's where we'd all be, planting rice or burning sugar cane. *If* the Japs decided to let you live, that is. They're a barbaric race. They always have been. That's all there is to it." The Pastor of St. Lucy's turned and faced Chester. "Now I am not going to tell you again. Move that goddamn jap car!"

*   *   *

Two months later Father Schuler was given his own parish, St. Marcelline, in Schaumburg. Chester had never heard of Schaumburg. He looked in an atlas in the rectory's library. No Schaumburg. He went to the Kroch and Brentano's bookstore in nearby Oak Park and bought the latest metropolitan map. Finally he found it.

"But that's all farmland," he said to Father Schuler as they said their goodbyes.

"Once upon a time," Father Schuler replied. "Not any more. Look, I have really enjoyed working with you, Chester. You're just like every new priest, only more so. You're even more serious than I was when I was fresh under the collar." Father Schuler collected his thoughts. "But that's good—being serious. Seriousness leads to quality. Even so, Chester, let me give you some advice. Learn to let go. To loosen up. It's going to get rough around here. Rough enough without blowing up every little problem into a crisis."

An uneasy feeling came over Chester. "What do you mean?"

"Just that the Monsignor is getting old and it's all slipping away. And he knows it. Like sand through his fingers. Oh, he doesn't let on all that much, but, trust me, he knows."

"What are you talking about? Knows what?" Chester nearly screamed these words.

"Well, think about it, Chester. For one thing, the Cardinal's closed or combined all the parishes east of here. St. Martin's, Precious Blood, Blessed Virgin Mary, St. Thomas, Resurrection. For another, I am not being replaced. St. Lucy's is down to two priests, the Monsignor and you. When I first came here, there were six. Do you think the Monsignor is happy that at what should be the pinnacle of his career he gets to preside over the funeral of what for decades was one of the premier parishes in the archdiocese? That he likes managing decline? He's the past. Guys like you are the future. And he knows it."

Guys like me? "At least Monsignor Maguire knows what he believes in," Chester replied. "Me, I'm not even sure which century I'm in."

"But don't you see?" Father Schuler said, "that's just what's needed now. *Tabula Rasa*. Make it new all over again. When this place closes—I give it two years at most—you'll be right out there with me in some place that just a few years ago was nothing but corn and alfalfa. It'll have some glitzy

name like Hanover Acres or Cottonwood Estates. Just hang
in there, Chester, just hang in there."

Hanover Acres? Cottonwood Estates? Saccharine
names. Chester envisioned himself in front of starched and
powdered white people, crisp, antiseptic, successful, sure.
The statues used to be in the front of the church, in the
sanctuary, he thought, not in the back, in the pews. A long
year ago Chester would not have seen anything wrong with
the portrait Father Schuler painted.

"Do you remember that conference I attended a
while back?" Father Schuyler asked. *"The Cardinal's
Conference for the Future: Lift-off for the Seventies"*?

Of course Chester remembered. It was March.
Monsignor Maguire was in Sarasota. Chester had had to
handle things himself. It seemed that Mrs. McGrath never
stopped knocking at his door. The telephone rang like an
alarm clock every other minute. Chester also remembered
that, after his return from Sarasota, Monsignor Maguire
spoke barely a word to Father Schuler for weeks. "What was
that all about?"

"Well," Father Schuler replied, "it has to do with
demographics." He looked kindly at Chester and laughed.
"The baby boomers like yourself coming of age. The kinds
of clothes you wear, which brand of toothpaste you buy,
and, of course, your automotive predilections." They both
laughed. "Anyway, the Church has to adjust to the changes
that are just around the corner. I suppose that's the gist of it.
If you see a hurricane coming, you'd best get out of the way."

Chester did not understand these last words, but he let them pass like a distant parade.

"As you and I know only too well," Father Schuler went on, "Monsignor Maguire is fond of saying that the Catholic Church is the most successful business enterprise of all time. What does he call it?"

"'The longest running show ever.'"

"Exactly! Well, I'm overjoyed, of course, with my own parish, etcetera. But, still, I am going to miss the old neighborhoods."

Chester was puzzled by Father Schuler's use of the plural: *neighborhoods*.

Another distant parade. "You can always come back to visit," Chester said.

"Well," Father Schuler replied with a sad shrug of his shoulders, "with apologies to Gertrude Stein, that's true only if there's a here here." Father Schuler laughed and Chester laughed with him although Chester did not know why he did. "At the conference," Father Schuler continued, "we learned all about 'Wide Wipes'."

"'Wide Wipes'?"

"One of the giant soap companies, Proctor and Gamble, I think it was, lost millions of dollars on a product called 'Wide Wipes,' which are, or rather were, sanitized squares of tissue paper pre-moistened with a perfumed antiseptic. The idea was that 'Wide Wipes' would replace good old-fashioned toilet paper. 'Wide Wipes' was packaged in an attractive container designed to sit on top of the toilet. It came in a rainbow of colors and scents. Well, everything was done according to the book: market tests in San Bernardino, California and so forth. Then a nationwide advertising campaign: full page ads in newspapers and magazines, free coupons, television and radio commercials. The professor who explained all this to us, a Pierre DeVere, couldn't resist saying that the *bottom* line was that 'Wide Wipes' went right down the toilet. One of the greatest marketing disasters since the Edsel. You do remember the Edsel, Chester, or was that before your time?"

Chester laughed. Of course he remembered the Edsel, the horsey car that Ford introduced when Chester was in sixth grade. Its front looked like a vacuum cleaner. Charlie Sims, who was in eighth grade, said that the front was supposed to look like a vagina. Chester didn't know what a vagina was but he soon found out. "What's the point?" Chester asked.

"The point is that there has to be some underlying reason to compel people to change their ingrained habits. Old-fashioned toilet paper works just fine. There really is no reason to replace it. For all the talk about 'creating need', the truth is not that need is created, but, rather, that formerly unrecognized needs come to the surface. They were there all along, but ignored, because satisfying them was not feasible, either because of technology, economics, or politics. This professor quoted Gandhi: 'There go my people; I must hurry and catch up with them, for I am their leader.' Let the people decide. That's what it's all about, Chester. Close knit neighborhoods and hence close knit parishes are things of the past, anachronisms. People are running to the suburbs.

They're running away from as much as they are running to and towards, but they're running nonetheless. The Catholic Church has to stay one step ahead, for we are their leader."

Chester did not know what to make of all this. Like a child poking a stick at a dead animal, he considered Father Schuler's words. "Perhaps the professor confuses cause and effect," he suggested.

"It doesn't make any difference," Father Schuler answered. "We can lead, or we can follow. We end up in the same place."

"Cottonwood Acres? Hanover Estates?"

"That's what the people want."

"What if the people are wrong?" Chester asked.

"The people are never wrong," Father Schuler replied with a certainty that sent chills down Chester's spine. "The people are a force of nature."

*   *   *

As the Second World War drew to a close the International Harvester Company perfected the mechanized cotton picking machine. Soon its most expensive model was six times more cost-effective than the worst paid human being. So the sharecropper who had migrated from plantation to plantation, essential for his labor while despised for her skin color, who always was and always would be without place, was now without purpose. Let the niggers go North! the white South chanted in a great chorus of glee and anticipation. Let them big bucks sit in the front of your buses, lunch counters, and movie theaters and rub knees with your fair Yankee daughters. So it was the sons and daughters of Nat Turner and Gabriel Prosser, of Denmark Vesey and Henry Highland Garnet, left Mississippi and Alabama, Georgia and Arkansas, for the promised land cities of the North. This was to be the greatest migration in history not fueled by war or famine. The second greatest would be that of white northerners who fled Chicago and Detroit, Cleveland and Newark, for newly made places called "suburbs." The concept is not new. As barbarian hordes menaced Rome in the Fifth and Sixth Centuries, the intelligentsia moved from the banks of the Tiber to estates in the country. Behind walled compounds the plutocrat and his family went on in their pretend world of comfort and isolation. They diddled; Rome burned. Now Blacks came North and Whites fled. Intermediaries greased each step of the way. In the Reconstruction Era a century before they were known as carpetbagger and scalawag. Now their names were real estate broker and mortgage banker, road builder and mall developer. Both sets of migrants heard what they were predisposed to hear. Black Americans heard that the days of Jim Crow were over. The Supreme Court had spoken. The Restrictive Covenant was a thing of the past. The fleeing Whites heard, "Move, before it's too late." Resegregation became a self-fulfilling prophecy. Americans of African descent moved to the promised land cities of the North only to find that the promised land itself was moving. Once again they would have to cast down their buckets where they were. Would they bring with them, like a hangover, the unrooted culture of sharecropping: migratory, masochistic, and mean? They were used to the white man's leavings. If whitey now abandoned neighborhoods like Austin, could they be of much worth? Better, no?, to do what true Americans do: use up and throw away. And then move on. One hundred years after Appomattox, Africans came and Europeans fled. As the Whites saw it, they were being driven from hearth and home, like the yeomen in the Eighteenth Century when the commons in Kent and Yorkshire were enclosed. The inflationary spiral of the nineteen-seventies and eighties would more than compensate financially so far as housing values were concerned, but this was a fact not to be admitted. What the refugees remembered was that they had lost it all. It was an invasion, an occupation, an expulsion. The White community was obliterated, its front porch way of life destroyed. For generations they had been city folk. Their fathers, grandfathers, and great-grandfathers had walked the same sidewalks and streets. Now they were cast out into the amorphous glob of suburbia, to places with silly names and no corner stores, where garages were attached, where there were no front porches. They had barely escaped with their lives as the tidal wave of black engulfed their patrimony. They thought of themselves as refugees like those seen in newsreels. Their pushcarts were station wagons and their portmanteaux minivans, but they were refugees nonetheless. In breakfast nooks in split-level homes with yards of tiny trees and streets without alleys, in anonymous and stoopless cookie cutter places, they would pass down, one generation to the next, their legacy of loss, misconception, and fear. In gated communities far from the ravages of their plundered city homelands, the refugees worried: could it all happen again? Would distance, their great protector, keep their new first class cabins secure? Or was the whole damn ship sinking?

*   *   *

The following months brought the hurricane Father Schuler saw coming. One by one the families of the parish fled. First the lawyers and the doctors, then the teachers and government employees, finally the factory workers. For the most part the elderly, mainly widows, stayed. Mrs. DeBose in her grand home on Midway Park. Mrs. Zack in her country cottage on Race Avenue.   And a handful of others. Barbara Jean Benedetto, who everyone knew was crazy. She'd marched into Cicero, Illinois, with Dr. King and got herself arrested. The hurricane lasted eighteen months. One hundred and twenty thousand Americans of European descent fled as Americans of African descent arrived. The first of the new immigrants had garages burned and windows broken.

Chester made a belated attempt to confront the whirlwind head-on. When he wasn't in Florida, Monsignor Maguire hibernated in his quarters. He had issued Chester explicit instructions: Chester's sermons were to make no mention of the ongoing neighborhood exodus. The Monsignor made sure everyone knew where he stood. A black woman and a young black girl approached the communion rail. Monsignor Maguire skipped over them, like a jump shot in billiards, he boasted. Chester had not witnessed this sin. As the congregation had dwindled to less than one-third its former size, there were now only two Sunday Masses. Chester presided over the earlier Mass. That Sunday he had gone to the Field Museum of Natural History afterwards to view an exhibit of Inca artifacts. In the afternoon, upon his return, Mrs. McGrath was waiting for him.

"It don't seem right, Father," she said. "I know they're pushing us out and all, but still, it don't seem right." Chester's confrontation with his superior was brief. Chester banged on Monsignor Maguire's door until, at last, it opened a crack. The Pastor of St. Lucy's whiskeyed voice snarled, "What is it this time?"

"It's about Communion." Chester looked directly into Monsignor Maguire's bathrobed and bleary eyes.

"An important Sacrament," Monsignor Maguire said.

"Is it true you refused to give Communion to a woman and her daughter?"

"Of course I refused. They weren't Catholic."

"Just how did you know that?"

"I have my ways. I've been doing this a lot longer than you. Call it instincts. Mind your own business." The door slammed shut.

It took some doing, but the next day Chester learned the woman's identity. Pamela Singleton. She had bought Dr. Sinclair's house in the 5700 block of Ohio Street. Chester dropped a note in her mailbox asking that she call. After dinner that evening his telephone rang.

"This is Pam Singleton." The crisp words brought forth an image of a middle-aged woman with her hair drawn into a bun. A bookkeeper, Chester thought. Funny, her voice didn't sound black. Perhaps there was some mistake. But there wasn't. "I got your note. You asked that I call. I'm calling."

"Ah, yes." Chester fumbled. "Thank you. I was hoping we might get together." He felt clumsy. He had no idea what he should say next. "To welcome you to St. Lucy's," he finally blurted.

"Don't you think I've been welcomed enough?"

"Oh, that *was* a dumb thing to say! I'm sorry."

"Not at all," the woman replied, "I'm just being overly sensitive. I'd be happy to see you. Why don't you stop by?"

Dr. Sinclair's house! How strange now, after all these years, that it belonged to someone else! It was an imposing frame home, one of the oldest in Chicago, circa 1870. The architectural books referred to it as "in the style of a Tuscan villa." Chester pushed the button in the middle of an ornate brass ornament that looked like an inkwell. He was studying its details of filigree when the door opened. A slender woman in her early thirties smiled at him. She sparkled. She was of medium height with a strong round face. Her nose seemed almost too perfect. She wore a simple white blouse with long puffy sleeves and blue jeans. Her skin was the deepest black Chester had ever seen. She had radiant white teeth. Her black hair was braided in closely knit rows. Bright green earrings danced at the sides of her head.

"Please come in, Father." Chester remembered the house from when he was a child. The great entry hall with an ornate curving staircase of African mahogany. Massive pocket doors, cherry and black walnut. Fireplaces with mantels of Carrera Marble. Up and down gas and electric light fixtures with etched glass globes and filigrees of nickel plated brass. Ceilings twelve feet high.

Pamela Singleton showed him to the front parlor. "It's the one room I have somewhat put together!" she laughed. "All I have to do is slide those doors open"—she pointed—"and you'd see a mountain of boxes, nothing but boxes. I don't know where all the stuff comes from. We Americans sure know how to accumulate! 'O, say can you shop?' That should be our national anthem, no?" She shook her head slowly and laughed. There was a gentle warmth about her. Chester settled into the sofa. Already he was at ease. "They say that Black folk only like brick houses," she went on. "I don't know how such stereotypes take hold, Father, do you? The three little pigs perhaps?"

Chester thought he was in a movie. This was not at all what he had expected. Pamela Singleton was nothing like the middle-aged matron he'd envisioned. He looked around the room. There was a beauty in its simplicity. Its furnishing were sparse, but he could see that they had been chosen with a discerning eye.

"Well, they must have been three artistic little pigs!" he said. Pamela Singleton laughed. Then neither said a word for long moments.

"I wanted to apologize for what happened yesterday," Chester said at last. "At Mass. I wish I had been there."

"I appreciate your apology, Father. Thank you. As for your being there, however, it wouldn't have mattered one way or the other."

"What I meant was that I wish you had come to the eight o'clock Mass, the one I say."

"Oh, I get it," the black woman responded sharply. "One Mass for the colored folk, another for the real Catholics. Separate but equal, is that it? Except that us darkies get to get up early." She had changed. Or had she? Chester was overcome with strange feelings, feelings he did not understand. Then she seemed to change again, back to her former self. "You must forgive me, Father. It's just that white folk are always telling us where and how to live and what to do. We get tired of it all."

Chester felt stupid and small. He didn't know what to say. "I'm sorry," he managed at last. "All of this is quite new to me."

"Well, it's new to me, too," Pamela Singleton responded. "Some misunderstanding is inevitable, I suppose." She pulled herself erect. A serious look spread over her face. "Therefore, Father," she teased, "it pleases me to tell you that, after due consideration, I have decided to accept your *second* apology." They laughed together now.

They talked for an hour. She and her daughter would not be back to St. Lucy's, at least not for a while. She'd continue attending her former parish, St. Josephus, but she hoped, nonetheless, to see Chester again. Some skinny white guy with pimples and red hair was urging her to lead a protest march in front of the Cardinal's residence but she had refused. "I'm tired of all the shouting," she said. "Most of the time it's just for show. All I want, all *we* want, is a decent place to live. Is that asking too much?" Once more Chester didn't know what to say. So he listened. "What I mean," she continued, "is that it's about time to get beyond color. It's a real shame that the white folks are running. That's not our fault. It's not what we want; most definitely it's not what *I* want. I'd like my daughter to grow up with all kinds of people. That's the wave of the future, isn't it? What do you think?"

"I don't know," Chester replied. "I'd like to think so."

"All we can do is hope—and try," Pamela Singleton said. "That's why I don't want any part of picketing the Cardinal's mansion. For the life of me I can't see what good it would do. All that Bradley Jakes wants is to keep the pot boiling. What's the Cardinal supposed to do? Give Monsignor Maguire a soul transplant?"

"I wouldn't object!" Chester said.

"You know, it's funny, but I wasn't all that surprised. I looked at him as Ashley and I approached the communion rail. I thought he was drunk. I should have just turned back."

"No, that's not right," Chester replied. "You shouldn't feel that way. God's house should be open to all."

"There's generally a big gap between *should* and *is*," Pamela Singleton said. "Something black folk know only too well. Strange, but in a way I'm glad Ashley was there. We talked a lot about what happened. Ashley said she likes our old church better anyway. She said she would pray for Monsignor Maguire." Pamela Singleton served coffee and pound cake her mother had made for her new home. Chester helped tuck her daughter into bed. There was a clear sky as Chester walked back to the rectory and, rare for Chicago, he could see the stars.

Chapter Twelve:
Ash

Marguerite
Mabouhey
1989

She could not love a white man. She would not love a white
man. Not after what they had done. No. How could she?
How could she even think of such a thing? She would never
love a white man. Marguerite waited in the verandah's
darkness, Father Chester and the American called Travers
silhouetted by the fire's dying, just far enough away that
their words could not reach her. She would have gone to take
her sleeping daughter, but she was unwilling to see the
American up so close so soon again, so soon after their hands
had touched in the netting. She sat there alone on her
verandah, in the dark, smothering feelings that stirred
within, that would spring to life the way new shoots of green
struggle towards sun through thickets of weed.

Over the clearing came wind from the ocean, rustling grassland and forest. Marguerite sat there, hidden in shadows. It was the blink of an eye, the beat of a heart, the cry of one word, no, no, no, sounding like a great door closing, a prison door closing, yet it was already five years, five long years, years when each new day dawned a new dying. They had killed Schugay, the blackest boy with the biggest heart. The white man had killed him. Schugara would never know his laughing eyes; Schugay's hands would never reach his daughter to the star-crowded sky to beg the moon god's blessing. For Marguerite every day was a deafened echo, every night an empty bed. The white man had killed Schugay. No. She would not love a white man. How could she even think of such a thing?

In the shadows on the verandah her anger flamed, as if the fire dying in the middle of the clearing found new life in her soul. Across the way one of the silhouettes reached to stroke her sleeping daughter. Marguerite looked closely. Father Chester. *His* white hands could bring comfort and blessing. He was one of them. She could see in the surreal light of the fire's ebbing that it was Father Chester who was speaking. She could see that it was the white man who listened. Then she saw the silhouette of the priest stand, his arms extended, his hands open. Blessed are the peacemakers, she thought. For me, there is no peace; my inheritance is the dirge of bitter ash. I shall never love a white man.

BOOK TWO: DISCOVERY

Chapter Thirteen:
Gone

Chester O'Reilly
Chicago; Hanover Park, Illinois
1971–1975

"Brothers and Sisters in Christ," Chester began his sermon the Sunday after his visit with Pamela Singleton. "It is Jesus' commandment that we love one another. He did not say that we should limit our love to the Catholic. He did not say that we should limit our love to those whose skin color is the same as ours. He said, simply, that we must love one another. We must love the Jew no less than the Christian, the Protestant no less than the Catholic. We must love black people the same as white. We must love one another. This is what Jesus commands us to do." Chester paused. The congregation was now one-quarter its former size and he knew there would be even fewer families in the Sundays to come. He was no longer so naive as to believe that his words would make much of a difference, but he felt, at least and at last, that he had to try. The faces that remained looked up at him, but most seemed frozen as if already far away.

"It is said that we live in a 'changing neighborhood', and this is said as if change can only be for the worse. Yet we know that it is in the nature of things to change. To change is to grow. To change is to adapt, to evolve. It is our duty to see to it that the changes we are experiencing are for the better. Black families"—there he had said it!—"are moving into Austin. Only a few of them are Catholic. But they are all God's children. It is Jesus' commandment that we love them. It is a sin to treat them differently because their skin is black. Make no mistake about it. This is a moral issue. Sin is sin. It is not our job to judge. That job is already taken. That job belongs to Someone Else. He will judge us and he will judge us all, white and black, and, when he does, he will judge us, in the words of Dr. Martin Luther King, Jr., not on the basis of the color of our skin but on the basis of the content of our character. Now may Jesus Christ, Son of the Father, and our Redeemer, be with us all, now and forever, in the name of the Holy Trinity, One and Indivisible, world without end. Peace be with you. Amen."

That evening Monsignor Maguire made a weak attempt to chastise him. Chester had been to the cinema with Father Sanders, an assistant pastor at St. Edmund's in nearby Oak Park. They had seen a Japanese film, *Brothel 8*. It told the story of a farm girl sold by her family to serve in the government run brothels that accompanied the Japanese armed forces during World War Two.

"Monsignor Maguire always said the Japanese are barbaric," Chester said on the ride home. "Perhaps he has a point."

"We should hold the sons responsible for the sins of their fathers? Is that what you're suggesting?" Father Sanders replied.

"Not exactly," Chester said. "But what if the sons continue to benefit from their fathers' sins? What then?"

"Are you proposing that we give California back to Mexico?"

"Maybe not such a bad idea, Father," Chester answered. Jonathan Edwalds' father was sitting in his rocking chair on his Race Avenue front porch, the red cooler at his feet. "I have never succeeded in thinking of one good thing that came from California, and I have been trying to for years!"

The other priest thought for a moment. "California is giving the nation right turn on red."

"Literally or metaphorically?"

"Both." Father Sanders laughed and Chester laughed with him.

Now Monsignor Maguire wobbled at the foot of the rectory's staircase, hanging on to its post as if it were a streetlamp. "I heard all about your sermon on sin, Father," he said. "Apparently you have forgotten that disobedience is a sin, too." Chester pushed by him to go to his room.

"Father Sanders has already heard my Confession," he said. "Besides there are worse sins than disobedience."

"Satan disobeyed," Monsignor Maguire shouted back. "Adam and Eve disobeyed."

"The Japanese you are so fond of didn't." Chester went to his room and slammed the door behind him. An hour later, as he was reading his breviary, Mrs. McGrath knocked at his door.

"Mr. Burdine is here to see you, Father, if it's not too late. He's been calling all afternoon."

"No, it's all right," Chester said. "Tell Mr. Burdine to wait in the reception. I'll be right down."

Jack Burdine had gone straight from Austin High School to the *Chicago Daily News*, starting as a janitor and working his way up to pressman. He had been at the newspaper ever since—thirty-four years. He was a paunchy man in his fifties. What remained of his hair, on the sides of his head, was a silver fleece. He had a large nose and bright blue eyes. Except for his head, his skin was as white as white paper. For some inexplicable reason, for Jack Burdine was the lightest of drinkers, he was iodine red in color from the neck up. His wife, Marcey, joked that her husband was thoroughly patriotic.

"What can I do for you, Mr. Burdine?"

"It's about your sermon today, Father," the older man said. "Me and da missus have been talkin' about it ever since dis morning. Marcey said I should come see you first ting."

Chester sensed the other man's anxiety. "Well, I'm glad you did come, Jack. I promise that I will appreciate sincere praise."

Jack Burdine did not catch Chester's attempt at humor. "Oh, it was a good sermon, Father, the words and all. For sure it was. I'm not saying anything different. I mean, it sounded good and everything like dat. But you see, Father, the ting about it is dat I got three daughters. Never was blessed wid a son, Father, but I wouldn't trade dem for da world, Father, not for da world."

"I'm sure you wouldn't," Chester said softly.

"An' you knows, Father, well, when all da big shots started leavin' an' such, da missus, God bless her, Father, she's a fine woman, well, she says how we was goin' to stick it out. Fiona Mulroney told her, 'It's one ting to have them move into your neighbourhood, it's anudder to be nice to dem,' but my Marcey ain't like dat, Father. We'll get by; somehow tings would work out. Dat's what she said, my Marcey. She's da tough one, Father, she really is. Me, I'm just a cream puff compared to her! So I went along. I mean, we been in da house ever since we was married and all like dat. But all da time I was feelin' like we was makin' a mistake. I mean half da houses on our block are already sold and people's just waitin' fer dem to close and de udder half, except ours and old Mrs. Sweeney's, dere all up for sale, Father. You'd think somebuddy named 'For Sale' was running for Mayor the way de signs are all up and down de street. And de block across from our alley, Father, Parkside Avenue, dat's all gone."

Gone. Can one small syllable contain such a world of loss? Gone.

"But surely Parkside Avenue is still there!" Chester joked.

Now the older man's turmoil expressed itself in anger. "Don't be making jokes about it, Father. It ain't funny. Dere's nobody left hardly. Our garage has been broken into and dey took my girls' bikes. Just before Tom and Mildred Casey moved, dey knocked Mildred down on her way back from da Jewels Foods and snatched her purse. Her ankle got busted up and all. Tings like dat never used ta happen around here, Father. You know dat. Austin! We don't want ta move, Father, we really don't. But I just don't know how I'd go on livin' if anything happened ta one of my girls, really, Father, I don't. You won't like dis here, Father, and it's a sin and all, I knows dat, but I will kill anybuddy dat touched one of my girls, Father, I really would and I mean it. Don't try to tell me nuttin' different."

Chester saw that Jack Burdine had tears in his eyes. He knew that he should reach out, that he should offer comfort, that he should provide answers. But there were no answers, none that he could think of. "We must leave judgment—and punishment—in God's hands," he said.

"Meanin' no disrespect, Father," Jack Burdine replied, "but dat's easy for you ta say. You don't have no daughters." The silence between them now was like grief. Tears poured down the older man's cheeks. Jack Burdine brought his hands to his face and sobbed. "All my life I've tried ta be a good Catholic, Father," he said. "I really have. Dat's how I was raised ever since I was a little boy. I don't want my Immortal Soul ta burn in da fires of Hell forever. I tole da missus she don't have nuttin' ta worry about cause a wife's duty is ta obey her husband. And so, no matter what, Marcey's soul is gonna be okay. Ain't dat right, Father?"

Chester had no idea what Jack Burdine was talking about. Then it came to him. His words from the pulpit that morning, which he had in their saying thought inspired and insightful, now seemed flaccid and faint. "This is a moral issue," he had lectured. "Sin is sin. Make no mistake about it. It is a sin to treat our new neighbors differently because their skin is black." In Jack Burdine's tears it came to him that what his sermon had accomplished was to increase Jack Burdine's turmoil. Now, thanks to Chester's lofty words, in addition to confusion, abandonment, and fear, Jack Burdine was assaulted as well by guilt, and for circumstances that were beyond his or any one person's control.

"You said it is a sin not to love 'em, Father, and, sure you're right and all, but you are askin' too much, Father, you may not know it, but you surely are. I drive to work late at night when I'm on da graveyard shift an' I see dem hangin' around on da corner, drinkin' beer and dressin' all funny, and dere's little children and all an' I kent help it, Father, but I don't love 'em. No, what I'm feelin' ain't nuttin' like love, far from it, Father, nuttin' like love at all. Why kent dey be like us?"

Chester thought of Pamela Singleton. "Maybe if you give it a chance."

"No, Father," Jack Burdine answered. "I kent. I just kent. I never taut I would say dis, Father, but I'm afraid. Me, an ex-marine. I'm afraid."

"It is natural to fear the unknown."

"Well, you're wrong dere, Father. I can tell you dat much. It ain't da unknown dat I'm afraid of. It's da known. Just drive east of here, Father. It's all tore up. You know dat, Father. The neighborhood by Garfield Park used ta be all so grand. We used ta sleep dere outsides in the park sometimes when we was kids, before dere was air-conditioning, on dose real hot summer nights, Father, before dey moved in and pushed us out over here. Jess look at Garfield Park now, Father, all tore-up. Dey throw garbage out de windows and everythin' like dat."

Chester uttered a few more clichés, about casting the first stone, about hating the sin but loving the sinner, about Ruth and the alien corn. But he knew he was just going through the motions. He could not find it in himself to condemn the simple man whose soul cried out in pain. The largest pile of dirty clothes always was the in-betweeners. Might as well get on with it. Jack Burdine had stopped crying. He raised his head and looked at the priest the way a patient in a cancer ward looks at her doctor.

"When we are faced with conflicting responsibilities," Chester said, "we must give priority to our primary responsibility. Your primary responsibility is to your family. As God watches over His people, as the father of your family, you must watch over your wife and daughters. God will not punish you for doing what in your heart of hearts you think best for them." There. It was done.

The older man sprang to his feet. "Oh, thank you, Father. Thank you. Marcey said you'd have da right answer.

You always was da smart one, Father, even when you was workin' over dere at Freeman's Clothing on Chicago Avenue. Thank you, Father, thank you." Happiness bubbled on Jack Burdine's face like that of a child's on Halloween. "Curtis Champion was by again just yesterday. He says we still got time if we hurry. We should list da house before it's too late, he says. You know him, Father. He used ta have his office over dere on Waller Avenue across from where Mahoney's Flowers used ta be."

"Yes," Chester replied. "I know Curtis Champion of Champion's First Choice Realty only too well." For years one of Monsignor Maguire's golfing buddies. Chester remembered what one of St. Lucy's most stalwart parishioners, Barbara Jean Benedetto, had told him. Curtis Champion had warned her that she should get her house on the market "before it's too late." Her stately Victorian was on Superior Street, just one block south of Chicago Avenue. The black tsunami had breached the natural barrier of the Lake Street Elevated embankment six blocks to the south; soon, he said, it would jump Chicago Avenue. If Champion's First Choice Realty listed her house immediately, Curtis could still tell black families they were moving into an "integrated" neighborhood.

"And they are," Curtis laughed to his wife, Roseanne, in their new home in Hoffman Estates, one of the instant subdivisions that were sprouting like weeds on the former farmlands to Chicago's west. "It's integrated from the time the first black family moves in until the last white family moves out, usually six months." For Curtis Champion those were six fecund months. Yes, Chester thought, I know Curtis Champion only too well.

"Course he says we won't get as much as da first ones got," Jack Burdine said. "But, still, at least it ain't too late. Dat's what he says. Do you tink he's right, Father?" Chester did not answer.

After Jack Burdine departed, Chester sat in his rocking chair for a long time. Were front porch neighborhoods like Austin things of the past, anachronisms, destined by interstates and inner states of mind to go the way of the horse and buggy? Were Hanover Acres and Cottonwood Estates historical inevitabilities? Would Americans ever learn to live together? Or, constricted by economics and ethnicity, are we doomed to quarantine ourselves in paranoid enclaves of perceived self-preservation? Wasn't it his job to liberate people, people like Jack Burdine, from the imprisonment of the past, from the imprisonment of fear? Chester thought of the look on Jack Burdine's face as the older man waited for Chester's *magisterium*. Who am I to have such power? Chester was supposed to be God's intermediary, but he knew, despite the Cardinal's hands, despite the incense and holy water, that he was simply a man. Had he done the right thing? Or had he given into weakness and rationalized his capitulation as mercy? It had all been so easy that morning pontificating from the pulpit. But, face to face with Jack Burdine, he was quick to blink. Was there any hope? Was there any hope at all?

*   *   *

A few days later Mrs. McGrath knocked on Chester's door. A Mr. Luther Custis Towe was on the phone. "Pam Singleton suggested I call." The voice was strong, with a slow Mississippi accent. "I'm with the Learning Network. I've been trying to reach the Monsignor, but he hasn't returned my calls."

Chester knew of the Learning Network. Some sort of African school on Fulton Street, just south of the Lake Street elevated. Chester had stopped Bradley Jakes at one of the community meetings the organizer always seemed to be calling. Bradley Jakes was dismissive: the Learning Network was an affront to the community. It drained students and resources from the public system. It was not community-based, but rather the plaything of a few disgruntled teachers. Parents had little say in its curriculum. It was just more flimflammery foisted on the politically immature and culturally disadvantaged. "Another red herring of false hope," he said with a cynical sneer that Chester found repellant.

"What do you mean?" Chester asked.

"Such elitism only serves to distract people from what's really going on, from the real problem."

"I'm not sure I understand. What is the real problem?" Chester asked.

"I'm surprised you don't know. The real problem is *racism*."

"Are you still there, Father?" the black voice now asked.

"Yes, forgive me. How may I be of help?"

"Well, Monsignor Evans downtown told me to get in touch with the Monsignor. I'd like to make an appointment to see the convent."

"The convent?"

"Well, yes. I mean I know that it's Siena High School now, but it's hard to think of it that way."

Chester understood what this meant. For nearly a century Siena High School sat, like a medieval fortress, at the northwest corner of Washington Boulevard and Central Avenue. It was an impressive structure that educated Catholic girls, including Jack Burdine's daughters. It had been sold to the Board of Education of the City of Chicago two years before. It had taken less than two years for Austin High School, three blocks away, to resegregate from all-white to all-black. The campus at Washington and Central would be used as an auxiliary Austin High site for a year before it would be abandoned and boarded up. Monsignor Evans, who handled the Archdiocese's real estate, was thrilled at the one million dollar price tag the Cardinal had negotiated with the Mayor, the more so because his files contained an environmental audit warning that the auditorium required asbestos abatement that would cost twice that amount. Checkers, Strawn, and Calahutty, the archdiocese's law firm, had made sure that the "as-is, where-is" clause was ironclad. Siena's nuns were moved out of the convent on Midway Park to St. Catherine's in adjacent Oak

Park. The former convent became the replacement Siena High School to accommodate the diminished and diminishing student body of the daughters of the families who had as yet not fled. When Siena High School was downsized and relocated, the Cardinal had promised that it would not close in his lifetime. Its new location on Midway Park was to be permanent. Chester remembered the dinner a few months before to celebrate the successful completion of the new Siena's fundraising drive.

"Are you telling me that the convent is now for sale?"

"Oh, you didn't know? Well, that's what Monsignor Evans said. Perhaps he's mistaken."

"No," Chester replied sadly. "If Monsignor Evans told you the convent is for sale, then the convent is for sale. When would you like to see it?" Today the convent, tomorrow the sanctuary, school, and rectory, Chester thought as he hung up the phone.

*   *   *

In the nineteen-sixties the Polish nation, whose people knew well that that government which governs most, governs worst, took the first steps towards liberating themselves from communist rule. It would take three long decades more for Poland and its Eastern European neighbors to rise up and free themselves, but rise up and free themselves they did. In the United States, bastion of capitalism, however, public education remains under the tyranny of centralized bureaucracies. In Chicago and other large cities, public schools cream off their middle and upper class students into "magnet" schools, which receive a disproportionate allocation of money, attention, and resources. In this they are akin to the specialty stores which existed in communist countries, whose access was limited to the *nomenklatura*.

In affluent communities, public schools work well. Students arrive well-fed, well-nurtured, prepared, and motivated. To apply the same model to devastated neighborhoods does not work. Students who live in the war zones that many poor communities have become need schools to be nurturing, caring, safe places, small in scale, intimate in scope, substitutes for endangered and near extinct hearth and home.

Many who support publicly funded education are unable to conceive of an alternative delivery system. They have before them the successful model of food stamps, which are vouchers for food, but they choose to dismiss the analogy. The thought of government run grocery stores is absurd. Cabbage would be rancid; milk, sour. Broccoli would be infested with worms.

The affluent thrive in skyscrapers. Why shouldn't the poor? For half a century, the poor were housed in multi-level projects, centrally controlled by public housing authorities. Despite exemptions from property taxes and water bills, and billions of dollars in taxpayer subsidies, high-rise housing projects for the poor were hellholes. It took housing professionals decades to admit the truth: that which works well for the affluent does not necessarily work well for the poor. Anyone today advocating housing the poor in high-rises would be told to have his or her head examined.

Education, it is thought, is different. Public education has to be controlled by the state and only by the state. "Power to the People!" stops at the schoolhouse door. Schools have to be identical. No child may be left in front. Each school must have its own gymnasium, computer laboratory, athletic field, swimming pool, library, cafeteria, teachers' lounge, and parking lot when what is needed above all is intimacy and caring. The wealth of the black and brown communities, its grandmothers and great-uncles, is dismissed. What could women and men who conquered Jim Crow possibly know that would be of use in the age of computers, celebrities, and cell phones? No, schools cannot be cottage industries. It is an absurd idea.

If only more money were provided! This is the chorus primeval of those who defend government school monopoly. In Kansas City, Missouri, in the nineteen-eighties, public school funding was *quadrupled* overnight. So the courts had ruled. The bureaucracy squandered the windfall. Year after subsequent year test scores stagnated; drop-out rates increased. Clearly the *delivery* system which works in affluent communities is ill-equipped to meet the needs of the nation's urban poor.

Each year politicians and union officials in America's cities dance the kabuki dance of pretense. We care more about the children than you do. Do not. Do too. Strikes are commonplace, settled once unions' demands, for engineers, for janitors, for bus drivers, for cafeteria workers, for secretaries, for therapists, for administrators, for teachers are reduced from rapacious to inordinate. No one is ever sufficiently overpaid. Bureaucrats at the top of the system view themselves as C.E.O.'s of great enterprises. They point to their overblown budgets to justify their obscene salaries. Yet they know the whispered truth: the children of the ghettoes are impossible to teach. Their absentee fathers are junkies, in prison, or on parole. Their mothers are whores. Keeping the bastard children in their seats is accomplishment sufficient. Just ask the teachers: most of their own children attend private schools as do the sons and daughters of politicians and the cognoscenti. "Do as we say, not as we do." Schools do not open on time and seldom with books, paper, pencils and teachers for all. Generations of Austin's children, like those of America's outer cities nationwide, do not learn. They cannot read a newspaper. They cannot balance a check book. They think that Brussels is a vegetable and Colombia a brand of coffee.

*   *   *

Once the Learning Network had settled into the convent, Chester became a regular visitor. He would hear of a used set of encyclopedias and show up, arms full and face beaming. He enjoyed the quiet bustle of the place.

Soon Chester was teaching a poetry class for six of the older students. He certainly had the time. St. Lucy's congregation had dwindled to fewer than thirty families, stalwart and steadfast, but insufficient, Chester knew, to sustain the parish. Chester presided over the one remaining Sunday Mass; Monsignor Maguire stayed hidden in his room. He reminded Chester of Miss Havisham in *Great Expectations*, and, although Chester tried not to despise the disheveled phantom he heard poking around late at night, he did. They had stopped taking their meals together when Father Schuler left. Mrs. McGrath left Monsignor Maguire a tray outside his door, while, alone in the dining room, Chester ate with a book for his tablemate. No one was surprised when finally the parish was closed.

Everything was sold. Statues. Holy water founts. Pews. Candlesticks. Even the banner of the St. Lucy's Holy Name Society. Gone. As Chester took a look around his empty room, he thought back to Jack Burdine: "It's gone, Father, all gone." Chester had already packed the Datsun 510 station wagon with his belongings and he knew that his room was empty. But he returned anyway, for a last look, staring out the front window for long moments. *For all the sad words of tongue and pen*, Jon Greenleaf Whittier's words came to him, *the saddest are these: it might have been.*

"I don't think so," Luther Custis Towe said a few days later. Chester's poetry class had just ended.

"You don't think what?" Chester asked.

"I don't think it might have been." Chester had driven in from his new assignment as Assistant Pastor at St. Ansgar's in Hanover Park, one of the new western suburbs. It was late in the afternoon and they were alone in the convent's kitchen.

"What do you mean?"

"Just that neighborhoods like Austin were written off years ago. And the riots didn't help any, either." Luther was referring to the burning and looting that had exploded on the south and west sides of the city the night Dr. Martin Luther King, Jr., was assassinated. "People like Bradley Jakes tried to make it sound like the looters and arsonists were revolutionaries, but they were just a bunch of hoodlums." The teacher poured himself a cup of coffee. To Luther, after twelve years in Chicago, Bradley Jakes was a familiar type, one of the interchangeable white misfits who styled themselves "community organizers," skipping from one changing neighborhood to the next, spewing revolution as they pocketed paychecks from the guilt money largesse of downtown philanthropies. As Luther saw it, these ne'er-do-wells could not make it in the white world so they tried their luck in the black. Theirs, he thought, was the dialect of self-righteousness and anger, of outrage and vituperation. Revolution was the answer. Luther was convinced that to self-appointed "activists" like Bradley Jakes, African-Americans were indeed important. To follow orders. To serve, if the revolution ever came, as cannon fodder. Chester also knew Bradley Jakes. A skinny stick of red hair, scraggly and unwashed, his face a permanent and acned sneer, Bradley Jakes had appeared in Austin as the first black families were moving in. He set up a paper organization, the "Assembly for a Better Austin." Chester, like everyone else, found the name offensive. As the neighborhood suffered resegregation, twenty-four year old Bradley Jakes became the resident expert on all things Austin. He was quoted frequently in the *Chicago Tribune* and the *Chicago Sun-Times*. Bradley Jakes was a regular guest on public service discussion shows televised on Sunday mornings. Chester remembered how Pamela Singleton sneered when she mentioned his name. Chester also remembered one meeting the year before held in the Austin Town Hall. A replica of Independence Hall in Philadelphia, the Town Hall had served as Austin's city hall until Austin was forcibly annexed to Chicago in 1899. Pamela Singleton and one of her few remaining white neighbors, a woman named Peggy Smith, had set up the meeting to deal with the neighborhood's rising crime rate. They were especially pleased with the big turn-out. One hundred and forty Austinites, white and black together!

Chester said the opening prayer. Peggy Smith, dowdy, messy, chain-smoking Peggy Smith, whose fulsome hairdo looked like the tip of an exploded cigar, stepped to the microphone. Before she could speak, however, Bradley Jakes ran to the front of the room. On his cue a group of surly young black men marched into the auditorium. Their clothes were dirty. They wore sunglasses and baseball caps with visors angled to the side. Inchoate sounds gurgled as they marched from the rear of the room, punctuated with audible words: "motherfucker," "shit," "cocksucker," "nigger." They brandished handlettered signs: "STOP RACISM NOW!" "DOWN WITH THE KLAN!" "BLACK POWER!"

An infestation of television people sprouted. Cameras applauded as Bradley Jakes spewed forth his venom: the pretend issue of crime was racist. Mrs. Sweeney had brought the latest attack on herself: she had been stupid enough to carry a purse! She should have known better. So what if she got mugged? There were larger and more important issues to be concerned with.

The damage was done. What remained of the meeting was a shambles. One by one the white Austinites, dressed in their work clothes, and their new black neighbors, dressed in their Sunday best, headed for the exits.

"I wonder," Chester mused. "What ever happened to Bradley Jakes?"

"Last I heard," Luther said, "he was selling hot tubs in the suburbs."

*   *   *

Chester and his sanity survived six months at St. Ansgar's. Each week fewer and fewer of its parishioners attended his Mass. "Nobody's into ghettoes or any of that civil rights stuff anymore," Father Schaunessey, St. Ansgar's pastor, lectured him. "It's all passé. The sixties are gone, thank God, and forgotten. The rest of us have gotten over that nightmare, but *you* keep reminding people of things they want to forget. You keep scratching at a sore. Ease up on the social conscience stuff, for crying out loud. To be blunt, I myself find it boring. How do you think the average lay person must feel? And, for God's sake, stop talking about that school all the time! So they got themselves one place where they're not killing or raping each other. What does that have to do with St. Ansgar's? You're in the suburbs now. Act like it. You have a job to do here. Do it."

In January Chester gave a sermon in honor of the birthday of Dr. Martin Luther King, Jr. That did it. Father Schaunessey would tolerate Chester's disobedience no longer. The following Wednesday Chester drove downtown to learn his new assignment. As the wasteland of Chicago's west side passed by as he drove eastward on the Eisenhower Expressway, Chester wondered if he should give it all up. He wasn't much good as a priest. But what else could he do? Teach Latin at a prep school?

Father Raulston showed Chester to a conference room. "I didn't know you had left the seminary, Father," Chester said.

"Yes. The Cardinal thought it best for me to come downtown to help straighten out some of the younger fellows like yourself!"

"Well, in my case, it's not the first time."

"No, I suppose not," Father Raulston answered with nostalgia. "Well, anyway, I've had a devil of a time, if you'll forgive the expression, trying to figure out what to do with you after your, shall we say, *stand-off* with Monsignor Maguire and your...your present St. Ansgar's...*situation*, shall we call it? But I believe I have come upon the perfect solution. I hope you like warm weather."

It turned out that when Mrs. Anna May Bell Castle, widow of Arthur McArthur Castle, president of the National

Bank of Austin, died, in 1925, she established a sizeable trust fund, its only beneficiary the Archdiocese of Chicago. Mrs. Castle's altruism stipulated one condition: the Archdiocese was to provide, in perpetuity, a priest "to work abroad among our darker brethren." The priest provided was to have "roots in the Austin community."

"Well, that's certainly you," Father Raulston laughed. "For fifty years now this Father Malcolm Somebody has been down on some island some place in the Caribbean. The Cardinal couldn't remember exactly where. We haven't heard from this Father Malcolm in years. We haven't wanted to. His assignment was to disappear. To do whatever it is that missionaries do. No news would be good news. And there has been no news for quite a satisfactory while. Just his being there, wherever there is, qualifies to keep the trust department at Austin Bank happy and, if the trust department at Austin Bank is happy, then the Cardinal is happy. Wherever he is, Father Malcolm's service in this regard has been exemplary. When we got his letter a few weeks ago, it took quite a while to figure out who, exactly, he is. That's how exemplary. Well, there's no getting around it. Father Malcolm writes that he is dying. You are the ideal replacement! The Cardinal sees divine intervention in all this. All you have to do, the Cardinal says, is go there and stay alive. If you leave immediately, Father Malcolm might hang in there long enough to show you the ropes. If not, well, just do the best you can. Emulate this sainted man, as the Cardinal thinks of him, now that he does think of him, and don't bother us. If you must, write every few years. And do try to keep in good health. The way things are now I have no idea how we'd ever find a replacement for you! Please try to make that my successor's problem!"

"I'll do my best to stay alive," Chester said.

"Good," Father Raulston answered. "I will say many prayers that you do."

*   *   *.

Chester's grandmother sat at the kitchen table, peeling potatoes. They knew this would be the last time they would see each other. Chester told his grandmother of his doubt, but also of his hope, that his life would have meaning, that he would, somehow, make a difference. The world would be a better place for his having lived.

"But you are a priest!" his grandmother exclaimed, as if his priesthood in and of itself were the solid coin of worth. His grandmother believed and the sun of her faith, there, for a moment, gave Chester life. Not many more words passed between them as their last meal together came to an end. Chester looked around the basement apartment for the last time. He felt the wonder of joy and the celebration of strength. He thought of his mother and father, of his brother and sisters. He remembered the smells of cinnamon and honey, the babushka women who sold flowers after Mass on the steps of St. Lucy's, the hot dog man who pushed his shiny cart up and down Central Avenue April through October, umbrella and spindly tires. He remembered the fitting rooms and cutting table at Freeman's Clothing on

Chicago Avenue, the war stories on Jonathan Edwalds' front porch, the six packs of Old Style, the farmers who sold corn and tomatoes from the backs of pick-up trucks under the el. Chester remembered hopscotch and bicycles in bright Austin summers. He saw fireflies in gangways and fireworks on rooftops, double dutch girls and stickball boys; he remembered hockey on roller skates with tin can or baseball. All these memories and more, inchoate as anger, as clear as imagination, sounded like heartbeats.

There were tears in Chester's eyes and in his grandmother's as they held hands and hugged each other. Then his grandmother knelt before him and asked his blessing. Chester made the Sign of the Cross over her. He said the Latin words and he was at peace.

No one could tell him about the island of Mabouhey. It wasn't even on the map, at least not on any of the maps Chester found in the Chicago Public Library, either the Austin branch or the main downtown library, nor on the maps of the Newberry Library on Bughouse Square. At least Frederique was on a few of the maps, although none of the atlases or travel guides he studied made mention of it. All Chester knew was that Frederique was in the southern Caribbean and the island of Mabouhey somewhere nearby. He had no idea what he should take with him, and no one could tell him. So he filled a large steamer trunk with books. Aquinas. Boethius. Dante. Wordsworth. *The Encyclopedia Britannica*. Norton Anthologies. Chester wrapped a typewriter inside sheets and then anchored it between the *Random House Dictionary* and *The Complete Works of*

Shakespeare. He packed twelve boxes of typewriter ribbons, a dozen in each box and forty reams of plain white paper. He wrapped his chalice and vestments in clothing to place on top. Father Schuler had given him a *Physician's Desk Reference* and this he carried with him in a large duffel bag, with shoes and some additional clothing, along with a small pharmacy of ointments, pills, and potions. He had one day to go and one last goodbye to make.

"What are these?" Luther Custis Towe asked as Chester threw two silver keys onto the kitchen table. "These, Director Towe, are the keys to the Learning Network's own official limousine, courtesy of one Chester O'Reilly. A tried, true, and trusty 1969 Datsun 510 station wagon, guaranteed to get you there in all but the coldest of Chicago's winters."

"Thank you," Luther replied. "Thank you very much. When are you off?"

"You're welcome. Tomorrow."

"To save the darker brethren?"

"Something like that. I must admit that I rather hope they might save me!"

"Oh, no," Luther replied. "It is you who must carry the white man's burden. All the movies tell us so."

Chester laughed. The secretary, Miss Lill, came into the room. "The children are ready now," she said. Luther escorted Chester to a large room at the front of the building, formerly the convent's chapel. The sixty-three children of the Learning Network stood in rows. They were blue-black and black, coal black and coffee colored, brown and yellow, and there were Barbara Jean Benedetto's two children who seemed in their whiteness but a lighter ebony shade. A boy, twelve years of age, stepped from the group, one of Chester's poetry students, Pharaoh Perkins. Chester smiled. "We will miss you," Pharaoh Perkins said. "This is for you from all of us." Then he stepped back. Now the magical words of Louis MacNeice washed over him as the children's voices, as pure as the morning's first light, blended together:

> *The sunlight on the garden hardens and grows cold.*
> *We cannot cage the minute within its nets of gold.*
> *When all is told,*
> *We cannot beg for pardon.*

> *Our freedom as free lances advances towards its end.*
> *The earth compels. Upon it, sonnets and birds descend,*
> *And soon, my friend,*
> *We shall have no time for dances.*

> *The sky was good for flying, defying the church bells,*
> *And every evil iron, siren, and what it tells.*
> *The earth compels.*
> *We are dying, Egypt, dying.*

> *And not expecting pardon, hardened with heart anew,*
> *But glad to have sat under thunder and rain with you,*
> *And grateful, too,*
> *For sunlight on the garden.*

Images washed over him like a rainbow. Chester felt all kinds of feelings he had not felt in years. He was alive. He knew it. He could feel it. There was hope, as sure as a star, as perfect as sunlight on the garden.

"Father Chester, would you step forward, please?" Keenesha Taylor, ten years old, smiled at him. Chester rose from his seat and walked to the front of the room. "Namaste! Father Chester!" Keenesha Taylor said as she placed a leather rope with an ebony figurine over his head. The stone face of the akua'ba radiated in the middle of his chest. Then another of the students, Sonceray Jackson, as tall as his waist, handed Chester a package. It was wrapped in iridescent silver with a bright green bow. Chester set the package on one of the desks to remove the wrapping. It was a set of three of Chinua Achebe's novels: *Things Fall Apart, Arrow of God, A Man of the People*. Then there was a party. Cookies and cakes, ice-cream and soft drinks. One by one the students hugged him.

"Thank you for Achebe," Chester said to Luther as Chester was leaving. "And thank you for the poem. Here there will always be sunlight on the garden." Luther smiled. "But I thought yours is an Afro-centric approach," Chester teased. "To what tribe does Louis MacNeice belong?"

"To the tribe we all belong to. Brother MacNeice belongs to the human race," Luther answered. "You see, blackness is a state of mind. It is a political and ethical construct. There have been white folk down through the ages who were black on the inside, which is where it counts. William Wilberforce. William Lloyd Garrison. John Brown.

Viola Liuzzo. Knowledge is power. Would you have me deprive the children of *Sunlight On The Garden*?"

"No," Chester said emphatically. He felt a clear certainty. "I would never do that."

Chapter Fourteen:
Faith

Travers Landeman
Mabouhey
1989

As Travers listened to Chester's story, the empty years of his own life paraded before him. In an unconscious monochrome he had gone from one same day to the next. If the unexamined life is not worth living, neither is the life that provides nothing to examine. Travers had not questioned. He had accepted. He had gone through the motions. Why had he settled for a maid instead of a mate? The wasted years! Why had he pushed his nephew away? If we live without others in our life, he thought as Chester's story unfolded, we do not live.

The low rumble of thunder came from over the horizon. Chester reached to stroke the face of the sleeping child. "When I left St. Ansgar's," he said, "I was drowning in despair." The words hung like smoke between them. I know all about despair, Travers thought. "The theologians tell us that despair is a turning away from God," Chester continued. "It is an insufficient faith."

"I have never understood faith," Travers said.

"Nor did I." Chester laughed. "Even when I was in the seminary. Faith, they said, was giving up and giving in—to God. No matter what. A deranged mother kills her infant and drinks its blood. We must trust in God. An earthquake kills thousands. We must trust in God. I watched as all the good men and good women ran. The doctors, the lawyers, the professors, the butcher, the baker, the truck drivers, secretaries, salesmen. Fear is the most fatal of fevers."

I fled too, Travers thought. "Uncle T, maybe we could go to a movie sometime like when I was little?" I too ran away.

"They fled," Chester continued. "They gave up their homes. They abandoned a rich way of life, a way of life they loved, that went back generations. Yanked themselves away, roots and all. Why? They had faith. They took their bibles and prayer books, crucifixes, and rosary beads with them. To start over in stark places, paved over cornfields! The parishes and parking lots were new. The catechism was the same. Faith, I began to learn, is not enough. It's easy to believe so long as we do not act. To act is to love. True faith is love in action. We must share, we must help, we must reach out."

That would not be a good idea. Chester's haunting words in his sister's garage. *I have my ways.* What ways were those?

"Inclusion, not exclusion! Most lives are wasted, skimming from 'What if?' to 'What a pity!' From 'If only I could!' to 'If only I had!'"

"Yes," Travers whispered. "Yes." Shadows flickered at the jungle's edge. In a scurry of breeze, treetop high, leaves rustled, branch by branch.

"The dry rot of wasted lives! Believers every one! We must move beyond belief. We must cast off the burglar bars of our merchandized lives. Every day I learn this anew: that love is faith incarnate. Luther Custis Towe taught me this. Can you imagine? A black man and a non-Catholic! He believed in children, so he loved children, so he started a school. Faith manifested in love manifested in action. That's what faith is. That's what love is. That's what life is. Luther's faith and love just rolled along like the big Mississippi. We are all tributaries, you see. Luther started upstream, way, way upstream!"

On the mat next to Chester the young girl turned in her sleep. Again, in the darkening of the fire's dying, came the sound of distant rain. "That is the story of my priesthood," Chester said.

"But you are still a priest!"

Chester thought back over the many long years to the last time he had seen his grandmother: *But you are a priest!* "Perhaps," he replied. "But that's not what's important."

"What is?"

"That I am a man." There was a quiet intensity to these words. Chester looked away from the fire for a moment. Then he turned his gaze to Travers. "Remember what I said in my sermon at St. Lucy's? *The job of judging belongs to Someone Else?* But I went on judging just the same. To me, Monsignor Maguire was nothing more than a drunken racist, a petty tyrant. Now I have come to feel pity for him. He was as much a lost soul as I. I was imprisoned by doubt; he, by fear. Where was there love to set us free?"

"But Monsignor Maguire was a drunken racist and a petty tyrant!' Travers exclaimed.

"He was also a man. But I tossed him into the garbage heap like a worn-out shoe. No one is beyond salvation. No one is beyond love. It's not just that damnation is a lot more fun, it's that it's also a lot easier. Keeps us, the holy ones, holy, damning others less worthy than ourselves! Salvation is too egalitarian. History is one great bloodbath of the saved versus the unsaved. Killing is less trouble than loving by great measure. I should have reached out to Monsignor Maguire. It was my job to love. After all, I was a priest."

"You still are."

"Perhaps, but there's a difference now."

"A difference?"

"The difference is that now, I hope, I am a human being first. We must strive to be human beings first. We are all members of the same tribe. There is sunlight on all our gardens. It was Father Malcolm who taught me this. He did not say, 'Follow me.' He said, 'Walk along beside.'"

"Father Malcolm?"

"Marguerite's grandfather. This lovely child's..." Chester stroked the face of the sleeping girl. "This lovely child's great-grandfather, Schugara's great-grandfather. 'We must search for *a* way,' he said, 'for *the* way does not exist.'"

Again Chester began to raise himself. Again Travers took him by the arm. "I would like to know more," he said. "Tell me of your coming to Mabouhey. Tell me about Father Malcolm."

Chapter Fifteen:
Peace

Chester O'Reilly
Mabouhey
1975

From Chicago Chester took the train to New Orleans, a swamp of a city on a sewer of a bay. There he boarded an aged tramp steamer scheduled to hopscotch from island to Caribbean island, including at some point, depending on weather and currents, the island of Frederique. The ship, if it could be called that, was named the *Caribbean Star*. For the most part its captain, one Oswego Tobias George, remained drunk in his cabin. Chester was assigned a small room near the boiler with barely enough room for himself, his trunk, and his duffel bag. Now and then a clap of water came against its one small window to leave behind short-lived blisters in a skin of grime. Like a wounded animal scraping across the desert, the *Caribbean Star* pulled itself forward.

Night and day metallic gurgles shivered through Chester's cabin. He felt as if he were trapped inside the artery of a dying heart.

He had finished reading *Things Fall Apart* on the train. Now he lay on the cot in the dingy room, a naked light bulb swinging from the ceiling like a dirge. He opened *Arrow of God* but concentrating was not possible. He returned Achebe to the duffel bag. The seas were not rough, but they were not calm either. Gray rainy days followed one another like forgotten dreams. Most of the time Chester stayed in his cabin. Trays of mysterious and flavorless food were brought to him by a young man who couldn't have been more than nineteen years old. His name was Paolo; like Chester he had been orphaned at an early age. Sometimes when he was off duty Paolo came to Chester's room. Chester listened as Paolo bubbled on about music. He played the guitar and was determined one day, someday, to leave the likes of the *Caribbean Star* for the coffeehouses of New Orleans or Santo Domingo. The few times Chester ventured out of his cabin all he could see were shrouds of mist. The weary vessel dug itself forward. Then, without warning, late one afternoon, as twilight approached, there were angry winds and great walls of water.

In a delirium of pain Chester rolled in his bed. His breaths came in sharp stabs. He thought his stomach would explode. Into the night like angry lovers ship and sea struggled. Then the storm slipped away and, in the reassurance of dawn, the sky was new, deep and white. The *Caribbean Star* slid over the still water like a song. Liquor flowed as the men told tales of hurricanes past and it was good, so good, to be alive. Chester too was laughing on the deck, dancing in the sailors' triumph. Then everything was a blur. He could not remember how it was he returned to his room. Sometime in the night Paolo entered. His body lay next to Chester's and his lips were at Chester's neck. One of his hands rested at Chester's waist. There was a gentleness to this touching that was like soft music. In the dream-world of near-death and resurrection Chester did not want the music to stop. He gave himself to Paolo's scent: a field of wheat newly wet with rain. Then Chester came awake. He pulled himself to the edge of the bed. Paolo reached for Chester's hand as Paolo's blond hair fell over his soft brown eyes. The sweetness of his face reminded Chester of a flower.

"Please want me," the young man said. "I thought we were going to die."

"I thought we were going to die, too," Chester said. Then he brought Paolo's hand to his lips and kissed it. "Lie back down," he said. Paolo started to unbutton his shirt, but Chester stopped him. "Lie back down," he said again. Then he put his arms around the young man's body and held him close. They fell asleep in each other's arms as the *Caribbean Star*, brave and unbroken, kept into the night.

*   *   *

Chester spent one night on the island of Frederique, in the Papagayo Hotel, a hut really. He thought about the hurricane's aftermath, how he had held Paolo in his arms, how Paolo felt and smelled. I have been a hypocrite, he thought, remembering the night he had come upon Easy in the seminary's showers. He fell to his knees and prayed. Night came, reaching out to him like his grandmother's arms. He went into and out of sleep. He heard again his grandmother's voice: "You are a priest!" He struggled through the dark, puzzling over his sexuality. He remembered Diana Weyer eating ice-cream in Merrick Park those many years ago and he remembered the tightness he had felt when he'd heard Easy's moanings. Does it matter? Does it matter at all? His religion taught that homosexuality is a sin. But now in this night Chester refused to think of sin in such simple terms. He had held Paolo in his arms, nothing more. He had summoned the strength to keep his vow. Wasn't the triumph, not the temptation, what mattered? But suppose he hadn't? Suppose that the young man had come to him and they had shared the life of their bodies? What then? Chester could no longer think of such comfort as sin, not any longer, not from this night forward. I will no longer judge, he said to himself. "But you are a priest!" his grandmother's voice echoed again. No, he thought. Not anymore. From now on I will be a man.

*   *   *

In a small boat, water sloshing in its bottom, a man named Hernando took Chester from the island of Frederique to the island of Mabouhey. Father Malcolm was sitting on the shore with his feet curled under him. As the small boat approached, a young man, nineteen or twenty years old, helped Father Malcolm to his feet. The old priest swept the sand from his clothing with both hands. Chester stepped to the shore, duffel bag over his shoulder.

"I am Father Malcolm and this is Christian." Father Malcolm reached out his hands to Chester. The few strands of the old priest's hair were bright white. His face, neck, forehead, and pate were bronze. He had the bluest of blue eyes, fierce and alive, and his sharp nose, slightly off-center, jutted from his face like a hook. He was wearing tattered pants whose leg bottoms were rags, a tattered shirt thinned by washings, and sandals made of banyan leaves and the treads of old tires. He wore no collar, no ring, no cross. One of his gnarled hands rested on the young man's shoulder. The other gripped a mahogany walking stick. Father Malcolm was of medium height. He carried his many years on the small frame of his wiry body as if they were not there at all. What was most noteworthy was that Father Malcolm's face was painted with bright colors, greens and reds, blues and yellows, sharp and geometric.

Chester had worried about this moment. Should I fall to my knees and ask for blessing? he had wondered as Hernando's boat neared shore and the old priest and the young man materialized from jungle and sand.

"Welcome to Mabouhey," Father Malcolm said. "I am dying."

Chester did not know how to respond. He stood there as Father Malcolm waited. Then, with the studied slowness of his years, the old priest removed his hand from his companion's shoulder. Two men came from the jungle. They wore only skirts and sandals. They stood there waiting, like bookends, black bodies burning blacker. Behind them Chester saw the green glaze of jungle, hardened in sunlight, netted in gold. The voices of the children of the Learning Network came to him: "And grateful, too, for sunlight on the garden."

"Namaste!" Chester said, cupping the akua' ba the children of the Learning Network had given him and then letting it loose to swing back and forth.

"Namaste, Mabouhey!" the old priest and his companions replied, their joy racing through the jungle. "Thank God it is you who has come," Father Malcolm said. "Thank God it is you who has come. He works in mysterious ways."

*   *   *

One of the men lashed Chester's duffel bag onto a mule and they set off into the jungle. In the distance the heartbeat of drums began, more alive with every step. After two hours they entered a clearing where the people of the village had gathered, seated on mats around a central fire. It was a great feast: pineapple, mango, papaya, potato, corn, fish, duck, turkey, pheasant. From earthen mugs they drank a steaming beverage. Soon stars began poking through the evening sky. The people sang and danced. Many fell asleep in the open, their arms around each other. Chester was taken to a small hut and soon he too was dreaming dreams that can only be dreamt close to the sea. The fire waned to a bed of whispering embers. Drums faded into a faint throbbing and soon into silence. Then, in the night, while dreams ruled over them like the ocean, came a great trembling. Men, women, and children woke from the ground or came running from their huts to gather again in the clearing.

"Katausa!" they shouted. They took each other's hands and waited, turning in the direction of the great volcano. Brief blazing arcs burst from its top, a vortex of shooting stars. Do I dream? Am I alive? Chester sat with his legs crossed beneath him. A girl ten or eleven years old, the color of coffee with cream, with long black hair, a beautiful child who would grow into a beautiful woman, came to him and sat on his lap. The men began to chant and the women to sing.

The men chanted:

> Sannu! Sannu! Come Away! Come Away!
> Yauwa sannu! Come away!

The women sang:

> Barka da yamma! Let peace return.
> Keep us, Katausa, awake in your dreams.
> Teach us, Katausa, to love like the wind.
> Don Allah! Let peace return.

The men chanted:

> Sannu! Sannu! Come Away! Come Away!
> Yauwa sannu! Come away!

The women sang:

> Barka da yamma! Let peace return.
> Keep us, Katausa, awake in your dreams.
> Teach us, Katausa, to love like the wind.
> Don Allah! Let peace return.

As one:

> Na gode! Come away! Come away!
> Na gode! Come away!

The volcano seemed to heed their incantations; its roarings ceased their song of fire to return the night and all of the night's spirits back to the rightful rule of the stars. As the chant-song ended, Father Malcolm seated himself beside Chester and the sleeping child.

"You know, I was sent here many years ago, as punishment for my transgressions. I had taken to drink, too much, much too much. They were building churches so fast, all over the west side, carving parishes out of parishes, until there was a church on every corner. The money poured in but it was never enough. The Cardinal always wanted more." The old priest shook his head slowly; there was a deep sadness to his every word. Chester looked from one end of the clearing to the other. People were returning to their huts, or giving themselves back to sleep next to the dying fire. "All that was a lifetime ago, another time in another place," Father Malcolm said, "and now I am dying."

Once again Chester did not know how to respond. He could see starlight dancing over the old priest's face as they both sat in silence. Then, without conscious thought, words came from him: "I have been afraid to love."

"There is no greater sin," Father Malcolm said softly. "I know this much about you, though, already: you will come, as I have, to thank God for this place." The old priest steadied himself to leave, but Chester held forth his hand in restraint.

"Tell me more, Father, please. Tell me about Mabouhey."

"As you wish," Father Malcolm replied. "I came here, I was sent here many, many years ago. 1925. I was like you, not many years out of the seminary. A true believer. Only problem was that nobody *here* had asked me to come. Wasn't *their* idea. Even so, I was determined. I would show them, the savages as I thought of them then, that is. They must be made to see the error of their ways. I would lead them forward. To the truth. To the *One* Truth. All they had to do was what I commanded. Well, it was a rough first year, let me tell you!"

"What did you do?"

"Well, the truth of the matter is that all the time I was preaching, the villagers were doing, but I was too blinded by my own ego to see. Theory and practice! Everything was backwards. I had it all down pat: Jesus said we must love one another. Visit the sick. Clothe the naked. Feed the hungry. Here I was, a guest really, basking in the sin of pride. It took me some time to realize it, but that's what it was: pride. My way or no way. I had *the* answer. The people simply looked at me with a sort of pity. They couldn't have been more understanding. They constructed a hut to serve as the chapel. I taught the young men to serve as altar boys. At Mass there would be two or three women in attendance, sewing or pounding corn, until just before the elevation of the Host. Then the entire village would rush in like carnival goers. Eventually I found out that what fascinated them so much was the altar boys' shaking the communion bells. They thought the bells were the voice of the Great Spirits."

The old priest paused. A wide smile came to his face. "Well, you can imagine how I reacted! Blasphemy! Horror! Making the Eucharist into a spectacle! The people gave me these hurt looks. The last thing they had intended was disrespect. They were doing their best to accommodate me—a strange white man—who had shown up like a ghost out of thin air! It was impossible to stay angry with them. Little by little, I, who was to have shown them the errors of their ways, began to see the folly of mine. It was a gradual thing, like a child learning to walk. Somewhere along the way, I'm not sure when, exactly, I became one of them."

Chester did not know what to make of this. There was a serenity about Father Malcolm that was overpowering. Chester was reminded of Father Raulston's quiet intensity and he vowed that he would listen before he spoke, that he would observe, study and learn, before he would attempt to teach. Maybe faith only comes by living, he thought, maybe it is only by doing that doubt is banished.

"Many years ago," the old priest continued, "a great hurricane came across the island. The chapel was one of the few structures that survived. The people took its salvation as a sign. There was much weeping, for many were killed, among them one of the council's elders, one of the most revered griots..."

"I'm sorry, Father," Chester interrupted.

"Ah, oh, yes. A griot is an historian. A griot learns at his father's and grandfather's knee, at his mother's and grandmother's, he remembers and memorizes, to recount the people's story all the way back to the dawn of memory, to the time from across the water, to the time of Kima and before. The griot had perished, but the chapel survived. So it was decided to use it as the taroumpa hut, for the taroumpa hut had also perished."

"The taroumpa hut?"

"I thought you might ask," the old priest laughed. "You might think of it as a meeting hall, city hall, and church all combined into one. So the chapel was transformed into the taroumpa hut, for, truly, we did not need two churches. That's about the one time, really, that I did play an instrumental role in changing the village's way of life. It was quite a change. It just came to me. A vision. The six remaining elders came to my hut. They said the Spirits had spoken and that I should take the griot's place on the council. I didn't know how to respond. It was a great honor, but I did not think myself worthy. I should say that fifteen years had passed by then; I was still a relatively young man. Another consideration, I thought, was my skin color. 'But that is only on the outside,' they said."

Chester remembered Luther Custis Towe's words: "There have been white folk down through the ages who were black on the inside, which is where it counts." Here, too, he thought, studying Father Malcolm, there is sunlight on the garden.

"'Does not your Jesus teach that we are all God's children?' the elders asked," the old priest continued. "Of course they had me there. So I agreed." Father Malcom raised himself to leave.

"But you haven't told me what it was you changed!"

"Ah, yes, that," Father Malcolm replied, touching the tips of the fingers of both hands to his cheeks and sitting back down. "I refused to have my face scarred. I couldn't understand how such a gentle people could practice such barbarism. But I had to have the traditional markings on my face, the elders said. The Spirits were calling me to the taroumpa hut. To serve, my face must be scarred. It had always been so."

"What did you do?"

"When the day for the ceremony arrived, I went to the taroumpa hut with my face painted like a human

Picasso. I stood outside the door. I wore the correct shells on ankles and wrists and the proper herbs and flowers around my neck and in my hair. I carried the traditional ceremonial spear and shield. I had bathed my body in coconut milk. The people gathered, standing or sitting, watching and waiting and wondering. One by one the elders came to the door of the taroumpa hut. Each looked me up and down before returning inside. I waited in the full sun. The hours passed. The paint melted into my skin, but I remained as erect as a Hausa warrior. At last a great cry came from inside the taroumpa hut. The villagers began singing and shouting, especially the women, as the elders came to the door and extended their arms to me. I went inside."

"It was a great thing you did."

"It was not of my doing. Remember, Chester, we are intermediaries. I'm sure you were taught that much in seminary. Ours is not the glory. God spoke *through* me. Why I was chosen, I cannot say. Perhaps God chooses us all, all the time, only we are too wrapped up in our own petty worries to pay attention. I say this with all humility, for I had not thought the matter through beforehand. I don't think it was the fear of the physical pain of having my face slashed, but, of course, it is not possible to know such a thing for certain. When the elders came to me, I heard words come from my mouth as if some Other Voice were speaking: 'We must not mutilate our bodies,' I heard this Other Voice say as clearly as I am speaking now. Ever since, from that time on, many years now, there has been no mutilation on Mabouhey. Not of the men. Not of the women."

"The women?"

"In many African cultures the puberty rite for girls requires the mutilation of their genitalia. Mabouhey, it pains me to say, was no exception. No culture is perfect because human beings are imperfect. The challenge is to make ourselves and our culture less imperfect, little by little. The culture we shape shapes those who are to follow. That is why humility is one of the great virtues. Identifying problems is always a lot easier than devising solutions. Frequently the cure turns out to be worse than the disease."

"I'm afraid I am not following you,"

"Scarification and female genital mutilation had been a part of this village's way of life told and retold by griot after griot, generation on generation. The village and its people survived. They survived flood and hurricane. They overcame enslavement. They did not merely survive, but did so in as near full happiness as any culture that has ever been. It has taken me many years to understand this. On Mabouhey people care about and take care of one another. They share. A person's worth is not measured in material things, but in qualities such as generosity and caring. Theirs is an idealized Christianity, one that never lost its soul. Every adult is parent to every child. It requires wisdom—and, equally important, courage—to abandon customs that have existed for centuries, to see through new eyes, to recognize that not all that has been handed down is necessarily good, that not all customs are for the better. It calls for trust and understanding to know which is which, strength to keep the good and jettison the harmful and in so doing not destroy the fabric of society. When you tamper with myth, you are performing surgery on the soul, and you had better know what you're doing."

"How do you do that?" Chester asked. "How do you know what you're doing?"

"You don't," Father Malcolm replied. "This is where humility comes in. The people of the village leave such matters to their elders, men, and for the past twenty years or so, men and women who have weathered life's storms to practice wisdom in so far as it is possible for human beings to develop such a god-like virtue. The elders never make a major decision without a great deal of thinking and praying, much drinking and smoking and dancing. We take time, as much time as is needed. Sometimes we are in the taroumpa hut for days. We wait for the Spirits to speak. When we are of one mind and one heart and one soul, the rightness of our decision is apparent to all and there is great rejoicing."

"Somewhat like the Supreme Court?"

"If you like," the old priest replied. "But the difference is that those who go into the taroumpa hut are bound only by their hearts and minds to do their best for what is best for all. There is no written set of rules. The Supreme Court didn't abolish slavery. In fact, the Dred Scott decision sanctioned re-enslavement. Despite treaties and laws, the Supreme Court didn't protect Native Americans. A better analogy, I believe, is Jesus and His Apostles."

"Judas was one of Jesus' apostles."

"Yes. If even Jesus can make a mistake, what makes us mere mortals believe that we are infallible? The problem with western thought is precisely this: its underlying arrogance, its misguided certainty that, if only we tinker long enough, we human beings can devise the one perfect system. One size fits all. Process becomes more important than the end result. Is Mabouhey a democracy? The definition of *democracy* could be stretched and stretched, but by any recognizable measure, no. Are the people happy? Without doubt. Is Mabouhey a civilized place? Without question. Here there are no locks on doors. Which is more important? The journey or the destination? Process or end result?"

"I should say," Chester replied, "that this is the perfect opportunity for me to practice humility, to admit that I have much to learn before attempting to answer such questions!"

Father Malcolm laughed. Again there was thunder in the distance. "I sense that your soul has been the scene of many a battle," he said. "But it is getting late and I am an old man. We will continue this conversation, I am sure, many times." The old priest steadied himself on Chester's shoulders. Then he stood before Chester and raised his hand in blessing. All the while Father Malcolm's granddaughter had slept in the younger priest's lap, but now she stirred, rubbing her eyes with both hands.

"Come along, Marguerite," Father Malcolm said. Hand in hand the child and the old priest walked across the clearing to Father Malcolm's hut. A woman appeared in the doorway. Dazzling stars sang silent songs as Chester fell asleep next to the slumbering fire.

*   *   *

In the months that followed Chester marveled at the simple beauty of life on Mabouhey. The woman he had seen that first night in the doorway of Father Malcolm's hut was named Carisa. She was Father Malcolm's wife. The girl who had fallen asleep on Chester's lap, Marguerite, was their granddaughter. Chester did not find this knowledge troubling. He could feel their love. Can love ever be a sin? He would not think so.

Chester helped Father Malcolm teach the children, writing, numbering, caring. He thought of Luther Custis Towe, of the mission statement of the Learning Network: *We like ourselves. We respect others. We learn to deal with conflict. We reach our goals through persistence and determination. We accept the consequences of our actions.* Men and women worked in the fields, tending to long rows of vegetables, bananas, and coffee. They fished, hunted, and worked in a great thatched hall, sorting, measuring, packing. Once a month a ship from Frederique came to empty the warehouse in exchange for canned goods, tools, and housewares. A month after Chester's arrival a man and a woman came to him, the young man named Christian walking behind. Chester remembered Christian from Chester's first moment on the island; thereafter he had seen him working in boats, weaving repairs in the butterfly nets, singing. Christian had large brown eyes. His teeth were perfect white rows. There was a gentleness to him that reminded Chester of a feather.

"This is our third son," the man said. "He would like to live with you." Christian stood behind his father. Chester saw him raise his head to look over his father's shoulder directly into Chester's eyes. "Please want me." Chester remembered Paolo's words that night on the *Caribbean Star*. "Please want me." Now Christian's soft eyes spoke Paolo's words to him.

"I must speak with Father Malcolm," Chester said.

"That is good," the woman replied. "That is as it should be. We will return in the evening." As they departed Christian turned his head back to look again into Chester's eyes. "Please want me."

"I have been here many years," Father Malcolm said, as he and Chester sat in rocking chairs on his front porch. "Carisa came to me six months after I arrived. We have three children and seven grandchildren. My Marguerite is as pretty as a flower." The old priest stroked the hair of the coffee with cream colored child who bounced on his lap. He set her down. Chester watched as the child chased a butterfly across the grassland. "I don't believe I have told you," Father Malcolm said, "but the people here are Hausa. Their songs trace their ancestry all the way back to Kano."

"Kano?"

"Kano is a city in what today is Northern Nigeria," Father Malcolm said. "Two hundred years ago the Hausa were a mighty people. Then they lost a war to the neighboring Fulani. The Hausa king escaped into the jungle, but his eldest son, Kima, was captured. These are the songs the people sing by the fire."

I must write this down, Chester thought. Then he was unsure. Would the written word contaminate and constrict?

"Kima was one of the lucky ones. He was sold into slavery."

"That doesn't sound lucky to me," Chester said.

"Such a point of view is incurably western," the old priest replied. "You see, if Kima had been captured a generation before, he would have been tortured to death. Slavery was a small step forward on mankind's slow journey towards light. The Hausa have the most beautiful song about the chains that bind the slaves together as they are marched to the ships." The old priest closed his eyes and sang: "*Zoom, gulley, gulley, gulley, zoom, gulley, gulley.*" From inside the hut Carisa's voice answered: "*Tra, la, la, la, la, la! Tra, la, la, la, la, la!*" Then, from far and near, the same syllables resounded, the deep voices of men followed by the honeyed voices of women:

Zoom, gulley, gulley, gulley.
Zoom, gulley, gulley.

Tra, la, la, la, la, la.
Tra, la, la, la, la, la.

"What the song celebrates is that the pain of the chains is a reminder of life and that where there is life, no matter how crushed or how broken, there is hope. This is what the griots teach us. Are you familiar with the middle passage, my son?"

"The middle passage?"

"The slave trade was a triangular trade, global in its reach. Ships would leave the ports of England laden with fabric and utensils, technological wonders like the compass, plus, of course, firearms, for the coasts of Africa to be traded for human cargo. That was the first leg. The second leg—the middle passage—was transporting Africans captured or sold into slavery to the plantations of the New World, where the ships loaded tobacco and corn, potatoes and furs for the third and final leg back to Liverpool, London, and Bristol. Then the cycle continued. This is what the griots sing about their ancestors, packed in chains in the bowels of the ships, in stench and filth:

This is the middle passage,
The memory and promise of home.
Will darkness unlit by starlight
Give way to dawn?

We must hold close to each other, no matter,
Until after the water ends.
We must love one another surely—
Stronger than chains.

Flat and fearing: we dance!
Chants! Rainforest! Drum!
Until the darkness relents,
Hold hands! Hold hands!

We are home.

As the griots tell it, Kima lived to fight another day. The slave ship carried him to Jamaica. Years passed, but finally he escaped, fleeing to the mountains. He was one of the first Maroons."

Father Malcolm saw the puzzled look on Chester's face and went on. "In Jamaica escaped slaves hid in the mountains. Eventually there were so many of them that for over a century they constituted their own nation within a nation. The British, after many losses, decided to leave the Maroons alone. A peace treaty was signed, which permitted the Maroons to stay where they were. A year after his escape Kima returned to the plantation where he had been enslaved, killed its owner, and freed the remaining slaves. They fled to the mountains to join the Maroons, but Kima and twenty-eight others of the Hausa tribe were determined to return home, to the Hausa kingdom in Africa. They made their way to a fishing village on Jamaica's north coast, which, in his honor, has been called 'Runaway Bay' ever since. Kima stole a boat; he and his people ended up here on Mabouhey, over two centuries ago."

"An amazing story!" Chester said.

"You must write this down," Father Malcolm said. "It is something I should have done a long time ago. Now you must do it for me." There was a confused look on Chester's face. "We can learn from books as well as from the griot," Father Malcolm continued. "Western civilization doesn't have to be destructive. The problem lies in its chauvinism, its insistence that it has all the answers. It leaves no place for the heart. Stripping away its arrogance is a large task, I admit. Remember, it's not the prophets who lead us astray but their disciples. Jesus was angered at the moneylenders in the temple, not at Mary Magdalene. His followers today? Sorry men in expensive suits who drive Cadillacs and rant against food stamps. Yes, you must write down Kima's story, but, in doing so, you must be sure it doesn't degenerate into dogma. Dogma is death."

Chester thought of Father Raulston and he also thought of Luther Custis Towe. Then he saw Christian standing on the other side of the clearing.

"The young man named Christian wants to live with me," he said.

"Do you want to live with him?" the old priest asked. He waited as if he had inquired about the time or the weather, but, to Chester, the question went to the depth of his being. He was face to face with himself and for the first time he did not want to turn away.

"Yes."

"Christian wants to live with you." The question was posed as a statement. Chester nodded his head. "Then where is the problem?" Chester said nothing. Father Malcolm continued. "You see, when it comes to sex, the only taboo the Hausa have is against abstinence. They believe that celibacy is unnatural. They do not understand celibacy for the Hausa believe that having sex is rejoining God. Their culture makes no distinction between heterosexuality and homosexuality. They judge not so that they be not judged. Jesus, remember Him? put it the same way: we are commanded to love one another."

The next day Christian moved into Chester's hut. Within the year Father Malcolm died, his grave high on the side of Katausa, marked with a simple cross. The elders came to Chester. They painted his face, and he took Father Malcolm's place on the tribal council and went into the taroumpa hut. The years passed one into the other. People danced and died and wed. Time was the most considerate of jailers.

Chapter Sixteen:
Doubt

Joe Rogers
Mabouhey
1991

It is my policy to avoid the clergy at all cost. As a child, I had the good fortune to be raised a Unitarian. Unitarianism is the uncola of religions. Unitarians compensate for their lack of dogma by flirting fanatically with the social issue of the day. United in anarchy the Unitarian army marches from yesterday's topic of outrage to tomorrow's, waving the latest issue of *The Nation* and singing *The Ballad of Joe Hill* or *We Shall Overcome*. When I was nine years old, my parents made the mistake of insisting that I continue to accompany them to the Little Church On The Side Of The Hill — Unitarians have a predilection for cute church names — if *and only if* I really wanted to, out of what they called my own free will. I was old enough to decide for myself. This momentous announcement was made with Unitarian conviction, which is pedigreed pride, descended from a distinguished lineage of New England unction. Thanks but no thanks, I said. I preferred to stay home reading comic books in my bedroom.

Please understand: I loved my mother and father. As the years have passed, I have come to appreciate them even more. Mark Twain observed that he was amazed at his father's ignorance when Mark Twain was nineteen but even more amazed by how much his father had learned by the time Mark Twain turned twenty-one. So it has been with me. My parents fed me. They clothed me. They did not extinguish even one burning cigarette into any part of my youthful flesh. They were nice to each other and to me. (In the pantheon of virtues niceness has no altar: go figure!) So, when I tell you that I can to this day see the shock on their faces at my unexpected and disappointing decision, please do not think of my parents with contempt. It had not occurred to them that lips brought close to the Unitarian chalice would choose *not* to partake of its proffered wine of doubt, incredulity, and righteous indignation. As I have grown older, I have come to understand that all religions suffer from an acute paralysis of cognitive dissonance. Each flavor strives mightily to pretend at tolerance when each is partisan to its one and only lock on truth. Does Bloomingdale's shop at Macy's? What the world needs is for the Grand Mufti of Mecca, the Chief Rabbi of Jerusalem, the

Pope, and the Archbishop of Canterbury to play pinochle on a regular basis. Stoically my parents pretended to respect my decision. In turn I thanked them for their misplaced trust. Sunday mornings they spent in The Little Church On The Side Of The Hill denouncing the Rosenberg verdict while in my room Superman and Spider-Woman battled the forces of evil to preserve the American way of life. You can well understand my anxiety, therefore, at Smith's insistence that we take the mask I had stumbled upon to "Father Chester," whoever he might be. "You take the mask to Father Chester," I implored. "Let me take my entourage back to Frederique. I am their gaggle-meister."

"No, señor," Smith replied. "Dat will not be de way of de doing. De mask eet has come to you. You must take eet to de Padrecito. Deese ease de way of de doing." So Hernando's mules truckled us through the jungle's chiaroscuro, my ankle swelling, as we bounded along. At last, as I have told you, we came to a clearing where huts circled an open fire. The strangest person I have ever seen appeared before us, hands extended in greeting. He wore some sort of sarong, green into blue into yellow. He was bare-chested except for an ebony figurine that swung from his neck on a leather cord. His hair, full, brown, and streaked with silver, reached to his shoulders. His cheeks and forehead were leathery lines between stripes of bright colors. He looked like a pirate in an Errol Flynn movie. You expected one eye to be covered with a patch, but both burned a soft hazel brown, alive, alert, on fire. He wore sandals with straps laced up over his ankles.

"I am Father Chester," he said at last. "I do not see many Americans. I have been expecting you. Please bring the mask inside." He noticed the surprised look on my face. "Drums," he said simply. We entered a large round hut. There was no altar inside. There were no statues, no benches, no prayer books. A large mat covered the center of the floor. There was a small table. Just below the high dome of its thatched roof, windows, as if holding hands, ran all around, one into the other, in a ring around the rosie of sky.

"This is the taroumpa hut," the priest said. "It is the house of the Spirits, of those who have gone on before." We sat, legs crossed. Three men entered, each blacker than the one before. Then three women joined us. Men and women alike wore sarongs and sandals. That was it, except that each had a necklace, too, of shells and of leather, with stones and wood carvings. From outside drums pounded. The men and women started to chant. Steaming mugs were passed around and a great pipe of burning ganja. They all sat with their eyes closed, so I closed my own as well. Visions of my mother and father ran through my mind. I saw golden cities and the dreamworld of rivers and valleys. I rocked back and forth with my left leg tucked perpendicularly under my right to cushion my tormented ankle. Pain faded as if I were suddenly out of its range. I saw the smiling faces of people I did not recognize who spoke to me in languages I did not know. As one we came to our feet dancing. "Father of Water and Father of Wood," a woman shouted, "guide us. Show us a way." "Mother of Earth and Mother of Sky," one of the men chanted, "'protect your children." "As the leaves are many..." Another voice. "...So the tree is one." Now there was a soundtapestry of drum, chant, flute, and song.

"Lord of Here and Lord of Hereafter, we honor you."

"We speak your names."

"Kima."

"Katausa."

"Jesus."

"Malcolm."

"We praise you." "We honor you." "Hear us." "The fire which warms us." "The sea which feeds us." "Water of river and water of rain!" "Starlight and moonlight!" "Speak to your children!" One by one the men and women fell to the floor, exhausted. Inside and from without drum and chant faded to murmur.

"Sun! Sun! Sun!" The words came from me and then I too fell to the floor. I do not expect you to understand any of this. I do not understand it myself. We drank from the mugs; we smoked from the pipe. We did this a lot. Then all of us who were in that room were not in that room. We were in the mind of God. This sounds crazy, but it's the best I can do. Stick with me here. We were all drunk, you say. Entranced in narcotic stupor. Perhaps. All I know is that I heard voices I did not recognize in languages I do not know and yet I understood with an understanding that, as I have heard and can now attest, surpasses all knowledge. Now and then someone jumped to her feet to dance in a susurration of music and chant. We did not speak and yet we spoke. We were one. Lords, gods, and ghosts! Hosanna in the highest! Even so and thus it was: we had decided. The mask was a sign; I was its messenger. The time was upon us. From the people's long struggle, from the time of Kima, from the time of Malcolm, in the shelter of the gods of forest and mountain and rain, Mabouhey would take its rightful place in the family of nations: the Commonwealth of the Island of Mabouhey was born.

*   *   *

"You see," the priest explained the following afternoon when I finally awoke, "until recently the Generalissimo left us alone. We were, as he saw it, just a bunch of savages on an island too small to matter. But then the airport went in on Frederique and that professor started digging around. Hernando opened his guest house. It is becoming, I fear, a different story. Sometime I must tell you about Mabouhey, our history, the ways of our people. It is a way of life that must be preserved."

I am not easily impressed with what people say, a legacy, no doubt, of my youthful taste of Unitarianism. But these were determined words and they moved me. We were in a small hut. I sat on a bed, my left dangling over its side. The priest, who, as I said, looked like a voodoo man, stood in the doorway. Now he entered and sat in a rocking chair.

"That is why it was decided to become our own country. Last night, in the taroumpa hut, the spirit house of those who have gone on before. You remember. The mask is a sign. You are its messenger."

Things happen to me, I thought. Why? "How does one go about doing that? Becoming a country?"

"I have no idea," the priest answered. "But, if we listen, the Spirits will show us a way. They always do. They did last night. Do you remember?"

Yes, I remembered. I wasn't sure what I remembered, but I remembered. "Why was I there?" I asked.

"You were chosen by the mask," Father Chester replied. There was a matter of fact tone in his voice as if he were reviewing multiplication tables with a child. "To come to us."

"Why me?"

"I haven't the foggiest idea."

"But I did not ask to be chosen!"

"Did you ask to be born? Don't you believe in miracles?"

"After last night I'm not so sure!"

"Believe! Believe!"

"Why should I?"

"Because there is no other choice."

"Belief requires action. If we believe, we must act."

"Precisely!"

"Not my long suit. I am more acted upon than acting."

Father Chester paused. "I was once a lot like you."

"How so?" As soon as these words were out of my mouth, I regretted them. Some doors are best left unopened.

"I too had nothing to believe in."

Now I paused. "I believe in vodka!"

"So I have heard," the priest responded. His serious demeanor made it clear that he was refusing to be a co-conspirator in wit. "Surely there is more to life than vodka!"

I thought of my parents; I thought of Val. I thought of Zero and "Sister Loltun" and Jimmy. I nodded my head.

"Then you must help us."

"I'm not sure I'm following."

"If your definition of life begins and ends with vodka, there is no point to your being here, taking up space, using up oxygen. Life must go beyond vodka. We must love one another, which means we must help one another."

"But I have no desire to be Kazimierz Pulaski or the Marquis de Lafayette!"

"My guess is that they didn't either. It is not my decision to make. It is yours. Crawl into your bottle and stay there if you like. Do not expect me to applaud." He rose from the rocking chair. "Let me look at your ankle."

"It was injured when I was chosen to find the mask," I said with what I intended as permissible irony. "The subsequent jaunt through the jungle didn't help either."

"Or last night's dancing."

"Or last night's dancing."

"Christian should examine you."

A few minutes later he returned, the man called Christian at his side. Christian was the most beautiful man I had ever seen, a manly man in his thirties. He had a full, round, black smile, as bright as the brightest day. I know you say: men are handsome, not beautiful. But Christian had such a glory of face and body that I can only describe his power and grace as the perfection of masculine beauty. He was an ebony butterfly made of iron.

"I am Christian," he said simply. "Let's have a look." These last words leapt across continents and sea. Christian's strong hands wrapped themselves around my ankle. I winced in pain.

"I did not mean to hurt you," he said softly. "Your ankle is broken. I will have to set it." He turned to face Father Chester. "I am worried about infection. We must send for Marguerite."

There was in the woman's name the power of song. Yes, yes, I wanted to shout. Send for Marguerite. She was as yet but a name, like a blossom whose existence, though unseen, perfumes the full forest. As parched earth cries out for rain, I longed that this word, *Marguerite*, become flesh. Marguerite would save me. From what?

"You know how Quince feels about Americans," Father Chester said.

"I need Marguerite to assist me," Christian replied, "to make sure nothing goes wrong." These last words tolled like a funeral bell.

"What does that mean?" I shouted. "'...nothing goes wrong'?"

"I am sorry I could not get here sooner," he said. "But it will be best if Marguerite is here as well."

"I don't mean to be unappreciative," I replied. I swung both my legs over the side of the bed and sat up. "But it is *my* ankle. I'm attached to it, you might say. There must be a hospital in Frederique City. If it's all the same to you..."

"Yes," Christian interrupted. "There is a hospital in Frederique City. You are welcome to go there if you like. But that would not be wise. It would take half a day to get you to the coast. You would have to be carried on a stretcher. You can no longer walk and even riding a mule is out of the question. Then, once we get you to the coast, you would have to wait for Hernando's boat. How long? Who knows? I am worried about gangrene. Still..." He turned and walked out of the hut. Gangrene! Wait! I wanted to shout. Come back! I knew nothing about gangrene. I didn't need to know. The sound of the word says it all. Onomatopoeia if ever there were! Imagine a cheese called *gangrene*. Would you eat it? Sweat bubbled on my forehead. I felt dizzy and lay back down.

"I know you did not mean it," Father Chester said, "but you have insulted him. Christian could feel your mistrust. I could feel it. That is so like Americans! You give blind obedience to anyone who has the right piece of paper. You look to paper for protection."

"And?"

"And, instead, you should put your trust in people. Christian does not have it in him to do you or anyone harm. He has been taking care of us, all of us, for many years. He studied for five years, for five very long years, at St. James Medical School on the island of Dominica. Those were long years, very long years." The power in these words was like a force of nature. Father Chester started for the door. Then he turned. "We will do whatever it is you want. As you observed, the ankle is yours. But you must make up your mind quickly. I could see that Christian is worried."

I tried to lift myself. The priest blurred into a wild figure silhouetted in the doorway. "We should send at once for Marguerite," he said. "The sooner she gets here, the sooner Christian can start."

"Yes," I said, weakly. Fever seized control of my body. "Send for Marguerite." I fell to the soaking bed and slipped like a dream into darkness.

Chapter Seventeen:
Journey

Marguerite
Mabouhey; Miami; Chicago
1982

Sandward

In mouth of wave children dream
Of wings and fins, of the unseen seen.
Things of the sea,
They too come poured forth
Sandward
To where we are:
Caught on the shore.
Then they laugh back once more
With the undertow into the sea,
And look!

Where did the last wave go?
What will the next wave be?

As a child Marguerite liked to play in the water. In the mornings, when the first boat came in, she would run to its side and lean over. In the early sun her long black hair swirled like sparks from a fire. On the bottom of the boat the fish lay exhausted, their eyes silent moons, their shimmering bodies silver, green, and yellowy blues. Some jumped like corn popping. Marguerite wondered what it would be like if she were taken from her world of land and plunged into the depths of their watery home. She imagined herself waving her arms and legs as if motion itself were an affirmation of life. Sometimes, as if she were stirring a pot of her mother's auyama soup, Marguerite poked with a stick, careful to stab in between the slithering fishbodies. Then, one by one, the other boats would pull alongside. Gideon, as tall as a palm tree, the father of Schugay, the black boy who followed Marguerite around as if he were her shadow, would lift Marguerite by the waist to swing her high in the air, laughing.

"You are the fish-girl," Gideon always said. "You are the girl of the sea."

In the shade of the giant eucalyptus tree Marguerite cleaned the fish with the old women and younger boys. The heads and guts of the fish went into buckets which she and Schugay carried to the fields for fertilizer.

"I would like to go to the sea and fish with the nets," she told her mother when she was fourteen. "You are the one who goes to the taroumpa hut. Ask. Ask the Spirits for me."

Icolyn was sitting in front of their hut, making sandals. Skins of dogs sat at her feet; a cutting board rested in her lap. Yes, Icolyn was the woman who went to the taroumpa hut—when Jericho, Marguerite's father, was near death from the fever. Icolyn had done everything she could, and so too Christian, back for the summer from learning the medicine ways of the white man, but still Jericho's fever would not let go. Icolyn went to the taroumpa hut. Had a woman ever gone to the taroumpa hut before? No griot could say. Icolyn stood at the door, her face painted with the mask of the moongod. Her ankles were braceleted with her grandmother's cowrie shells and she prayed to Carmenya's spirit to speak for Jericho. Had not Carmenya herself died of a broken heart when the fever took Moraldo, Icolyn's grandfather, to the other world? Then Icolyn prayed the Prayer of The Father, as Malcolm, Jericho's father, had taught her, many years before, and stepped inside. The next day Jericho's fever broke.

So now again Icolyn went to the taroumpa hut. She drank and she smoked and the Spirits came. Marguerite was leaning over the side of a boat at the place of many rocks, there where the water is white, her long hair floating in the seawind. Red tears fell from a wine red rose into the turquoise sea. This is what Icolyn saw. There was a man, a white man, in the water; Marguerite reached over the side of the boat and then Icolyn could see no more. The following day Marguerite went to the sea to fish with the nets.

When she was not on the sea, Marguerite went to the village school, where Father Chester taught of women and men of the past, of cities and civilizations, of machines and miracles, of a larger world, a world which to Marguerite was full of wonders, despite the priest's cautionary tales of war and greed. She spent long hours in the village's library, which Father Malcom, her grandfather, had started. Once it had seemed enough to go to the sea and fish with the nets. Once it had seemed enough to move beyond the confines of her designated role, to say that I am as good as anyone else, I shall not be held back, I shall go to the sea and fish with the nets because I can, but a time came when Marguerite began to think of herself beyond the context of place. She needed a larger stage, a bigger world, if only for a taste of time, for, even as she imagined metal cities fingering the sky with glass, as she imagined the rush of electronic miracles and the frenzy of concrete forests, she knew that the day would come when her wonder at such wonders would dissolve like raindrops in the full day sun, that memories of Mabouhey would call her home, that she was and always would be a fish-girl, a girl of the sea. Yet she longed to see the other world, too, to satisfy the wrenching need to know. When she turned eighteen Marguerite's grandfather came to her in her dreams.

Marguerite remembered bouncing on the holy man's knee when she was a child. She saw his white hair and leathery face. She remembered how he laughed and danced and sang, how her playmates ran to "Pa-pa Malcolm," how the gleam in his eye for her came from deep in his soul. She knew that the Spirits had sent him to her from the peace of the other world.

"Grandpapa came to me last night," she told her father. "I said that you are well and that mother too sends blessings."

Jericho looked at her. She was the first of his and Icolyn's three children. He remembered with shame his disappointment at the birth of a girl, but he also remembered, as the years passed, how his love for Marguerite had grown into the strongest tree, for the first of his children was blessed with a special blessing. She was the sparkle of sunlight, yet she was strong with the strength of a thousand rivers. Marguerite's was the will of the autumn wind.

Jericho was lying in his hammock, in the lazy part of the afternoon, in the siesta time before he would return to the warehouse, where he worked with bags of burlap and bushels of grain. Now Jericho look at the beauty of his daughter and saw her strength.

"What is it my father said?" he asked.

"He said that I should learn the ways of the white man," Marguerite answered. Yes, she thought, you have known of my need, I have made no secret that I must go beyond. Grandpapa came to me in my dreams as if I had willed him to do so.

"I do not want you to leave this place," her father said. He folded Marguerite's hands inside his and carried them to his heart. "You are here. You will always be here. But should you go, you must promise me, as you love your grandfather and honor his memory, you will return. You must promise me."

"I will return, Papa," Marguerite answered. "I promise." I have this need to go beyond, yet I know that once I have seen what there is to see, my need to return will be as strong as the ocean pulling back from the shore. "I will return," Marguerite said again. For a long moment, a time that would end, the world was Jericho's arms.

It was a great matter that had to be decided, one that called for the most careful of thought. It had to be looked at the way one looks at the clouds or the ocean, the way one looks at a newborn child. Jericho and Icolyn brought Marguerite to Father Chester. She had studied the books in Mabouhey's library, he said. She had a mind like the blackest soil, but there was little more that he alone could teach her. The following evening Icolyn took her daughter to the taroumpa hut. Six weeks later she was on a boat to Miami on her way to Chicago.

*   *   *

In Miami Marguerite went to the Greyhound Bus depot, a suitcase firmly in each hand. In a great cavern where people greeted and parted, she kept to herself, studying the mosaic of travelers. Once before she had taken Hernando's boat to Frederique City, but she had not spent the night there. Its loud sauntering men reminded her of the roving black birds that circled high over Katausa, pinpricks of black heads on nervous black bodies, darting from side to side looking for prey. Yet she remembered too the children of Frederique City, who were happy, on buses and motoconchos, smiling, or skipping along on streets and sidewalks, laughing. But the fatherless children of Miami were not happy. They sat like discarded dolls on the wooden benches in the hum of the waiting room with sad silent eyes and small nervous bodies. Their limbs jerked like the hands of a dysfunctional clock.

"You shut up. You bad! I tole you. You shut up." On the bench across from Marguerite a large black woman, obese, grabbed the wrists of a young girl, seven or eight years old, and shook her. The top of the woman's head was a bubble of visqueen blue plastic; grease seeped from around its edges like oil through the leaky gasket of a misfiring engine. "You bad," the woman said again. "An' shut up. Ah better not hear nuttin' from you and ah means it!" She let go of the child's wrists with a violent shove. The girl's body slammed into the curve of the bench. Her mother menaced before her, a large brown pocketbook of patent leather over her right arm like a weapon. "Ah'm goin' to the ladies room," she said. "You better not move a muscle til ah gets back. You hear me?"

The fat woman crushed a cigarette against the side of the bench. A puddle of chewing gum wrappers and cookie crumbs, of candy wrappers and cigarette butts, sprouted underneath and in front of where she had been sitting. The child peeked tentatively from inside the question mark of her curled body, wiping tears from her cheeks with her sleeves.

Marguerite had not witnessed any of this, for she had turned to study a large banner that hung from the ceiling against the far wall. It was an advertisement for a local television news program. Two smiling faces, one black, one white, one male, one female, displayed the whitest teeth Marguerite had ever seen. Fascinated with the faces' plastic perfection, she had neither seen nor heard the woman and her child. When Marguerite turned around, the child was alone and crying. Marguerite picked up her luggage and went to her.

"Oh, you are such a pretty young lady," she said, sitting down next to her. "What is your name?" The girl looked up but did not say a word. "My name is Marguerite. Do you like my name?"

The girl looked at Marguerite with wide, sad eyes.

"Let me guess what your name is," Marguerite said. "Is you name Susan?" The child's head moved from side to side. "Maybe your name is Mary. Mary is such a pretty name." Again, no. "Rebecca?" No. "Well," Marguerite said with a smile, "I give up. You know what my name is. Why don't you tell me yours? Please?"

The child stayed in her world of silence.

Marguerite reached into her purse. "Would you like some candy?" She unwrapped a coconut-chocolate-peanut butter bar. The girl nodded her head and reached out one of her small hands.

"Thank you," she whispered.

"Now will you tell me your name? Please?"

The child looked up from her candy and opened her mouth. "My name is..."

"Cloetha!" The fat woman stood in front of them, hands on her hips. "Cloetha, chile! How many times have ah tole you not to take candy from strangers!" With her right hand the woman grabbed what remained of the candy bar from the child's hand and threw it to the floor. Then with her left she gave a sharp slap to the right side of the child's face. In the next instant she turned her fury to Marguerite, who was trying to stand up. But the large woman stood too close; Marguerite was penned into the bench like an animal in a cage. "An' you," the woman bellowed, "how dare you be touching my chile? Ah ought to get the police. That's jess what ah should do!"

Clawing around the bulk of the loudmouthed woman, Marguerite managed to slide to her feet. The young girl curled against the back of the bench, crying. "Yes," Marguerite said, "Yes. Why don't you do that? Let's get the police." The sobs of the child gave fuel to her anger.

"What seems to be the problem here, ladies?" The policeman was a tall black man in a crisp uniform. There was a bored look on his face.

"She be touchin' my chile, officer. That's jess what she be doin'. Ain't that right, Cloetha?" The woman reached behind her and yanked her daughter to her feet.

"This woman hit the child, officer," Marguerite said. "I was just trying to help."

"Whose child is it?" the officer asked.

"Mine!" the fat woman shouted triumphantly. "Mine. Cloetha's mine." She jabbed a finger into Marguerite's chest. "An' she be touchin' her."

Marguerite felt a chill race through her body. This cannot be happening, she thought. This cannot be happening. Seeing the child alone and crying, she had assumed that she had become separated from her mother or father. Instinctively, Marguerite had gone to give comfort until parent or guardian returned. There should have been warm welcomes and introducings, sharings of hellos and thank yous. Instead, this.

"You see, officer..."

"Did you touch the child?" the policeman interrupted.

"Ah, shit. Dis here bitch jess gonna lie like the 'ho that she is," the woman interrupted his interruption, spitting her words. "Ah ain't got time for dis here crap. Ah got me a bus to catch."

"Well, go on along then." The policeman's words were without energy. Nothing would come of any of this, he knew, if the fat woman were to file charges, except a lot of paperwork. With one hand the woman dragged the girl along by the wrist as she headed for the exit.

"You go on touchin' other folk's chillren, bitch," she yelled over her shoulder, "and you sho' nuff' gonna git yourseff what's coming to ya."

The policeman looked at Marguerite. "You're not from around her, are you, ma'am?"

Marguerite lowered herself to the bench and shook her head. "I was only trying to help," she said softly. At the far end of the room the young girl disappeared through the exit. Her wide eyes looked back over her shoulder into

Marguerite's for an instant of light. Then she was gone. Marguerite started to cry. "I was only trying to help," she said again.

"Well, ma'am," the policeman replied gently, "the child does belong to someone else."

On the bus to Chicago Marguerite sat next to a window with an empty seat beside her. Miami slid through the twilight, a gauze of smoke and grime. Along Biscayne Boulevard stick figures of ragged men and yellow women dragged cardboard boxes. Others pushed shopping carts piled with aluminum cans and scraps of clothing. Sunken faces sat on corners, lay in gutters, or leaned against the sides of buildings. After a short while Marguerite curled herself as best she could inside blanket and pillow. Chicago waited, a day away. The policeman's words came to her: the child belonged, a possession, like a toy. Marguerite saw the child's last desperate look and felt unclean. She should have run to her. And then what? She would have been arrested for sure. My God, she thought with a foretaste of dread, what kind of people are these?

*   *   *

There was a palpable energy to Chicago: crisp men and women purposeful in gaze and gait. Luther Custis Towe had arranged for Marguerite to stay with his Auntie Rose and her husband, Zion, until Marguerite could find her own lodgings. Auntie Rose, Luther said, as he and his wife, Juliette, accompanied Marguerite from the bus terminal, had a heart as big as Texas and was famous, as well, for her down home cooking. Auntie Rose put both feet in her sweet potatoes.

"Come in, child! Zion, you help this child with her things." A pert bundle of smiles opened her arms. Marguerite let the woman's warmth radiate into her as her husband, a large black man with tufts of gray hair and a bushy mustache, took her suitcases to disappear down a hallway.

"This is my Auntie Rose," Luther said. "My favorite Auntie Rose."

The brown-black woman smiled. "And just how many Auntie Roses do you have, Luther Custis Towe?"

"Oh," Luther replied, "it's quality we're talking about here, not quantity!" They sat in the dining room of the tidy bungalow. Ribbons of stained glass edged the doors of a built-in china cabinet; oak beams crossed the ceiling, a medallion of plaster anaglyph in its center. Etched orange crystals, suspended in midair, glowed. Zion blessed the food, giving thanks for Marguerite's safe arrival. Then there were bowls of string beans, mashed potatoes, black-eyed peas, rice, sweet potatoes, collard greens, and cornbread muffins. Like heavy laden barges platters passed back and forth, heaped with ham hocks and fried chicken.

"What's the matter, child? You eating like a skinny bird." A hurt look stretched across Auntie Rose's face. "Zion," she commanded, "put some sweet potatoes on that poor child's plate."

After offerings of bus stop sandwiches and wilted salads, the flavors of Auntie Rose's cooking were like streaks of sun after days of cloudy rain. But the sweet potatoes sat on a corner of Marguerite's plate, untouched, until the rest of her plate was clean and Marguerite could avoid them no longer. She pushed the tines of her fork to them. With a reluctant touch she brought a spot of orange to her mouth. Cinnamon, molasses, and marshmallows blended into a creamy sweetness unlike anything she had tasted before. Sweet potatoes, she knew, were cousin to the yam, but she could detect no trace of the strawlike flavor she remembered from Mabouhey. Enthusiastically she pushed her fork into the mound of orange. Then Marguerite realized that Luther, Juliette, Auntie Rose, and Zion all were staring at her.

"What is it, child?"

"Well, Auntie Rose, what I was wondering is how, exactly, do you put your feet in the sweet potatoes? Is it something like squashing grapes to make wine? However you do it, it sure does give them a wonderful flavor!" Zion roared. Auntie Rose and Juliette reached for their napkins. Luther laughed so hard he had to stand up. In an instant it came to Marguerite why they all were laughing. "Oh," she said, spooning herself a generous second helping, "where I come from we have a different saying. On Mabouhey we say 'You dropped your hand in this one!'"

*   *   *

Marguerite had come to Chicago to study the ways of the white man. But where was he? Where Auntie Rose and Zion lived there were no white men. It took Marguerite two weeks to locate an apartment, a two and one-half room "studio" close to the Central Avenue elevated stop and within walking distance to the Learning Network. In this time the only white person she encountered was the rental agent at CityFront Realty. A wiry black man had shown Marguerite the apartment with instructions to deliver the rental application to the CityFront office on Washington Boulevard. To either side of its entrance garbage assaulted skeletons of threadbare bushes prickly with thorns. Marguerite pushed a once white button beneath a sign lettered with grime and graffiti. Then she waited. Finally, there came a buzzing, acrid, ugly. Inside, the worn carpeting was dirty, a faded blue spliced with strips of gray duct tape. A rancid odor like stagnant water came to Marguerite's nostrils; she reached into her purse for a handkerchief. Dull metallic buttons dotted a bulletproof plastic cubicle, grimy and opaque. From within a white woman in her fifties told Marguerite to deposit the rental application and twenty dollars in the mouth of a metal tray which slid out of her plastic prison like the jaws of a prehistoric beast. Then the white woman barked through the intercom: "Come back in an hour." That was all she said.

It was late August. Along the lakefront Chicago gave itself to the sun in shorts and roller skates, jump ropes, bicycles, and frisbees. Here on Central Avenue from Washington Boulevard to Jackson Boulevard women crossed their arms around their handbags like footballs clutched close to their bosoms; men leaned against lamp posts begging for bus transfers and cigarettes. The streets were garbage and the sun was harsh. Marguerite walked the few blocks south to Columbus Park. She turned west and came to its reflecting pool. She stood at the edge, watching the ducks, brown and white and gray mallards and then, on the other side of a high chain link fence, she saw them. White people. They were dressed in loud colors, shorts and shirts, culottes and blouses, plaids, stripes, and paisleys. They rode around on small carts when they were not hitting small white balls with wooden or metal sticks. There was a carefree manner about them as they chattered to one another in quick bursts of words like sudden gusts of wind. The men had red faces; their thick bodies were without necks. The women and their perfect hair floated like clouds.

Marguerite stood at the fence, her fingers gripping the wires of nothingness, but the golfers paid her no attention. She did not know it, but she was alongside the fairway of the seventh hole of the Chicago Park District's Columbus Park golf course. Here she watched in fascination as the white men and white women paraded past: bankers, lawyers, secretaries, housewives. Every once in a while a group of black golfers came along to intrigue her for they seemed no different than the white golfers. Then a mixed group appeared, a black man and a black woman, and a white man and a white woman. They seemed to be the best of friends; Marguerite wanted to run to them, to talk, to listen, to learn, but she could see, as heads turned in their direction and as eyes wandered to them, that they already were the targets of attention and objects of conversation of the other golfers, white and black, as she knew that her own eyes were wondering too, so she turned away. She was nearly back to the pond when it happened. A blur of a young man came running, grabbed her purse, and pushed her to the ground. In an instant his blue coat disappeared over the slight rise that Jackson Boulevard makes as it flows into the park. A man helped her to her feet.

"Are you okay? Are you all right?"

"I think so," Marguerite answered, sweeping the dirt from her skirt. "He took my purse." The rent money, she thought. The rent money is gone. A police officer appeared to write answers in a small notebook. A black man about twenty. A blue jacket. Her purse. Her rent money. The interrogation continued for fifteen minutes or so until a police car arrived, the lights on its top flashing like the guns of a battleship. In the back seat, hands cuffed behind him, as sullen and fierce as a stray dog, a young black man in a blue jacket stared through windowpane eyes.

"Is this your bag, ma'am?" A second police officer held up Marguerite's purse.

"Yes," she answered softly. The officer handed Marguerite the purse. The young man in the blue jacket was taken from the police car and made to stand before her. "My money is gone," Marguerite cried. "My rent money is gone."

"Fuck you, you 'ho," the young man shouted. "Dere weren't no money, you lyin' bitch. You better watch out, 'ho. Fuck you."

"Shut up, you piece of shit," the first officer said. She shoved her nightstick into the young man's ribs. "Put him back in the car."

As he was dragged into the police car, her attacker shouted more angry words: "You gonna be sorry, you fuckin' 'ho. I'll get the word out. Ain't nowhere you gonna be safe, bitch. I'm gonna git you, you fuckin' liar."

Marguerite was taken to the police station to file a written complaint. On the way she asked the policewoman to stop at CityFront Realty.

"Your application has been approved," slurred the white woman from inside her plastic cocoon without raising her head. "I need the first month's rent to hold the apartment. You pay the month and a half security deposit when you pick up the keys. When do you want to move in?" There was no life in these words.

"I've just been robbed," Marguerite said. "My money is gone. I am on my way to the police station now to make a report." Marguerite pointed towards the waiting flashing lights. "Can you keep the apartment for me for a while until I figure out what I am going to do?"

A bored look came over the rental agent's face. A likely story, she thought. Funny, the woman was dressed well, clean, not too flashy. Bit of an accent. Probably illegal. But she didn't look like a druggie. Probably her boyfriend was. Betcha he took the money. Maybe one of her kids stole it. What difference did it make? If it wasn't one story, it was another. The rental agent had heard them all, frequently several times in the same day. Probably the police waiting outside needed her for something, if she wasn't being arrested herself. For what? The rental agent paid closer attention. Yes, that was it. She was a whore, walking the strip by the golf course for paunchy suburban fathers and husbands to get their tickle on. Always a mistake to rent to whores. Whores came with pimps and pimps caused trouble.

"Look, lady," the rental agent said. "This is a business we're trying to run here. Come back when you have the money—all of it. If the apartment is still available, you can have it, but I'm afraid I'm going to require double security in addition to the first month's rent; that's four months upfront cash." That'll do it, the rental agent thought. That'll make her somebody else's trouble for sure.

Marguerite felt more anger. "Why must I pay a double security deposit?" she asked. "That isn't fair. It's not my fault I was robbed."

"Don't give me any more of your guff. Fair is what I say it is. You don't like it, go somewhere else. It's a free country." It had been hard, very hard, to find anything even tangentially habitable. The small apartment CityFront offered not only was affordable, it was also bright and somewhat clean. Even so, in that moment, Marguerite vowed that she would not give the uncaring woman inside the plastic cage even one penny of her money. It was not Marguerite's money, not really. It was a sacred trust, the manifestation and representation of her people. She would not leave it in a place of such disrespect. She put the anger out of her.

"May I have my twenty dollars back, please?"

"You gotta be kidding, lady," the rental agent sneered. "Just where do you think you are? You take up all my time and cause all this trouble and have the gall to ask for money? Get outta here or I'll call dem police outside inside here and have your damn ass thrown in the slammer twice as long. Scoot."

At the police station Marguerite waited on a crowded bench for nearly an hour. People argued and pushed against each other. Telephones drilled and uniforms loitered. She signed many papers. Then one of the officers offered her a ride home. As they exited the building, Marguerite saw the young man in the blue jacket leaning against the side of the building across the street.

"Oh, that's what we call an I-Bond," the police officer explained. "It means he showed proof of identification, so he's released until the preliminary hearing. Crazy, no?"

In her bedroom at Auntie Rose and Zion's, Marguerite threw herself on the bed. She did not come out for a long time. At dinner she told Auntie Rose and Zion what had happened.

"It's a jungle out there," Zion said.

"No," Marguerite replied. "You are wrong. It is not a jungle."

Chapter Eighteen:
Back to the Future

Albert Sidney McNab

New York, New York; Athens, Ohio; Pennsylvania

1991

After three M.A.F.I.A. years Albert Sidney McNab knew his days were numbered. "I shall be re-unemployed," he said to himself. "Either that or I shall murder Carlo, and the better angels of my cockroach self forbid homicide. I shall not kill." He came home, soaked his feet, and ate as usual in front of the television. Further proof of the superiority of the cockroach, he thought. It was a stunning epiphany: cockroaches do not watch television. Do worms? Giraffes? Hummingbirds? Enough. One of these days he would break his cursed televisual addiction. Four hours later he cleared his bed of clothing and dirty dishes and went to sleep. He was dreaming of sandy beaches and blue skies when the telephone rang him awake.

"This is A. T. and T.—U.S.A. direct," a crisp voice with a British accent said. "A collect call to a Mr. Albert McNap from a Mr. Ragweed Jones. Will you pay for the call?" Ragweed Jones. *Who* is Ragweed Jones?

"Who?"

"A collect call to Mr. Albert McNap," the voice repeated.

"Yes, yes. I know who *I* am. Well, I think I do. Most of the time, anyway," Albert said with exasperation.

"That's all well and good," the operator replied. "But what I need to know is will you accept the charges?"

"The charges?"

"For the call. To a Mr. Albert Sidney McNap."

"So you have said."

"Well?"

"Well what?"

"It's a straightforward question. Will you or will you not accept the charges?"

Albert decided to stall. "Who did you say the call is from again?"

Garbled Caribbean voices thrashed about on the line. Finally the crisp voice returned. "A Mr. Ragweed Jones calling. I ask you again: will you pay for the call?"

"How much is it?"

"I can't give you that information," the crisp voice said with its own edge of exasperation. "You have to get that information from your local telephone company. Do you or do you not want to pay for the bloody call?"

Yes, yes. Of course I want to pay for the call, Albert thought. Let me pay for the call. Please. Let me pay for this, let me pay for that, let me pay taxes and surcharges and taxes on surcharges, and surcharges on taxes on surcharges, let me pay, let me pay, let my money go, let it fly away, let me pay. I am losing it, he thought, this time for sure. Should I pay for the call? Who is this Mr. Ragweed Jones? The name Ragweed was vaguely familiar, or was it? No. Even *I* couldn't forget a name like Ragweed. Haywood, perhaps. That's easily forgettable. Ragweed—never! Probably some salesman pushing timeshares. Then it dawned on him: the free breakfast at the New Papagayo Hotel! Some sort of slide show. Was it possible he had won something?

"But where is he calling from?"

"A Mr. Ragweed Jones calling a Mr. Albert McNap from the Peoples Republic of Frederique. This is it, mate: will you pay for the bloody call? Yes or no?"

He should have made the connection sooner. "Yes, yes," he shouted. "Of course I will pay for the call." Foreplay and all.

"Praise be. Go ahead."

"Hey, mon, why you no take me call without all de dis and dat?" a hurt voice asked. "Dis ease de Ragweed Jones calling, mon, de Ragweed hisself and none de other." Albert couldn't remember who, precisely Ragweed Jones was, but he knew he wanted to talk to him.

"Oh, sorry. I was sound asleep, well, not sound asleep, but asleep." What does that mean: *sound* asleep? Never mind. Now's not the time. "Thank you for calling."

"You do remember me, mon, don't you sure enough?"

"Of course," Albert lied. "How have you been?"

"Not too good, mon. Tings here dey be rougher and rougher. Rougher and rougher. De prices dey go up and up and de exchange it goes down and down and de money, mon, it ain't worth de paper, it ain't worth de ink on de paper, mon, dat's how rough it is sure enough."

It's the same all over, Albert thought. No one has enough money. Why don't they make more of it? "I am sorry to hear that." This call is going to bankrupt me, he thought. "What is it that I can do for you, Mr. Ragweed?"

"Oh, mon, don't be calling me dat, mon. I ain't no mister, mister, not for de dozen of de meatie pies, no sir. You jess call me 'Rag,' okay?"

"Okay, Rag," Albert replied. A sick feeling returned to his stomach as he remembered all the money he had wasted two years before, on his first trip to Frederique and Mabouhey. On his return to New York, for weeks, a spate of collect calls, whispered hints, teasing promises, and Moneygrams disappeared into the Caribbean void, then nothing, lots of nothing.

"What I's got to tell you, mon, is dis. My girlfriend she works in de bank, de bank on de square dere in Sharpston, and de other day, she took in dis note, mon, it was a hundred dollar note, but it was old, real old, so old de green eet was more like de yellow. My girlfriend say dat a friend of hers say it worth more dan a whole lot more dan de hundred dollars it say, mon, like de daily double square in de Jeopardy and it had markings on it come from de bank dere in someplace dat start with an 'O', mon, I can't sure how you say it.".

Albert Sidney McNab felt a thrill of intrigue. "O-HI-O?"

"Yes, mon, dat be it: O-HI-O, and dat dere O-HI-O, mon, I remember dat dat's where dat man you was looking for is from, and dat's what I have to tell you, dis here what I just said, as sure as de fish in de net."

Albert tried to think. An old one hundred dollar bill. "How old, exactly?"

"Well, mon, I don't really sure. I don't really certain. Dat's all I can be telling you now, mon, cause dat's all dere is to say. The farmer has to plant de seed but de seed grow when it wants to. If you send me two hundred dollars, mon, den I will send you de note cause my girlfriend, she taked it and put in de money."

"Just how do I know you will send me the note once I send you the money if I were so inclined?"

"Well, mon, I hope you don't be saying dat de Ragweed is de crook, cause if dat's how you feel after everything and all, well den, mon, we can end dis here conversation ready and right now, as final as de dead rat. De Ragweed ain't no crook, no sir, and dat's a fact, yes sir, like the tourist wid de sunburn."

"I will tell you what I will do," Albert replied. "Let me do some more poking about up here. Call me in a week. Maybe we can do business."

"Okay, mon, I will do dat, if de bill is still around by den. I do not guarantee eet, mon. You know how de money eet goes. Like de young girl wid de old rich mon in de wheelchair."

"That's a risk I will have to take," Albert said.

The next afternoon, for the second time in his life, Albert Sidney McNab was on a Greyhound bus to Athens, Ohio.

* * *

With self-satisfied pride Arnie Williamson showed Albert Sidney McNab around Ohio Valley Screw and Superior Manufacturing. "You saw all of this two years ago," the former accountant, now Chief Executive Officer, said. "When, when... the first time," he stammered. "Of course I don't mind showing you around again, if it's really necessary. What is this new development you mentioned over the phone?" Arnie Williamson tried to say these last words casually, but the investigator detected an edge of panic in his voice.

"As I said," Albert replied, "I am not at liberty to discuss the specifics or even the parameters of the specifics must less the specifics of the specifics or their parameters at this juncture. I may well be on a wild goose chase and it would be unwise to rock the apple cart as matters now stand until a comprehensive analysis of all data is undertaken and the potentialities of all probabilities evaluated." He gave a serious look to the earnest thin man beside him as they passed a cluster of machines. In white gowns attendants attended. Dials turned. Satisfied cows, the machines hummed, row upon row. After three M.A.F.I.A. years Albert had the lingo down pat. During the interminable bus ride from New York he had practiced silently in an effort to achieve the right mix of technical jargon, cliché, and pregnant pause. Now, despite an unplanned belch at the end (he shouldn't have chanced that third chicken salad sandwich in Harrisburg!), he had no doubt that his words had achieved their desired effect of seemingly unintended intimidation.

"Of course, of course," Arnie Williamson replied, convincing himself he understood every word of the fat man's peroration. He had determined in his own mind that Albert worked for a secret government agency, most likely the C.I.A. He had suspected as much two years before; now he was certain. The rancid raincoat smushed over the fat man's right arm like a dead animal in the middle of the road! The polyester plaid pants, the beltless waist grabbed frequently between thumb and index finger! The horror of the fat man's oversized shirt which, despite its paisley, failed to camouflage splotches of ketchup, mustard, mayonnaise, and various gravies. The most that could be said of possible normalcy was that both his socks were the same color. The same, yes, but also green.

"Let us resume our peregrinations," Albert commanded. With a thrust of his arm like a fascist salute he pointed.

"Oh, that," Arnie Williamson replied. "That door leads to one of the basements. We don't go down there."

"Oh, we don't, don't we?" the inquiring mind of Albert Sidney McNab inquired. "Long past time then that we do."

"I have no idea where the key might be," Arnie Williamson said, trying to appear calm. He knew he had nothing to hide. Yet there was something in the fat man's demeanor that put him off balance. Maybe, Arnie thought, I am feeling guilty at not feeling sorry when Travers disappeared. Yes, I mouthed perfunctory and proper platitudes of sympathy, especially to the grieving widow, who had, he remembered, promptly fled to California. Arnie Williamson's first thought when he learned of Travers' disappearance was that things would run a lot smoother without Travers Landeman around and they did. "Perhaps Madge Drayback knows where the key is," he said, inspired.

"Perhaps she does," Albert agreed, rubbing his protruding stomach in a manner that Arnie Williamson found upsetting. Madge Drayback? Albert wondered. Who is Madge Drayback? Then he remembered. The prim old lady, gray hair pulled into a bun. The office manager. She reminded him of his mother, God rest her soul. Madge Drayback had the same quiet efficiency. A hard worker. Dedicated. Loyal. And what had it behooved his mother, those forty years of dunking pickles at Chestaway Confections and Condiments in the lower east side on Bile Street? Bad back, ruined feet, and heart attack at age 67! A workhorse led to slaughter! Madge Drayback approached. Yes, she was just like his mother! At the basement door the gray haired woman fumbled with various keys. Eventually one slid into the dusty lock.

"Lucky you are here this week," Arnie Williamson said as he pulled the door open.

"And why, may I ask, do you say that?" To Arnie Williamson Albert's tone suggested that Arnie's words were a confession of the most heinous crime.

"All I meant," Arnie replied defensively as they descended the stairs, "is that this is Madge's last week. After forty-five years Madge is retiring. God knows if we would have found the right key a week from now."

"We could have smashed the door, or summoned a locksmith." As soon as these words were out of his mouth, Albert realized how insensitive they sounded. The old woman wasn't even out to pasture yet! Why should he care? How come he always had to care about people like Madge Drayback? She was so much like his mother! That had to be the explanation. He turned in the middle of the stairway. "I apologize," he said. "That wasn't very nice."

"Oh, not at all," the gray haired woman replied. "I'm used to it."

I'm used to it! The nobility of the strength of the suffering! Enjoy your retirement, dear lady, Albert thought. May you live another thirty years! My mother, God rest her soul, never got the chance. A workhorse led to slaughter! Tears came to his eyes. Down a hallway there was another door.

"Stand back!" Albert commanded as he pushed the door open and flipped a light switch. He peered inside. There, in distinct if faded silhouettes, footprints in the dust led from the doorway to end in front of a rectangular shape, waist high, that was covered with a shroud-like cloth. Arnie Williamson and Madge Drayback waited as the fat man retraced the faded footprints. Then, like a bullfighter's cape, the covering cloth swirled in the air; the room filled with snowflakes of dust. The investigator knelt in front of the uncovered object—a safe! Its door came open at his first touch. Arnie Williamson and Madge Drayback looked over his shoulders. Empty. Albert Sidney McNab felt his hands around the safe's insides. Empty.

"I had no idea this safe existed," Arnie Williamson said. "You've got to believe me."

"Whether I believe you or not is of no consequence. Yet." Albert said. "What I do know with certainty is that another piece of the puzzle has been locked into place. The Cartesian emptiness of this safe explains why you uncovered no evidence of embezzlement when Travers Landeman disappeared. He had no reason to embezzle. It wasn't necessary."

"But how do you know that there was anything in the safe?" Arnie Williamson asked. Once again the fat man had made him feel like a criminal. "Of course, I never even knew it was here. The safe, that is. No one knew, right, Madge?"

"That's right, Mr. Williamson," Madge Drayback lied. She remembered standing in the very same spot, thirty odd years before, Travers' father's eyes burning into hers.

"So, how do you know there was anything in the safe?" Arnie Williamson asked again.

"Oh, I know all right," Albert answered. "I know." Then he saw that Madge Drayback's face was a mask of fear. Of all the people he had interviewed two years before, she was the only one who had shown the slightest compassion for the missing businessman. Did her agitation now reflect concern for her missing and presumed dead boss? Or was she thinking of her own fate? Was she worrying now that after forty-five years of sweat and sacrifice, her pension might evaporate like a politician's promise to lower taxes? Suppose the Ohio valley businessman were alive? Could Ohio Valley Screw and Superior Manufacturing survive his rebirth? Could she? Did the prim officer manager want her former boss dead or alive? Madge Drayback adjusted a hair pin at the back of her head.

"Well, to tell the truth," Albert Sidney McNab lied, "I am not certain that there was anything in the safe." He saw a glimpse of relief sweep across Madge Drayback's face. The thrill of compassion coursed through Albert's ample body. He thought again of his mother. A workhorse led to slaughter!

*   *   *

Albert Sidney McNab threw his clothes on top of the bed. The room, a "businessman's special," in the Sweet Valley Motel and Truck Stop was as shabby as his suitcase. As he packed, he catalogued the slim information he had. One: the possibility that Ragweed Jones had not lied, that a vintage one hundred dollar bill, perhaps a gold certificate, had appeared, like a new planet, on the island of Frederique. And that proved...? Perhaps a lot. Perhaps nothing. Two: footprints in the dust and an empty safe. He thought of the ballyhoo a few years before over the discovery of Al Capone's safe in the Lexington Hotel in Chicago. On prime time a pompadoured personality, a reborn Hispanic, presided, bejeweled and breathless, as its massive door was exploded open to reveal its secret contents: empty beer bottles, pages of old newspapers, and a moldy toothbrush. The critics howled; the pompadour laughed all the way to the bank. Ah, yes: money, money, money. It—whatever it is—always comes down to money. Capitalism's oxygen! Albert started to fantasize about all the things he could do with twenty percent of three million dollars: he could buy things. Like what? Well, nice things. Like...some new clothes, except that he didn't want new clothes. You had to take care of new clothes. You couldn't just throw them on the bed. New clothes were almost as much bother as pets or children, and he didn't want them either. A car...except that he had never learned to drive. Well, then: he could move out of his crummy neighborhood...except he didn't want to move out of his crummy neighborhood. He liked his crummy neighborhood: serendipitous sidewalks of polyglot patter where one size did not fit all. Okay. He could buy himself a new pair of shoes, ComfortWalks, even if they did cost $135 a pair. So: he would chase all over the hemisphere risking death again by mule and mosquito, for a pair of ComfortWalks? Fine. Make it two pairs, one brown and one black.

Then it came to him how ridiculous his daydreaming was. I'm getting all worked up over money I don't have and can't figure out how to spend even if I did have it, he thought. I could always give it away. He remembered his mother. All she ever wanted was a Craftomatic Adjustable bed. Is that asking too much? Well, it was too late for her, wasn't it? Then he thought of Madge Drayback and he vowed that she would not also go gentle into that good night Craftomaticless, not if he could help it. What he should do, he thought—a much better bet, a surer payoff—was return to the Big Apple and slip on the front steps of the Park Slope branch of the New York City Public Library. He would have the shoes and Madge would have the bed. A much better option indeed! For too many months his warnings had gone unheeded: the steps were faulty, cracked, uneven, crumbling, a menace to the limbs of the literate few. This flagrant danger was compounded by the fact that the handrail had been removed when the entrance was made handicapped accessible and never reinstalled completely— to no avail he had called attention to the possibly not so insignificant gap. A lawsuit and settlement just waiting to happen! Why not his? This he thought is *terra cognito*, not some fantasy island! I prefer prosperous to Prospero, he chuckled. Enough of wild goose and mule and shark chasings! Steps and missing handrail beckon! Fear not, Charleston Travers Landeman, he said to himself, as he threw the remaining clothes into his suitcase, fear not Albert Sidney McNab, be you alive or be you dead. Live in bliss or rest in peace! There is a world elsewhere and its name is Park Slope!

Albert grabbed the suitcase and started for the door when he saw a cockroach scurry across the wall. He dropped the suitcase and sat on the edge of the bed. No, he thought. He could not fake a fall on the steps of the Park Slope library. It wouldn't be right. M.A.F.I.A. or no M.A.F.I.A., he thought, I shall survive. He could hear Carlo Franco Weberelli taunting, yes, survival of the fattest! These ruminations and more were jumbling together when the telephone rang.

"Ask Arnie Williamson about the pictures," a woman's voice said.

"Pictures? What pictures?"

"He'll know." Renee Carter, one of Magnolia Williamson's canasta circle, hung up the phone. Gossip abhors a vacuum.

So the game *was* afoot! The thrill of the chase! The end-all and be-all? Fuck the money. Doesn't the Bible teach that the love of money is the root of all evil? Money is like the revolutionary in exile, he thought, promising peace and happiness, wonderous good things. But open your arms and voilà! Slavemaster. Lenin. Castro. Besides, all Carlo ever seemed to do was fight with "theinsurance." Atlantis Fidelity was quick to take premiums for all sorts of policies: fire, flood, earthquake, "mine subsidence," whatever that was. Payouts, well, payouts were a different matter. Did Albert really want to enter the world of litigation? Never to return? Suppose he did and did. Suppose he found the missing businessman and by some miracle Travers Landeman was returned, suppose Atlantis Fidelity were forced to honor its end of the bargain, suppose that after lawyers, expert witnesses, accountants, expediters, and taxmen were done pawing over the payout and by some miracle a surprising bounty was his and his alone, did he really want to spend his life in the back seats of limousines, in tailor-made suits, in posh places, hobnobbing with the obsequious and scheming? He had done quite fine, thank you, so far. Chess in the park with Max. Evenings and weekends at the Park Slope library, a comfortable chair, wondrous galaxies in the cosmos of books, hushed smiling faces as he entered and left. He was lonely much of the time, true, but there was nothing that money could do about that that he was likely to trust. Still: once started, best finished, no? He was hot on the trail of the missing businessman. He could feel it. He would see things through. Why not? When the time came—*if* the time came, he would do what he would do. Comme çi, comme ça. He dialed the front desk.

"I've decided to stay a day or two longer," he said.

*   *   *

He would confront Arnie Williamson that same afternoon. Pounce into his office unannounced. Catch him off guard. Make him sweat. Just as he had learned in his correspondence course: **Secret Techniques of Private Investigation in 30 days**. Money well spent!

"I know all about the pictures," he shouted as Arnie Williamson struggled to rise from his chair. "Now why don't you tell me what you know?"

"Well," Arnie Williamson fumbled, "I didn't think they were that important. The pictures, that is. Besides I thought that out of respect for the dead..."

"But we don't know with certainty that Travers Landeman is dead," the fat man interrupted, "do we?"

"No."

"This time tell me everything you know! Everything!" Albert banged his fist like a gavel. Rumbles from the epicenter waved across the desk's surface, toppling a spiral bound report to the floor. Arnie Williamson reached over the side of his chair.

"It was a few days after...after Travers went missing," he said, repositioning the report on his desk with geometric precision. "These appeared on my chair. I don't know how they got here." Arnie Williamson reached for his keys, selected a thin silver one, unlocked a bottom drawer, and removed a manila envelope. The picture quality is only so-so, the investigator noticed at once. My photos are much better! Better framed, more properly aligned. Albert studied the photos. No doubt about it. Travers Landeman *en flagrante delecto.* Not bad for a middle aged man in a gray flannel suit, or rather, *not* in a gray flannel suit!

"I will take these," Albert said, eager to crush any resistance from Arnie Williamson, who sweated like an animal in a trap on the other side of the desk. But there was none. "There must have been some follow-up." Arnie Williamson waited as the Falstaffian figure before him slid the manila envelope into the green pouch that served as the fat man's briefcase. Pimpled with flecks of mashed potatoes, it bore an advertising slogan from a Bronx funeral home: *Leave The Rest To Us. Money Back Guarantee!* All Arnie Williamson wanted was for the mountain of flesh to go away. His headache intensified as the purple shirt, red pants, and green socks waited like a hallucination for his answer.

"Yes. There was a phone call a few days later. I ignored it."

With new eyes Albert looked at the tweed jacket and silver cuff links sitting before him. The pastepot of fashion had called their bluff! "Well done!" Albert extended his hand. The surprised Arnie Williamson rose and shook the catch basin paw that reached over his desk. Its fingernails reminded him of the uncleaned backbones of shrimp. He slumped back into his chair. "And whom have you told about this...this tyro attempt at Malthusian extortion?"

"No one," Arnie Williamson lied. "No one at all."

"But of course you are lying!" The investigator deposited both paws on Arnie Williamson's desk to bulge forward like a dam on the verge of collaspe. Arnie

Williamson pushed back in his chair, away from the menacing avalanche of clashing colors and bad breath. "You told your wife for one!" Albert had great confidence in this deduction. Of course the wimp had run home to momma! The fat man waited as the sartorial correctness in front of him slumped deeper into the Naugahyde cage of his high-backed chair. It was quilted, the fat man observed, in forest green and gold piping. *No detail is too small or too insignificant. Chapter Nine: Attention Must Be Paid!* "Tell me, please, who else partook of your consommé of spilled beans?" Albert congratulated himself on the "please." He was good cop and bad cop in the same sentence! *Chapter Six: Vinegar **and** Honey!* Money well spent indeed.

"I didn't tell anyone," Arnie Williamson protested. "Just Magnolia. Honest. I swear it. I'm telling the truth."

"But of course you are," Albert replied. "You were lying before. It is now that you are telling the truth. And the missus—Magnolia is it?—told her pinochle club!"

"No, you are wrong there," Arnie Williamson said. "Magnolia plays canasta."

*   *   *

On the bus back to New York Albert Sidney McNab relived the triumph of his interrogation of Arnie Williamson as well as of the subsequent interrogation of Arnie Williamson's wife, the Magnolia Blossom, as Albert thought of her. He was sitting in the last row, where a small bathroom left space for three seats across. The advantage of the extra room, not quite sufficient for him to recline fully, was offset by concomitant olfactory assaults, as, to his amazement, one after another of his travelmates managed to squeeze themselves through the small door. No pain, no gain, he thought, as he finished another bag of Crumpy's Old Fashioned Garlic Flavored Potato Chips. He blew into the empty bag and then clapped it between his hands, a trick he had been perfecting since first grade. The demise of the bag gave but a pitiful burp. Not one of his better efforts and, he feared, of no impact at all in motivating his fellow travelers to more stoical bladder control. A utilitarian as well as an aesthetic failure! This is the way the world ends? His implosion disappointment was short-lived, however, as he savored his dual triumphs. Arnie Williamson had finally told the truth. Of this Albert had no doubt. The Magnolia Blossom, he had anticipated, would stand behind her man. How far behind?

Albert had interrogated her in what she called her "Florida room." He had no idea what that meant. The room looked nothing like a penis to him. Magnolia had succeeded in getting a peek at the photographs after much cajoling of the fashion plate. She had also succeeded in persuading her husband to keep his mouth shut regarding their existence, sound advice, which, regrettably, she herself did not follow. Arnie knew and she knew that the dead are best left dead, even if they aren't, technically speaking, dead, "if you know what I mean." The last thing Ohio Valley Screw and Superior Manufacturing needed was the resurrection of its founder's great-great-grandson, "if you know what I mean."

"Please, have another chocolate cherry," Magnolia invited. The fat man consumed the entire box as she prattled on. Yes, there was no question about it. Travers was better left dead, even if he weren't. "This resurrection business," she said, "is overrated." A lot of hype. Lazarus came back from the dead. For how long? She hadn't seen him around lately. What it boiled down to, then, was this: Lazarus got to die twice. We all should be so fortunate, "if you know what I mean." Arnie and the Magnolia Blossom had batted these and other cogitations back and forth. No, Ohio Valley Screw and Superior Manufacturing did not have three million dollars just lying around to give back to Atlantis Fidelity Insurance, not any longer. Arnie had used the money for special bonuses for all, starting with himself. Arnie and the Magnolia Blossom agreed. They would tell no one about the pictures. It was the lure of a moment's glory, she said "if you know what I mean," that did her in. At canasta the week following Arnie's revelation she let just the tiniest hint escape from her lips as Renee Carter poured Kahlua into coffee. Renee was glowing in triumph: once again she had finished in first place. This would shut her up good. So it was that the Magnolia Blossom uttered the fatal words: "I have news." *Gold discovered at Sutter's mill!* Albert thought, *if you know what I mean*. Magnolia Williamson had folded her arms as Renee and the others went through the ritual of delicious supplication. "Arnie has some pictures," Magnolia finally confessed. Within hours beauty shops and diners exhilarated with the news. The pictures were of Travers and two women. Or, perhaps, of Travers and a woman and another man, possibly Arnie Williamson. There were whips and chains. Someone who claimed to have seen the photographs swore there was a syringe on the night stand next to the bed.

One result of this hysteria was that Corinne Landeman packed her bags and moved to California. This was seen as civic improvement. For too many years Corinne had been envied the largesse of the "Reinvestment Development Partnerships Effort"'s booty. More recently she had been resented because of the even greater good fortune of widowhood. The double whammy, as Renee Carter called it, brought into question the existence of God. A second consensus emerged as well. Whoever had taken the pictures had mighty poor timing. Everyone had a good laugh at Corinne's expense, and that *was* something, of course. Given Travers' demise, however, what use were the pictures other than valley-wide and too short-lived titillation? "If you know what I mean." All this the Magnolia Blossom had poured forth to the rumpled stranger with mixed feelings. She delighted in being the center of attention, but she was fearful, too, that the investigator's poking around might bring changes to her world and she was, now that her husband had ascended to Travers' throne, happy with her world just the way it was. If only her canasta buddies had kept their big mouths shut!

"But don't you see," she tried, in closing, "none of this makes any difference. Not any more." Big deal. Someone was trying to blackmail Travers. So what? The boat had been missed. "That puppy won't fight any more, if you know what I mean." The tip of her tongue slid between the lavender strips of her lips as she gave the fat inquisitor what Magnolia thought of as her "come-hither" look, like Marlene Dietrich's in *The Blue Angel*. Every day Magnolia practiced this look in front of a mirror while riding her exercycle and watching dating game shows.

The photographs prove something else, Albert Sidney McNab said to himself as the bus droned along on the interminable interstate otherwise known as Pennsylvania. The empty safe indicates that my good friend, Travers Landeman, had the means. Albert petted the green pouch in his lap. These photographs, poor quality and all, prove that he had the motive. It was only a matter of time until Carlo dispensed with the fat man's services. This Albert knew as surely as his chessmate, Max, knew biscuits and buns. It was time to go out on his own! He would cut his own deal with Atlantis Fidelity Insurance. Then it would be back to the future, to Ragweed Jones and the islands of Frederique and Mabouhey!

Chapter Nineteen:
The Poisoned Tree

Travers Landeman
Mabouhey
1989

Instinctively Travers felt that Father Chester's story would change him, would help Travers give birth to the new self he felt stirring within. In the uncharted territory of the soul, Father Chester had gone on before. On the mat next to the priest the child curled herself in sleep. "Schugara, Schugara, Schugara!" the priest sang, stroking her cheek:

Hush, little baby, don't say a word,
Mamma's gonna buy you a mockingbird.

"You know, Schugara was one of the first babies Christian delivered. He had returned from Dominica only a year or two before...before Marguerite went away. He had been gone for five years, years when I remembered what it was to be alone." I have been alone, Travers thought. I am still alone. "Time is a thief who robs us all, saint and sinner alike," Father Chester said. "But I have found that here on Mabouhey time is a gentle thief, the most considerate of pickpockets."

"I'm not sure I understand," Travers said.

"It's hard to explain. Perhaps you have to live it. When all is said and done, time is the universal currency, the only true dollar, yen, pound, or peso. Would not the millionaire who dies at forty trade place with the pauper who lives to eighty-five?" Again the priest reached to the sleeping child to stroke her cheek. "On Mabouhey we keep time in our pockets. One day is pretty much like the next. Or it was until the airport was constructed on Frederique. We began to see young white people with tents on their backs, camping by the sea, 'like spiders in the evening dew,' the people said. Then Hernando built his guest house. These changes came like the wind. How many more? The people wondered."

Travers thought of his own withered life. "No man is an island," he said. "Perhaps no island is either."

"Perhaps. The taroumpa hut was filled with unanswered questions for many days." The priest paused. "Do you remember Marguerite? She helped you with your netting."

Many times yes. Travers nodded his head.

"Finally the Spirits spoke and we were of one mind. Marguerite, the fish-girl, the girl who would go beyond, the granddaughter of Father Malcolm, the daughter of Icolyn and Jericho, would go to Chicago to study the ways of the white man. She would return to help us prepare for the changes that were coming. That is what we decided. That is what the Spirits spoke."

Marguerite. In a hunger of anticipation Travers waited. But the priest did not continue. He took the sleeping child in his arms. "I think of Schugay to this day," he said. "We will all always think of him. He is in our hearts." Schugay? Who was Schugay? Who was he to the sleeping child? Who was he to the woman named Marguerite?

Father Chester stood. "Now it is I who am tired," he said. "Sleep ceases the conquest of grief if only in the space of dreams." Somewhere near a bird gave song. "Let me walk you to your hut," the priest said.

"There is no need for that," Travers replied. "If I may, I would like to sit here a while longer." Then he added, in words that came like the surprise of a rainbow, "To be reacquainted with the stars."

"As you please." The priest turned. He cradled the sleeping child, the child named Schugara, in his arms. With slow steps he disappeared into the night.

*   *   *

Overhead there were new stars. As Travers returned to his hut he knew that Father Chester's story had changed him, had touched something long buried to reach back over the many dead years, to rekindle the brightness of his youth, when all of his fears and all of his failures lay in the future. "The greatest sin of all," Father Chester had said, "is the failure to love." Travers had not then responded, but now, as he lay on the simple cot, inside the tent of the netting that the woman named Marguerite's hands had touched, it came to him. The greatest sin, like all sins, begins with self. The deadly hit parade down through the ages of envy, greed, pride, and their compatriots was the expression of the gluttony of the self, while the greatest sin, the failure to love, was its starvation. I must love myself first, Travers thought. It must begin with me. But how? My life has been one of denial, of turning away, of fear, of molding myself to others' expectations. I have gone along to get...a long lostness. He took his nephew's tote bag and held it in his hands. Matt is gone; there is nothing I can do for him, not any longer. I would go to the ends of the earth if I could to help him, but it is too late. Too late! He returned the tote bag to its peg. The record button is permanently pushed in, he thought. Yes, and we can push the rewind button any time we choose, to live it all over again, all of our mistakes, all of our should haves and did nots. But there is no fast forward and no erase. Life is a stripped down model. He reached under the bed and carried the duffel bag into the full moon night. No one stirred. He approached the remains of the fire. Handful by handful he fed the gutted Bibles and prayer books to its embers, which, sloughing off slumber, flashed short-lived bursts of light. This is the trauma of birth, Travers thought, as the shells flamed like the passing of days. Then he returned to his hut and put the empty duffel bag under the bed. He lay down again but could not sleep. He was too new, too alive. He came from the hut to follow a narrow path he knew not where. Every few steps in the jungle's undulation came the spiderweb light of stars and moon. Bushes and branches brushed against him. Then, in the crystal night, sharp and pure, he saw her.

Marguerite stood on the shore. Waves expired in gentle lappings, bathing her bare feet up over her ankles. She did not hear Travers approach. Facing the sea in a forest of stars, she did not see him. Marguerite's body was turned slightly so that her long hair came weaving around her waist. She was the brightest of visions in the surest of dreams. Travers stopped at the jungle's edge, watching Marguerite. To go forward would be trespass, a violation of what he did not know, but he would not retreat. He had had enough of retreating. So he too stood transfixed, like a conquistador who has hacked his way through the jungle to at last set eyes on the sea. Long minutes later Marguerite turned. The scarring of her face glowed. Travers went to her.

"I felt that someone was here," she said.

There was a sharp edge to her words. "I did not mean to intrude," he said, "but I did not want to go away either." He reached for her hand, but she would not let him take it. Instead, Marguerite sat down on the shore. Travers sat beside her. "You are beautiful," he said, after a long silence had passed between them.

"No." This one word came as death comes, certain, irrevocable. "Once I *was* beautiful, but now I am scarred." She touched the right side of her face.

"No. Do not say that. That is not right. You are the most beautiful woman I have ever seen."

Marguerite gave a cynical laugh. "I had forgotten how superficial Americans are."

"But you *are* beautiful!" Travers said.

"Americans are also predictable. Your every thought is a cliché. You know nothing about me, nothing at all. Please go. Leave me alone." She slid herself to the side so that there was more space between them. Travers' former self started to move, to raise himself from the sand, to do as he had been asked, to comply with her wishes. *I am sorry—* the words formed in his mind. But he did not say them. Instead he heard these words: "It is you to whom your face is scarred. To me you are beautiful."

"My face is none of your business. I have asked you to leave."

"I have as much right as you to be here."

"Yes, I know all about your rights. Americans have so many rights. You are from the land of equality where everyone is superior."

"I said, 'As much right.' I did not say, 'more'."

"Why would you stay where you are not wanted?"

"Talk about a cliché!" Travers answered. It was a new voice. "We must decide our own place, not give in to others who would do so for us, who would fix everyone's place at the table. I am just now beginning to learn this."

"I hate Americans," Marguerite said, "and the ways of Americans."

"Your grandfather was an American."

"How do you know?"

"Father Chester told me."

"Father Chester had no right to tell you anything about me." Marguerite pushed herself to her feet. Anger flamed her face in moonlight.

"Please stay," Travers said. It was a gentle plea. Marguerite looked down at him.

"If there were pity in my heart," she said, "I would pity you. Father Chester should not have asked me to help you with the netting. You..."

"Father Chester knew exactly what he was doing," Travers interrupted. "The only way to overcome our demons is to confront them face to face. The greatest sin of all, he has taught me, is the failure to love."

"So now I am a sinner! What arrogance!"

"You say you hate Americans. Father Chester is an American."

"Father Chester *was* an American." Marguerite turned and stepped a short distance away.

"If we fail to love," Travers said, "sooner or later we hate."

Marguerite turned and faced him. "It is a sin only if we act. Our thoughts are our own." The night in his sister's garage flashed in Travers' mind. Once again his nephew reached out to him. Once again he turned away. "The poisoned tree always bears fruit," he said.

These words came to Marguerite with great force; her legs collapsed beneath her. Tears filled her eyes as she fell to her knees. Travers kept his distance. He said nothing more. Traces of light reached from the water's edge as they sat there neither together nor apart. Slowly the light separated into new births of color. Marguerite stood. Without looking back she walked along the shore until far in the distance she turned into the jungle.

Chapter Twenty:
Delirium

Joe Rogers
Mabouhey
1991

Native Americans, the Blackfoot, the Huron, the Crow,
believe that the real world is the world of dreams. It is the
waking world that is the world of fantasy. I did not know
that I had fallen into delirium. I did not know that my ankle
was broken, nor that the man called Christian feared
amputation. I remembered Father Chester sending for a
woman named Marguerite. Yes, I had answered, send for
Marguerite. Her lovely name stayed with me like a song. I
could not move—there were ropes at my wrists and
ankles—and yet I was moving. I remember bouncing along
as if I had returned to my mother's womb. The sounds of

birds came crying and shrill. Monkeys jabbered. Mists of sun swirled, yellow piercing into the greenest of greens. How much time passed I cannot say. Then there was a softness of voice and a vision bending down, a silhouette that blurred into and out of darkness.

Under a willow tree Val danced. "Dance with me. We know not when the music stops. Dance with me." A long skirt washed at her ankles. It was mauve and pale green, a weave of glistening stars. With the sweep of the willow tree's branches Val's long hair swayed, red into gold into light, an alchemy of moon. From about her neck flowers poured bathing her bare breasts. "Dance with me." As gentle as a sigh, a soft breeze came in elegant arcs, the lace of the willow tree easy, sweeping easy, one edge of night sky to the other. There were flutes and a harp and a far tambourine. "Dance with me." In the frozen light of the fullest of moons, in the mothering night of the willow tree's song, Val danced. She danced rhythmic and slow, like cradling arms sheltering a newborn child, like patience itself and understanding. There was time and more time and all the time that will ever be. "Dance with me." Oh, make it so that our eyes do not open, make it so that the day is held from us. Let dreams keep away death. Spirits of Crow, of Blackfoot, of Huron shall triumph! I know it. I can feel it. I shall will it so that it shall be so. *Listen! Listen!* The night sky's eagle takes wing as our grandmothers promised. No eye will open while the sun is marauding. We shall hold the day only in the cave of pretending, long, long ago. Cry no more women stirring pots that are empty. We shall be freed from the prison of sun. No one will cut up the land. Never again will the sky and the river be parted, nor mother earth bleed from knives made of paper. The world of the day is but dust. The eagle's wing shall shade us from harm. River and sea, mountain and meadow shall once again breathe the songs of our fathers and all the earth's bounty restored in our souls. The waters shall be crowded with fish and the fields with fowl and buffalo and we shall go forward forever in the womb of our mother's dreamings. "Dance with me!" Val danced. With harp and flutes and a far tambourine Val danced. In the moon's liquid silver Val danced. In the sanctuary of willow and night Val danced. In a long skirt that washed at her ankles, her bare breasts bubbled with flowers, rhythmic and slow, Val danced. Then as I told you, as we all will be, just like that she was gone.

Chapter Twenty-One:
Searchlights on Prison Towers

Marguerite
Chicago, Illinois
1982

After her assault in Columbus Park Marguerite's life became a nightmare of looking over her shoulders. Like a torture of thieves, courtroom proceedings assaulted her. There was a motion for a change of venue. There was a motion for a new judge. There was a hearing to determine mental competence. There was a demand for a jury trial. Finally an earnest young assistant telephoned: the case had been settled. The young man in the blue coat, whose name Marguerite had burned in her memory, had pled guilty and would be sentenced to five years. At last! An end to the endless treks to the monolith of concrete that housed the circuit court, to the crowds and the waiting, to burning eyes, to smells, to garbage, to graffiti slashed into benches rubbed dull from waiting, to sagging shoulders and surly glances, to the wash of the unwashed, to the languor of the downtrodden and the snarls of the dispossessed, to the fear on faces of victims and witnesses alike, to the insolence of the accused, to the lethargy of judges, to the stupor of lawyers and clerks, to the boredom of bailiffs and deputies! At last! Marguerite would put the bad dream behind her. The police officers had encouraged her to do her duty and what had it gotten her? Months of catching her breath when a footstep came at a corner, of not sleeping, of fear. Well before five years passes, Marguerite reassured herself, I will be back in Mabouhey.

"This is good news," she said to the crisp voice on the phone. "Now I will be safe."

"You should still take precautions," the voice replied. "You should still be careful."

"You said it was a five-year sentence. Surely now I am safe."

"You don't understand," the voice came at her. "It's a suspended sentence."

"A suspended sentence?"

"It means," the voice, now weary, explained, "just what it says. The sentence is suspended."

"This cannot be," Marguerite protested in futile horror, "this cannot be. Demetrius Jefferson, who stole my money, who knocked me down, who threatened me, he's...he's going to go free? It cannot be. No!"

"I'm truly sorry. But you must remember. Demetrius Jefferson did not have a gun or a knife. All he did was knock you down. You said that it all happened so fast you couldn't make a positive identification, so it was just the word of the white golfers..."

"What does that have to do with anything?"

"It's their word against his. There's no hard evidence."

"I do not understand any of this," Marguerite cried.

"Well," the voice responded with exasperation, "this is Cook County and that's how it goes. There's not much point in letting this thing hang around. Your money was taken, yes, but you weren't injured. We have to give priority to more serious cases. The backlog is getting longer and longer."

Marguerite hung up the phone. After the assault, she had given up on finding an apartment and had settled, instead, on renting a room in one of the rooming houses that line Huron Street. She had enrolled in the Registered Nursing Program at Loop College. Three afternoons each week she volunteered at the Learning Network. Did Demetrius Jefferson know where she lived? She looked over her shoulder and did not carry a purse.

Two weeks later, as Marguerite was on Waller Avenue walking home, she was grabbed from behind. A hand came over her mouth as lips brushed wet against her ear. "If you make a sound," they said, "I will rip your heart out." There was a sharpness against her waist. Marguerite was dragged down an alley and into a garage. Demetrius

Jefferson ripped at her clothes and then he raped her. Marguerite looked into his dead eyes. When he was through, he took a knife and cut deeply into the right side of her face.

"I tole you I was gonna get you, bitch. You happy now?"

Marguerite's arms were pinned beneath her, but she managed to slide the right one free. Its hand clawed about in the rubbish that covered the garage's floor, old newspapers, greasy rags, empty cans, broken bottles and then...something solid! A brick! She hit Demetrius Jefferson on the side of his head. He fell to his right, holding his bleeding head with both hands. The blood that poured from her cheek burned into Marguerite's eyes so that all she could see was blurred red and blurring. She crawled on her hands and knees. She reached out until her fingers found him. She brought the brick high over her head, over and over, many times, pounding the wetness her clawing fingertips felt in the rags, in the trash, among the broken bottles. A gurgle came from Demetrius Jefferson's throat and Marguerite knew that his head was crushed beyond all further crushing. She crawled to the garage door and slid herself under. At the corner of Parkside and Erie children bounced and bobbed at the side of an ice cream truck. As the ice cream man bent over and then raised up he saw Marguerite crawl from under the garage door and collapse into the alley.

*   *   *

In the hospital Marguerite went into and out of sleep. The children from the Learning Network sent homemade cards to stand like candles on dresser and window sill, of bright crayon colors, of tin foil, doilies, and ribbons. Images of Mabouhey and of Gideon's son, Schugay, wandered through her mind.

Schugay ran to her, the white sand like sugar washing over his ankles. His black, black hands lifted her to the sky and his thick lips nibbled at her neck as he and Marguerite lay on the mirror where water meets shore, touching. Marguerite put her hands together around the small of Schugay's back and then her body was his body, her breathing was his breathing, and they were one.

"Do not leave," Schugay said.

Why could she not just stay with him? As a child she would not stay on the shore; she had had to venture out. Now a new world beckoned and she would not turn away. Men go forth and no one wonders. This is something I must do, the way a painter paints or a dancer dances. The why of it is not to say. I must go, Schugay, or my love for you will wither like a butterfly in a glass jar. "Wait for me, my Schugay. Wait for me. I will return and we shall never again be parted."

Schugay leaned to his side and spat. The ocean ran to their feet and retreated. "The white man is the devil," Schugay said.

"Do not speak that way," Marguerite answered. "My grandfather was a white man. Father Chester is a white man."

Schugay brought her hands to his lips. "You are right," he said. "It is the ways of the white man that are evil. Their world is the hyena world, the world of the vulture and scorpion, the world of the snake. If you go, you will be destroyed."

"I am strong," Marguerite said. "I will not be destroyed."

"You will not be the same. Do not go."

Marguerite kissed Schugay's strong black hands. Tears came to her. "Father Chester says the world is getting smaller and smaller. There will be many changes. We must be prepared. We must arm ourselves with knowledge." She stood, bent over, and kissed him full and sweet. "I will count the days until I return. Wait for me." Marguerite ran into the sea and Schugay followed. They swam far out to a sandbar where they lay together again and spoke no more of her journey.

Two days passed and Marguerite was able with unsure steps to carry herself to the bathroom's mirror. Her head was a nest of bandage. She remembered when she was a little girl and Jericho first took her to the great warehouse, huge and dark. Giant spools of fabric, like silent ghosts, stood guard. She had been afraid. She closed her eyes. Then Jericho lifted her in his arms, laughing, and carried her back into the jungle's green song. Would she ever find light again? What she saw now were ugly blisters where her lips had been. And my eyes? Searchlights on prison towers.

Another day passed and her bandages were removed. The right side of her face was the corner of a dirty handkerchief, a fusion of sores, of curdled skin, pimpled and sick. Forehead and cheek surrounding her right eye angled into spidery webs. "You will be changed," Schugay had said. "You will be destroyed." She saw Schugay's face in her mind and what was left of her own in the bathroom's mirror. Schugay would no longer love her. He would never love her again. He had begged her not to leave, but she left. She left the blackest boy with the biggest heart and he would never love her again. She fled from the mirror, threw herself on top of the bed, and hungered for sleep. In the world of dreams she was unchanged and Schugay would love her forever.

*　　　*　　　*

The next day a white man in his early thirties came to her room. He was dressed in the finest clothes Marguerite had ever seen. His suit, smooth and refined, fit like a second skin. His manner was as crisp as his garb. He introduced himself.

"I am Merrill Forbes, Merrill Forbes the Third, actually. These are from all of us at Forbes, Morgan, Dixon, and White." The young man displayed a bouquet of roses, long stemmed, bright in their redness, and laid them on the side of her bed. Marguerite was sitting, propped against the metal headboard, reading. She did not know what to say. Who was this person? What did he want?

She found the ease of Merrill Forbes the Third's demeanor irritating. In its excess his smoothness grated.

Now, without asking, the young man seated himself on the side of Marguerite's bed, his fingers playing with the stems of the roses.

"You see," he said, "Forbes, Morgan is one of the city's premier law firms. As such, of course, we are a member—a founding member, actually—of the Chicago Council on Foreign Affairs. When my father, we call him Number Two—he's the senior *and* managing partner—well, when he saw the article in the *Tribune* he got on the horn in a hurry and, of course, I wasn't about to spin my wheels, not when Number Two was calling. So here I am!"

Merrill Forbes the Third looked at Marguerite with a smile as dazzling as a movie star's. "We are all so sorry, you see," he continued. "We at Forbes, Morgan take a particular interest in our foreign guests. When something like this happens, it's a real black eye...I mean it's a real black mark, image-wise, for the entire city. That's all the more reason your suffering should not go without recompense." Again the smile.

"What is it you want?" Marguerite asked.

"I want to be your advocate. You are not an American so you are not cognizant of your rights, all of your rights. You may not be a citizen," the attorney said, as if summing up for a jury, "but you are a human being!"

"I am sorry," Marguerite said, growing tired, "but I do not understand."

The young man leaned forward. "Look," he said, "you came here to study. To learn. To improve yourself. You never hurt anyone. You were just minding your own business. And you were exceptionally beautiful, in the flower of your femininity. I can still see that. The more precious the jewel, the ugliler the flaw!" He reached into the inside pocket of his jacket and wrote in a small notebook.

Marguerite turned her head into the pillow, smothering her scars. She wanted Merrill Forbes the Third to leave.

"Someone should pay," the lawyer continued. "Someone should pay for what happened to you. Perhaps the homeowner of the garage. If the garage door had been secured, well, this might have been avoided." The lawyer gave the room a wide sweep with both hands. "There is no doubt the homeowner was negligent. The legal question is to what extent was that negligence responsible for what happened to you. There is a chance we might break new ground here, set a new precedent. It could all be quite exciting. Of course, the main complaint will be against Cook County. Demetrius Jefferson should not have been on the street in the first place. We will also look into bringing suit against the manufacturer of the knife that did *that*"—Merrill Forbes the Third pointed at her face—"as well as the store where it was purchased, but, as I said, the main action is against the county. That's where the deep pockets are. We should know. You see, Forbes, Morgan maintains an excellent relationship with Warner Tully—he's the States Attorney—and I am confident we can get him to see things our way. No one wants a thing like this hanging around, especially when the primaries are just around the corner."

Marguerite did not want to sue anyone. All she wanted was to be left alone. She pushed a button at the side of the bed to summon a nurse.

"There's no charge to you at all," Merrill Forbes the Third went on. "None whatsoever. Forbes, Morgan is willing in this case to work on a contingency basis, which is contrary to our normal policy. We will keep one-third of the settlements we engineer. After reimbursement for expenses, of course. All of this is standard and there's no need to bother you with details you wouldn't understand anyway. I know this is foreign to you, but if I didn't do everything in my power to see to it that your rights are defended, well, I wouldn't be doing my job." Again there was the smile. "When the Good Lord closes a door, he always opens a window. I am your window. Of course it's hard to see this right now, but a day will come when you realize that this isn't as bad as it seems, not really all that bad at all. I have represented lots of women in similar situations who do—especially you people—but it takes time. We could very well be talking big bucks here. Big big bucks."

Marguerite saw Schugay's white, white teeth and the sunburst of his smile. Tears came to the edges of her eyes. "You will be changed," Schugay had said. "You will be destroyed." Schugay would no longer love her. He would never love her again.

A nurse came into the room. "Did you want something?" she asked.

Marguerite moved her head from the pillow. "Make him go," she said in a hard voice. "I want him to leave."

"Fine, fine," the lawyer said, straightening his tie. "Of course you are tired. I'll just leave my business card here on the window sill. Think about what I said. I'll get back to you in a few." Again, the smile. Marguerite did not see it, for she had turned her face fully into the pillow.

"You must leave now," the nurse said.

Merrill Forbes the Third started for the door. Then he turned. "One more thing," he said. "Watch carefully what they do to you here. Or, even more importantly, what they don't do." Then he was gone.

"The hyena world," Schugay had said. "The world of the vulture and scorpion, the world of the snake."

"Please give those flowers to someone else," Marguerite said to the nurse as she took the lawyer's business card from the window sill. She ripped it into small pieces, letting them drop like dead leaves into the waste basket at the side of her bed. She turned her head again into the pillow and finally there came the silent music of sleep. The next day, the day before her discharge, a young woman from the states attorney's office came to her room. "I have good news," she said. "We have decided to drop all charges against you."

*   *   *

While Marguerite was in the hospital Luther moved her belongings into Auntie Rose and Zion's spare bedroom. Everyone insisted, and Marguerite agreed: she'd feel safer at Auntie Rose and Zion's. On Mabouhey the question of safety did not exist. Yes, there were sharks in the ocean and snakes and scorpions in the jungle, but there were no human predators. Now, as Luther drove her from the hospital, Marguerite cringed at every stoplight. She checked and rechecked that the car's doors were locked; each pair of walking eyes menaced.

"Maybe you should carry a gun," Zion suggested a few days later. "With the hours you keep and all." A gun! Is survival so ensured life worth preserving? "Lots of ladies are these days," Zion said. "They make a real nice one called the Lady Earp, fits snug in the palm of your hand. You could get some training."

Marguerite had come to Chicago to learn. She would observe the customs of Americans, their ways, their values. In the abstract there was something to be said for their deification of the individual, but Marguerite came to realize that on a practical level the American cult of the individual, however noble as an ideal, meant each for himself, each for herself, and each against all. You're on your own, kid. Money, lots of money, will protect you. It will permit you to live far from festering places in various stages of abandonment where crime is an elemental force, the at least one less place setting at every table. Yet traffic goes in both directions; the asphalt that takes the law-abiding citizen away also takes the predator to. No one feels safe, not really. Politicians postured about unity in the community, but Marguerite saw no sign of either. "Don't ever let anybody come up on you," Auntie Rose said. "Don't ever let anybody come up on you." Everyone Marguerite met wanted to live some place else. It was bad, real bad where they lived. Put your trust in the gun, Zion said. To Marguerite there was something repugnant about owning a gun. She tried to think clearly. She had been in Chicago all of eight months. She spent her afternoons in the Austin branch library on Race Avenue. There were, she quickly realized, certain public issues that were for Americans as unchanging as the seasons: abortion, gun control, capital punishment. Increasingly she came to understand that the democratic clash of ideas, extolled and idealized, was a game without rules, where nothing was out of bounds. It was not a democracy, as she understood it, but a plutocracy of money, of pollsters, of television, of scandal, titillation, and tripe. Somehow, although Marguerite wondered for how much longer, the dinosaur republic blundered along with more and more heat and less and less light. Fanaticism poisoned every issue. In the great mudding which passed for discourse, supposed dialogue degenerated into personal attacks. Nothing was off limits. Insinuations were bandied about in unsubtle code: vote for this candidate "before it's too late," support so and so because "she's one of us." Nobody listened to anybody else. Nobody respected anybody else. It was the ethos of suicide. What was most frightening to Marguerite was that Americans accepted this barbarism as normal, not just as the way things were but, from what she could tell, as the way things were supposed to be. Americans, she decided, are the least introspective of people. To question was unpatriotic. Everything American was the biggest, the greatest, the best that ever was or would be.

She read as much as she could about guns and gun control. In the *National Review* she read that a government ban on firearms would disarm only the otherwise law-abiding citizen. In *Harper's* she read that the Second Amendment to the American Constitution does not guarantee an individual the right to own a machine gun. In *Ladies' Home Journal* she read about brassiere holsters and designer pistols. She would not carry a gun. Yet she could not say why not. Of course the decision was easier knowing that Zion had not one, but two, firearms in the house: a shotgun and a revolver. But carrying her own gun seemed a surrendering to fear, a giving up of faith and hope, a bonding with the forces of force, an abandonment of reason.

No, she would not carry a gun.

*   *   *

A week later Marguerite returned to Loop College. A banner hung over the doorway of the first classroom she entered:

WELCOME BACK, MARGUERITE!

Her classmates bustled around her, like drive-by shootings their eyes stealing furtive glances of her face. Marguerite had not found it easy to adjust to the strange world of the American classroom. Most of the students had little enthusiasm for their studies. Many of the teachers were dispirited and dull. But there were students who worked as hard as she did and there were teachers who gave genuinely of themselves. She eavesdropped in the cafeteria as her fellow students gossiped about their instructors. The majority of students fixated on grades, not learning. As a result, the classrooms of the less demanding instructors were enrolled to capacity. Paradoxically this did not mean that attendance in them was high, for their pandering professors dismissed mandatory attendance as the heresy of elitism. Merely enrolling and showing up for one or two classes guaranteed a passing grade. The happy consequence of full enrollment in such masquerades was that the other instructors' classes had fewer students; their smaller class size, coupled with their caring professors' intensity, took Marguerite on a joyous journey of the mind. She exhilarated in the pleasure of learning. She was reminded of Icolyn teaching her to make auyama soup, of Gideon who taught her to fish as if she were a fish herself, and of Father Chester's library.

She had been attacked at the beginning of the Fall semester and would therefore not resume a full schedule until the following spring. This provided time to sample classes already in session. She sat in the last row, in sunglasses, with a kerchief loosely at her neck. The classes had baffling colonated names. American Literature: Chauvinism as Poetic; Western Civilization: Apotheosis of Power; Psychology 101: Heterosexual Myth and the Origins of Psychosis. Not all were as silly as their names suggested, but many were, and, after one visit, she did not return.

She was angered most by her experience in a sociology class, *Contemporary Culture: Majoritarian Miasma.* Twenty minutes late its professor, Dr. Lenell Jerkers, strode into the classroom like General Douglas MacArthur landing on Luzon. He wore a multi-colored dashiki with kente cloth draping his right shoulder. On his head sat a yellow pillbox, crescent moon and stars on the sides, Arabic lettering across its front. His legs were stockings woven with shells and little bells. His feet were sandals. His left hand carried a staff, intricately carved, shining in polyurethane sheen like gadgets Marguerite had seen advertised on television. His right hand waved a Koran as if it were for sale. He was a middle-aged brown man of medium height and, as Marguerite quickly realized, of less than medium intelligence.

"As-Salaam-Alaikum!" Professor Jerkers saluted with fist raised. He sat on the top of his desk, feet dangling.

"Wa-Alaikum-Salaam," eight of the sixteen students in attendance responded without enthusiasm.

"Hautep! I see we have a sister, a fine young sister, new to our assembly," the professor said. "Sister, why don't you bring it on up here so we can get a better look at you?"

"I have trouble with my eyes, sir," Marguerite said. "It is better for me here. The light is less glaring."

"By all means," the professor replied with a deprecatory wave of his left hand. Marguerite knew he was annoyed. He was one of those men, she understood instinctively, who demands immediate and full obeisance from the female, especially when other men are witness. "By all means," Professor Jerkers repeated. "Brother Malcolm said, 'By any means necessary', but I will leave it at that, 'by all means'." He attempted an indulgent smile, but Marguerite had lowered her head.

Her failure to appreciate what the professor saw as magnanimity and wit on his part was as irritating as a stone in his sandal. He would cast it out. "I am sorry for your disability, sister. To achieve a more complete comprehension of how the oppression of the racist, imperialistic, and capitalistic system of the white man functions, I find it efficacious to utilize examples from real life, to mine the soil of the people who struggle against daunting odds for survival in spite of the deck that the Jew and the white man has stacked against us. How is it that you became disabled?"

Marguerite did not think of herself as disabled. She cringed at the word. She was as able as ever. "I am not disabled," she said.

"Okay. 'Have it your way,' sister, as Burger King says." The professor paused, expecting laughter; he was annoyed when it was weaker than he felt his wit deserved. "Let me rephrase. How is it that you are disfigured?"

Disfigured. An ugly word. A titillating jolt coursed through the room as the students turned to stare at her. Marguerite did not think her personal affairs were any of the professor's business. She did not want to be grist for his venomous mill. "I would rather you not ask, please," she replied. There was a weary determination to her voice.

Professor Jerkers sprang to his feet, smashing his fisted right hand into the palm of his left. "Bourgeois sensibility!" he exclaimed. "Exactly what we were analyzing last week. Bourgeois sensibility! You have nothing to be ashamed of, sister." He looked at Marguerite. "It is a shame that you were not with us then. I have no doubt that your consciousness would have been awakened from the slumber of its bourgeois sensibility had you been in attendance. You have, I repeat, nothing to be ashamed of. It is important that you understand that. You are a victim, nothing more. We are all victims. Victims of the Jew and his pretend sympathy! Victims of the white man!" The professor went to the chalkboard. "Here, let me illustrate." He drew a white circle at the top of the board and a smaller triangle near the bottom. He wrote the word *Africa* in the circle and the word *Europe* in the triangle.

"Africans are sun people," he lectured. "Europeans are creatures of ice. Deprived of the warmth of the sun, huddled together like hibernating beasts in the dreary wetness of Saxony and Wales, of Bohemia and Transylvania, the neurological system of the white man is stunted. This leads to melanin deficiency, cause and effect, effect and cause! Hence the white man is bleached, emaciated. His is a race of albinos. They need to be put back in the oven. Especially the Jew. In their thin-lipped inferiority they lash out. They oppress." With a flourish the professor turned to face the students in self-congratulation. His face was beaming. "This is the paradigm," he said. "Hautep!"

"The white man is the devil," Schugay had said that day on the beach. Marguerite would not, could not, give herself to such hatred then, as much as she loved the laughing black boy whose lips were sweeter than the ripest berry. She looked now with disgust at Professor Jerkers. She wanted to leave, but did not want to call additional attention to herself.

The professor was not through with her. Seated back on his desk, he had babbled on while her thoughts wandered, but now, suddenly, Marguerite realized that the entire class was once again staring at her.

"Well?" the professor demanded.

"Well what?" Marguerite replied.

"Are you going to tell us? As I have just finished explaining, had you paid attention, the false concept of the individual is a perversion, seeking to deny us, sons and daughters of the mother continent, our true African roots. Individuality is an aberrant idea imperialistically imposed by the European aggressor, by the lackey Jew. It seeks to divide us, the true Chosen People, by eviscerating the soul of our original and pure Saharan and sub-Saharan essence. It seeks to destroy our unity. Our *umoja*. We can all see that you are polluted by European blood, sister. Was your great-grandmother raped by the slavemaster? The preponderance of melanin in you may yet overcome the stain of the inferior hemoglobin infecting you, but only if you nurture the nexus. This you must do. As Soul II Soul puts it, 'Be selective, be objective, be an asset to the collective'." Professor Jerkers paused but Marguerite remained silent. "We are waiting, sister. What happened? Tell us." The professor walked towards her.

"I do not understand any of this," Marguerite said. She reached for her things and started to rise. Now the professor stood next to her.

"Tell us," he demanded again, the words hissing from between clenched teeth. He bent over close to Marguerite's face. "Tell us."

"I will tell you this." Marguerite got to her feet. "You are a bigot and a fool. You are a part of the problem, not a part of the solution. How dare you attempt to use me like a frog in a biology experiment? I am a woman, a black woman, and strong, yes, but, first of all, I am a human being!"

Professor Jerkers stepped from her and leaned against the back wall. "Now, now, sister," he cooed. "I get it. That time of the month, is it?" He glanced at the other students for approval, but their faces turned quickly away. Marguerite walked to the door and slammed it behind her. The professor returned to his desk. "I guess the period is over," he laughed, holding his hands to his stomach. The students rose from their desks and started for the exit. "Get it?" Professor Jerkers leaned against the chalkboard. Saliva slid from the corners of his mouth. "The period is over," he repeated. "The period is over."

*   *   *

Schugay's letters came, one after the other, each more questioning and worried at the urgency of her silence, but Marguerite did not, could not, answer. She took his letters from the red-ribboned bundle she kept in the dresser's bottom drawer to read over and over. Finally, in her tears, she brought herself to the small desk in front of the bedroom window. Bundled like elves in brightly colored snow suits, children played in Chicago's November cold.

"*My Schugay,*" she began, as she always had. "*You were right when you said I would be changed. I cannot find it in my heart to let you go on believing that what we had once will remain. I shall return to Mabouhey, as I promised, but we will not return to each other. I read and reread your letters with pain, for I have waited to write you longer than I should have. If you love me as you say you love me, and as I know you loved me once, do not write again. Keep me in your heart the way you remember me. Let me go as I must let go of you. Farewell.*

Marguerite

She looked at her signature: *Marguerite.* Not *Your Marguerite* as she had always written before. She threw herself on the bed, weeping.

She dragged herself through each day, through visits to specialists who poked at her face like cheery robins pecking at crumbs, through classes at Loop College and field practice at West Suburban Hospital in nearby Oak Park. As frequently as possible she was at the Learning Network, where she could be a child again if only for a few hours. She would not think of Schugay. Yet, as the days passed after she had sent the letter, the last, last letter, she hoped that in spite of her words Schugay would write again, that he would smother the anguish of her damaged soul with such a deluge of love that she would dare once more to hope. Perhaps Schugay had adjusted to her absence, had come to terms with the distance and time that separated them, had given up counting the days until her return. She remembered Schugay's strong arms, the beauty of his shoulders, and her heart beat faster. Had he found someone else? Maybe that would be for the best. She pretended to find solace in such thoughts even as her soul cried the eternal tears of lost love. She studied her face in the mirror, kerchiefed and kerchiefless. If she turned her head just so, and held her neck at a certain angle, she looked no different than before. But Schugay would turn away from her like a fish from its shadow. In the first power of their new love he had begged her to stay with him, he had begged her not to go. No, the scars on her face would be a constant reminder of her turning away. She had allowed the spell of their magic to be broken: fine crystal shattered on cold marble floors. She would not weaken. She would not answer his letters. Slowly Schugay would forget her. By the time she returned to Mabouhey his heart would no longer be hers. A week passed and then another. Schugay could go to Frederique City, she could not keep herself from thinking, to the American Express. He had called once, two months before, before what had happened, on her birthday, even though they had agreed that they would only write, international calls so very dear. But he had surprised her, if only for a few moments, and the remembrance now of his wired words and pausings was a knife in her heart. The days passed and the telephone was silent.

She tried not to be out late, alone, on the streets, but there came a night when her ride did not come and she found herself walking home alone in the murky gauze that is Chicago's December twilight, which came, as the sun fled, like strips of dirty bandage. Marguerite hurried her steps. She darted her head from side to side. Yes, she would make it. Yes, she would be safe. She was at the front door of Auntie Rose and Zion's, keys in hand. Her body tensed. Were those footsteps behind her? Before she could turn, embracing arms came to take her. Then, like a whisper, the smells of Mabouhey! Sweet lips nibbled at her neck. Schugay! Schugay! Schugay!

Chapter Twenty-Two:
A Blanket of Stars

Schugay
Mabouhey; Chicago
1982-1983

Schugay went to Hernando's boat every day, but there were no letters. Hernando laughed at him: Marguerite had found herself a rich white man. Schugay was a fool to have permitted her to leave. She had found herself a rich white man.

Schugay wrote:

My Marguerite,

I could not sleep last night. I went to our place, there at the water and I swam out to the sandbar (do you remember?) and I sat there thinking of you. I asked the stars, "Stars, are you watching over Marguerite? Is she asleep in her bed? Does she dream of me?" But the stars did not answer. Marguerite. Marguerite. Marguerite. I wrote your name in the sand and I put my hand where I had written and whispered your name. I prayed that the Spirits would look over you and keep you safe and keep you warm and keep you mine.

Every day I go to meet Hernando's boat. I wait and I watch as the boat comes from the sky but Hernando and his brother do not wave back and I know that my heart will be stone for another day. Yet I wait until Hernando's boat is at the shore and I run to it and ask and there is no letter. Maybe tomorrow there will be a big bag full of your letters, one after one, like little fish all in one net. That is what I tell myself.

Love and love and love again. And one more time. And another.

Your Schugay

And then Hernando's boat was coming and Hernando and his brother were waving, the spot of white dancing between them. Schugay ran into the water and swam to the boat and put his hand on its side, pushing the boat, swimming along its side until the water was shallow enough to stand. The white paper came like a bird to his hand and the dark clouds of Marguerite's words stormed in his heart. No. No. No. It cannot be. It cannot be. Schugay clutched the white paper and fell to the water.

Then he was on his feet, wounding the sand with angry footprints until he was far from the boat and no one could see him. He fell to the sand. No. No. No. It cannot be. She has gone and found herself a rich white man, he heard

Hernando laugh. No. No. It cannot be. Schugay's face was a sea of tears. His heart ached with the worst ache there is, the worst wound of all, the pain of too late and not enough and it cannot be. No. No. An hour passed and then another. *Do not write me again.* The words were prison bars. *If you love me.* Oh, yes, yes, yes, I love you. Do you not know, Marguerite? Have you forgotten? *Keep me in your heart.* But you are in my heart, you are in my heart forever. "...*the way you remember me.*" Why does she say this? "...*the way you remember me?*" If she has found herself a rich white man, why does she ask if I love her? Why does she tell me to keep her in my heart— oh! I could do nothing other!—"*the way you remember me?*" Hope, like music, came to him. He brought the letter to his lips. I must go see Father Chester, he thought. Father Chester will help me. Father Chester will know what to do.

Words like tears poured from the black boy's heart.

"You have always been strong," Father Chester said. "But now you must find a deeper strength, the strength of unselfish love. Yes, you love Marguerite. But do you love her enough to let her go?"

"I do not understand," Schugay cried. Marguerite was walking in front of him, dangling a bucket at her side. Her long black hair played with the breeze. It was enough to walk behind.

"Love is not possessiveness. Love is not enslave- ment. Love is freedom. We must choose love freely. We must move to the side, get out of its way, and let love be. Love is. We cannot will it. We cannot control it. It is the mightiest of rivers and the calmest of seas. Is your love for

Marguerite pure? Will you risk everything for her —even a heart that breaks worse than any bone can ever be broken?"

"No one has loved as I have loved," Schugay said, tears streaming his face full and flowing.

"Then you must let her go if that is what she asks of you."

"But she asks if I love her," Schugay said, pushing the white paper into the priest's hands. The shipwrecked sailor clings to the stick though the stick be but splinter.

"Our son would like to live with you." Yes, I remember, Father Chester thought. I remember what it is to love with a love that is young once only, and I know what it is to love with a love that stays young forever. The years he and Christian shared sang in his heart like the sea.

"I will go to Frederique City," Chester said.

"But there is something I must tell you first," Schugay said. "It was in my heart that you were the devil."

"Now in your heart there is only room for love. Let love be."

It had been many years since his last visit to Frederique. Chester had forgotten how tawdry and desperate the larger island was becoming. Gutters were papered and bottled with garbage. The men kept their hands close to their pockets. The women either did not carry handbags or clutched them close to their shoulders.

"You can place your call now." The young man in the American Express office pointed to a desk in the corner, beneath a poster that boasted Chicago's skyline:

CITY OF BIG SHOULDERS

"Yes, yes." Luther's voice came to him. "I will accept the charges." A pause. "It has been a long time," Luther said.

"Yes," Chester replied. "Letters are not the same. How is Marguerite?" The waiting between them now was the silence that hangs between thunder and lightning.

"Marguerite is very strong," Luther said.

"Do you know who Schugay is?"

"Marguerite used to talk about him all the time." Another pause. Then: "Marguerite does not want anyone there to know."

"You must tell me," Chester said, his words the tin cup of a blind man.

Schugay was waiting as Hernando's boat came to the shore. Chester stepped into the water. Then he and Schugay walked on the beach.

"Do you love Marguerite?"

Every day since her letter came I have died a thousand deaths. "Yes. Yes."

"For better? For worse?"

"A thousand times yes."

"In sickness and in health?"

"Yes, yes."

"Then you must go to her," the priest said. "Then you must go to her at once." He did not say anything more.

*   *   *

He saw her. She wore a pillowly coat with a bulky hood that hid her face, but Schugay knew it was Marguerite. She reached the front door and he was behind her. His arms wrapped around her waist, his lips at her neck the wings of a hummingbird. Marguerite held his body close, her head against his chest, like an infant at her mother's bosom, and then she took Schugay's hand and they went inside. Marguerite sat on her bed with her body turned and buried her face in her hands.

"I thought I had lost you forever," Schugay said. "I cried a thousand oceans."

"You must forget me," Marguerite said. Oh, my Schugay, I will never stop loving you though the world turns to ice and no birds sing.

"That I cannot do." He was standing next to her, the strength of his hands on her shoulders. Tears filled their eyes. Schugay turned Marguerite towards him. She would not raise her head, but buried it instead against her right shoulder. Schugay untied her hood and brushed snowflakes from her coat. Then he brought his hand to her face and lifted her to him. Marguerite's scars shone through her tears, a blanket of stars.

Arrow to rainbow,
From under thunder and shadow,
The nightingale sings.
Wandered in desert, we come upon water.
Wounded in winter, we enter on spring.

Schugay fell to his knees and buried his face in Marguerite's lap. "Tell me tomorrow," he whispered. He brought Marguerite's face close to his. Their tears were as where river meets sea. Then night came and took them, and they stayed in each other's arms and would not let go.

*   *   *

Auntie Rose got up early the next morning. She set four places on the dining room table. She took tablecloth and china from the breakfront, crystal, cloth napkins, silver napkin rings. "A woman knows," she said to herself, "a woman knows." She knocked at Marguerite's door. "It's okay now," Auntie Rose said.

In the middle of the night Marguerite told him, one word of pain following another. Schugay stroked her face with the back of his hand as she lay against him. Moonlight came across her breasts. "Promise you will never leave me," Schugay said. "Promise."

"This is Schugay," Marguerite said to Auntie Rose and Zion as they gathered in the dining room.

"Yes, yes," Auntie Rose beamed. "I am Auntie Rose and this is Zion."

"Pleased to meet you," Schugay said.

"Likewise," Zion mumbled in a low, gruff voice. He pulled his chair from the table and sat down. "Don't rightly understand why we ain't eating in the kitchen like we always do, this being breakfast." Auntie Rose looked at

Marguerite and Schugay and winked. "Let us bow our heads," Zion said. Under the table Marguerite's hand found Schugay's. "We give thanks to Thee, O Lord," Zion prayed, "for what we are about to eat."

"Amen!" Auntie Rose said. Marguerite and Schugay opened their mouths.

"I wasn't finished," Zion continued. "And let us follow in your holy ways, Lord, and avoid the path of sin and damnation. Let us keep thy commandments, Lord, and stick to the path of righteousness!" Silence like a shadow.

"AMEN!" Zion said. The crystal glasses at his place setting trembled.

"Amen!" Auntie Rose said again and Marguerite and Schugay echoed her: "Amen!"

"Now," Zion said, "we are not going to speak about this again, but this is my house and in my house we do what the Bible says. You know what I'm talking about. That's all I'm going to say. Now, let's us eat. What did you say your name was again, boy? Steven?"

"My name is Schugay." He looked at Marguerite. "You tell them," Schugay said.

"Schugay and I are going to get married!" The dining room of the golden bungalow filled with sunlight.

"None too soon!" Zion said.

"Shut yo' mouth," Auntie Rose said. "Oh, thank you, Jesus," she shouted. "Thank you, Jesus." Auntie Rose jumped from her chair and leaned over Marguerite, hugging her shoulders. Then she put her lips on Schugay's cheek as tears came to her face. "I am so happy for you," Auntie Rose said. "I am so happy for you both. This calls for a celebration. Zion," she commanded, "bring Cousin Jamesia's wine up from the cellar."

Zion pushed his chair back from the table. Moments later he returned with a large green jug, its pig-snout cork wrapped in tin foil. "May you be blessed as we have been blessed," Zion said, raising his glass. He put his arm around the small brown woman who stood at his side. "If you have one part of our happiness," Zion said, "your hearts will sing forever."

*　　*　　*

Green, glass, and golden the Garfield Park Conservatory was an ocean of lilies. Marguerite and Schugay stood between Laredo Taft's statues of Helena and Hector. Reverend Augustus White, pastor of the Greater Rose Church of God in Christ, whose father had married Auntie Rose and Zion, pronounced wise words and Marguerite and Schugay jumped the broom. Then Luther Custis Towe gathered the children of the Learning Network, white shirts and white blouses, and their voices came like sunlight on the garden:

Let love be in all its splendor,
In every heart, in every home.
Let love be forever under
Every star and every moon.

Let love be everywhere and always:
Let love be.

Let love be in every dawning
Of each day's journey into night.
Let love be with the breath of morning
On every wing of every flight.

Let love be everywhere and always:
Let love be.

Let love be in towns and cities,
In farms and valleys, on the oceanside,
Let love be the nights and days
Of every parent's every child.

Let love be everywhere and always:
Let love be.

Let love be in every meadow,
In every pasture, in every plain,
Let love be with all its rapture
Before and after every rain.

Let love be everywhere and always:
Let love be.

Let love be at every table,
In every room, in every bed.
Let love be beyond and brimful
In all that's thought and all that's said.

Let love be everywhere and always:
Let love be.

Let love be wherever hands labor,
Let love be where seeds are sown.
Let love be where grain is gathered,
Let love be where rivers flow.

Let love be everywhere and always:
Let love be.
Let love be for Marguerite and Schugay.
Let love be.

Let love be everywhere and always.
Let love be.

Let love be.

*   *   *

One mile to the south the rental car of the Nelson family of
Timberlane Trails, Tennessee, headed for the Independence

Boulevard exit of the Eisenhower Expressway. The brochure Mrs. Nelson had propped against the dashboard stated that the Garfield Park Conservatory was "Chicago's best kept secret." "'This time of year,'" she read at Jeanette, age 11 and Paul Jr., age 9, "'thousands of lilies are in bloom.'" Heads conquered by portable radios, her progeny sat like insects in the back seat, moonfaced and silent, as Malcolm X College and the Garfield Exterminating Company passed by. "'Over one hundred varieties of lily'," their mother continued. "'A must-see for the horticulturist'." Mr. Nelson turned the car into the conservatory's parking lot, which, Mrs. Nelson saw with disappointment, was nearly full. Then in the late afternoon sun the Nelson family set foot on Chicago's west side.

"There's no charge," a young black woman at the lobby counter said to Mr. Nelson as she handed him brochures. "There's a wedding just ending. They're mostly in the main room. But there are two other rooms, so, by the time you've seen them, the party should be over. Walk right in. You'll be just fine." She gave a big smile. "Marguerite and Schugay jumped the broom!"

Blank looks. Better not to ask, Mr. and Mrs. Wilson each thought. The Nelson family started for the interior entrance door.

"Oh, you don't have any bubbly! We can't have that now, can we?" Like a magician, a tuxedo lowered a tray scintillating with glasses of champagne. The Nelson family froze. They were at the entrance. The doors were open. The feast was spread out before them.

"No, thank you," Mrs. Wilson said.

"No, thank you," Mr. Wilson echoed.

The tuxedo gave a wide smile, white teeth in a black face, thin black bowtie and magnetic eyes, and then, with a flourish, twirled his glimmering Aztec calendar high in the air to dissolve into the crowd.

The Nelson family had never seen so many black people. They were so well-dressed. The children so well-behaved! Mrs. Nelson gave her pocketbook a tight clutch under her shoulder. Mr. Nelson felt for his wallet. The Nelson children remained as before, snatched and invaded by WCKG, *Chicago's best rock and a whole lot more coming at'cha!*

"And I was so looking forward to seeing the lilies!" Mrs. Nelson cried as their rental car fled from the parking lot.

"Harriet," her husband replied, "it is best not to take chances. It is best to stick to your own kind." In the back seat the mannequin heads of Jeanette and Paul Jr. nodded like yo-yo's.

*   *   *

When you walk through the front door you can tell if a house is a home of love and that is all you need to know. Now to the abundance of Auntie Rose and Zion's love came the bounty of Marguerite and Schugay's. Theirs was no cloistered virtue. Theirs was a love thought lost, a love reborn as the sun after eclipse blazes anew. Marguerite returned to her classes at Loop College, Schugay walking her to and from the Central Avenue elevated stop. Barbara Jean Benedetto paid Schugay in cash to join her construction crew, demolishing, hauling, sweeping, hammering. Zion and Auntie Rose taught Marguerite and Schugay to play bid whist with a six card kitty. Once a week the four of them bowled at Austin Lanes on Division Street. Auntie Rose and Marguerite played together in garden and kitchen while Zion and Schugay tinkered with engines in garage and side driveway.

On weekends Marguerite unfolded Chicago's wonders: the green jewel of its lakefront, its grandeur of buildings, the Art Institute and the Field Museum, the Shedd Aquarium, the Museum of Science and Industry, the DuSable Museum. Schugay did not let go of Marguerite's hand. On the way home they would stop at Hermione's, the Jamaican restaurant on Chicago Avenue, to buy ganja.

Summer and autumn passed. Like an uninvited guest winter returned and Chicago, so recently green and so recently golden, trudged about dreary in gray like a prisoner. Schugay had never known such cold; Marguerite layered him with underwear and outerwear, in thermal socks and insulated boots, but some part of Schugay was always cold. He counted the days until they would return to Mabouhey. There was snow and more snow and wind and more wind and there was ice. Day after day the sky was a hangover. Then, as gradual as a glacier, Chicago stirred, a cranky old woman waking from cumbersome sleep. A vomit of decayed snow stained sidewalks and streets like dirty sheets and pillow cases. In Chicago March is the cruelest month.

Zion screwed the cap back on the bottle of cognac and rose from the table. He extended the flat of his hand for Schugay to brush with a slap.

"Guess that'll teach the women folk a thing or two!" Zion exclaimed. "A Boston! Take the A train to Evanston! Seven no trump, bid and made!"

"Isn't that the train that stops in Uptown?" Schugay asked. He stood and shook his waist from side to side. "On its way to Boston?"

"This one sure did," Zion said. "Lordy, lordy!"

"Shut yo' mouth!" Auntie Rose laughed. "You'd think nobody ever made a Boston before. You want some breakfast in the morning, Mr. Cardshark," she said to Zion, "you'd better help clean up this mess." Auntie Rose turned to Marguerite. "You children run along now. Zion and me can handle this."

Marguerite opened her mouth to protest, but Schugay grabbed her by the hand. In the bedroom his lips came to her neck, but she reached her hands to his shoulders. "Wait until they are in their room," Marguerite whispered. Schugay turned on the radio. He walked to the dresser to return to the bed with ganja and rolling papers. Like a cashier counting money his fingers worked the paper and crushed leaves. Then he inhaled the sweet smoke deeply into his lungs. He handed the spliff to Marguerite. But Marguerite shook her head.

"I will not be smoking for a while," she said. She reached for Schugay's hand and brought it to her stomach. Schugay smudged the burning ganja into an ash tray and fell to his knees. His lips began at her ankles and went along the insides of her thighs until they rested on her stomach. He put his large hands on either side and held her. Then Schugay rested his head lightly on her bosom as Marguerite's hands played with his hair.

"Let's make a brother! Let's make a sister!" Schugay said.

"One at time, please," Marguerite laughed. They held each other and kissed, their hands speaking to every part of their bodies. Then Schgay was inside her. The soft sounds of spring rain came against the window. Night like an ocean held them in dreams.

BOOK THREE: REBIRTH

Chapter Twenty-Three:
The Gruntings of Wild Boars

Peter Comora ["Pack"]
Chicago
1983

It was time to round up the usual suspects. Sergeant Peter Comora, age 46, balding and overweight, a white man who smoked a pack of Camels a day, put his feet on his desk and leaned back in his chair. He had graduated from the police academy twenty-two years earlier, rode a squad car in the Englewood district for ten years, and then transferred to narcotics. Narcotics was where the big money was. Peter Comora—"Pack" to his buddies—mined the mother lode of coke, smack, and crack on Chicago's west side. His nickname as well as a very slight limp in his left leg was the legacy of a raid on the old Ye Fong men's club in Chinatown shortly before his transfer to narcotics. Somebody hadn't paid somebody and the joint was raided. Gambling. Opium. Prostitution. Peter Comora emptied two firearms, only one of which was regulation. "PISTOL PACKING PETE!" the headline on the *Chicago Sun-Times* blared the next morning.

District 15, the Austin District, was "the most west and most best" of the mother lode. "Most best" because a high level of organization ruled. There definitely was a there there. And a yours, a mine, and an ours. Wilfredo Chapman, "One Ear Willie," was in charge from Roosevelt Road on the south to Madison Avenue on the north, from Kedzie Boulevard on the east to Austin Boulevard on the west. North of Madison to Division Street "Skeedoobee Brown" governed. Division Street to Grand Avenue was the fiefdom of one "Player Dog" Spraggins. There were spotters on corners and rooftops, retailers in vestibules and gangways. Enforcers patrolled with walkie-talkies; resuppliers cruised in Sevilles and deuce and a quarters. Skeleton men and scarecrow women parted with crumpled up paper and pitiful change. "Blow" was bliss. "Rock" brought dazzle, escape, and oblivion.

It was called *getting high* and for very good reason. Without drugs it was a broken bottle world, with the shells of burned out cars and the hulks of boarded-up buildings, mailboxes smashed and front doors shattered, piss in carpetless stairwells: burglar bars, locks and chains, falling plaster, leaky faucets, no hot water, rotting porches, rats and roaches, sirens, drive-by shootings, social workers and ankle bracelets, long lines and questions that poke like a stick in your gut. Too many babies and never enough Pampers. Everywhere graffiti and everywhere garbage, nowhere a paycheck, nowhere a smile. You too deserve a break today. Close your eyes. Let go. Get gone. *I'm loving it.*

It was again those damned elections. You couldn't turn around without some damned election for something, dogcatcher, whatever taking place and taking over. Pack opened the top drawer of his desk, fumbled around, and carried a small plastic bottle to the water fountain. *Valium: prairie yum-yums.* This would do the trick. Take just enough of the edge off to give you a real good feel good feeling. Lord knows he needed it. Thelma was back in court, Roland, the youngest of their four children, needing braces, Margaret, the oldest, contact lenses. Pack swallowed two of the yellow pills. I shouldn't bitch, he thought, as a soft glow simmered through his body. The commander of the district, one Captain Lester O'Rourke—unusual surname for a black man—spent most of his time on the golf course or lecture circuit. The B.N.I.C., as Pack and his buddies thought of him—the "Big Nigger in Charge"—had hit it big the year before. A *Sun-Times* columnist, one Sally Clark, had ventured forth from the safety of the lakefront to be hypnotized as the B.N.I.C. dispensed his bogart wisdom. Her *Sun-Times* panegyric was followed by a by-line in *Time* wherein the bedazzled Sally presented the gospel according to Lester. She pinched herself at her good fortune: *Time* was just the beginning; she'd get a book deal out of this even if she had to let Lester bed her again. There Lester was technicolor in *Time*, as handsome as a movie star, as crisp as a marine on a recruiting poster, saying, with some coaching, although Sally denied it, all the right things. Taxes didn't need to be raised. It was simply a matter of managing resources effectively. More bang for the buck, Sally had Lester saying, taking the risk of a politically incorrect pun. What was needed was modern police methodology and an end to the coddling of criminals. All the blather about social programs was a lot of hooey. Lester O'Rourke, for one, was sick and tired of welfare. People should get off their duffs, go out, and get a job. What it boiled down to was this: lots of people are just plain lazy and just plain losers. They are happy to live like pigs. Wouldn't find Lester O'Rourke living in the sewer. He might have to work there, but he didn't have to live there. Where Lester O'Rourke lived, lawns were mowed. Within a week of Sally's second panegyric the commander of the 15th District registered with a speaker's agency and the money came pouring in.

That the B.N.I.C. stayed in his new world of glitz suited Pack and his buddies just fine. There was a place for everyone and everyone knew his place. One Ear, Player Dog, and Skeedoobee handed Pack or his partner, Ollie, thick envelopes in Columbus Park or in front of the Austin Town Hall. But now, once again, the damned elections would interrupt the orderly working of crime and the cosmos. Citizens would vote for the City Council, the Metropolitan Water Reclamation District, the Cook County Board. Who should run the jails? Who should be City

Treasurer? Secretary of State? What about judges? Municipal Court, County Court, Circuit Court, Appellate Court, Supreme Court. You understand the offices and their functions. You know of each and every candidate. You are qualified to decide because you have five fingers on your right hand and five toes on your left foot. The Clerk of the Circuit Court! Now, there's an important office! Wouldn't want to make the wrong choice there! Today's candidate for county sheriff was yesterday's candidate for alderman. Tomorrow's candidate for Attorney General today runs for City Clerk. There is a blitz of offices and candidates, the musical chair game of parties and politicians, whose faces stare during elections from trees and lamp posts and afterwards from gutters, who are on your side and my side and everyone's else's, who care, who will make a difference, who are for change, who are tough on crime, who will crack down on waste, who abhor fraud and mismanagement, who love America, who will balance budgets and lower taxes, who are for everything good and against everything bad, who will solve all problems and put an end to all worries, who are straight shooters and fair dealers, and who will, whether elected or defeated, begin their next campaign the morning after the votes for this one are counted. This is known as *democracy*. It is the hope of the world.

The thing about elections, as far as Pack was concerned, was that they interfered with his business, the business of crime management. From City Clerk to Recorder of Deeds every candidate ran against crime. Television ads showed prison doors slamming shut and keys being thrown away. Each candidate was tougher than the next. Would-be state senators insisted on life imprisonment for auto theft; candidates for city council outshouted one another in support of the death penalty.

Now the election for States Attorney was proving particularly troublesome. The incumbent, one Warner Tully, a former commander of the Wentworth police district, and, more to the point, a golfing buddy of the B.N.I.C., had pulled off an upset four years before. That stunning victory, as the newspapers called it, was due in large part to a gruesome television commercial which featured women being raped, pedestrians shotgunned, homes invaded, and shoppers mugged. Loud rock music like the soundtrack of a pornographic movie pulsated as red images collaged across the screen. These were interspersed with photographs of a stern Warner Tully, all brass and braid in his commander's uniform, his name in bold letters trailing the bottom of the screen: **WARNER TULLY.** Mayhem, music: **HAD ENOUGH?** Mayhem, music: **FIGHT BACK!** The slogans flashed like traffic signals. The ad could run for ten seconds, twenty seconds, thirty seconds. It was thought of as brilliant. In political science courses and campaign seminars around the country the ad was Exhibit A. It had set a new record for effectively reducing attention span. But that was four years ago. Now, no matter how Warner's consultants cooked the numbers, it was clear that crime continued on its upward course. What was of greater importance were perceptions and perception-wise Warner Tully had an even bigger problem. That damned ad! Everybody remembered that damned ad! His opponent, Naomi "No-Nonsense" Clarke, a member of the school board, was rebroadcasting the ad in slow motion, which made it appear that it was Warner himself who was doing the raping, shotgunning, invading, and mugging while the stretched-out soundtrack whined like a sick dog. **IS YOUR FAMILY SAFER THAN IT WAS FOUR YEARS AGO?** There was a shot of his opponent in a rocking chair next to an infant's cradle, billy club in her lap. Then: **THE HAND THAT ROCKS THE CRADLE CARRIES A BIG STICK! WE NEED "NO-NONSENSE NAOMI!" NAOMI CLARKE FOR STATES ATTORNEY! "NO-NONSENSE NAOMI" NOW! "NO-NONSENSE NAOMI" NOW!**

The customary reporters, newspaper, television, radio, had been alerted, the ones least likely to ask in-depth questions. All Pack had to do now was figure out the who, what, where, and when. He knew the why. Why? Because the American way of life that begins in the attached garage and ends in the hot tub must be preserved. Why? Because we are engaged in a second great Civil War, the War Against Drugs. Why? Because the wrong people's drugs are forbidden. Why? Because Pack was just doing his job, just following orders. And the biggest why of all: because Warner Tully lusted after the governor's mansion but first had to be re-elected States Attorney and because Warner Tully was a friend of the B.N.I.C. That's why.

Too bad things had been so quiet. The Peace of Westphalia, Pack called it. One of the few things he remembered from his history class at Bishop Weber High, the Peace of Westphalia fascinated Pack with how it had, for centuries, kept the German states under the control of a few who lived in luxury while the many scratched for a living or starved. Predating One Ear, Skeedoobee, and Player Dog by three centuries, the German princes, gang leaders, as Pack saw them, were confirmed by the Peace of Westphalia as tyrannical and absolute rulers of their separate and delineated fiefdoms. They had pioneered absolute control through blind obedience and total terror. The more things change! Pack thought: their Twentieth Century westside Chicago counterparts had become as reliable as clocks. One Ear, Skeedoobee, and Player Dog had grown up; they had come of age. They stopped killing each other. They settled down to business. They had finally learned that making money—real money—was better, way better, than spilling blood. They lived the good life. Moved to the suburbs. Supported the United Way. Made campaign contributions. Who said the homies in the hood were lazy good-for-nothings? One Ear, Skeedoobee, and Player Dog could tell you better: their army of teenagers and pre-teenagers spread across Chicago's west side like intestines, supply meeting demand. The pay was good, the hours flexible and, most important of all, there was the camaraderie of belonging. Selling drugs was not just a business, it was, the first time for many, a family. There were eager replacements for those who suffered the occupational hazards of incarceration or death.

There was, Pack thought, that Jamaican place on Chicago Avenue, Hermione's. Never hurt to bust

Hermione's. Nobody much minded if you busted the Jamaicans. On Chicago's electoral map the Jamaicans did not exist. Very few of their very few registered and even fewer voted. They did not count for they were not counted. One Ear, Skeedoobee, and Player Dog left the Jamaicans alone too: marijuana was the hind tit on the junkie hog. Too bulky. A kilo of cocaine took up the same space as a pound of marijuana: $20,000 compared to $500.00. You do the math. So, no big deal to pick on the Jamaicans: One Ear, Skeedoobee, and Player Dog couldn't care less. Besides, Hermione was used to her once or twice yearly busts, just another cost of doing business, like payroll taxes. No, not this time, the voice from downtown said. This time we need something bigger, more dramatic. "No-Nonsense" would see right through another raid on Hermione's. Why, she will ask, is the place still in business if it's been raided eight times in the past five years? No, something sexier is required, a lot sexier. You know the turf. You know the players. You figure it out.

What is needed, Pack said to himself, is some harmless nobody, some nobody nobody sent, a nobody connected with nobody, a nobody we can harass and hassle and then let go once the spotlight ceases to drift back into his nobody life. Pack parked his unmarked car across from Hermione's, studying the men and women entering and leaving. He had, he told himself, a special knack, a sharp eye for just the right type. He should have been a casting agent, he thought. Finally he saw them: a strong man as black, no, blacker, than the ace of spades, at his side a beautiful coffee with cream colored woman, thin and graceful, with flowing black hair. The contrast would look great on television! Then the woman turned: the right side of her face looked like a piece of raw meat! Perfect! On television the man would look menacing; the woman, deranged. He followed the couple a few blocks until they entered a well-kept bungalow on Ferdinand Street. An easily fixed problem: empty a few cans of garbage on the front lawn, break the windows. He drove back to Hermione's.

"Hey there, my man," he said to Winston, Hermione's partner. "If you want to avoid trouble, tell me what I want to hear. You remember that dude was in here black as the blackest nigger's ass? Half hour ago? With the hot-shot broad with the long hair and messed up face? You sell 'em anything? A dime bag?"

There is a god after all, Pack thought as he returned to his car. Everything was falling into place. Best of all the black as the ace of spade dude and the bitch with the messed up face were foreigners! Legal? Illegal? He didn't know and he didn't care for it didn't matter. Everybody hated foreigners. Taking away jobs while red-blooded Americans rot on welfare. Let some pimply ass lawyer try to make his bones on this one! Perfect! An ongoing undercover investigation. Surveillance of a well-known drug hangout. Exited suspiciously. Witness interrogated. More than enough for a search warrant. As tight as a nun's cunt. Bet that bitch with the messed up face gives good head, Pack thought. I know one thing, that's for sure, he laughed to himself as he drove to the station. She's sure gonna give good head on television! Perfect!

*   *   *

There was never enough money and there was always too much money. You had to be careful about cash. That's how they got Judge Leo LeFavre, poking around in his garbage, snooping at the butcher's and auto repair shop. Not depositing cash, not leaving a paper trail, that wasn't good enough, not any more. Now you had also to be careful about what you paid for with cash. You couldn't just drop by your friendly Buick dealer, drop down a bundle, and tool away in a Park Avenue. Good old Leo, he's too smart, they'll never get Leo. That's what everyone said. Well, Leo was now a long term guest of Uncle Sam in Terre Haute, Indiana. Leo's babysitters and grocer, the owner of the gas station which serviced his cars, the clerks at the private schools his children attended, all were subpoenaed and all testified to being paid with c-a-s-h. Cash. The be-all, and, if you weren't careful, the end-all. Pack couldn't simply hand Thelma a fistful of hundred dollar bills and tell her to go away until the middle of the next month. So the cash piled up in the coffee cans buried behind the cabin he and Ollie had on Gull Lake in Kalamazoo County, Michigan. Saving it for the big five and five. About all Pack could do for the time being was pay for a blow job here and a quick trip to Vegas there. Pocket change. Except, of course, for the speedboat. It was Ollie's idea and by the squeeze of a whore's tit they'd gotten away with it. When Pack was on the speedboat, skimming along at twenty knots, every bone in his body rejoiced. It was better than sex. It was better than sex, booze, weed, and rock and roll combined.

Pack didn't think of himself as corrupt. The way Pack saw it he was expected to go to work in the sewer every day and not get dirty. No way. There were rules and it was his job to see to it that the rules were enforced. That was the easy part. The hard part was knowing which rules really mattered and, if they mattered, when. This took years. The rules weren't the same for everyone. Different strokes for different folks. Mr. and Mrs. Two-Bit, for example. Go to work, come home, shovel snow, take out the garbage, walk the dog, go to church. You don't see them getting tax breaks for moving their factory to Mexico. The chumps, that's what "Cinch" Magruder, Pack's first partner, called them. The chumps. There were chumps and there were champs. "You wanna be a chump or you wanna be a champ, kid? You decide."

Cinch taught him the ropes. It started with a cup of coffee here, a sandwich there, a pair of slacks, then a suit. Some kids broke into John Yong's store. A window broken, a radio snatched, maybe two. "I missing TVs, many, many." To get along, go along. Cinch selected an eighteen inch with remote, Pack, a Panasonic stereo. Before long it was honest to goodness greeno dinero. So it began and so it continued. It was supposed to be easy. There were the good guys and the bad guys. Us versus Them. There had been a time when

Pack knew who was who. Now all he could do was follow his own rules: you did what you could get away with so long as you didn't hurt anybody who was anybody and you took care of your partner. You didn't see nothing nobody who was anybody didn't want you to see. You went after the punks and you steered clear of priests and politicians. So what if the padres were diddling little boys or the politicos lined their own pockets? What did that have to do with the price of frijoles? No money for him and Ollie there. The truth of the matter was that everything was a joke. They let the perps out before you finished the paperwork. Before the politicians got hooked on this War on Drugs crusade, Pack remembered, the police had had a fighting chance. Now the system was as clogged as a backed up toilet. Never mind. Shit anyway. The numbers were staggering. The perps were marched in in the morning and out in the afternoon. The jails were full; some do-good somebody went to court; the judge said, "Let my people go!" The Constitution forbids cruel and unusual punishment; rapists and murderers must not sleep on the floor. Besides room was needed for others. Always. The line at the front door was longer and longer. Knock an old lady on the head, get arrested. Go home and wait for trial. Show up if you feel like it. Tell the judge it wasn't you. Go back home and wait for a court date to open up. Don't call us. We'll call you. When and if there's room. If the file hasn't been lost. If it is remembered who you are. If we knew who you were in the first place. If the witness is still alive. If the victim will testify. Ten year sentences became two years actually served. It was all a crap-shoot. Everybody knew the system was on life support. Everyone from policeman to probation officer swept back the sea. Little by little everyone compromised. Patchwork here. A band-aid there. The ship is sinking; the best we can do is keep it afloat for as long as we can and pray for a miracle.

The world of drugs is a world of cash. Everybody was elbow deep in cash. Why not Pack? Why should he be left out? So what if he worked in narcotics? Trouble was that's where most bluebellies draw the line. Something doesn't sit right, doesn't feel right, doesn't fit. Maybe it is the January junkies under viaducts and in gangways, fingers and toes and sometimes themselves dead from frostbite. Maybe it is the underwear children, runny noses, corkscrew legs and sleepwalking arms, eyes wide like spotlights scarring your soul. You bust the door: bedmamma zonked, television blazing like the eye of a demon, the grunge dust of corn flakes and cracker crumbs from kitchen to bedroom, of potato chips, popcorn, and cookies, ground in like sawdust: horizontal holes where the air is piss. You are not my son. You are not my daughter. Bang 'em and bust 'em. For what? For why? Pack was sick of it. He was sick to what was left of his soul of it. Once, a long time ago, before he knew better, he got involved. Her name was Sara. She didn't want to leave her babies.

"Please, please, don't take away my babies."

"You should have thought about your babies before making your lungs a blasting furnace," he said.

"I'll go clean. I'll do the program. Don't take away my babies." Sara looked at Pack. A glint of life worked through the milk glaze of her eyes' despair. He threw her in the back seat and started for the station, but, as he passed St. Anne's Hospital, something inside him gave way. He pulled to the curb.

"Go in there," he said. "They'll help you in there." But in there they hadn't helped her. In there there was a waiting list so long they had stopped taking names. She went back to the gutter and o.d.'d a month later and they took away her babies after all. What did any of it matter? To get along, go along. So Pack went along. He had migraines, his back hurt, he drank, all he and Thelma ever did was fight; they divorced. There was only one way out and that was to die. I will die until I'm fifty-five, Pack decided, and then I will be reborn. All I have to do is keep in shape. But he hadn't kept in shape. He smoked more, he drank more, he whored more, he junk-fooded more. Still, there was breath in his body. That was the important thing. There were more and more coffee cans and fewer and fewer years. The trick was surviving. The trick was sticking it out to the big five and five.

When Ollie's Uncle Newton was on his deathbed, Pack and Ollie gave Ollie's Aunt Martha ninety-seven thousand of their coffee can dollars. "Buy Uncle Newie a speedboat," Ollie said. Uncle Newie had always wanted a speedboat. Might be just the thing to make him snap out of it. Might be just what the doctor couldn't order. Inside his oxygen tent the eighty-six year old man trembled his left hand a few inches above the sheets. "Just one thing, Auntie," Ollie whispered. "It's kind of delicate, I know, but *if* Uncle

Newie doesn't make it, make sure it's in his will that he leaves the speedboat to me, okay?"

The speedboat was their one big splurge, the chance they'd taken and gotten away with, as slick as a good shit first thing in the morning, Ollie said. The cabin was nothing special, nothing to draw attention. But the speedboat was something else. A real pisser. Now three years had passed since Ollie's uncle died and, as far as the speedboat was concerned, everything was as quiet as Uncle Newie's grave. A chump or a champ, Cinch Magruder said. You decide.

*　　　*　　　*

The police powers of the State are always to be feared. History is replete with fugitive slave laws and Nuremberg decrees, laws against witches and laws against homosexuals. Laws may ensure liberty but they may also enshrine tyranny. If the law does not protect the individual, it loses its kinship with divinity. The question becomes not "Why me?" but "When me?" Now, in our own time and place, the War on Drugs makes a shambles of the law for it is a war of the State against its own people. It is a crusade of cultural chauvinism, a theocratic war of belief against heresy. Methadone is good; heroin, bad. Alcohol, yes; marijuana, no. The War on Drugs erases the distinction between self-regarding conduct, which should not be the province of law, and conduct which directly affects others, which is its rightful realm. The War on Drugs has nothing to do with the state's duty to protect the life and property of its citizens. Anything that gets in its way, including the Constitution of the United States, suffers its friendly fire. Coffee, tea, alcohol, nicotine, red meat, salt, white sugar, television, and a whole pharmacology of sanctioned drugs are permitted while the War on Drugs disembowels the nation in a futile attempt to proscribe other poisons. Like Prohibition in the nineteen-twenties, the War on Drugs codifies the tyranny of the majority. I may pursue happiness on Via Viagra; you may not take the Highway Hashish. The Constitution of the United States is dismissed. It is no longer the state's duty to prove guilt; it is the citizen's to prove innocence. Without the nuisance of arrest, the cash of druglords is confiscated as a *de facto* tax, an efficient if hypocritical symbiosis that is a boon to police and druglord alike. Police departments help themselves. The druglord, inconvenienced, goes about his business as usual. Prisons overflow with the penny ante pusher; teenagers and preteenagers parade into the pipeline of penal profiteering: Crime 101. Murderers and rapists are set free so that society might be protected from the suicidal choices of those who stick needles in their arms, or snort powder up their noses, or inhale the wrong kind of smoke. With its insatiable constituency of prosecutors, drug czars, defense attorneys, and privatized prison profiteers the prison-industrial complex rules. Of the nation's fifteen million users of illegal drugs fewer than one million are incarcerated at a given time, and this, the concomitant corrosiveness of selective enforcement, further eviscerates respect for the law. Athletes who snort cocaine and movie stars who syringe are pampered, their brave struggles against addiction celebrated on tabloid TV as they enter their fourth spa treatment. The War on Drugs marks the advent of the new normal: perpetual war in foreign places distant and near. It is fought as all wars are: on the backs of the poor. Pestilence conquers the land. The ghetto is terrorized by this Second Civil War. Bodies are searched and urine extorted. Homes are invaded, automobiles seized, property destroyed. Washington dollars assault the 'hood to cordon off this morning this block, this afternoon that. You or you or you, eeny, meeny, miney, moe, oh, what the hell why not take all of you? are arrested in "sweeps," in "weed and seed" programs. Weed whom? Seed what? The overtime gestapo from faraway whiteland invades, gangbanging the streets to protect you against your son, your neighbor, your momma, your self. If you were a right-minded citizen you'd live somewhere else, somewhere decent. But you are poor and you are black and the sausage must be ground. So what if you lose your job in the suburbs—by the time you are processed the bus link has stopped running. In war, there are casualties. You should be proud to play your patriotic part. There were drugs on your person or in your car or in somebody you knew's crib and even if there weren't there had been yesterday or the day before or will be tomorrow. And where, exactly, does your baby momma live? The absence of negation constitutes guilt. There is a vast system of spies and snoops and in schools children are exhorted to rat on their parents.

Said the American colonel in VietNam: "We destroyed the village in order to save it."

*   *   *

Outside the golden bungalow on Ferdinand Street units from the Metropolitan Drug Enforcement Unit, the Chicago Police Department, the Cook County's Sheriff's Office, the Drug Enforcement Agency, and the Bureau of Alcohol, Tobacco, and Firearms gathered. The night glistened with the shine of alphabetized jackets: MDE–DEA–ATF. The jackets carried submachine guns and wore bulletproof vests. They cut the electric supply line that went from the pole in the alley. They smashed through the leaded glass of the front door and the security gate at the rear.

Zion came awake into a world of dark noise and strange darkness. He pushed Auntie Rose to the floor. "Get under the bed and stay there." Zion reached into the closet for his shotgun. Marguerite and Schugay lay naked in each other's arms. Marguerite fumbled for her bathrobe. Schugay slipped into his shorts and opened the door. Groping and squinting he stepped into the hallway. Electrified sounds megaphoned from the feeding frenzy outside. In a blur of noise silhouettes of the invaders poured into the golden home. In dark confusion Zion came from his bedroom, shotgun raised. In the blast of its discharge he saw Schugay's face. Then Zion was grabbed by a robot-like figure and thrown to the floor. His hands were fastened behind him. In bathrobes and handcuffs Auntie Rose and Marguerite were dragged to the hallway.

"Sector one: all clear."

"Sector two: all clear."

"All clear: sector three."

"Sector four: all clear."

The walkie-talkie voices came from inside and out, from basement and kitchen. Then the electricity was restored. On her stomach Marguerite crawled to Schugay's body. Where his chest had been was now only red. Marguerite cradled Schugay's head with her shoulders and bosom as best she could, rocking. Tears streamed down her face. Short gasps of sounds came through her lips in a moaning of *no*'s. Marguerite did not know where she was. Auntie Rose fought her way to Marguerite's side. She touched her body to Marguerite's. Soaking in Schugay's blood the two women breathed as one.

Outside the members of the States Attorney's media team slapped each other's hands high in the air. A spotlight from a helicopter blasted at the bungalow's front door as policemen who looked like astronauts emerged with the handcuffed suspects, two black women and one black man. One of the women looked deranged. Then there was a corpse on a stretcher, blood soaking through its covering sheet. A D.E.A. agent walked beside, thrusting Zion's shotgun into the night sky as if it were a scalp. The air filled with guttural sounds like the gruntings of wild boars. Perfect! Filming at night was always tricky, but this time, this one time, everything was perfect. They had it all from every conceivable angle. Let "No-Nonsense" try to Willie Horton me now,

Warner Tully thought, positioning himself in front of a television camera with the triumphant tableau as his backdrop.

The story played as well as had been hoped for. Banner headlines. "Compelling" TV. A coordinated raid. Sixteen agents and officers. A S.W.A.T. team. A serious dent in drug trafficking. A body blow to the Jamaican cartel. Firearms recovered. An undisclosed quantity of drugs seized. The citizens of Cook County were safer and they had Warner Tully to thank for it.

Chapter Twenty-Four:
Salt into Salt

Marguerite
Chicago; Mabouhey
1983-1984

She would not bury Schugay there and she would not have her baby there. That was all Marguerite could think. There were five weeks to go, but she would not have her baby there and she would not bury Schugay there. Auntie Rose gave her a vase of purpled glass, an heirloom from the time of bondage, passed down from Zion's grandmother. Marguerite carried it to the funeral home and they gave her Schugay's ashes. In the smoke of the dying city she came up Central Avenue one last time. There was nothing of green. Sallow black faces waited for buses. Sidewalks howled in rubbish. The golden bungalow on Ferdinand Street cried one more time, one final time of anguish, and then Marguerite was on a bus to Miami and a boat to Frederique and then she was on Hernando's boat. Mabouhey came to her, floating on the water, and she thought she saw Schugay waving to her from the sand, the white sand like sugar. Marguerite stood. She put her hand to her forehead, but Schugay was gone, the white man had killed him, Schugay was gone forever. She sat down and put her hands to her stomach, remembering how strong, how gentle Schugay's hands were, how his fingers dug into her stomach lightly, lightly, and how he laughed and teased and said they would make many babies, many beautiful black and brown and brown-black babies. Marguerite would be like the old woman in the shoe except she would get prettier with each baby, Schugay promised, and he would always love her, Schugay would love her forever. Then he would go back to kissing her stomach and nibbling at her sides and make her promise that she would never leave him, that she would never leave him again.

Marguerite went to the side of Katausa and gave Schugay back to his ancestors. She moved into the hut across from the clearing, next to Father Chester and Christian. She taught the young children in the village's school and she assisted Christian in the clinic. Then it was time. A beautiful, beautiful baby girl with black, black skin and Schugay's laughing eyes. Schugara.

*　　　*　　　*

Every day she went to the sea. With Schugara at her breast Marguerite looked out to the sandbar. She waited and she looked out far but Schugay did not come. Hour after hour she stood there, her feet in the water at the ocean's ending, unmoving, as if she were carved of stone, as if she were a statue in a fountain, her tears flowing, salt into salt. Day gave itself to night and still she looked out to the sandbar and still Schugay did not come. First it was the children and soon thereafter everyone in the village who spoke of her as the woman who weeps and waits by the sea. The years passed because there was no other choice. Every day Marguerite went to the sea and looked out to the sandbar, but Schugay did not come.

Chapter Twenty-Five: Duty

Travers Landeman
Mabouhey
1989-91

When had Travers decided that he was not going back? At his nephew's funeral? When the photographs appeared on the passenger seat of his car? When he slapped Corinne? Certainly he knew by the time he emptied the safe. What did it matter? He was not going back. Ever. One step at a time. He had always had plenty of time but he had not realized it. He had never used it for himself. Now he would. First he would learn to love himself. Now that he was on Mabouhey a new tranquility came over him. He took long walks on the beach, occasionally venturing into jungle where there were caves and lagoons, where formations of earth hinted at civilizations past. The island was pristine in its solitude. There was wind-powered electricity for the warehouse and its machinery, but Mabouhey was unscarred by the technological ruinations of the Nineteenth and Twentieth Centuries. No telephones, no automobiles, no television. Could he stay on Mabouhey? The island and its people had reached deep inside him to set his new self free. Even so, it would be safer, would it not, to go on, to keep going? But then it came to him like the sun bursting through dark clouds: if we give ourselves to fear nowhere is safe. We must decide to be safe here and now. We must draw a circle around ourselves and declare it a liberated zone. He came upon Father Chester working in the fields. The priest wore a fulsome straw hat, no shirt, only shorts and sandals. As Travers approached, Father Chester stood to lean against a wooden hoe.

"Mad dogs and Americans," he said. "Keeps me in shape."

"There's no one else about," Travers said.

"It's siesta time. I'm about to take a break myself. Why don't we go to the warehouse?" They walked in the clear silence of the full sun. "You will be leaving us soon," Father Chester said as they rounded a bend and the warehouse came into view.

"Yes," Travers replied. "But, to tell the truth, I feel as if I could stay here forever."

"Mabouhey does tend to grab hold of you and never let go. Look at me. Exhibit A. Fifteen years and I feel as if I arrived yesterday." They came to the warehouse. Father

Chester motioned Travers to a table under a canopy striped in green and yellow. Men and women reclined in hammocks or sat at tables and drank lemonade or beer made from potatoes. "If you would like, Marguerite will bring us refreshments."

Since his first night on the island, when she had helped him with his netting, when he had come upon her in the shore's moonlight, Marguerite had stayed in his thoughts. On the beach, that first magical night, Travers sensed that her pain was a match for his own, but, ever since, he had seen her only from afar.

Marguerite brought lemonade but would not join them. Travers watched as she walked towards the forest. She reached the bushes that marked its beginning where she turned just for a moment. In that instant Travers' eyes caught hers but he could not tell if it was desire or despair that burned within. Then she disappeared, swallowed in green. Travers turned to the priest sitting across from him.

"I am not going back," he said. "Never."

"It is one thing to run away," Chester replied. "It is another to run to."

"I am coming to believe that it does not matter. I am going to draw a circle around myself and call it home."

"Only be sure your circle is not a wall," the priest replied.

"Will you help me, Father?" It was the first time Travers had called the American sitting across from him *Father*.

"We must help each other if we can."

"Is there a library in Frederique City?"

"Yes, as a matter of fact, there is. But why do you ask?"

"I should like to learn about places where there can be circles which are not walls," Travers replied.

"Then you should visit our library here on Mabouhey."

It had not occurred to Travers that Mabouhey had a library. "Yes," he said, "I would like that very much."

Travers was surprised and delighted. It was an impressive collection. Shelves and shelves, floor to thatched roof. He sat at one of the long tables clustered in a central area, encyclopedias and other reference books spread before him. Hours later he returned the books to their shelves. He had decided. He would make his way to Belize. The five days he had spent on Mabouhey had reached a new self inside him, a self that breathed the unhurried pace of sunshine spun days that are bright worlds of magic, as old and as new as each retelling of the griot's fables.

He went to the mouth of the river next to where the old women washed clothes and hung them over bushes to dry. He propped his back against a palm tree, poking a strand of grass between his teeth. A young girl splashed in the surf. Disappearing, he thought, was one thing; dying was another. He needed to die, to have everyone, Corinne, Arnie Williamson, Madge Drayback, believe him dead. But the thing of it was that dying required help. It wasn't something you could do all by yourself, he thought with a smile. He needed an accomplice and, most certainly, a witness. How could he work it all out? He could hide the money in one of the caves that pockmarked the cliffs hidden by jungle. He could fall overboard as Hernando's boat returned to Frederique and then swim ashore, retrieve the money, and make his way to the island of Tobraga, forty miles to the southeast, and then on to Belize. If his accomplice didn't slit his throat and feed him to the sharks. Maybe he should take Hernando into his confidence? Hernando seemed an honorable man. How could he know?

As he sat against the palm tree these questions and more mixed together in a blur of excitement so that, at first, Travers did not hear the shouts of the old women who had left off their washing and were running to the ocean waving their arms like the wings of angry crows.

"Kintura!" They shouted. "Kintura! Kintura!"

Travers looked to the sea. Her arms wrapped over a log, the young girl played in the water. The girl who had slept in Father Chester's arms that first night on the island, Schugara, Marguerite's daughter! Travers' eyes came as well to a triangle of gray slicing through the water. He jumped to his feet and ran to the ocean, reaching Schugara an instant before the jaws of the great shark opened. He pulled the child towards the shore as the old women screamed and as other women and men came running from fields and warehouse. Kintura's teeth came together, ripping flesh from Travers' left thigh; the water reddened. Now Schugara was in Travers' arms as he staggered onto shore, his left leg collapsing beneath him. Men ran to carry him back to the palm tree. Schugara stood next to him, her hand on his arm.

She would not leave his side. Travers saw the blood pouring from his thigh; he tried to stay conscious but the world closed like a lens into darkness.

"Schugara! Schugara!" It was Marguerite. She grabbed her daughter close to her bosom. "Schugara! Schugara!" Then she fell to her knees. Quickly she tied a tourniquet to the upper part of Travers' thigh. He was carried to the warehouse where Marguerite and Christian doused his leg with antiseptic and wrapped it with bandage. He was taken by stretcher to his hut and laid on his bed. Marguerite pulled a chair to its side and took his hand in hers. She lay the right side of her face against the cover and looked at Travers with burning eyes.

He came awake in the morning to searing pain in his left leg. Then he remembered Schugara and the cries of the washerwomen, he remembered the teeth of the shark, and he saw again the light in Marguerite's eyes as darkness had seized him. Now Marguerite stood at the side of his bed, her long black hair sweeping against him as she bent over to touch his forehead.

"I think your fever has broken," she said.

Travers pulled himself upright as best he could. "Have you been here all night?" he asked.

"Yes." Marguerite pointed to the other side of the room. "Christian brought a cot for Schugara. She would not leave you."

Travers looked at the softness of the sleeping child. "Schugara is a lovely name," he said. "Schugara."

"She is named after her father."

"You must have loved him very much."

"Yes." Marguerite saw the laughing boy, his flashing smile, his eyes bright, his teeth shining. He was there now in the small hut. Schugay had come back. His hands were on her waist and then they let her go. She heard Schugay's voice as deep as the forest night, as clear as the summer's rain. "Let love be," Schugay said. "Let love be." Marguerite reached for Travers' hand.

"Do not cry," Travers said. Marguerite sat on the side of the bed and they held each other. Travers stroked her flowing hair, wetting his fingers in the tears that flowed down her cheeks. "Promise me that you will never leave me," he said. "Promise that you will stay with me forever."

"I will never go back to America. Never."

"Nor will I. If you will have me, I will stay here with you and Schugara."

Nine nights later Marguerite took him to the place of many rocks, where the Caribbean currents churn the ocean into angry whiteness. "We will hide the canoe here," she said, "under this caoba tree." She pointed to beyond the white fury. "Once Hernando's boat is there, it will be swept around the bend. To return to search for you, Hernando's sons will have to fight the mighty currents."

*　　　*　　　*

Marguerite and Travers found Father Chester on the verandah of his hut, reading. "Grandpapa Malcolm spoke to me in my dreams," Marguerite said. "We will build our house on the other side of the island, on the side of Katausa, at the place where the breath of the Spirits sings without sorrow, near to the mouth of the cave in Katausa's side where drawings on the walls call to us by those who were here before. The sheltering ledge will protect us. Grandpapa said that Katausa will not become angry with us. There we will not be found." She handed the priest Travers' duffel bag. "Use this as the elders think best." Chester looked inside: bundles of green, each with a rubber band in its center. "We have kept what is adequate for our needs," Marguerite said. "Namaste, Mabouhey."

In the days that followed Travers wondered at the world's newness. One day at a time, he told himself, one day at a time. It takes years for the boy to grow into the man; grow into your new self one day at a time. But he could not restrain himself. He greeted the gift of each new day as if he were a blind man restored to sight. He refused to look backwards. He had thought it all out, for once. Madge Drayback could retire in security; Corinne would excel in her role of grieving and rich widow; that other world would go on fine and feckless without him. Good riddance. *Requiescat in pace,* Charleston Travers Landeman. *Bienvenidos al mundo, Quince.* Marguerite had selected his new name. *Quince.* It was a lucky name, she said. The old woman who lived in the cave said so. A chance had presented itself; he had seized it by the scruff of its neck, he had buried his teeth in it, and he was not letting go. There was no going back nor did he want to.

The natives called the mountain Katausa, or Great Angry One. Its fires within slept an unquiet sleep. The griots told of the river of fire than ran to the sea and made the sea boil, of the great clouds of steam, blood baptized by sea and reborn as rock, there by the caoba tree that drinks at the forested place of moss and root.

"We began at the end," Marguerite said, "we shall end at the beginning." On the side of Katausa they built their house, singing over and into the valley. In the night Marguerite came to him in softness and shadow. Starlight and moonglow danced like fireflies over their bodies. Many mornings they did not stir until after the sharpest sun. Then they ran to the sea and played in the water like children. One day, as the house neared completion, Quince saw him, coming up over the rim of the mountain. He walked alongside a mule that carried yet another window. Quince shielded his eyes. The mule trudged slowly up the slope of the volcano. The young man walked with a natural grace.

"You don't go to church much, do you, Uncle T?"

"I don't go to church at all."

The youth and the mule were directly in front of him. Quince waved. The young man left the patient animal, which was only too happy to pause for a while. One of Marguerite's brothers, Papuch, came to stand beside Quince, a cutting tool in his hand.

"I am Mateo," the young man said. "May I take some lemonade when I am in the house, Señor Quince?"

"Of course," Quince answered.

The youth turned to Marguerite's brother. "And perhaps a small glass of your potato beer, Señor Papuch?"

Papuch laughed. "I do not think that would be a good idea, Mateo. The sun is high in the sky; the day is still long before you."

"No harm asking," Mateo replied.

"No, no harm at all."

Mule and youth resumed their slow passing. Travers, for that's who he was in this moment, watched with a heavy heart. Could he ever forget? The passion and promise of a life cut short because of his fear, his stingy fear. "No harm. No harm at all."

At last they moved into the house that lunged from Katausa towards jungle and sea. Marguerite and Quince had a large bedroom at the rear. A second bedroom was for Marguerite's aunt, Eshmaya, and a large ebony man, Morimbo, who seemed half Eshmaya's age. There was a third bedroom for Schugara and, at the front, a great gathering room. There were bathrooms and a kitchen, with water diverted from the stream that ran from Katausa. Swathed like a rainbow in the colors of jungle and sea, a wide shelf of balcony on thick caoba stilts wrapped around three sides of the house with the fourth anchored into the rock of the volcano's side. The house had a high dome of thatch for its roof. There were openings for windows in many places, filled in with glass as Marguerite's brothers and their mules went down and back up the volcano. They brought in a generator and drums of gasoline, electronic gadgetry, wires, speakers, batteries. Quince would have music but he would not have television. He had left behind forever its ugly world of murder and greed. He hated all it stood for. It was the world he had left behind, the prison from which he had escaped, a reminder that men and women measure out their lives with credit cards; it was the talisman of a world where cardboard potatoes are poured from boxes. He sent for books: Dickens, Thackeray, Eliot, Trollope, Hardy, Twain, Wharton, Wright, Baldwin, Achebe, Bellow, Lessing, Gordimer, Emecheta.

His hands returned to life. A workroom was added beneath his and Marguerite's bedroom, a rope ladder connecting. With tools made for hands Morimbo taught Quince to make tables and chairs. He experimented with clay and with canvas. He made kites. Quince gathered all who would come whenever they would come. He read to them, and they told him stories. Together they worked and sang. Together they ate and danced. The island days and volcano nights flowed into each other, a journey without destination. In the evenings they gathered on the balcony to watch the sun's farewell. They ate and they drank and they smoked. Quince sat in a rocking chair made with his own hands. Mozart or Pink Floyd, Ravel or Bob Marley embraced them. Slowly, slowly the sun dissolved into sea, shimmering orange, reds, and yellow. Stars came into focus one by one; the beauty of the world was slow and sure.

*   *   *

Two years passed. The windmill neared completion. Soon the generator's smells and noises would belong to the past. Any day now the solar panels would arrive and there would be plentiful hot water. Was Quince the same person as Charleston Travers Landeman? It was hard to think so.

Quince sat on the balcony in his rocking chair reading Richard Wright's *The Outsider*. A train crashes and a new man is born. Each new day gives a second chance, Quince thought, is another world, a new world if we will it so, waiting for the explorer's reach, waiting for discovery's dawn, yet we squander time as if we have an endless supply of full tomorrows. Each new day we are born again or we are never born at all. One day we wake up and we don't. Quince went to the kitchen. Marguerite and Schugara rolled out thin doilies of dough; bowls filled with the blackest of berries waited like armies assembled for battle.

"Would you bring me, please, the apron that is in the bedroom closet?" Marguerite asked.

As he reached for the apron, Quince's eye caught a corner of blue on the topmost shelf. Matthew's cassettes! He nestled the blue bag under his left arm as he returned to the kitchen.

"Thank you. What are you carrying?"

"My nephew's music. I would like to know what he liked, what he listened to. I don't know how to say this exactly but I feel that by listening to his music some part of him will go on, will become a part of me."

"You must stop blaming yourself," Marguerite said. She looked at Schugara, busy filling doilies with berries.

"There must be an end to grief." She pulled Quince's body close to hers. Schugara looked up from the pastries. "There are children present, well a child present!" she teased.

Marguerite pulled herself from Quince to rejoin flour and rolling pin.

"You can't be claiming her all the time," Schugara laughed. "It's important that she spend some quality time with her daughter!" Quince walked to the young girl. Bright sun filled the happy kitchen.

"Schugara! Schugara! My Schugara!"

"Want a taste?" Schugara popped one of the berry-laden pastries into his mouth.

"Is it true what they say, Papa?" Quince looked at the smiling child, as black as the rarest pearl. He pretended to have serious thought.

"Yes," he said at length. "It is true. The blacker the berry, the sweeter the juice!"

"If the men folk would leave the women folks alone," Marguerite interrupted, waving a wooden spoon, "we could do some righteous cooking!"

"You were the one who asked for help."

"Oh, shush now," Marguerite replied. "Go back to your reading." Then from deep in the valley the pounding of drums sounded, faint at first, then loud and louder, like the pistons of a powerful locomotive. Marguerite put the rolling pin to one side and listened. "There is a white man in the village," she said. "And another on his way."

"There have been white men before," Quince responded. "Let them come. When they do, I shall be out on the sea, to the keys beyond Tobraga. I shall fish with the nets like the fish-girl they sing of in the griot's stories."

"Tell me again, Mama, how Grandma Icolyn went into the taroumpa hut," Schugara asked. "Please?"

Quince walked to the balcony. He put the blue bag on the small table next to his rocking chair. Then he reached for the bag's zipper. *The Journal of Matthew James Calkins.* As he turned the pages, all of Travers' pain, all of Travers' grief, returned to mix with anger as red as Katausa's lava. Travers' heart pounded and his breaths came in sharp jolts. Again he saw his nephew standing next to him in his sister's garage. "No harm," he heard himself say, "no harm at all." Matthew had reached out, and Travers had let him drown. Matthew had also reached out to others, most of whom had also turned away. But there was one who did not turn away. There was one who pounced like a rabid wolf. Something had not been right there in his dead nephew's house after the funeral and now Travers knew what it was. "Matthew told me about his poems," he remembered Father McArtle saying. Yes, and about this journal, too, no doubt. "I'm sure we can find the funds to publish a small memorial volume." In a grotesque tableau the hope on the faces of the dead boy's parents flashed once again, this time like a curse: "Oh, could you? Would you, Father?" In angry questions Travers' anguish boiled. Can we ever escape the past? Does it ever let go? Are we doomed forever to march to its drumbeat? In the valley below the earth was fresh. The new day waited like a canvas on an easel, but now the only colors there were were red and black, which swept over him in a great wave of rage and death. Marguerite and Schugara began singing; the honey of their voices flamed his turmoil. Words pounded in his brain: "No harm. No harm at all." I must go back, he thought, as images of Matthew, Marguerite, and Schugara blurred together. I must go back. Then his body struggled with sweat as fever took hold. There was a numbing pain in his chest. His dead nephew's diary crashed to the floor as Travers went back into darkness.

Chapter Twenty-Six:
The Congo Bongo Coco Tour

Albert Sidney McNab
Frederique
1991

Albert Sidney McNab did not like airplanes. It was, *prima facie*, unnatural for tons of metal to go arrowing through the air to say nothing about the fact that airplanes treat their customers like cattle. He was herded from one line to the next, squeezed into a narrow tin can, and fed slop on a tray.

"What alimentary crime will it be this time? What's on?" he amused himself. Crisp uniforms wheeled carts down the aisle. He unwrapped tin foil from a plastic tray. Ah! Green wrinkled balls, sickly white paste, pressed breast of brown cardboard! Albert was determined to allocate the parsimonious packets of salt and pepper equitably, but the green got too much black and the brown too much white. We must entertain ourselves as best we can, he mused, for time is fleeting and we know not when the grim reaper calls! The airplane rattled in a pocket of turbulent air. Just so, he continued to himself with satisfaction. The shaking put him at ease for it reminded him of his apartment. He opened a small foil packet. "Dairy DeLite," he read. "Soybeans. Polyunsaturated hydroglycerin palm oil. Contains no known dairy products." Such a relief! Somewhere a cow lives! Let the Hindu rejoice! A second thought: had not political correctness in this instance gone too far? Then it occurred to him that milking a cow is not the same thing as killing it. Do Hindus drink milk? Do they eat butter?

Ragweed Jones greeted him as soon as he exited the terminal, which Albert thought resembled a chicken coop. The airline treated me like a cow. Am I now to be a chicken? Ragweed Jones carried a cardboard sign on a three foot bamboo pole: **McNap.**

"You must be the Ragweed," Albert said. The man *did* look vaguely familiar.

"I am, Señor McNap, Ragwildo Spinoza Francisco Castiña y Jones. None de other and none de less. Ragweed Jones, at de service of you, *para servirle.*"

Chapter Four: Sizing Up The Suspect! Albert studied the short man. Five feet six, no, five feet seven. Slight build. Happy-go-lucky face. Oh, dear! An ugly mole as big as a dime at the back of his neck just peeking out at the collar! Wavy black hair. Black eyes set deep below a nondescript forehead. A thirty somethingish Mexican-Cuban-Puerto Rican-Columbian-Dominican-Honduran-*Hispanic!*—that's the word—*Hispanic* male. This is hard work, Albert thought.

"May I take your picture?" he asked. I should have thought of that sooner! Ragweed Jones threw his head back and placed his right hand over his heart.

"But of course. *Para servirle!* At de service of you!" Albert pushed the red button on the top of his camera. The salesman had called it a "Ph.D." camera. So simple to use! A week later his chessmate, Max, explained that "Ph.D." stood for "Push here, dummy." He was led to a waiting car that looked like a small tank. "Dis is de Lada," Ragweed Jones announced with pride. "Eet is Russian. Dey make dem like de bomb."

Its driver, whose picture Albert took at once, threw Albert's suitcases into the backseat. Albert squeezed alongside. Then they were off into the neon and noise of Frederique City, Frederique, viscid in the Caribbean night. Streets and sidewalks crowded with black bodies, swaggering and sauntering, baskets on heads, sandals and bare feet on cobblestones. The driver pounded the middle of the steering wheel. He leaned his head out the window: "Give up de way dere! Cummin' on true! Give up de way dere!" Two huge speakers jammed into the space below the Lada's rear window blasted:

> *We should have no fear.*
> *So much, so much, so much love.*
> *It will make you understand.*
> *Love is just the answer, yes.*
> *There is no time for regret.*
> *Let me tell you now:*

Love is just the answer, yes.

Clouds of smoke came from the front seat: the sweet smell of ganja. Ragweed Jones turned to extend the spear-shaped burning. But Albert's arms were pinned to his sides by the back of the driver's seat on one side and by his luggage on the other, so, instead, thoughtfully, Ragweed leaned his face close to the American's. A burst of exhalation filled the fat man's lungs. Tears came to his eyes. His breathing came in sharp jolts as the Lada's front seat squeezed against him. I am a huge grape stuck in a wine press, he thought. He wondered: what kind of grape am I? He tried to remember what, precisely, he knew about grapes. Not much. There were red grapes and white grapes though the white grapes were more properly described as *satin* grapes, to be precise. *Chapter Eleven: Precison! Precison! Precison!*

Brightly dressed colors sauntering washed around the amber-eyed beetle as it crawled upstream. Probably there are black grapes, too, Albert's rumination continued. Not me, though. I am a big fat juicy white grape, stuff of the finest Chardonnay, that's what I am. Well, to tell the truth, more of a medium-priced Zinfandel. Those were the two types of white wines Zimmerman's Value Liquor—"The Pour To Always Have With You"—sold around the corner from his apartment, except, of course, for the gallon jugs labeled, simply, **WHITE WINE**. Yes, that's it. If I am any kind of wine at all, I am a gallon jug of cheap white wine. This *is* ridiculous, he thought, even for me! Making happy faces with peas and presumed mashed potatoes on the plane: that was one thing. He tried to move first one, then the other, of his legs. All he accomplished was a constricted buttwiggle. He thought of the horrible pictures he walked by in the subway on his way to Washington Square to play chess with Max: photographs covered entire walls, glaring and grainy, of calves imprisoned in their own feces. "I shall never eat veal again," he had vowed, followed by wondering if the righteousness of his pledge was invalidated by the fact that he detested the taste of veal. Is there no grace to be found anywhere? Are our motives inevitably ulterior? He hated lima beans too and brussels sprouts. As soon as he returned to New York, he would visit the Park Slope library, carefully, to research how vegetables are grown. They too might well be subjected to concomitant cruelties. Some he knew are tied to stakes. Asparagus, broccoli...who could know the precise ingenuity of their possible tortures? He hoped no one was cruel to cauliflower, for he thought it the most noble and delicious of vegetables. Albert envisioned terrorist squads in defense of vegetable rights invading supermarkets to spray cabbage and celery with red paint. Or would they use green? Do vegetables feel pain?

> *Justice, Mr. President, is what the people want,*
> *Just and equal distribution of the wealth,*
> *Blow the trumpets far and near,*
> *Gonna be war, war, war, rumors of war.*

Ragweed Jones and the driver argued. Like toy rockets angry words lurched through the white smoke. "Is de *Congos*," the driver insisted.

"No. You are wrong like de red light dat is stuck. Eet is Cedric and Yvonne Myton. Dey de ones be doin' dat singing. *War, war, war, rumours of war*. Ain't dat so, Mr. McNap?"

Albert had no idea what the argument was about. "I should think you're both right," his ganja voice replied from the backseat as, with exaggerated finesse, the driver performed the miracle of a U turn and, to the blasts of *War, war, war, rumors of war*, brought the Lada to stop in front of a cheerless three story building, possibly white in color. Many of the neighboring structures were in various stages of construction *interruptus*. Those that were not suffered a malnourishment of paint. Behind their iron masks, windows were missing or cracked, some of the cracks crisscrossed with strips of silver tape to look like vertical sardine tins. Over the faded door, possibly yellow, dusty lettering grunted the building's name: *Casa Carnival*. It looked like a Styrofoam wedding cake on the verge of collapse.

"Dis ease de place of my friend, Magdaleña," Ragweed Jones boasted. "Dere ease no danger here. Here we have safety." As soon as he heard these words, Albert felt a chill. He was barely able to survive the motions of welcome. At the first opportunity he asked to be taken to his room where he immediately locked the door. He propped a chair against it and a small table. The room, when he finally got around to noticing, was comfortable in a cozy sort of way, without a doubt to be preferred to the motel rooms he was used to, like the one in the Sweet Valley Motel and Truck Stop. Perhaps there were cockroaches in *Casa Carnival* too? He threw himself onto the bed where his large body heaved like a beached whale, wetting its cover into a pool of sweat. *Danger. Safety. Danger. Safety.* The metronome of survival! He had been driven forwards and backwards in the pulsating night. He was God knows where, with complete strangers. With complete *black* strangers! They could have slit his throat at any time! He saw his dead hulk tossed into the gutter like an empty jug, labeled, simply, WHITE WINE.

> *Blow the trumpets*
> *Far and near,*
> *Gonna be war, war, war,*
> *Rumors of war.*

Then, in an instant, his fear vanished. Why had it not occurred to him that he could have been in danger? The most basic precautions, which he followed by instinct in New York, he had thrown to the wind. He had simply followed Ragweed Jones' instructions: himself, his suitcases, his money pouch squashed together in the back seat of the Lada. A Russian car at that! It could have been a garbage truck on its way to the city dump! Two BLACK men with faces like those that jump out at you from F.B.I. posters as you wait to buy stamps. He had vanished into the night with complete strangers! He hadn't even asked to see identification! But his throat *hadn't* been slit! He wasn't a wine bottle discarded in the gutter! He had been welcomed with genuine warmth. "Here we have safety," Ragweed Jones said. Now in the cozy room, in the reassurance of the ceiling fan's hum, Albert realized that he believed. He believed and he trusted. From below music reached him:

> *We should have no fear.*
> *So much, so much, so much love.*
> *It will make you understand.*
> *Love is just the answer, yes.*

He opened the windows and lay on the bed. For the first time he could remember he felt he belonged. The broomsounds of nearby sea came with the chorus—*so much, so much, so much love*—to carry him into sleep.

*　　*　　*

In the midst of a tidy jungle they had breakfast on a patio surrounded by high stucco walls, pieces of jagged glass protruding at the top like alligators' teeth. Albert was too big to fit into any of the chairs; Ragweed Jones found a board, the ends of which he anchored on top of two large flower pots turned upside down. The American was dressed in an oversized bright green shirt with red polka dots, pastel yellow walking shorts, orange socks, and basketball shoes. The left shoe was white with purple piping; the right was also white but instead of purple piping was measled with red circles the size of quarters. These he had purchased especially for the trip, making good his promise to himself of two years before. He had intended to buy tennis shoes, but the salesman had convinced him to reject footwear of such lesser strength, syringes in the sand likely to be of lurking if unseen danger. Forlorn strays, the hybrid set, for it could not be called a pair, was marked down ninety percent and that, of course, had clinched it. Albert thought that wearing mismatched shoes might start a new fashion trend. Or was it a matter of style? Fashion or style? Fashion you buy; style you are born with. Clearly, he decided, it was both. Elbows on the table, a large fringed circle of a straw hat on his head, he looked like a trained bear in a circus as his bulk hung over the edges of the sagging plank.

"It's decided, then," he said between mouthfuls of egg, papaya, mango, and toast smeared with guava jelly. "We are off to the Crimsontown Trust and Building Society first thing. Afterwards we shall seek out a zoom lens for this state of the art photographic wonder." He patted the Ph.D. camera that swung from his neck, accidentally activating the red button to memorialize the mango slices.

In the vault of the Crimsontown Trust and Building Society Ragweed Jones opened the safety deposit box. Albert took a magnifying glass from his pocket. Ragweed pinched the faded green paper daintily up to the light. Yes! There was no question about it. A gold certificate issued by the Federal Reserve Bank in Cleveland, dated 1929. Face value: one hundred dollars. Present value? There was no telling. Albert would pay the full price that Ragweed Jones had asked. Haggling, he had decided, would vitiate the spirit of camaraderie he believed essential for the successful completion of his mission. This, like the money spent for the camera, correspondence course, plane ticket, and shoes would be money well spent. He would violate his most sacred of principles and pay full price! Historic moments, clearly, called for decisive action. He remembered an old joke: why did God make Gentiles? Answer: somebody has to pay retail! Albert Sidney McNab would be true to his ethnic heritage.

"Señor Ragweed, I will pay you the two hundred dollars you are asking," he said, as he squeezed himself into the torture chamber of the Lada's rear seat. Lada's engineers, he had no doubt, moonlighted as KGB agents at Lubiyanka prison.

"But, Señor, dat was being de price when you were in New York. Now you are come all de way here. We have all of de expenses." A mosquito attacked Albert's left leg, just above the ankle. He felt the insect brush against his skin and land, like the astronauts on the moon, he thought. He was helpless as the mosquito assumed the devouring position to plunge its fangs into what Albert was certain was the yummiest of flesh. Soon, he feared, the mosquito's entire family would join the feast. Smorgasbord time! He let out a small howl.

"But, Señor, dere ees no need to be so angrified. You must not be to yelling like de dog. After all, eet ees only de fairness. You eat a lot of de food, Señor, and de gasoline for de driving here and de driving dere ees not cheapy also. Dere should be de more so of de more so." The mosquito was not through. Albert was certain he could feel the blood draining out of his leg. How symbolic! Gouge the tourist! You are never going to see him again. Unlike the mosquito, one hit is all you get. Then, again, perhaps Ragweed did have a point? His room at *Casa Carnival*, as Albert saw it, was luxurious, ceiling fan and all. The food, too, was superb and served in the loveliest of gardens! Too bad he was watching his weight! The diet would have to wait again.

"How much more so of the more so?"

"Well, Señor," Ragweed Jones replied, as the Lada pulled in front of *Casa Carnival*, "you get de valuable bill of de money, full accommodation at Magdaleña's, all de meals inclusive, a sightseeing trip to de rain forest at Loiza, and a night out of de night life, all of dis, Señor, oh, let us not forgetting de drive here and de drive dere, what ees called de *ground transportation*, everything, Señor, for six hundred dollars, which is only five hundred dollars more dan de bill. Yes, a bargain, you say. But de Ragweed wants to you to come back again and again, like de lost chicken." Albert detected the reconnaissance of another mosquito. Yes, it was landing! Alert!

"That seems fair," he said with relief, as the Lada burped to a halt. "But please get me out of here!" Too late. Scratching his leg, Albert struggled from the Lada. Like radioactive freckles, half a dozen red welts purpled the flesh above his ankle.

"Oh, Señor, you must not to scratch," Ragweed Jones said, hurrying him inside. "De scratch eet ees no good, Señor, like poking de snake with de stick."

Magdaleña smeared a mucilaginous porridge of crushed weeds and household ointments on his neck, arms, and legs. Then the American fled to his room. He lay on the bed with the windows shut and tried not to scratch. Of course they want to get as much money out of you as they can, he thought. That should come as no surprise. But then he wondered: where was his gratitude of the night before? Is not Ragweed Jones entitled to homage for not having slit my throat and dumped my body into the gutter? That's your problem, he told himself. It's either one extreme or the other. Just because Ragweed and his entourage are not the James gang doesn't mean they are Carmelite nuns either. What exactly is a Carmelite nun? Less penance? Fewer rosaries? Oh, shut up, he said out loud, treating himself to the tiniest touch of a scratch. Ah! A moment of relief for an eternity of suffering! Credit cards! Federal deficits! He reached for the best seller he had started on the plane: *Grow Rich and Die!* It chronicled the stories of men and women who shuffled off their mortal coils within days of inheriting great wealth, or of winning lotteries, or after having triumphed on televised game shows. Before long his left leg was a blotting rash, red and raw.

Ragweed Jones returned a few hours later. The bad news was that there was no such thing as a zoom lens for the Ph.D. camera. The worse news was that the cheapest camera *with* a zoom lens would require the expenditure of one hundred and forty-five of the fat man's fast disappearing dollars. They will get it all out of me yet, Albert thought, as he handed Ragweed the money. This is the slow torture method. Perhaps having my throat slit would have been better after all.

*   *   *

The following evening he was taken on the "Congo Bongo Coco Tour." Ragweed Jones insisted. After all, it was already paid for, "totally included, Señor, like de dog with de fleas." Magdaleña brought along a friend of hers, Esmerelda, a large, happy woman from Mabouhey about the same age as Albert.

"Oh, I am so honored to meet you at last!" Esmerelda said as she and Albert squeezed against each other in the Lada's rear seat. "Few foreigners know so much about our culture! Tell me how it is that you are so well-informed, particularly about our music!" Ragweed had told Esmerelda that he and the driver had found out that the American *was* correct: Ragweed and the driver both were right. Cedric and Yvonne Myton performed under the stage name *The Congos*.

"De Congos and dey be one and de same, like de chicken and de egg," Ragweed told her. "Dat fat man dere must be de man of de magic if he best be knowing deese things so much." Albert had no idea what Esmerelda was talking about, so he did not respond. Instead he gave her a sincere, weak smile.

"*So much, so much, so much love,*" Esmerelda sang. "*It will make you understand.* It is one of my favorite songs."

What a lovely voice! Albert thought. He looked at the happy woman sitting next to him. I have read about a soul-mate, he mused. Is there such a thing as a grape-mate?

"De Congos-Maytals!" the driver shouted.

"De Mytals-Congos!" Ragweed laughed.

"You are much too modest," Esmerelda said in response to Albert's silence. "Modesty is so becoming in a strong, smart man like yourself. May I call you 'Al'?"

Albert thought Esmerelda's nose was cute. It reminded him of a mushroom. Esmerelda took his hand and squeezed. He liked that, too, but he had no idea if he should say so.

"I have had the pleasure of visiting your fair island," he said, at last, in desperation.

"Well," Esmerelda replied. "You must return soon. Mabouhey is a place of magic. A magical place for a magical man!" She squeezed his hand again. "Our way of life goes back many generations, to the time of Kima. We do not think of the past as separate from the present, nor of the present as distinct from what is to come. Past, present, and future are all part of a larger whole. Someday I shall visit your country, as you have visited mine, so that I may study *your* philosophers." She looked directly into Albert's eyes. "I have no doubt that we have much in common."

"I am going on a diet tomorrow!" Albert replied. Esmerelda paid no attention to this insensitivity. Instead, she gave his hand another squeeze. "The problem," Albert said, "is that I never get any exercise. Except for walking to the subway. I go to the park to play chess with my friend,

Max. He drives a bread truck. You'd be amazed what Max knows about bread—especially white bread!"

"How interesting!" Esmerelda replied. "On Mabouhey Father Chester and I have been chess partners for many years. So, you see, I was right. We do have a lot in common!" She gave Albert's hand another squeeze and this time he squeezed back.

So it came about that Albert Sidney McNab didn't much mind as he parted with dollars in one tourist trap after another. Scantily clad women circumnavigated their navels with tassels of silver and gold. Like the cartoon character Spider-Woman a bikini-girl, spray painted silver from the top of her shaved head to the bottoms of her bare feet, paraded about exhaling bursts of fire. There was limbo dancing with flaming poles a few inches from the ground. "Put your hands together," hosts commanded, and, with genuine enthusiasm, Albert did—when they were not reaching for his wallet to pay for yet another round of drinks. Ragweed, the driver, Magdaleña, and Esmerelda seemed to have the most wonderful of times and to tell the truth Albert did too.

Hours past midnight they brought him to a happy place where, in smoke and dim light, black faces chattered like chopsticks. Black bodies brushed together in a frenetic blur of sound. A singer sang. Drummers drummed bongo drums, small, medium, large. There were guitars and tambourines, marimbulas, a xylophone and a keyboard. Albert had barely seated himself when a great roar came from the crowd as the words of Jimmy Cliff filled the room:

Sitting here in limbo,
But I know it won't be long,
Sitting here in limbo,
Like a bird without a song...

Esmerelda jumped to her feet and reached her hands to him. Albert looked sheepishly at Ragweed, who came from around the table to pull him to his feet.

"Dere ees only one of de things to be doing so now," Ragweed said grandly. "Dat ees to shake your boo-tay." And so Albert Sidney McNab did, to the delight of Ragweed, the driver, Magdaleña, and, especially, of Esmerelda.

Sitting here in limbo,
Waiting for the dice to roll,
Sitting here in limbo,
Have some time to search my soul...

Albert waved his arms and jiggled his feet and jerked his head around. He looked like a polar bear shaking himself awake after a long hibernation. Jimmy Cliff grabbed him and did not let go even as strong black arms lifted him so that his happy feet could dance on the top of a table.

I can't say what life will show me
But I know what I've seen,

I can't say where life will lead me,
But I know where I've been
Sitting in limbo,
Limbo, limbo,
Sitting here in limbo,
Limbo, limbo, limbo...

In his hothouse room as dawn arrives, Albert Sidney McNab falls asleep, Congo Bongo Coco, and dreams of mushrooms.

* * *

Four days later Ragweed Jones returned to "good news, yes, and bad news, too, yes of de course," but also, he exclaimed, "even more so good of de good news." Albert was in the garden, fly swatter in hand. He wore a helmet with lavender netting that dropped over his face like purple rain. His arms and legs were wrapped in sheets and pillow cases. He looked like a mummified beekeeper. The first good news, Ragweed announced with breathless excitement, was that the man in the lumber yard *was* correct. A white man was building a house on Mabouhey, on the side of the volcano no less. Just the week before, strange panels had been released by customs—something to do with the sun! Ragweed had crawled as close to the house as he could without risking detection. He had taken many pictures: of the white man sitting in a rocking chair, standing on the balcony, or leaning against its railing, of a beautiful woman with flowing black hair, of a girl about seven years old. The bad news was that the new camera and its zoom lens had fallen out of Hernando's boat. "Splash! Just liking that: splash!"

"I am mostly of sorry, Señor," Ragweed Jones apologized. "I have some disappointment." Albert waited in a bewilderment of anticipation. He saw himself as a general at command central and Ragweed Jones as a courier just returned from the front. So: there was a white man. Ragweed Jones had promised more good news though how it could compensate for the loss of the camera Albert could not imagine. The commander-in-chief, he reminded himself, must have nerves of steel! Spruance at Midway! Eisenhower on D-Day! He would suspend final judgment until the courier's report was complete.

"But I am promising to you more of de good news, Señor. De camera wid de zoom zoom, Señor, eet fall out of de boat on de way over to dere, not on de way to de back. So dat's de good news, mon, don't you be seein' dat?" The commander-in-chief most definitely did not see that. But he withheld comment. Nerves of steel, he said to himself, nerves of steel! Ragweed waited. After long moments Albert nodded his head.

"Well, mon, you see, like de pig hiding in de bushes, de Ragweed Jones, mon, he used de udder camera, de one wid de red button and eet could did work mon, as sure as de tire wid de patch. Of dis de Ragweed has none of de doubt. No, sir, mon. None of de doubt at all." Ragweed Jones reported all of this with the enthusiastic certainty of a used car salesman. Albert, after a few desultory questions, decided he would just have to accept Ragweed Jones' optimistic prognosis, at least for the time being. What choice did he have? It was the fog of war.

"But why do you be wanting to deese pictures, mon? You be to wanting dem very of much. Yes, very of much." More money, Albert thought. I can feel it in my bones. He is going to ask for more money! I am a big fat cow at milking time. I should have gone myself. Now, that's a ridiculous idea! He remembered his trip to Mabouhey two years before. He had circum-mule-gated the entire island, it seemed, from village to jungle, with mosquitoes aplenty but little else. Mabouhey wasn't a suburb, not by a long shot, but it too was bus-deficient! Albert thought of Percy Armond Lutton, the teen-aged gardener, the fallen ladder, and the confiscated film. He remembered his suburban sore feet. On Mabouhey it wasn't only his feet that were sore. "You be to wanting de pictures very of much," Ragweed Jones said again.

"Yes. I do be to wanting de pictures very of much."

"De development of de pictures here, Señor, ees costing much of de money, mon, very much much of de money."

"Surprise! Surprise!" Albert shouted. "How very much much of the money?"

"De chemicoos, mon, dey costing expensive. Much much of de money."

Albert looked directly at what he thought of as Ragweed Jones' cash register face.

"Thirty of de dollars, Señor!"

Thirty dollars doesn't seem like much much of de money, Albert thought. Still it is probably best to go through a dance of outrage. "THIRTY DOLLARS!" he yelled, clutching his chest with both hands. He turned his body around wildly as if looking for a suitable place to die. Ragweed Jones put on a hurt look. Magdalena came running from the kitchen.

"What is it?" she asked. The fat American had plopped himself down in the middle of the narrow path that led to the rear gate, crushing sentries of lilies that fringed its border.

"All right den," Ragweed Jones said. "Twenty-five of de dollars. I will work eet for de free." There was the pretense of a pause on Albert's part.

"A deal!" Ragweed helped him to his feet.

"Oh!" Magdalena sighed, kneeling over the crushed lilies. "My poor babies are wounded and hurt." She steadied the green stalks before returning to the kitchen, her left hip barging against the penitent American. Ragweed Jones shrank into the shadows. Then Magdalena was back, slender sticks in hand. With thin green threads she ministered to the injured lilies. "Flowers too have feelings," she said. If we can't eat animals and we can't eat plants, Albert wondered, what can we eat?

Albert Sidney McNab wavered between exhilaration and despair. As long as he parted with money, life in *Casa Carnival* was like a sailboat in a steady breeze. His appointed role, clearly, was exchequer of the purse—his. Well, he comforted himself, it would all be over soon. Besides the sums involved weren't all that much: five dollars for milk, sugar, eggs; ten dollars for screening, nails, and furring strips so that he could open his windows without further fear of the plague. Needs arose. He had money. Money was made to be spent. It was better, he sensed, to go down with boughten friendship at his side. He would provide.

Two days later the photographs were ready. Ragweed Jones brought Albert to a small shop inside a cavern of yellow concrete. Albert handed Ragweed the twenty-five dollars. Ragweed Jones, in turn, handed the money to the man in the stall, who disappeared behind a curtain. The American felt a shiver of shame course through his body. So: the "chemicoos" *were* expensive after all! He felt cheap, but he also felt reassured. Maybe, he thought, the money that dribbled away every time he turned around wasn't what mattered. Maybe it wasn't what mattered at all.

Ensconced again in the Lada's rear seat, Albert studied the photographs. There was a picture of a white man. That much could be determined. He was about the same size and shape as the missing Charleston Travers Landeman. That much could also be determined. The man wore a full beard—salt and pepper? He had a moustache. Two years had passed since the businessman's disappearance. Physical characteristics can change in two years. *Chapter Three: The Element Of Time.* Maybe, he thought, an F.B.I. computer could establish with certainty that our Ohio friend is the man in these photographs. I surely can't. There was no choice in the matter. He would have to traverse ocean and jungle and risk death again by mule and mosquito to confront the bearded man face to face. Right back where I started from, Mabouhey, here I come!

Chapter Twenty-Seven:
Denouement

Joe Rogers
Mabouhey
1991

I have an idiosyncratic nose. Some scents, no matter how strong, I miss altogether—the smell of garlic, for example. I simply cannot detect the smell of garlic while other scents as slight as a whisper overpower me, like the fragrance of roses, which springs like a rainbow to fill me with music. As I came awake in a strange bed, tented with gauze to allow the discernment of strange blurrings and nothing more, my nostrils filled with the most alluring scent, a scent I cannot describe for it would be like trying to describe the sudden appearance of a new color. Not green, nor blue, nor red, nor yellow, nor purple. An entirely new color. A color that should have been there all along. That's what the loveliness of this new scent was: the birth of a new color.

"You have been asleep for two days." It was a soft, lovely voice, in some way I could not fathom, a familiar voice. It came to me from the past and it called to me from the future, promising a perfection of all things womanly and warm. I sat up and reached my hand to the flimsy but impenetrable wall that separated us as her hand parted the netting. The right side of her face was seared burgundy brown, the petal of a wine red rose.

"I am Marguerite," she said. "I doubt that you remember."

"I do remember and I don't remember," I said. "Where am I?"

"You are on the side of Katausa at a place called Schugara. It is named after my daughter." I rubbed my face. I was very hungry. Before I could speak, however, a young girl, bright and black, the deepest night jeweled with the most radiant star, entered the room carrying a tray. "Schugara," the woman named Marguerite said, "this is Mr. Joe Rogers. He is from Chicago." In this last word there was a sharpness of pain that cut with the precision of a surgeon's knife. There was a snake among the roses.

"Hello," I said, putting from my mind the bitterness of this one word, *Chicago*, that hung over us like a curse. "Pleased to meet you."

"And I am pleased to meet you too, sir." Schugara smiled and skipped away. I studied the room. A simple space, but with the most glorious of views: windows, windows everywhere framing sky, sea, and jungle.

Furniture of fresh wood, a table, a dresser, a rocking chair.

"How did I get here?"

"Quince, my husband, came down with the fever after...after he found that." Marguerite pointed to a notebook with a blue cover that lay on top of the dresser. "The tale it tells is a tale of betrayal." I did not know how to respond so I waited in silence while Marguerite paused to compose her thoughts. A funny, familiar feeling came over me, like the feeling I'd had when I first met Zero. Go along for the ride, I'd thought then. Now I was God knows where and it seemed, *wise* is not quite the word, it seemed *natural* to let be what would be, not to stand in the way.

Marguerite's hair shimmered with light. She had a perfect grace. It took just a moment before her face played tricks with your eyes and she seemed a perfect loveliness, lovely beyond loveliness, her face perfect and whole, her eyes looking deep in your soul. You knew it and felt it and there was nothing you could do about it. I tried to pull my eyes from hers, but they drew me back like a bird returning to its nest. I think that when the body recovers from illness there is a part of us that is so happy to be alive for a bit while longer that all our senses are heightened. Our eyes are eager. Our ears, aware. To have stepped back from the brink! To see Marguerite! I admit it. I would have done anything she commanded. She had cast her spell upon my all too willing self.

Distant drumsounds came strong and stronger bringing tears to Marguerite's eyes. She stood at the side of the bed in the mystery of her sex, in the mystery of herself. There and then I decided I would love her if only from afar. She had a husband named Quince. She had a daughter named Schugara. Mine would be a selfless love and it would not matter that she would never know. If I am delirious, I thought, why not love? Marguerite would provide focus, structure, meaning, purpose. Soon I would return to Chicago. Why not let the days of my recovery float along on the golden wings of love?

"How did I get here?" I asked again.

"I was going for Christian," she answered, "even as the drums began calling for me. I arrived at the village just as Christian was starting. We drained the infection and set your ankle. You were carried here on a stretcher. Quince's fever would not break and Christian would not leave you in case..."

"In case he had to chop off my foot." I finished the sentence for her. She looked at me with wide eyes but said nothing. The dishes on my tray were empty now. Survival whets the appetite, I thought. Vegetables, rice, pieces of chicken, bread. A five star meal! Because I was alive to eat it.

"You must rest now." Marguerite took the tray and departed. I hobbled on one foot to the dresser, snatched the blue notebook, and staggered back to bed. I propped myself against the headboard and began to read.

"The tale it tells is a tale of betrayal." So Marguerite had said. *Betrayal.* The softness of the word lies and mystifies. The notebook was a diary recording the life of one Matthew James Calkins. Who was Matthew James Calkins and how did it matter that he had been betrayed, for he had been betrayed, that much was certain? He was young; he was betrayed. I finished reading, on the last page these final chilling words: *There is too much pain. I am so tired. Goodbye.* Yes, we are each of us imprisoned in our own world of hurt and need, of dream and desire. Everything depends on whose ox it is that is being gored. I did not know Matthew James Calkins. I had no idea who he was. Why should his story matter? Of my own free will, if there is such a thing, I had gone to the dresser. I could have stayed in bed. I could have minded my own business. But now I was witness to a tale of betrayal. I did not know exactly why the story mattered. Yet I believed it did. If we believe, Father Chester had said, we must act. But how? Knowledge is complicity. Children are hungry in Calcutta and on the west side of Chicago but as long as we don't see them they don't exist and we can cling to the essential rationalization which has separated man from beast down through the ages: the rationalization we call *civilization.* Opera, theater, museum, restaurant, and yes, bookstore are safe. The belly when it belongs to someone else is déclassé. We all get to die. Death: our shared humanity. So what's all this ruckus about keeping the planet going? It too is going to die. Okay. Let's say we stop over procreating. We stop polluting. We conserve natural resources. Good old Mother Earth lasts another two million years instead of just another two hundred which is the most she's got left the way we're going. In two hundred years, none of *us* will be alive. What we're talking about then is somebody else's troubles. In the words of Lily Tomlin: no matter how cynical you become, it's never enough to keep up. The solution? Eat, drink, and be merry. Hello, vodka!

I slipped lower beneath the sheets. You know better, I thought, or ought to. What it's all about is not brute survival. It's about happiness. And happiness is not something you can go out and buy, seventeen trillion television commercials to the contrary. The real trick is to go on as if it all *does* matter. To choose the side of truth, the side of beauty, the side of justice. To make room for others at the table. To do what you can do when you can do it. To leave the sidelines. To put yourself in the game! As simple as that?

The notebook! I had better return it to the dresser! But, halfway there, I stumbled, crashing to the floor. Then Marguerite was next to me helping me back to bed. She replaced the blue notebook on top of the dresser.

"Thank you," I said, feeling stupid, and awkward, and cheap. Marguerite looked at me with eyes whose sadness came as water from the deepest well. She sat on the side of the bed.

"Father Chester says we are going to have visitors. They will take him away. He says he must go. He will leave me."

"Who?"

"Travers."

"Travers?"

"Travers is Quince, my husband. My second husband."

Then it all came out in a torrent of tears: how she had loved, how she had lost, how she had found love again. She reached for my hand. Our fingers touched. Ever since she could remember, Schugay had loved her. He was the blackest boy with the biggest heart and Schugay loved her. Oh, how Schugay loved her! They were young together. She had gone to Chicago, Schugay had begged her not to go, but she had gone, and they had done this to her. [She touched the right side of her face.] In Chicago's nights she cried, for she knew that Schugay would no longer love her, would never love her again. But Schugay did love her. He came across the ocean to come to her like the sun and he did not care that her face was scarred for he had thought he'd lost her forever. To Schugay she was still as beautiful as the first blush of sun in the early sky. Schugay was the whisper of night. And Chicago had killed him. It would have been better if Schugay had not loved her so much, if he had not come across the ocean, if he had found another though the world turn to ice and no birds sing. For years Marguerite waited on the shore as if she too had died. She held Schugara in her arms but Schugay was gone, he was gone forever. Then a man named Travers came to the island, his soul as scarred as hers. When Travers saved Schugara from the great white shark, Schugay returned from the other world. Schugay put his hands on her waist and softly let her go. "Let love be," Schugay told her. "Let love be." The past two years she had returned to life. She and Quince and Schugara lived and loved on the side of the volcano as if time would last forever. Quince had promised that he would never leave her. Now he would break that promise. She had left Schugay; now Travers would leave her. When he read his nephew's diary the heaviness in his heart flamed his soul into anger. He would return. It was his responsibility to his murdered nephew. It was his responsibility to himself.

Before the crag-like figure of Time, hooded and carrying a scythe, march men, women, and children. "Time goes, you say? Ah no! Alas, Time stays, we go."

"I have an idea," I said. "Listen closely."

*   *   *

My grand plan? Simply this: a search party was about to arrive in pursuit of one Charleston Travers Landeman. Fine. I would become he. We were, Marguerite agreed, about the same age and height. We were both Americans. If I wasn't the missing businessman, who in the heck was I? How else to explain my strange presence on the island of Mabouhey? On the side of Katausa? At a place called Schugara? We are predisposed to see what we expect to see. Our world is a pigeonholed place. Remember my first impression of Zero? He was black, he did not speak the King's English: therefore he would push a broom. All that was needed now was for me to fit into a preconceived role. A line from *Hamlet* came to me: "The lady doth protest too much." Protest too much I would. The more I insisted on my own identity, the more it would seem I was lying. They—whoever they were—could give me back my true identity once we were in the good old U. S. of A. "Told you Unitarians would never name a child *Charleston*."

I struggled to my feet. Marguerite helped me out of the bedroom. We entered a large living area which thrust like one of the wings of a boomerang over the edge of a ravine. Muscular black men pushed table and chairs to the sides of the room. All this while sounded an increasing pounding of drums as if Mother Earth herself were one big heart. New smells came to my nostrils the way spring returns to the winter-worn-weary.

"I will leave you now," Marguerite said. "I must see about Quince. Christian says his fever should break soon." She turned. An undercurrent of skirt whispered between her legs. I settled into the softness of pillow. It had been many years since I was last on stage, since my college days. I had played the role of Rosencrantz in *Hamlet*. Rosencrantz, you may recall, was one of Hamlet's schoolmates. The role of Rosencrantz, the director insisted, is of *structural cruciality* to the theme of the play. That's how he put it: *structural crucialty*. And *Hamlet's* theme? Betrayal. In passing myself off as Travers Landeman, I would be as compelling as the ghost of Hamlet's father. At my direction a table was positioned with a tape recorder to bathe me in Mozart. Next to it sat liquid proof of the existence of God: a bottle of *Potempkin*. Suddenly, like the stopping of a heavy rain, the drums ceased. A large black man entered the room.

"I am Morimbo," he said. "Ragweed Jones is coming." I took a good look at Morimbo. It was as if he had been sent from central casting. He might well be the most gentle of giants, I thought, but how could you tell? The guy on the can of peas is supposed to be jolly, too, ho, ho, ho, but I wouldn't want to come upon him in a dark alley, would you?

"Who is Ragweed Jones?" I asked.

"Ragwildo Spinoza Francisco Castiña y Jones. They are my friends," Morimbo said.

"They?"

"Ragweed and his twin brother, Adolfo. They are my friends."

So: Smith had a brother! A twin! Well, I had never told him about my family either.

"Ragweed has with him a fat white man, an American." I reached for the liquid silver on the table beside. "Show them in," I said.

*   *   *

I have never had a close relationship with anyone who is a twin. We live in a politically correct age and no doubt it is an azygous error to admit that I am glad I am not a twin. Of course, how can one know for certain? Our individuality is an off the rack suit not of our choosing, but we pretend it's tailor made. Smith's twin brother entered. He was accompanied by one of the strangest persons I had ever seen, and an American at that. I didn't know we still came that way. He was a fat white man layered in a tent of khaki. He wore mismatched athletic shoes. His socks were orange. A helmet skirted with lavender lace covered his head, giving him the appearance of a Mayan god.

"I had to improvise." These were the first words I heard from Albert Sidney McNab, for such I soon learned was his name. He removed the helmet to fuss with its lace. Then he stood before me as if posing for a portrait. Finally he pulled one of the chairs close and sat down, balancing the laced helmet on his knee as if it were the most delicate of pastries and he the proudest of pastry chefs. He was in his own world and it appeared to be a nice one.

"I must look into patenting," he said. "Look, here you will see that the netting is removable. I had little holes drilled into the headpiece. I put strips of Velcro all around on the inside of the rim. That turned out to be crucial. Finally I sewed small dots of Velcro into this lovely lace, like puffs of purple pussywillow, and, voilá!" With outstretched arms the fat man presented his offspring for my inspection and approval. I was back in fifth grade. It was Valentine's Day. Mary Sue Gannon, pigtails and freckles, showed me the valentine she was making for her mother. In the reddest of red crayons Mary Sue had drawn a raggedy heart and then smudged a glob of masticated chewing gum, like a gray wart, onto its center. She still had to draw the arrow. It would go right through the gum. I'M STUCK ON YOU! Mary Sue's labored printing boasted across the top. I told her that *I* would never give *my* mother a glob of already chewed chewing gum. *Pukey* was the word I used. In tears, her pigtails and freckles fled out of my life forever. My father had taught me that honesty is the best policy but I decided right then and there to find out what the next best policy is. So I lavished praise on the marvel of Velcro and lace. Clever and yet practical. Patenting should definitely be pursued. Smith's brother stood behind the fat American as watchful and patient as a nanny.

"I believe I know your brother," I said, once I succeeded in returning the soon to be patented contraption to its glowing inventor.

"Ho, Señor," he replied. "Dat ees very too good. Yes, I know this. I am the Ragweed. You must to be the one who drinks de vodka." Smith's brother extended his hand. The upper half of the fat man's body swiveled like the turret of a tank.

"Ragweed," he said grandly, "we need a moment." It was as if he had remembered these words from a Cary Grant movie. A fat Cary Grant in bright orange socks if you can so imagine. I savored the incongruity. Incongruity demands sustenance. I reached again for *Potempkin*. "Perhaps you would like some food," I said to Ragweed Jones, sweeping my free arm in the direction of the kitchen. Morimbo reappeared and the two of them departed, chatting in patois like long lost brothers.

"Now to business!" the fat American declared. He fumbled about in the many pockets of his khaki tent to finally extend a photograph. "Have you seen this man?" I studied the photograph. A blurred image of a man leaning over a balcony. He may have been white. He could have been anyone. Yet instantly I recognized the photograph's background: the balcony that reached into the valley below in the very place where I was, a place called Schugara. Yes, it had to be him—Quince/Travers, Marguerite's husband! Even though I had never seen him, I knew.

"Look, Al," I began. There was a minor earthquake on the chair beside me. "It is okay if I call you *Al* isn't it?" The fat man looked as if he were going to cry.

"No one ever calls me *Al*," he said.

"What do they call you?"

"*Hey, you* mostly. They call me *Hey, you.*"

I did not know how to respond. A sad silence waited. "Surely not everyone," I said at last. "Surely not Ragweed."

His face lit up. "Oh, no," he said. "Ragweed calls me *Mister* or *Señor*. It sure beats *Hey, you*, but it's a far cry from *Al*."

"Well, then, Al," I continued, "may I ask why it is that you are interested in the identity of this man? How do you know it's not me? Perhaps I decided to shave." I handed back the photograph to study his reaction. I filled my glass as his rambling story unfolded. He was a detective, well, not a detective, strictly speaking, not *exactly*. He was more of an investigator. Well, precisely speaking, not an investigator. Never mind. He had to get away from the M.A.F.I.A. You see, his feet hurt and his back was sore. Anyway, the man in the photograph might be the man who had disappeared from something having to do with some sort of S & M business in Ohio. There was an extortion attempt. But Albert Sidney McNab wasn't so sure, you see, about anything, really. Something didn't pass the smell test. He would shoot the moon, go for the whole enchilada, damn the torpedoes, and so forth. The Atlantis Fidelity Insurance Company [!] would pay him a whole lot of money, though, truth to tell, he didn't need the money. He was worried about his mother. Except that his mother was dead and it was all his fault. A Craftomatic bed had killed her to say nothing of the fact that she might lose her pension. Between swigs of *Potempkin*, as clear as the sound of a silver bell, I did my best to follow what he was saying. Finally he came to a stop like a car that has run out of gas. Well, more like a bus. "Suppose the man in the photograph *is* alive," I said, "and suppose it's *not* me. What then?"

Al looked confused. "What do you mean?"

"Simply this. Say you actually found this man, assuming again, that he's not me. He walks into the room right now. So?"

"So...I go back to New York and claim my reward."

"As easy as that? I doubt it. What you'd have to do is bring him back alive, as they say in the movies. To do that you'd need your own army. And, if your man, again assuming it's not me, were to get killed while you were trying to return him, well, then, he'd be dead just the same. You'd have a devil of a time trying to prove he died later rather than sooner, after rather than before, wouldn't you? At any rate, it wouldn't matter. He'd be dead. It doesn't sound to me like anyone wants this guy alive. They'd all gang up against you, the S & M outfit in Ohio, most of all."

"And what about Madge?" Al replied as if in a daze.

"Madge?"

"Madge Drayback. The office manager. Well, the former office manager. She's retired. And she doesn't even have a Craftomatic bed." Like the one that had killed his mother? I thought it better not to ask.

"Precisely," I said. "You don't want to do that to Madge do you? Take away her pension? Leave her without a bed?"

"No," he said. "No."

Everything was swinging along as coolly as a hammock in a breeze. All that remained was to tie up a few loose ends. Ah, to play a benevolent god! To say "It shall be so!" and have it be as said. Puck in *A Midsummer Night's Dream*! Al would return, with or without me, Marguerite and Quince/Travers would have each other, Madge Drayback would keep her pension and possibly get a new bed in the bargain. I would return to Chicago to reacquaint myself with *Ketel One* and *Grey Goose*, my noble doings on Mabouhey at a place called Schugara untarnished by reward or recognition. But then, as if struggling through thick smoke, a voice came from the balcony. It was an American's voice, a voice I had not heard before.

"I don't want to hurt Madge either. But I must go back. There is no other choice."

*   *   *

Quince—Charleston Travers Landeman—entered the room, holding on to Marguerite's arm. Her face was a waterfall of tears. Smith, Ragweed, and Morimbo followed to spread blankets and pillows; a bamboo pipe of burning ganja was passed around as platters of bread, meat, fruit and vegetables sailed through smoke like freighters through fog. There was music, strange music, like the sounds of rain, wind, and forest. Here, as near as *Potempkin* and I can remember, is what happened. Marguerite's husband went to Albert Sidney McNab, and extended his hands with his wrists together. "Now I am called Quince," he said. "But once I was Charleston Travers Landeman. It seems I am to be your prisoner."

"All you have to do now, Al, is bring him in," I said.

"Do I have to?" Al asked.

"Isn't it rather late in the game to be asking that?" Quince replied. "Of course you have to. I surrender; you bring me in; you claim your reward."

"I'm not so sure," Al replied. "You say you are Travers. Maybe you are. Maybe this other man is." Here he pointed to me. "None of this makes any sense. The fugitive is supposed to resist. Chapter Eight warns against the setup. This very well could be a ruse. The fugitive is supposed to run away. Perhaps it is best if you *both* stay right where you are. You would have me take away Madge's pension. I can do without the shoes." This last sentence sticks in my mind. I cannot vouch with certainty that everything I am recounting here is entirely accurate, but those were his verbatim words. That's what the man said: *I can do without the shoes*. **The** shoes.

"Have it your way," Quince replied. "I'll turn myself in. Somebody else can have the reward."

"But first you must get off the island." It was Father Chester's voice. Where did he come from? When did he arrive?

"You would keep me here as a prisoner?"

We are all prisoners, I thought again, prisoners of self. To break out we must reach out.

"You are needed here," Father Chester said. "Marguerite needs you. Schugara needs you."

"See?" Al clapped his hands together. There was a small pop of a sound, like an exclamation point. A satisfied smile spread over the fat man's face as he fumbled through his many khaki pockets to produce in triumph a second bag of potato chips.

"As far as your reward is concerned, assuming of course, that you bring the right man back alive," I said as matter-of-factly as I could, "I wouldn't count on it, Al, not unless you've had a LaSalle Street lawyer review the fine print of your deal with theinsurance. What did you say its name is again?"

"Atlantis Fidelity Insurance." My ears hadn't deceived me! I thought of the Sisters of the Sisterhood. Terrorists my ass! Chicago's winter was in my veins. It was payback time.

"The way I see it," I continued, "is that Travers did in fact die. Charleston Travers Landeman died. Quince was born. Besides the entire idea of life insurance is repugnant. A wonderful deal! Except you have to die, so you won't be around to make sure that theinsurance keeps its end of the bargain. Such a deal!" I turned and faced Marguerite's husband. "Leave well enough alone. Stay dead. Look, Travers..."

"His name is Quince," Father Chester said.

"I like Quince a whole lot better too," Al interjected. "It's more refined. *Travers* sounds like the name of a species of crayfish."

"Scuttling across the floors of silent seas?" I added.

"Exactly!" Al said. A louder pop, a wider smile. "What does Morris here say?" Al turned to face the black giant.

"He is Quince," Morimbo answered.

Marguerite's husband had been pacing back and forth; now he turned and faced us. "My nephew killed himself," he said. "I could have saved him, but I turned away. I stood by safe on the sidelines. Matthew reached out to me, but I was trapped in my own petty fear. I did not give him a good shove over the side but I might as well have. Yet someone else did. You want me to stay here and again keep to the sidelines? Pretend that nothing happened? How many other boys will kill themselves? I didn't help my own nephew, but I must if I can reach out to save other sons of other parents, nephews, sons, and brothers, lest they become members of my all too grieving tribe. This is what I believe."

"You are the father of your own family now," Father Chester said. "Your primary responsibility is here." There was a terrible sadness to these words as if they were a debt of long standing demanding full payment.

"I am to do nothing? I am to turn away again?"

I filled my glass. "Sometimes it is best to leave such matters to God," I said. Me. Can you imagine?

Then Marguerite spoke: "If we leave God's work to God," she said, "it will never get done. It won't even get started." Her words were steel wrapped in velvet. I turned to look at Albert Sidney McNab. A cocker spaniel with a bone, he had found a third bag of potato chips.

"Why not let Al handle it?" I said. "It's his line of work. Is it justice you want, Quince, or revenge?"

Quince, for that's who he was as far as we all were concerned, myself included, reached for Marguerite's hand. "I turned away once," he said. "I am determined not to do so again."

"Leave the job to me," Albert Sidney McNab said. "This is right up my alley. I will see to it that justice is done. I will be as persistent as a cockroach."

"You will do this for me?"

"Count on it."

I stared at jungle and sea. We were all as silent as shadows. Quince and Marguerite left the room to return a few minutes later. Marguerite handed Al the blue notebook. Quince extended a fistful of oversized greenbacks. We all looked at each other as if we were cavemen around a fire.

"It's settled, then," Father Chester said. "This fine man, Albert Sidney, will take your burden, Quince, upon his worthy shoulders. Here," he added, "take this with you."

He reached into the side of his sarong and handed Al the mask I had discovered. I felt again a wince of pain in my ankle. "Keep it safe for us," the priest said, "for all of us. When the time comes, we will send instructions." Carefully the fat man tucked the mask inside one of his inner pockets. He brushed the top of his head with his right hand. He pulled himself ramrod straight. Then he stepped to the middle of the room as if he were Hamlet about to give the *To be or not to be* soliloquy.

"I am a simple man," he said. "I have lived a simple life. All I know about other people is they hurt me. I don't think they mean to hurt me, but they do. I have known for a long time that I'm ridiculous as far as other people are concerned, but to me I'm just myself—nothing all that special but content in my own way with my own life. Why do people have to hurt each other? Why can't we be more like cockroaches? There is too much pain the whole world over. This is something I know too well. But now I know something more. I know that there is love and I know that love must be. This here man"—he pointed to Quince— "loves this here woman"—he pointed to Marguerite—"and she loves him. They love each other. We can all see that. Can there ever be too much love? You, sir, the one that is called *Quince*. Are you Travers? What if you are? What then? What good is money if it gets in the way of love? What good is duty if it denies love? What good is justice if it takes away love? They say, 'Let justice be done though the heavens fall!' This is nonsense. We must figure out a just way where the heavens stay right where they are. We must love. I have learned this now for I have been a garden without flowers. Now I've witnessed love. I have heard the sounds of music, I have savored the taste of wine, and I know what it is to dance. You, sir," —he looked at me—"called me Al. You, sir" —he looked at the priest—"called me *this fine man*. I am one of you. The shoes are not important. The shoes are not important at all. I shall eat mushrooms."

Of these words I am also certain: he who spurned the shoes would eat mushrooms. That's what he said and I believed him, understanding without knowing, like the night in the taroumpa hut. Al went to Quince and took him by the hand. "I swear to you," he said, "that your nephew did not die in vain. I will make sure of that. It's my line of work. I found you, didn't I?" Then he walked over to me. "That goes for you, too. Double or nothing!" The fat man winked and I had the strangest feeling that he had never before winked in his entire life. Next it was Father Chester's turn: "The mask is safe with me. I promise."

That was about it. We ate and we drank; we smoked and we danced. Finally, we fell asleep. In the frolic of the morning that followed, birds jabbered high and low in the branches. The rising sun stoked greens—emerald and jade, myrtle and moss—into glistening gold. Albert Sidney McNab, the most unlikely of heroes, who would eat mushrooms and do without the shoes, was off. He and Ragweed Jones entered the glimmering jungle. Al stopped, turned, and, with a wave of lavender lace, was gone. I hobbled to a rocking chair and sat there in wonder, high on a balcony, on the side of a volcano, on the island of

Mabouhey, at a place called Schuraga. In the valley below people walked with a happy walk or tended to the earth, *plough down sillion shine*. From beyond the sea's silver song and forever of sky, the ceaseless new day reached out with a lover's arms.

EPILOGUE

From the *Cleveland Plain Dealer*, May 17, 1995, page three:

Settlement Ends Abuse Trial Against
Archdiocese of Cleveland
by Randall Stevens

Cleveland, Ohio—An out of court settlement with the Archdiocese of Cleveland was announced today by lawyers representing the "Ohio Valley Nineteen," nineteen families whose sons were allegedly sexually victimized by the late Arthur McArtle, formerly associate pastor at St. Canasius parish, St. Gabriel's parish, Mother of Sorrows parish, in Athens, Ohio, and chaplain at St. Francis' Home for Troubled Youth, also located in Athens. McArtle was being held without bond in the Athens County jail awaiting trial on eighty-eight counts of juvenile sexual offenses when he was found beaten to death in his cell this past January. Terms of the settlement were not made public. In the text accompanying the dismissal order, however, the Archdiocese acknowledged that it had not co-operated fully with law enforcement authorities and pledged to do so in the future. A spokesperson for the families, Albert S. McNab, said, "It is important that the Archdiocese has accepted responsibility for these tragedies. Confession is good for the soul. The families have done what we had to do. Two sons are no longer with us. We will always grieve."

*   *   *

From *The New York Times*, July 14, 1995, page two:

Mask Sets Record at Sotheby's
by Sally Clark

New York, New York—A pre-Columbian mask, believed to date to the Arawak era, circa 1100 A.D., approximately twelve inches high by six inches wide, was auctioned yesterday at Sotheby's for Ninety-Seven Million, Seven Hundred and Sixty-Five Thousand dollars. The successful bidder was the Komorado Museum of Kyoto, Japan. Spokespersons for Sotheby's said the sum established a new record for a pre-Columbian artifact. Of ebony, laced with silver, gold, and precious jewels, the mask was put up for auction by Mrs. Esmerelda McNab, United Nations Ambassador of its newest member nation, the Caribbean island of Mabouhey, which achieved full member status this past March. According to Ambassador McNab proceeds from the sale will be used to upgrade medical facilities on Mabouhey and to establish birth control programs as well as implementing environmental strategies for water treatment and recycling, including efforts to preserve Mabouhey's coral reefs, recognized as among the most pristine in the Caribbean.

"It has always been the Mabouhey way to share," Mrs. McNab said, in response to protestors from Columbia University, who denounced the sale as "cultural genocide." "We are happy to share a part of our heritage with our generous Japanese friends. Our history is an oral history; Mabouheyans do not place importance on possessions in and of themselves. The Spirits of the mask will continue to watch over us, wherever the physical object itself may be. Namaste, Mabouhey!"

*   *   *

From the *Chicago Tribune*, August 13, 2003, page six:

"Pack" Comora Paroled
by Myesha Myles

Chicago, Illinois—Former Chicago police sergeant Peter "Pack" Comora, convicted in the corruption trial known as Operation Deep Pockets, was granted a medical release from Oxford Federal Prison, Oxford, Wisconsin, yesterday after serving six years of his original fifteen to twenty year sentence. Comora was diagnosed with stage four lung, pancreatic, and liver cancer earlier this year. In 1997 Comora pled guilty to multiple counts of malfeasance and corruption, including the manufacture of false evidence and the shakedown of drug dealers in the 15th Police District in Chicago's Austin neighborhood, where he spent twenty years as liason with the Drug Enforcement Administration. Thirteen police officers, including Comora, six Cook County bailiffs, and former States Attorney Warner Tully also pled guilty to multiple counts of an assortment of crimes, including conspiracy, wire fraud, and witness coersion. Tully, who turned states evidence and whose wiretaps led to the convictions, served six months in the Terre Haute Federal Correctional Complex, in Terre Haute, Indiana. He joined the witness protection program in 1998 and was killed in a convenience store robbery in Fairfield, Wyoming, two months after his release.

NOTES

1) Chapter 5, p. 161. Malcolm Lowry, author of *Under the Volcano*, wrote that the novel's theme is "Only against death does man cry out in vain." He joked that he and his wife should be known as "Alcoholics Synonymous." See "Day of the Dead," by D. T. Max, *The New Yorker*, December 17, 2007, p. 76.

2) Chapter 8, pp. 199. The quotation is from *Personal Memoirs of U. S. Grant*, published by the Library of Congress, copyright 1990, by the Literary Classics of the United States, Inc., New York, New York, p. 419.

3) Chapter 11, pp. 269-270. See *The Promised Land: The Great Black Migration and How It Changed America* by Nicholas Lemann (Penguin Random House, 1991) for a detailed discussion of the development of the mechanized cotton picking machine and the migration of black southerners to northern cities 1940-1970.

4) Chapter 13, p. 307. See *Race Matters* by Cornel West (Vintage Books, 1994) from which Luther Custis Towe's statement that "Blackness is a state of mind. It is a political and ethical construct." is taken verbatim.

5) Chapter 21, p. 401. In his history of socialism, *To The Finland Station*, published in 1940, Edmund Wilson describes the railroad station where Lenin arrived on April 11, 1917, from the "sealed" train that carried him from Geneva to St. Petersberg as having "benches rubbed dull from waiting."

6) Chapter 23, pp. 445-446. See *The Rise and Fall of the Third Reich*, by William Shirer (Simon & Schuster, 1960). The reference to the Peace of Westphalia is a paraphrase of pp. 93-94.

7) Chapter 27, p. 521. The phrase *plough down sillion shine* is from Gerard Manley Hopkins' poem, *The Windhover*, written 1877 and published 1918. George P. Landow, Professor of English and the History of Art, Brown University, explains, the "work of the ploughman makes the plough shine from its polishing against the earth, and it also makes the sillion, the soil cut by the plough, shine."

About the Author

When Chicago's largest neighborhood, Austin—once a municipality in its own right—resegregated from 100% Caucasian to 90+% African-American in the years 1970-71, as 120,000 Austinites fled overnight, Joe English was one of a handful of residents who cast down their buckets with their new neighbors. As a minority in a majority minority neighborhood, English has, after forty-eight years, gained a unique perspective on the state of urban America. He maintains a residence in Austin but now spends much of his time in the Caribbean. He has two children, now in their forties, who were raised in Austin. English has a B.A. *cum laude* from Colorado College in Colorado Springs, Colorado, and an M.A. from Rice University in Houston, Texas. He is a Woodrow Wilson Fellow. His writings have appeared in the *Chicago Tribune,* the *Chicago Sun-Times,* the Chicago *Reader,* and *Co-Existence,* the literary journal which featured the works of Henry Miller.

About Carlos Barberena

Carlos Barberena is a Nicaraguan printmaker based in Chicago. He has had solo exhibitions in Costa Rica, Estonia, France, Mexico, Nicaragua, Spain, and the United States of America. His work has been shown in art biennials, museums, galleries, and cultural centers around the world. Barberena has received numerous awards, most notably the "National Printmaking Award 2012" awarded by the Nicaraguan Institute of Culture, Managua, Nicaragua. The frontispiece is entitled **Ofrenda** ("Offering"). www.carlosbarberena.com

Author's Notes

There *was* a Learning Network School. It *was* located in the building that formerly was Siena High School and, before Siena, the convent for the nuns of St. Lucy's Roman Catholic parish. From 1972 to 2011 the Learning Network (K–8) educated children, primarily from the economically disadvantaged neighborhoods on Chicago's west side, including Austin. Its track record was impressive. 90+ percent of its students graduated from high school. 70+ percent then went on to college and universities. Of the students who attended the Learning Network, out-of-wedlock pregnancies as well as incarceration in penal institutions were virtually non-existent.

The battle over using vouchers to deliver education to outer city students should focus on ensuring that for-profit corporations, which see the poor not as people but as profit centers, do not monopolize and control the implementation of vouchers. Instead, small, teacher-run schools like the Learning Network should take precedence, to gurarantee that the factory model of the public school system is not replaced with a factory model of private for-profit schools. The Learning Network was featured by the BBC (British Broadcasting Corporation) for its impressive accomplishments. Among Chicago's philanthropies and established institutions, however, the Learning Network was a prophet without honor in its own land. It was administered and and run by teachers. Its priority was students, not contractors, bureaucrats, administrators, and politicians. It was small; its student body never exceed 100. The Learning Network proved that it can be done. To do so, however, requires thinking in new ways, prioritizing intimacy, caring, and intensive individual student focus as the essential components of urban education.

*   *   *

The author is indebted to Richard Jung of Minuteman Press, Oak Park, Illinois for his formatting expertise.

*   *   *

The author welcomes comments: schugara@gmail.com

Also by Line By Lion

The award- winning novel by internationally acclaimed author Joao Cirqueira

Jesus Christ returns to earth and meets Magdalene, an environmental activist. who is fighting for a better world. Together they encounter an extremist ecological group plotting to destroy a maize plantation that they believe to be genetically modified, an uprising against a tourist development that is to be built in a forest reserve, and a racially motivated armed conflict that changes everything.

Though Jesus chooses to simply bear witness, seeking to bring about understanding and harmony, he cannot escape the hatred and blindess of humanity. And only a con-man will recognize Him for who He truly is. Their story, *Jesus and Magdalene*, is a modern-day retelling of the social and political conflict that has characterized history through the ages and is especially relevant to the headlines of today.